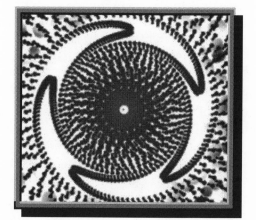

The Scribing of Ishitar

ASHES TO ASHES

By
Carrie F. Shepherd

CARRIE F. SHEPHERD

THE SCRIBING OF ISHITAR: ASHES TO ASHES
By
Carrie F. Shepherd
Copyright © Carrie F. Shepherd 2014
Cover Illustration Copyright © 2014 by Novel Idea Design
Published by Mythos Press
(An Imprint of GMTA Publishing)

Contact:
GMTA Publishing
6296 Philippi Church Rd.
Raeford, NC 28376

Printed in the U.S.A.

ISBN-13: 978-0692023402
ISBN-10: 0692023402

LCCN: 2013908871

Dedication

*For my parents, Jerry and Carolene Shepherd,
with all of my love.*

"Like the moon, a mother of light guiding me from above.
I sang words of your praise, incantations of love.
Conversations late into the night filled me with wisdom.
But in a moment of rage, I unleashed a plague of malevolence.
My tongue, a scalpel sliced deep into your heart.
Death took you into his arms and away from me.
Words are magic, speak them with care.
Once uttered a spell cannot be undone.
Think twice before you utter an oath.
That will leave you with only the memories of ghosts."

-Wade Nicholes

Acknowledgements

The greatest lesson that I learned during the publishing process of the first installment of The Scribing of Ishitar, Fall From Grace, is that, while an author might have a great idea, no one person can see the bigger picture. Such was true with Ashes to Ashes.

I would like to thank Brooke Funk and Gabby Raines, among others who have asked to remain anonymous, for providing me with their feedback and building the story to make it stronger.

Matthew 5:4
Blessed are those who mourn,
for they will be comforted.

CHARLIE

After climbing the hill on the north side of the pond at Liberty Park, Charles Hamilton lowers himself to the ground and removes his shoes and socks. Despite the fact that this has been one of the warmest spring mornings on record in years, the grass is cool on his feet.

It eases his troubled mind and calms his tattered nerves.

As do the sounds of the people on their paddle boats on the pond and the children running to and fro around him, their parents calling after them to mind their feet lest they fall.

The laughter of one particular child brings a smile to Charlie's face. It is a young boy's laughter and it reminds him, overwhelmingly, of his nephew, Mason.

In the distance, the peacocks are calling, screaming at those park goers who have ventured into Tracy Aviary. The chorus raises cries from the golden eagle which, in turn, excites the exotic birds in the surrounding cages.

To Charlie's left, his service dog—a long haired golden retriever named Rocky—pants in his ear as he sits patiently at Charlie's side. An old friend, Charlie finds comfort in Rocky's constant companionship. He knows that, with Rocky on guard, danger will have a difficult time should it decide today was the day it would seek him.

The week has been invigorating. It has also been overwhelming.

On Friday, he went to the bank to peruse the contents of his safety deposit box. He has a standing monthly appointment to do so and rarely finds anything within it that he didn't place there himself. During this particular visit, however, Charlie discovered that an old friend had visited the bank and added a puzzle box to his many treasures.

As luck would have it, a gentleman happened to be visiting the bank that day who made his living by studying ancient theologies. The man had recognized the puzzle box at once and proclaimed it to be an extraordinary archeological find. Upon sight, he had vehemently insisted that, should Charlie be able to open the box, he must show him what was hidden inside.

As curious about the man as he was the puzzle box, itself, Charlie had spent the afternoon with his strange new friend, working the puzzle while conversing on many subjects both large and small. In fact, he came to know the man well enough that, by the time the puzzle was solved and the box sprang open, he wasn't at all surprised to learn that Joshua Silverstone recognized the tome buried inside it for what it was and that he had studied the ancient symbols making up the language in which it had been written.

As excited about the find as Charlie, himself, Joshua pleaded with Charlie to allow him to translate the tome. Eager to know the secrets he held in his hand, Charlie more than willingly complied.

Though Charlie was certain the words within the pages were little more than the myth of the peoples of its time, Joshua insisted that the characters which made up the fascinating tale were littered throughout thousands of other tomes written in the same symbolic prose. And, interestingly enough, this tome, seemingly insignificant when you took the library of Raziel's Tomes—which was the name of this antiquated series—as a whole, had been missing since time out of mind.

In fact, it was believed that the copy in Charlie's hands was the only one ever bound. Because of this, the tome, according to Joshua, was priceless and needed to be preserved at once. "I will pay you whatever sum you like for this tome. If only to complete my collection. I shall even read you all of the rest, if that will entice you."

Charlie wasn't willing to sell Mr. Silverstone the book. Not at any price. Though he chose not to share this with Joshua Silverstone lest he received additional books and required the man's future assistance in translating them.

Now, Rocky lets out a long, low sigh, shifts slightly and lowers himself to rest his muzzle on his forepaws. As he does so, he growls low in his throat, warning Charlie that someone is approaching. That Rocky doesn't bark tells Charlie that he doesn't consider this person to be a threat.

Grinning, Charlie reaches forward and buries his hand in the fur between Rocky's ears to give him a good, hard scratch. It is as he is pulling his hand away that he, himself, senses the presence.

The scent surrounding the approaching party is blindingly familiar and it takes Charlie completely by surprise. It is the same essence which permeates from the letters and puzzles that he receives from time to time. It is the smell of the mud pots at Yellowstone National Park, though much fainter and more pleasing in its earthiness.

"Does the A stand for Azrael then?" He teases as his old friend lowers himself at Charlie's right to sit beside him. "Is this the riddle in the book which I am meant to solve?"

"It does." There is a smile to Azrael's soothingly deep voice. It forms itself around a strange accent, which Charlie is unable to place. It is similar to Joshua Silverstone's; yet, in a strange way, different. Though very heavy, it is melodic to the ear. "And it is."

"Have you come for me, then?"

More teasing. Azrael, in the story, is the archangel of death.

"Not today."

Charlie finds himself chuckling at this cryptic response. "Well then. After a lifetime of playing cat and mouse with me, why *have* you finally made yourself known?"

"To see if you enjoyed the spin of my yarn." Charlie feels him shrug. "To see if the secrets buried within it intrigue you."

"How was I to read it?" Charlie asks, grinning to himself. "The text, from what I understand, was more symbols than words. And certainly it wasn't in Braille."

"Let's not play unnecessary games with one another." Azrael chuckles under his breath. "I'm well aware that you had help with the translation."

"I did." Charlie admits, though how the man touting himself

as the archangel Azrael would know this compounds the mystery and increases Charlie's curiosity. He wonders if Joshua Silverstone's sudden appearance in his life was truly coincidental. Feeling rather silly, he realizes that this is a thought that should have occurred to him before. "My new friend tells me the tome is invaluable."

"It is."

"Why, then, would you give it to me?" He asks.

Azrael considers him for a long, almost torturous, moment. Finally he says, "Because you remind me of myself."

"Do I?" Amused.

"Yes." Azrael replies. "Myself before I was cursed by Noliminan to bear such heavy magic."

Charlie's brow furrows as Azrael says this. The sheer conviction behind the sentiment is overwhelming. He could almost believe that Azrael is speaking words of truth rather than playing a game with him.

Almost.

The tale is far too fantastical to actually believe.

"I don't trust myself anymore, you see." He explains. "I don't trust my true hearted opinion. I know too much and am stretched too thin. I am going . . ." he shudders, "insane."

"How am I able to help you?" Charlie asks, not dissuading his old friend from this contemplation. "What do you need from me?"

"My motives are uncertain to me." He admits. "Although I believe that sharing another piece of my history with you may ease my troubled heart."

"Perhaps." Charlie crosses his arms over his chest, suddenly chilled. "Or, this could be a monumental waste of your time."

"You may be right about that." Azrael agrees. Then, with an obvious smile around his words, "But, you are curious as to what happens to these characters in my tale? You do wish to know what secrets the remaining tomes—in the least those which hold any import—contain?"

Charlie is unable to deny this. Though Joshua has offered to read the tomes, he understands that he will learn more from listening to Azrael speak of the events within them than merely listening to Joshua reading them.

A lifetime of the pair of them playing at puzzles has taught Charlie the true depths of his friend's mind.

"I am." He admits. Then, teasing, "Though, this King of Lords bloke; I shouldn't like to stumble across *him* in a blind alley."

Azrael titters slightly at the pun and begins running his fingers through the grass. The sound of this simple gesture is oddly comforting to Charlie. "Nor should I."

"Which manner of God is he?" Charlie wants to know. "Which people worship him?"

"All people." Azrael mutters. "As to whom he represents, I should think you could consider him Zeus or Odin or Ra." Azrael raises his hand and sets it upon his own thigh. It is a lightly made gesture which is nearly impossible for Charlie to detect. "But if you paid even a small bit of attention to the telling of the tale, then you know the status of all three of these Gods is base and not at all as important as the mythology of this world would demand you to believe."

Charlie nods. He heard mention being made of a smattering of Gods and angels whose names he knows. Even Azrael's name comes from Charlie's Catholic based teachings.

"What *does* become of Loki after he eats Ishitar's pie?" That Azrael knows the answer to this query bears no question in Charlie's mind. He would have read the other tomes. Charlie is certain of it. "And what becomes of the young Prince of Providence?"

"You ask for the end of a story before you know the middle bits." Azrael's deep laughter is low and respectful. "What about this new book you are reading? The story of Gilles de Rais?"

"It's chilling." Charlie admits. He wants to puzzle over how Azrael knows he is recording that book, but understands the answer to this question will have to come later. "Do you believe—or I should ask, given who you are, I suppose—*know* if

11

the events described within it are true."

"You know I cannot tell you." Azrael sighs. "I can only speak of what others have told. Not what I, myself, bore witness to."

Then it's a game he still wishes to play. Charlie thinks, wearing a smile.

"If you lost your voice," Charlie asks, very haughtily, "how is it that you are talking with me now?"

"*Am* I talking with you?" Azrael asks him. "Or am I merely making you believe that I am talking with you?"

Charlie starts. It is true, given he is blind, that he cannot tell if Azrael is moving his lips. Nor has he heard even the faintest sound of his friend's breathing.

This is madness. Nonsense! Merely another riddle to add to the seemingly unending layers of the game.

"We digress." Azrael mutters, turning his face away. "And the day is getting away from us."

"Very well." Charlie's lips grow thin as he bites back a smile. "Tell me of all that came to pass after the revolution ended."

"The same thing that always happens." He shrugs. "Another revolution." Charlie is unable to suppress his smile. "But the revolution, itself, had little impact. It was the aftermath which, irrevocably, directed the course of history."

"By whose hand?" Charlie asks him. "Lucias' or Loki's?"

Azrael shakes his head. "Neither she nor he."

"Noliminan?"

"Not that worthy either." This time it is Azrael who smiles. "No. The events that changed the course of the worlds came at the hands of a most insignificant creature."

Charlie's smile grows. "A hobbit?"

"No." Azrael laughs at this Tolkien reference. The sound of it rattling between them brings Charlie an odd sense of peace. "But near enough to be the point. It was an elf."

"An elf." Charlie snorts and rolls his eyes.

"The first of his kind." Azrael's tone grows serious again. "And, at the time, he was little more than a child."

"I'm intrigued." And, much to his surprise, he is.

"Shall I tell you then?" Azrael asks, still smiling around his words. "The next bit of my story?"

"If you have the time." Charlie's voice sounds eager to his own ears.

"My dear, Charles." Azrael titters. "Must I remind you that I have nothing which I might call my own *but* time?"

"Then yes." Charlie nods at him. "Tell me the next bit of it." Then, remembering Raziel's words to Azrael at the beginning of the last story, "And leave not a single sordid detail aside!"

Iladrul watched with wide eyes as the two shadows collided. He wondered which of his father's friends would die defending him from the blonde haired demon. He was helpless to look away as the shadows twisted and turned in a clawing, fighting rage.

Soon the shadows loomed closer. As they passed Iladrul's open door, the young elf's fears intensified.

It wasn't an angel that the blonde haired demon was fighting. It was one of his kindred; another demon.

Iladrul understood, in his repugnance, that, no matter which of the battling figures won their hand to hand combat, his life was forfeit.

He threw away his blankets and flung himself to the floor. As swiftly as possible, he crawled under the bed and reached for the nearest blanket to pull it down as a shield that he could hide behind. He forced himself to lie as still as he could and he prayed to whatever God would listen that, no matter which of the two demons won their fight, they would not hear the pathetic sound of his fearful breathing.

Die proud, Iladrul, Wisterian and the other warriors always counseled him, *or don't bother to die at all. An elf who cannot die proud deserves to be damned to live with his cowardice.*

There was a final screech. It seemed to stretch into antiquity.

When the shrill cry ended, there was deafening silence.

Iladrul's heart was beating wildly and his shoulder length, copper hair became damp with sweat. He swallowed and curled into a ball as he listened to the silence echoing like thunder around him. He wished desperately that he had, for once in his pathetic young life, actually listened to his father and done as he had been told.

The sound of booted feet upon the marble tile almost made him cry out, but he swallowed his scream lest the demon who had won the argument hear him. He listened as the steps came closer, stopping at the patio door and then resuming themselves as the creature walked with purpose to his bed.

Iladrul laid his head on the side so he could see through the there were many more worlds and times to go, she was growing weary and afraid.

Sappharon had not told Na'amah who her father was. She knew that if Na'amah had this information she would seek him out. The demon didn't want to put any of the three of them in greater danger than they already were. So, instead, she told her daughter that if there ever came a time when Na'amah couldn't find her, she was to wait an appropriate number of years and then seek out Apprentice Lord Loki.

Loki, Sappharon promised her, would take Na'amah into his protection if she but asked him to.

"Perhaps it's time." She shivered.

This was a cautious thought, however. In order to find Loki, Na'amah would have to breach the gates which separated the Heavens and Hells from the mortal worlds. The risk was great that she would be seen and recognized for what she was.

Never mind that she didn't know, exactly, where Apprentice Lord Loki lived and would be forced to navigate the Halls of the Hells until she found his apartment. If she were lucky enough to actually make it through the gate, the chances of her reaching Apprentice Lord Loki were slim to none.

Yet, what other options were available to her? Was she to travel from world to world to the end of antiquity? Perhaps, even then, never learning what had become of her mother?

"No." She muttered to herself. "I cannot bear it. Not even a single world more."

Knowing the cost should she be discovered, Na'amah retreated into the cave to pack her trikla.

- 3 -

Wisterian awoke to the sound of screaming.

He flew from his bed, his white wings fluttering behind him, and ran to the doors leading to the balcony. Though they had been closed and locked when he had gone to bed the night before, they now stood wide open as the morning sun rose over the mountain on the other side of the great ravine.

He ran through the doors, stopping abruptly in horror as he turned toward the cries, his eyes landing upon a screaming, writhing mass of fire.

He had time to think, *Oh my Gods, someone put that poor creature out of its misery,* before the mass of fire exploded and was, then, simply gone.

In its place, at the foot of a stake mired with silver chains, was a pile of ashes. Surrounding them were scorch marks, which had been burned into the marble tiles.

He heard the footfalls coming from the opposite direction of the balcony. Whichever one of his warriors it was let out a horrified, inarticulate cry of despair. This was followed by, "What in the name of Loki's beard—?"

Wisterian looked upward, over the scorched outline of the pile of ashes, and met the gaze of the second in command of his Kinsgard, an angel by the name of Balean. He swallowed as he turned his attention to the closed glass doors that belonged to his son's apartment. Leaning against the marble blocks that make up the castle were two great black wings, carefully propped so they would draw attention.

"Oh my Gods . . ." Balean's horror was palpable as he ran over the scorch marks, kicking the ashes and scattering them, to grasp at the wings. In an unconscious gesture he thrust them toward Wisterian.

As If I can't see them with my own two glams.

"My Lord . . . ?"

Wisterian shook his head and darted forward. When he reached the doors to his son's bedchamber he began pulling on them violently. Relieved to find that he could not open them, and to see the curve of Iladrul's back upon the bed, the angel rolled his eyes closed and swallowed.

"Find Titheron." He barked to Balean. "Have him scour our borders. I must know how a demon has breached our walls."

Balean bowed. "Yes, my Lord."

Swallowing his distaste, Wisterian reached for the wings and touched them. They were as soft as his own, but that didn't surprise him. His best friend was a demon.

Or someone who used *to be my best friend.*

He shivered at the next thought that filled his mind.

He didn't know which demon these wings belonged to. They could belong to Jamiason as easily as they could belong to any of the others who had been exiled.

What if . . . ?

He couldn't believe that, but there was only one way to tell. He lifted one of the wings to his nose and breathed in the scent of them.

Not oranges.

His relief at the thought was momentary.

A demon had broached his borders. It could very well have been on Jamiason's orders.

He shivered again.

It was no secret that the demons, who were now cursed to live only in the darkness of the night, were jealous of the angels.

The demons' plight was anything but fair. Wisterian was the first to agree with them. Yet, fair or not, Wisterian and his people had not been the ones to decide the angels' *or* the demons' fates.

He looked upward and realized that Iladrul was standing behind his glass doors, watching his father with wide, frightened eyes. Frowning, Wisterian threw the wings to the ground. He hadn't realized that he was still holding them to his face.

He forced a smile and raised his hand to his son. Iladrul, reluctantly, raised a hand in response.

Thank the Gods, Wisterian thought as his eyes trailed over Iladrul's small face, *that for once in your damn life you actually listened to me and did as I commanded.*

Sappharon heard that damn whistle and grimaced.

"Come." Lady Lucias' tone was low. Sappharon would pay for her insolence later. She would make no mistake in thinking otherwise. "I'm in the middle of my instructions to Loki, but we can talk while I finish them up if you'll do me the favor of delivering them to him."

"Of course, my Lady," Metatron, always polite, always steadfast, replied with a thin, troubled smile. "It would be no bother to me."

"Very well." Lucias replied. Sappharon, who had yet to turn to face her Mistress, heard the smile in her Lady's voice and winced. "Sappharon shall make us lunch."

"I'm afraid that I am not here for pleasantries."

Of course you aren't. But do you have to say as much? Do you have to turn your Gods be damned sword deeper into her heart?

Sappharon would have destroyed him if she thought that she wouldn't be punished for the mere thought alone. Who in the name of all of the Gods that are or ever were would have known if Metatron sullied his pristine reputation for the purpose of having tea and sandwiches with Lucias?

"Sappharon, move out of Metatron's way." Lucias flared. "For the love of the Gods. What is *wrong* with you today?"

Sappharon turned toward her Goddess, flashing an angry, irritated grin. "Just a bad day."

"Very well, met paken." Used to Sappharon's moods, she assessed her demon with a dark, and doubtful, frown. "Put it aside for the nonce and allow Metatron to come in?"

Sappharon turned to the only man she had ever truly loved, raised her hands high, flew them to each side—looking nearly cartoonish, had she but known it—and forced herself to temper her madness.

Metatron slid past her and into her home.

She turned to follow the pair into the library. When they were nearly there, Lucias looked over her shoulder and gave

Sappharon an irritated smile. "I'm rather certain that Metatron means this to be a private conversation."

"Who else would hear it?"

Metatron pursed his lips and lowered his gaze, appearing to be both amused and frustrated with her. As for Lucias, she let out that whistle again. "Go to your room. If I need to share what's discussed with you then I shall."

More irritated than ever, Sappharon wrinkled her nose and did as she was bid.

-5-

"Sit, child." Lucias commanded as she slid around her massive desk and lowered herself into her seat.

Metatron shook his head. He had been able to stay his reaction to seeing her in her female form in front of Sappharon. Now, alone with her, he found that he could not force his gaze away from her perfectly made features.

"I know that you won't stay." Her dark eyes were dancing over his face, drinking him in. He wanted to reach for her, to comfort her. To show her the love that he felt for her that he had never been able to display when she had worn the face of his father. "But may we at least share a drink?"

"I'm sorry, my Lady." He shook his head. "The King of Lords will be angry enough if he learns that I have come to speak with you. I dare not tarry overly long."

She sighed, turning her face away from him as she did so. Even in this form she would not allow him to see her softer side. His smile, when she returned her gaze to him, was completely unguarded and without malice.

She found a smile for him as well and gave him an understanding nod.

"How is the carvetek mouk?" Her tone was silky. Her love for Noliminan was palpable despite her insult toward him.

"You know that he wouldn't tell me one way or the other."
Metatron offered her another tight smile. "Though, from what I
understand, he is well."

She nodded, seemingly not surprised. "He truly can weather
any storm."

"Given the majority of the storms are wrought at his
command, I suppose that he must." Metatron shrugged. "I loathe
to come right to the point, my Lo—" Irritated with himself, he
shook his head. "My Lady. But, as I say, if it is learned that I
have come to visit you, I shall be severely punished."

"Very well." She sighed. "What is it that you seek from me?"

Swallowing, he forced himself to raise his gaze. But only
slightly. Though he was here of his own accord, he was terrified.

"I seek your succor." He muttered and lowered himself into
one of the chairs on the other side of her desk. "I'm not . . . I can
no longer bear to serve Noliminan."

"Metatron." He swallowed, afraid of her hurtful words. He
didn't care for her tone. "You know that I cannot grant you my
succor."

More than anything, this response angered him. She had
never turned down any one of the angels or demons who had
come to her for help. Yet she was unwilling to aide her own son?

"I cannot—" He closed his eyes, shook his head and forced
himself to meet her gaze. "My Lady, I beg it of you. I cannot
bear to look upon Lord Noliminan anymore. Yet, I am forced to
pretend that I am in his fealty." His teeth clenched together. "I
loathe him. I despise the tasks that he orders me to do in his
name."

He had to look away again as memory upon memory of acts
committed at Noliminan's behest crashed down upon him,
crushing his already broken spirit. His task, as a member of the
Quorum, was to deliver the message of the King of Lords to
those who displeased him. Noliminan's anger, which came swift
and often, was almost always exacted at Metatron's hands.

Yet never so frequently, or violently, as it was delivered upon the members of the Quorum. It was these punishments, above all others, which Metatron was no longer able to bear.

He decided to share this with her. Perhaps the knowledge that her other children were being mistreated would entice her to spare and protect him.

"Especially when it comes to my brothers and sisters."

"What is it that he has, lately, done to your brothers and sisters?" Her tone was guarded, yet curious. As he had suspected it would be, the concern she felt for her children was palpable upon her expression.

"He loathes that Uriel and Mihr are female." His anger was rising. Not toward Noliminan, he was surprised to discover. It was rising against her. "What were you thinking? Turning them male when they were babes?"

"He never would have accepted them into the Quorum as women." She said simply. "I regret that decision not a bit. Someone needed to protect them. I knew that their brothers would. If they had been delivered to him as women, then he would have had Zadkiel expire their souls and he would have forced Raziel and I to try again."

"He would never—"

Seeing her eyes narrow, he stopped himself. Of course he would have. And he would have made either Michael or Metatron be the one to hold his sisters down as Zadkiel ran his finger over their brows.

"Yet you won't protect *me* from him?" Metatron growled at her. "You won't free *me* from his servitude?"

"To go where, exactly?" She asked him. Her expression was painful to look upon. "Do you honestly believe that he will let you walk free and unscathed into the service of another? Or into exile to serve me, for that matter? You are his property, Metatron. Nothing less and nothing more. If I were to grant you my succor, he would hunt you down and destroy you." She looked away from him then, her eyes flashing with the pain that

27

the truth of her words wrought within her heart. "If only to put me in my place."

"Do you not understand that whatever short time I would live as a free man—?"

"Trust me in this, Metatron." Her tone was heavy and her dark eyes were brooding. "He would sense your intentions. You wouldn't even make it to the door."

"My Lady, I—"

"I am not telling you no." She looked swiftly away. "I am telling you not today." She sighed and returned her gaze to his. "Think to the game of kings' castles, my son. And think to how I choose to play."

His lips pursed as he looked upon her. "My life isn't a Gods be damned game of kings' castles."

"I know it isn't." She forced herself to smile at him. "Please be patient. This is all I ask of you."

"I will." He rose to his feet and glared at her across her desk. "For now. Because you've left me no choice."

"I've left you no choice because you *have* no choice." She corrected him. "I do have a plan. Which, if it works out as I intend it to, will protect you. As well as your brothers and sisters."

Loathing the position that she was putting him in, Metatron had no choice but to believe her.

-6-

"Madness." I seethed as Ishitar reached upward to pick another gourd from Noliminan's forbidden fruit tree. "When your father learns what you have been doing, he's going to be furious."

"Do you intend to tell him?" Ishitar lowered his hand from the gourd that he was about to pick and assessed me with his light brown eyes. "Oh. That's right. You can't."

"Do not mock me, boy." I frowned at him. "You know well and good that if I wish to pass a message to him it will be an easy enough thing for me to do."

"It isn't your ability that I speak to." He shrugged and returned his attention to the tree. "You can't tattle on me because you genuinely care about the consequence if you do."

I didn't bother to deny this because, having watched him closely for the full of his life, I knew that it would do me no good. He is the one being in all of creation who understands me through and through.

"When do you intend to deliver this new pie?" I asked him.

"Soon." He muttered as he placed the gourd he had just plucked into the sack at his hip. "In fact, I intend to move in with Loki. In payment to him for the inconvenience, I shall gift him the pie."

"What are you thinking?" I admonished him. "Do you know what that will do to Zad and Zam?"

Ishitar turned toward me and assessed me with his contemplative gaze. It is a gaze that he uses to either study or intimidate and I have seen many a soul shatter when it is turned their way.

I, however, am used to his ways. His tactics rarely, if ever, work on me.

"They will be devastated." I advised him, not giving him the advantage by lowering my eyes. "Especially Zamyael."

He waved his hand at me. I glared at him.

"Never mind that Loki is an unfit choice."

"I have my reasons for choosing Loki." He advised me as he reached upward and pulled another gourd from the tree.

"I'm certain that you do." My lips thinned. "This doesn't mean—"

He turned to face me. His eyes were blazing with irritation. Gone was that contemplative, studious expression that he generally wore.

"Leave it, Azrael." He warned me. "You have no say in the matter and there is no argument you may share that will change my mind."

Understanding the truth of those words, I turned my back to him as he finished filling his sack with Noliminan's forbidden fruit.

-7-

When the angels of the second revolution were exiled, every one of them felt lost and confused. They were so used to the repression of the Sixty Realms that to find themselves in a situation where they would be allowed to not only create a new society, but also to govern it, had been overwhelming.

Wisterian was chosen to be their King because he had been the angel who had stepped up to lead the revolution and, as a result, their ruling Goddess, Lady Theasis, deemed that he should be the one to father the future Emissary Lord of the race they would create. The same was true with Jamiason when it came to the determination as to who would become King of the demons. This left over six hundred angels and five hundred demons who had completely lost their sense of purpose and self.

Balean breken Thyman, and his twin brother, Jeanir, included.

From a distance, the angels had watched the demons, under Jamiason's command, as they swiftly built a society that seemed to work for them. Each of the demons was raised up by James and directed to contribute by performing the tasks that he or she knew they would excel at.

The angels, however, were not as willing to fall into old habits. As a result, rather than immediately propagating their race, chaos had ensued.

It had been Balean and Jeanir who had finally approached Wisterian and told him that something must be done. And, after far too many cups and a mindless games of storming stones, the solution came all too easily.

Since the angels were not willing to play to their natural strengths, they would, instead, trust to their fates.

A ridiculous notion, Balean reflected as he tied the strap of his saddle tightly to his horse.

Especially given Jeanir, who had trained under Sirs Michael and Metatron, was now living in the whore's village, a stallion sent to stud, rather than swinging a sword or stringing a bow.

Balean shook his head and allowed his neck to bend backward so that he was staring at the ceiling.

"What a fucking mess." He muttered under his breath.

"Balean?" Zander, an angel who had pulled the black storming stone and, as a result, assigned the charge of a servant, gave Balean a wan smile. Here was an angel whose wings had been stripped from him because his child, who was a stable boy, had had the audacity to play boyish games with a Prince. "Are you alright?"

"Time will tell." Balean gave him a patient smile. He'd always liked Zander. He was an easy going bloke who, like Balean and Jeanir, had been human when he wore his mortal veil. Yet, now that he was wingless, Balean found it difficult to look upon him at times. "Did you hear of the morning events at the castle?"

"Ta." Zander looked swiftly away. "The young Prince . . . ?"

"He's well." Balean reached upward and clapped Zander's shoulder. "Safe."

"I'm relieved to hear it, Captain Balean." Zander swallowed and raised his gaze to meet Balean's. "The horses are ready."

Balean gave him a tight smile and watched with a heavy heart as the wingless angel darted away lest he say something which he may later regret. Balean shook his head when Zander closed the door to his small stocking room, wishing that he had never had that first cup or cast that first stone that had, in the end, fated them all.

Although he was grateful for another moment of reflection, the moment didn't last long. The elves' walls had been breached and there wasn't time for melancholy or regret over poor choices.

-8-

I watched Lord Loki with dire fascination as he slipped into Lucias' cottage, his eyes dancing around her sitting room, as they always did, so that he could drink in her essence before seeking her out. I knew that he was in love with the Lady from the days when I had been able to raid his thoughts. I also knew that he believed she was beyond him.

When he seemed content that he could mask his desire for her, he sought her out in the library. She sat, as she often did, on her favorite, high backed, leather chair, her feet tucked beneath her and a book in her hands.

Seeing her there, to him the perfect picture of beauty, he shivered. No amount of preparation ever seemed to truly ready him for the reality of her features. I suspect that he believed, as his eyes danced over the lines of her face, that he was a fool to have even tried.

"My Lady."

She looked up, her lips parting. She was surprised to see him, I knew. And, then again, as her lips curled into a smile, I realized that she was not.

"Loki." Her voice was sultry, causing him to shiver again as he stepped toward the chair opposite her, tugging on the leg of his trousers as if to use them to shield his obvious lust from her. "Metatron visited my abode this afternoon."

Loki, who was lowering himself into the chair, froze. Having watched him sit outside of her prison and eat Ishitar's pie, I knew he understood that she had been told by the Prince of Providence what had taken place at the Council meeting which had fated us all. Yet, she had respected him enough, until now, to never raise her son's name in his presence.

"He asked me for his succor." Her lips thinned. "He asked for release from Noliminan's servitude."

"I can't blame him for that." Loki replied, his tone heavy with harsh criticism, as he finished sitting down.

"I told him to wait."

Clearly surprised by this, Loki snapped at her, "Why ever for?! We could protect him."

"Not yet." She looked swiftly away. "We can. But we have to lay out a plan first."

"Such as?"

She looked at him. Her dark eyes were assessing. I sensed by his expression that he was, oddly enough, given the depths of his love for her, irritated by her regard.

"Raziel isn't right for my throne as Lady Regent." She finally said. "You should sit upon it instead." Her smile became true. "Lord Regent Loki. Has a rather nice ring to it, don't you think?"

"Right." He scoffed. "Noliminan will allow *that*."

"Mayhap not at the moment." She conceded. "But what if you have a Quorum of your own to serve you?"

"I will *never* bed Raziel." Loki growled at her. "You know I can't stand to even be in the same room as the cunt."

"Raziel is not the one who can breed archangels." She stopped him, her gaze leveling him. She didn't, I knew, appreciate Loki's distasteful insult toward the woman who had birthed her sons and daughters. "I am."

"Perhaps." Loki's expression took on an ugly quality. This time it was me who shivered. "But, even with the spell that allows you to return to your male form when it suits you, Raziel is required to accept your seed. Even if you raped her, she'd just root it out."

"I don't mean to use the spell." She looked away. As she did so, the tight expression washed out of Loki's features and was replaced with his general regard of longing for her. "And I don't mean to rape her." She granted him a coquettish smile. "I mean that *you* should sire them." He flinched backward as she turned her gaze to meet his once again. "And, I mean to birth them."

"My Lady . . . ?" His tone was heavy with surprise. "You cannot mean—?"

"Ta." She smiled softly at him. "I can and I do."

"But you have ever been faithful to Noliminan as a woman!" Loki cried. "Why, now, would you betray him?"

"He turned me from his servitude eagerly enough." She looked away. I sensed that Loki knew that she was lying. But he, clearly, didn't care. She told him what she needed him to know when he needed to know it and he was, for now, seemingly content with that. Besides, when she turned her gaze back to him, she spoke words he had ever longed to hear. "And I love you. I would proudly bear your children."

"I would eagerly plant them within you." His tone was thick with his lust. "If you aren't teasing me—"

"Never, Loki." She replied, lowering her gaze as her cheeks flushed pink. "You know I desire you. I've never hidden this fact from you." She raised her gaze again. "Do you deny that you desire me as well?"

"Never in life." He whispered.

"Well, then." She stood and walked toward him. When she was before him, she set both hands upon his shoulders. As he looked up at her, his senses were clearly no longer his own. When she straddled him and reached for his belt to unbuckle it, he appeared to lose all control. "Now seems to me as perfect a time to start as any."

"As you will me, my Lady." He responded to this as he reached for her hips, wearing a cocky, hungry grin under his ever so famous goatee. "I am, as I ever have been, yours to command."

-9-

After searching in all of the usual places, Faunus finally found Prince Iladrul in deep contemplation beside the river which ran through their lands. He sat on the very edge of the bank with his long, gray skirt pulled up to his knees and his bare feet dangling in the deep, white capped water of the river.

Relieved to have found his Prince, Faunus let out a grateful sigh and quickened his pace so that he might speak with the other boy.

"My Prince!" He called, "There you are!"

"Here I am." Prince Iladrul agreed, not looking away from the river.

"Tarna and I are going to play at swords." Faunus tried to engage his Prince. "Do you wish to join?"

"Not really." He replied, never looking away from the rushing water of the river.

"Then archery?" Faunus suggested.

"No." A little more irritably.

"We could go spy on the doxies." Faunus offered. "There's that pretty female one with the lavender eyes that you like—"

"I don't want to." He snapped.

Faunus flinched. He didn't understand this sudden disinterest in the doxies. Prince Iladrul had been the first of them to brave sneaking into the village unaccompanied by his father. As he had been the one to show the others where the doxies bathed. Since then, he and Faunus had taken every opportunity afforded to them to sneak into the forest so that they might hide in the trees and watch from a distance.

"Then we could tease the kitchen girls."

"What is *wrong* with you?" Prince Iladrul raved. "What don't you understand? The demons breached our borders! They killed our General at Arms! Yet, all that you care about is useless fawning over slaves and servants?"

Faunus recoiled.

"As you say, my Prince." He was cautious with his response. "But you should let my father know when you leave the castle grounds."

"Your father is not *my* father." Prince Iladrul snapped at him.

"Maybe not, my Prince." Faunus conceded. "But he is, now, the General of your Kinsgard. And he can't protect you if he doesn't know where you are."

"Perhaps I don't want to be protected." Prince Iladrul continued to stare up at Faunus. His brooding expression was now replaced by something entirely different.

It wasn't defeat, exactly. But it was an extremely near thing.

Whatever it was, Faunus didn't like it.

Having shared the cradle with Prince Iladrul, however, Faunus knew when to question the boy and when to let things bide.

"As you will, my Prince."

A strange shiver passed over the older boy's face before he looked away. Prince Iladrul was, clearly, finished with their palaver.

Faunus bowed to him again, though Prince Iladrul didn't see it, and turned away.

He hesitated for a moment, wondering what the right thing was to do.

He should speak with his father about his concerns regarding the Prince and he knew that. But his father had gone to the doxy village, presumably in seek of comfort from what he had seen. To go there without his father accompanying him could get Faunus into grave trouble. To interrupt his father if he were rutting with one of the breeding angels would ensure that his back was stripped.

He would wait, he thought. He would speak with his father when the General returned home.

This was his plan until he looked over his shoulder. Seeing Prince Iladrul so broken and small, he knew that his personal safety meant little and less compared to that of his future King.

Hoping the whipping he was liable to earn on his Prince's behalf was worth the effort, Faunus stepped onto the Great Road and began walking away from the castle grounds.

From where Prince Iladrul was sitting, the doxy village was two streams stemmed from the main river to the southeast. It was a pretty walk, with the river on one side and the forest on the other.

The forest also resumed on the other side of the river. It was on that side where Faunus and his friends usually approached on their ventures to spy.

When Faunus reached the bridge that crossed from the land of the freemen to that of the doxies, he stopped and looked toward the small shack where a guard should have been set. Given that their people had been attacked that morning, Faunus found it queer that the shack was empty. Yet, perhaps, this was merely because the angel on duty was securing the borders to the village.

Shrugging, Faunus looked toward the village, itself, to the many rows of cottages. They were built neatly together with only small gaps to separate them. Most of them had small back yards where the inhabitants could grow vegetables and many had flower beds neatly planted in front. Each cottage looked virtually the same; the only distinction being the odd porch swing or personal bric-a-brac chosen by the inhabitants to liven up, Faunus had to assume, a very dreary existence.

There was no luxury here, as there were for those born of the freemen and Kinsgard. What pleasures these folk found they made themselves.

While his father didn't own any of the breeding angels—purchase of the doxies was being saved for their children once they reached the age for such things—he did have one that he preferred. Though Faunus had only met her once, it had been at her cottage. Because of this, he knew exactly where to go to find his father.

He knocked, and he waited. Eventually she answered, at first curious and then smiling. Faunus smiled in return—an easy thing to do given that she was beautiful with her long brown hair and hazel eyes—and gave her a bow. "I seek my father, my Lady."

"I'm sorry, Faunus." She shook her head. "I believe that he's with Jeanir this afternoon."

Faunus continued to smile politely at her. She had said this with no jealousy. He didn't understand this, given she was his father's favorite whore. He supposed when he had whores of his

Balean's voice seethed with anger. In fact, he was angrier than Faunus had ever seen him be before.

Faunus braced himself as he turned to face his father. "Forgive me, Sir." He swallowed back his fear. "I wouldn't have come, but I think it's important."

"What do you know of important?" His father growled at him. His dark eyes were brooding and every line of his face was drawn in irritation.

"My concern is for Prince Iladrul, Sir." Faunus forced himself to hold his father's gaze. "Something is upsetting him."

His father's face transformed from one of anger and irritation to one of deep concern. "What, do you think, that might be?"

Faunus shook his head. He didn't know how to voice what he suspected.

"Out with it boy!" His father, not always a patient man, snapped.

Faunus shook his head again. But this time he found his voice.

"He's been distant. He won't train with us. He won't play with us either. He only sits by himself and broods." He lowered his gaze and swallowed. This he would be punished for and he knew it. "I asked him if he wanted to sneak to the river and watch the doxies bathe and he didn't even have an interest in that."

When his father spoke, his tone was bemused. "You shouldn't sneak about the doxies. You aren't ready for that."

Blushing, Faunus nodded. "Yes, Sir."

"Don't do it again." Still bemused, though the order buried within his words was clear. If he disobeyed he would regret it. He knew that and so promised himself he would no longer sneak through the forest to spy. "And tell your friends the same."

"Yes, Sir."

"How long has this been going on?" Now his voice was filled with concern again. "Prince Iladrul's behavior, I mean. Not your peeping."

"Since this morning." Faunus answered, relieved.

"Does this have to do with the demon, then?"

"I think so." Faunus nodded. "He seems . . ." He felt a strange satisfaction as he said the words. He wasn't certain where it came from, or why, and nor would he reflect on it. "He seems frightened, Sir."

General Balean nodded. "Go home, boy. You don't belong here."

"Yes, Sir." Faunus bowed to him.

His father turned away from him, ready to return to the angel within, and then froze. "Faunus."

"Yes, Sir?" Faunus, who was leaving, turned back to him.

"Best you don't tell anyone where you found me."

Faunus, taken aback by this request, stared at him with wide eyed confusion. Though he knew the consequences of class mixing, he had never seen them for himself and so took them far too lightly. He didn't understand what could happen to both Balean and Jeanir should Balean's consistent visits with his brother be discovered.

"Do you hear me?" Balean asked, impatiently.

"Yes, Sir." Faunus nodded as he decided whatever his father's reasons where they were his own.

His father glared at him in response. "I'll see you at supper."

-10-

Balean approached Wisterian very wearily. His King had been very moody all day.

Not that he didn't have good reason. Plenty had happened that day to put the Kingdom at risk. Balean, himself, had been out of sorts since seeing Titheron's felled body.

"Are you going to hover in the shadows all evening, Balean?" Wisterian, not looking up from the paperwork that consumed him, sighed after Balean had hovered at the door for far too long. "Or do you mean to palaver?"

"Forgive me, your Highness." Balean bowed to him. "I was lost in thought."

"You're lost in thought overly much these days." Wisterian raised his emerald gaze and pushed his long, copper hair behind his now pointed elf's ear. "You're not thinking of calling upon Sir Zadkiel I hope? I need you yet. I would hate to think you would permanently expire yourself a purpose."

Balean smiled at this and shook his head. "No, your Highness. Nothing like that."

"I'm glad to hear it." Wisterian nodded to him. "I would be lost without you."

"I appreciate your honor." Balean bowed to him.

"Then honor me enough, in like kind, to speak your mind." His wide mouth curled into a strange smile. "What troubles you Balean?"

Balean sighed, frowned, and bowed again. "I am concerned about Prince Iladrul."

"Iladrul?" Wisterian asked, his lips twitching. "Why?"

"My son," Balean gave him a tired, proud smile, "Faunus. He tells me that Prince Iladrul hasn't spent time with him and the other boys today."

"Is that true?" Wisterian asked, now visibly concerned.

"He is Faunus' best friend." Balean didn't know if this was true or not, though the two boys did spend the majority of their free time together. "My son would sense a change in Prince Iladrul if any of the boys were to do so."

Wisterian sighed and nodded. "I will speak with him."

"Thank you, your Highness." Balean bowed again, meaning to take his leave.

"How is Jeanir?"

Balean frowned at him. He had seen, for himself, by way of Zander, how Wisterian dealt with those who broke the rules and mixed classes. "Your Highness?"

"Where else would you go after a day such as yesterday?" Wisterian leveled his gaze upon Balean. "If not to take comfort from your brother and to gain counsel from our greatest warrior?"

Balean lowered his gaze. "I find myself a bit overwhelmed with my new station."

44

"You're up for the task." Wisterian lowered his quill. "Do you believe otherwise?"

"No." Balean's response was swift. He had nearly bested Titheron when the time for deciding which of them would be General had come. So that wasn't the problem. The problem lay in the fact that their greatest asset was living his life as a stud rather than as a soldier. "I don't, but . . ."

Wisterian cocked his head slightly to the left. His lips thinned. He waited, rather patiently, for Balean to continue.

"I merely wonder if now is the time to sit on politics."

"You believe I should put Jeanir in your place." It wasn't a question, though Balean nodded all the same. "He pulled his stone, Balean. The same as you."

"Are we to put our children's lives at risk because the storming stones decreed it should be so?" Balean asked him. "The vampires breached our borders. We're lucky it was only soldiers and angels who were slaughtered."

"I know you well, Balean." Wisterian sat back in his chair. "You wouldn't have come to me with a problem that has no solution."

Balean sighed his relief in response. "What if you were to purchase his doxy?"

Wisterian's green eyes narrowed.

"I know you have no interest in such things." Balean shrugged. "But Jamiason and Jeanir were fast friends. He knows the manner in which James strategizes better than any of us. And James is our enemy now." He swallowed. "I think you should consider purchasing Jeanir's eldest children for your son."

"He's too young." Wisterian barked. "He's barely found his hand."

"Your Highness," Balean tried to hold his frustrated tone. "Consider it an unnecessary precaution if you must." Wisterian's expression relaxed slightly. "Jeanir has been training all five of his children since they were born. The four boys can protect the Prince when he goes off to war. And the girl can become his taster to ensure that he's not poisoned."

45

Wisterian's lips thinned again. "Who would dare poison my son?"

"At war?" Balean shrugged. "Loyalties are going to be tested. It isn't going to be just elves and angels fighting at his side. You know we're going to have to call in our allies. With the humans fighting wars amongst themselves, who is to say what tricks they will play to garner power?"

"The Devonshires—"

He stopped midsentence. He knew that Balean was right. The Earls of Devonshire had long been their allies. They trusted the King of Devonshire, whose name was Jon, above all other humans. That didn't mean that the Devonshires didn't have enemies of their own.

"What does Jeanir's girl look like?"

"She's pretty." Balean assured him. "And the lads are strong."

"Have the boys see to their vasectomy." Wisterian looked swiftly away. "And pass the gold."

Balean narrowed his eyes. He understood the importance of ensuring that only doxy females breed. That didn't mean he was comfortable with the idea of cutting boys before they could become men.

Regardless of his personal thoughts on the subject, this had been something that all of the angels had agreed upon when it came time for the first male doxy to be sold upon the block.

"It will be done tonight."

"Do not speak of this to Jeanir." Wisterian rounded his gaze upon Balean. "He won't be pleased that his sons are being cut ten years too early."

Balean shook his head. He understood that Jeanir would be furious. He wasn't going to be the one to navigate that conversation.

"Tell the children's mothers to keep quiet as well." Wisterian counseled him. "Pay them extra gold if you have to."

"An easy enough thing." Balean grunted at him. "They all share the same mother and she happens to be my preferred whore."

Wisterian started at that. "You jest."

"Nit." He lowered his gaze, ashamed of his actions. "In fact, I think the girl might, actually, be mine. She has Faunus' look about her."

Wisterian, frowning, shook his head. Balean wasn't certain he cared for the tight lipped smile his friend was trying to hide.

"Come to me in the morning." Wisterian muttered. "I'll have my orders for Jeanir ready by then."

Balean gave Wisterian a cautious bow and backed, very swiftly, out of the room.

-11-

Ishitar knocked on the open door, smiling at Loki, who sat behind his desk rifling through paperwork. His dark brown hair was slightly disheveled and his purple eyes were bright with what seemed to be amusement. When he looked up and saw that it was Ishitar who came to call, his cocky grin widened.

"Your Royal Highness." He planted his hands upon his desk and stood before raising one of them toward Ishitar so that he could shake it. "How are you this morning?"

"Well." Ishitar stepped forward and took the proffered hand. "May I steal a shift of the shadows?"

"Undoubtedly." Loki replied, indicating one of the chairs on the other side of the desk. "May I offer you something to drink?"

"I prefer wine." Ishitar smiled as he lowered himself into his chair. "If you have it."

"I do." He nodded and stepped away. Ishitar watched him with keen interest as Loki set about his task. "How may I help you, your Royal Highness?"

"Please, Loki." Ishitar smiled up at Loki as he looked over his shoulder. "I prefer to simply be called Ishitar by you. Leave your fealty aside when we are in our privacy."

"Very well." Loki shrugged and returned his attention to the bar. "How may I help you, Ishitar?"

"I have very much appreciated your tutelage." Ishitar explained. "But I fear I need more from you."

"Such as?" Loki turned toward Ishitar, holding out a glass of wine. He, himself, had a glass of whiskey.

"Zadkiel is a bit . . ." He chuckled and shook his head. "I love my Da. Never doubt it. But every bird must eventually leave the safety of their preening parents' nest."

"Are you asking my permission?" Loki teased.

"No." Ishitar smiled at him. "Of course not. I am informing you that I intend to stay with you. I chose you because I can explain to my father that the reason I must is to learn my mother's arts. Otherwise, I'll be forced to live with him. And I require more freedom than he would, necessarily, afford me."

"I see." Loki lowered himself into his chair and crossed his arms over his chest. "My problem is that I don't know where to put you. Sam is in my old room and Aiken Darklief has been staying in Sappharon's when he isn't in the Oakland Grove."

"I regret that I will be displacing Aiken." He informed Loki. "But I've already made myself comfortable in Sappharon's room."

Loki's brow furrowed slightly as his purple eyes assessed Ishitar. Finally he smiled and shook his head. "Regret is unnecessary. Aiken is only here on occasion. He can sleep on the sofa when he pays a visit."

"I do hope that he doesn't mind."

"It's not a problem." Loki assured Ishitar. "Aiken has never been picky about bedding where he lands." Then with a furrowed brow, "How will Zadkiel take it? Your moving in with me?"

"Hard." Ishitar sighed and immediately changed the subject. "How is my mother?"

"Well enough." Loki looked swiftly away.

Ishitar's eyes narrowed and his smile grew tight.

"Aiken intends on making a stew for dinner tonight." Loki's tone was cautious. "It's been on the fire all day. You don't want to miss the first night of it. It's when it tastes the best."

Ishitar gave him a guarded chuckle in response. "What meat?"

"Lamb." Loki muttered under his breath. "Or, so, that's what he tells me."

"Then I shall pretend that he isn't lying." Ishitar winked at him.

-12-

Aiken shut the door to Loki's apartment, frowning.

A prince from one of the water fairy tribes had visited the Oakland Grove to look at his youngest daughter. He had hoped, desperately, that the pair would be a match. But the youngling hadn't been serious about the courtship and was there only upon the orders of his father.

The prince, himself, was still grieving the death of the woman that he had intended to marry and had no interest in replacing her given that his grief was still raw.

Aiken understood the youngling's position. Because of this, he wasn't offended by the boy's rejection of his daughter. But he needed to get her married off and he knew that she wanted desperately to marry a prince rather than one of the common people.

"Loki?" He called.

There was no answer.

That was alright. Loki was probably in the basement dealing with the damned.

He threw his bag of vegetables onto one of the chairs and made his way down the hall to the room where Loki allowed him to stay when he came to visit. When he reached the door he opened it, stopping short as his eyes fell upon a very tall, broad backed man wearing nothing more than his small clothes.

Smiling to himself, Aiken cleared his throat and said, "Loki is overly generous with his gifts these days."

The man started and turned swiftly around. The very moment Aiken saw his face he was overcome with embarrassment.

"My Gods." He said, shaking his head. "Forgive me, your Royal Highness. I was only teasing."

"Never mind it." Ishitar smiled at Aiken. "I should have locked the door."

"No, I—" Aiken lowered his gaze. "I should have knocked."

"On your own bedchamber door?" He asked as he reached for the white linen shendyt he was known for wearing and wrapped it around his hips. "I'm an unexpected guest and I've taken over your living quarters."

"They aren't really *my* living quarters." He shook his head. "I have my own apartment. I just prefer to stay with Loki when I'm visiting the Hells."

"I understand." The Prince of Providence smiled at him. "I hear you're brewing a stew?"

"It's lamb." Aiken grinned at him. "Whatever else he told you—"

"He told me it's lamb." Price Ishitar replied, clearly amused. "I hope you don't mind but I intend to redecorate your room."

Aiken looked around. He, himself, hadn't bothered. He'd always felt that it was Loki's place to disturb Lady Lucias' things. Given that Loki hadn't changed anything else in the apartment, Aiken didn't think that he would have wanted to change Sappharon's room either.

"It's your mother's home, so such is your right." He muttered. "By any road, these are Dame Sappharon's things."

"Oh." Prince Ishitar's lips twitched. "No wonder the place is so . . . eh . . . womanly."

"I see." Aiken winked at him. "You thought these were my things because I'm a fairy."

"The thought did cross my mind," Ishitar teased.

"Very nice." Aiken rolled his eyes.

"Sorry." He shrugged.

"Right." Aiken, smiling now, turned away. "I have vegetables to chop."

"Would mind my company?"

"Not at all." Aiken replied, surprised.

"Do you know how to bake a pie?"

Aiken shook his head.

Ishitar gave him one of his contemplative smiles as he pointed to a bag upon his bed. It was filled with the gourds he had picked from Noliminan's tree. Irritated by his antics, I shook my head.

"I mean to make Loki a special one to thank him for allowing me to stay with him. Would you care if I baked it while you finished the stew?"

"Certainly not." Aiken grinned. "He told me about your last pie. I would like to try a slice myself."

The Prince of Providence considered him for a moment and then gave him a slight nod. "Of course. But just a small slice if you please. The rest, you must understand, is meant for Loki."

"I only want a taste."

"Then a taste you shall have." Still wearing his contemplative smile. "But no more than a taste shall you crave."

Aiken furrowed his brow. Though he had wanted more than a single slice if the pie were good, suddenly the idea of more than just that one taste made his stomach churn.

A single slice, it seemed, would be far more than enough to quell his curiosity.

-13-

Iykva waited for thirteen days for an audience with Jamiason. This didn't trouble him, however. Audiences with a King are hard to come by in the most peaceful of times. These days, Iykva was lucky to have been granted Jamiason's attention at all.

The demons had been uprising for far too many passes of the sun for Iykva to count. Jamiason had seen it coming and had been able to quell it thus far.

Iykva knew that he would not be able to convince the demons to bide much longer. The time for war had come. The time to overtake the angels now that their earthen children were close to reaching adolescence so the demons and their descendants could utilize their strengths and farm them for harvest.

The doors to the great throne room opened and two childlike, dark haired vampires stood to either side. Iykva knew these two well; they were the first ever made. The twins, they were called more often than by their actual names. Had they been singletons, one of them would have been in line to become God of the vampire race once Jamiason deemed them ready. Because they were not, and because they had been made too young, it was the third that Jamiason had turned who would claim this honor.

Iykva had never seen or met Prince Paul. Though, gossip of Jamiason's fledgling *had* reached his ears. By all accounts the once human prince was a laughing, idiotic fool who was less than adequately qualified to rule.

Iykva rose from the chair upon which he had been waiting and swallowed his discord. Though he, too, was a demon rather than merely a vampire, he had heard rumors of the favor that Lord Evanbourough had bestowed upon Jamiason and his lineage. To displease Jamiason, or his fledglings, was to displease their God, himself. To displease Lord Evanbourough could bring about the punishment of the rising sun.

As his eyes fell upon Jamiason for the first time since their turning, Iykva was stricken by the changes that had overtaken him since their turning. James' blue eyes were preternaturally cold and appraising. The expression that he wore was stony. He was still, looking to be little more than a statue.

It was the other that commanded him; the fool of a Prince. "Come forward."

Iykva did as he was bid, looking to the left of Jamiason's throne. There was the other; the carrot top that he had heard about. How very human he looked with the tumble of copper hair over his brow and trimmed, bearded face.

THE SCRIBING OF ISHITAR: ASHES TO ASHES

Though pale, how easily must he be able to dwell, unnoticed, amongst his own kind?

Iykva loathed him for his all too human appearance, which would allow him to more easily beckon his prey.

Forcing himself to ignore his distaste for the Prince that would one day govern him, Iykva stepped before Jamiason's throne and bowed low, his left foot back and his black wings spread wide. "Your Highness."

Jamiason didn't respond or move. He merely sat and watched. His cold blue eyes and unmoving expression were unsettling.

It was the other, the one that had bid him to come forward, who asked, "What gift have you brought our King for his audience?"

Prepared for this eventuality, Iykva reached into the folds of his robes and brought out a rolled tapestry that had been woven by the mischief fairies of the Blackwood Grove. Knowing that Jamiason had once served the Emissary God of this race, and so had a fondness for these people, Iykva had bartered much to obtain this bit of artistry.

The other stood and stepped forward, taking the tapestry from Iykva's hand. He stepped toward Jamiason and unrolled it. It was larger than it appeared as a scroll and, because of this, Iykva was unable to see his King's face or expression behind it. He *was* able to see Jamiason's hand rise—ever so slightly—however, and wave his companion to the side.

The other nodded to Iykva and bowed.

"It pleases him." Prince Paul said as he took the tapestry from Jamiason and begin to roll it back into a scroll. "You may speak your mind."

Behind him he heard the light footsteps of the twins and the heavy clanking of the doors as the throne room was sealed shut. Iykva bowed to the other and then returned his attention to King Jamiason. He bowed to him again for good measure and began.

"I come before you to speak on behalf of our race." He said. "Not those made, but we true demons." Jamiason said nothing. Nor did his eyes—or any other part of him for that matter—

move. Yet, he was watching Iykva, so the demon knew that he was listening, and, more importantly, that he was hearing. "We believe the time for striking the elves has come."

Silence. No movement. Still just watching.

"Our army has trained and is ready at your will, your Highness." Iykva advised him. "We are strong and we can, and will, overtake them."

Jamiason continued to stare at him as Prince Paul spoke. "Do your people not think it wise to first meet with King Wisterian to discuss your demands? And then strike if they are not met?"

"Our demands are that they freely supplicate their children to our will, your Highness." He replied to Jamiason, not the other.

This was a nearly fatal mistake.

Jamiason's eyes widened and he bared his fanged teeth in a growl. Before Iykva had a chance to mark his anger for disrespecting his progeny, Jamiason advanced upon him and thrust the demon upward with hand clinched tightly around Iykva's neck, choking him. Iykva felt his feet dangling beneath him as his hands grasped desperately for the one around his neck, but he was helpless against the strength of his King.

He felt the grip release from his neck as he fell to the floor in a heap. Before he had time to even raise his head, Jamiason had returned to his seat and was staring at him, wearing that same, cold expression that had darkened his features before.

It is as though he hasn't even moved!

"You will address me directly, if you please." Prince Paul counseled him in a cool, somewhat amused tone.

"Yes." Iykva swallowed as he found his feet. He wanted to raise his hand to soothe his crushed throat but he knew that to show weakness would defeat his cause for seeking King Jamiason's audience. "Forgive me, my Prince." He bowed to Jamiason's companion. "I meant you no disrespect."

The vampire nodded and replied. "Regardless of what your demands are, Wisterian deserves the opportunity to meet them of his free will before we attack his people. He would grant us the same courtesies, were our situations reversed."

"Begging your pardon, my Prince," Iykva bowed to him again, "but he will not meet this particular demand with his free will."

"Which is when you may gather your army and strike the elves." The vampire said with his head cocked slightly to the side.

Iykva realized something of overwhelming importance in that moment. Prince Paul was listening to something. Yet when he turned his gaze toward Jamiason he noted that his King's lips were not moving. Rather, he was as still as he had ever been.

"If you mean to attack King Wisterian and his people, then his Highness first bids that you arrange a meeting between the two. King Jamiason will present your demands with a deadline. Should that deadline not be met, then you have my permission to proceed." His head straightened. "But not a single shift of the shadows before. Do you understand?"

"Yes, my Prince." Iykva replied, bowing. He had gotten what he wanted, even though it would be delayed.

Yet, perhaps, the delay was wise. Nothing good could come out of an attack made upon children. One God, or perhaps another, might be offended and exact his revenge.

"You are dismissed." Prince Paul said, raising his hand and waving it at Iykva to excuse him.

Almost offended by the rudeness of the gesture, Iykva bowed to him. He then turned to Jamiason, realized the demon King was still watching him, and bowed even lower.

He didn't like the darkness buried within Jamiason's cold blue eyes.

He didn't like it even one little bit.

"Your Highness." He turned to Prince Paul and bowed. "My Prince."

As swiftly as possible, he turned to walk toward the closed doors. The twins stepped to the center where they met, turned the knobs and pushed the doors open.

Iykva had never been so grateful to leave a room in the full of his immortal life.

-14-

"Leave us." James barked at the twins before turning to Paul. The twins, ever obedient, did as they were bid. "What do you think of Iykva's proposal?"

"That it's pure shit." Paul shrugged. "What else would I think of it?"

Jamiason felt his lips wanting to twitch into a smile. Now was not the time to be amused by Paul's infallible sense of humor and mortal bred ways, however. There were important matters to discuss. "What do you mean to do about it?"

"I told him we have to meet with the elves." Paul suddenly wore a confused expression. "What more can I do?"

"Maybe nothing." Jamiason pushed himself off of his throne and onto his feet. "Maybe much." His expression hard, he turned to face Paul. "I cannot condone it. You must understand that."

"I do." Paul looked swiftly away.

"Whatever you have to say to me," Jamiason's eyes narrowed, "say it."

"Louis says—"

"Louis says." Jamiason snorted and turned away from him. "Louis is possessive. And has long coveted your position at my side."

"Yes, your Highness."

"Stop it." James growled at Paul. "We're alone."

Paul's eyes darted to the door, where they both knew the twins stood, hovering on the other side so that they might eavesdrop. James waved his hand at the door, not caring if they overheard. They may be snoops, but they weren't spies. Anything that was said between Jamiason and Paul would remain between Jamiason and Paul.

"James . . ." Paul's tone was one of guarded disdain. "We can't stand against our own people to protect the elves."

"Standing against them and preventing them from making a fundamental—and unforgiveable—error are two different things." James responded to this, his pacing coming to a halt as he glared at Paul. "There is nothing overt that we can do. I agree. This doesn't mean we cannot act where we might."

Paul rolled his eyes and shook his head. "You and I?"

"And the twins." Jamiason shrugged.

"The twins." Paul scoffed. "You jest."

"Not about my twins."

Yes, the boys had been made into vampires at too young an age. But they were made with his God's blood. As such, they were more powerful than any other vampire—demon or otherwise—in any one of the many worlds.

Never mind that James knew, without any doubt, that they would never betray him.

"I do not understand your infallible faith in them." Paul admitted. "But I've little and less choice other than to trust you."

"No." Jamiason agreed. "You don't." He made his way to his throne again and lowered himself within it before turning to face Paul. "You and I must palaver with them. Employ them. They are stealthy and crafty. And, given their youth, they will be underestimated in their guile."

Paul rolled his eyes closed and bent his neck back. "Now I see."

"Good." Jamiason muttered. "Because I need you to see. I need you to understand." Paul raised his head and met Jamiason's gaze. "This is not a game, Paul. If we lose this battle of the wits with Iykva and his clan, we are, all of us, damned."

-15-

Loki sat back in his chair, sated from the last slice of the pie that Ishitar had baked for him. He wasn't one for sweets. As such, I suspect that his desire to eat every last bite of the damn thing was puzzling to him.

Smiling, he patted his belly. He was clearly full. After Aiken's savory stew and Ishitar's damn pie, how could he feel anything otherwise?

His burp, as he leaned forward to look at the paperwork on his desk, was followed by a crooked smile.

"My Lord?"

Loki looked upward and grinned at his demon. "Sam! You missed a wonderful meal."

"Forgive me." Samyael smiled at him. "I was distracted in the Courtyard."

Loki smiled warmly at him. "It *is* your day off."

"You have a guest." Sam advised him, still smiling. "Dame Sappharon."

"Sappharon?" He started. "Here?"

Sam nodded. "She tells me it is important that she speaks with you immediately."

Loki's brow furrowed as he considered how she had told Sam anything. Though he understood her sign language because of the time he had spent with Lucias, he had never taught it to his demon. "Send her in."

Samyael bowed and took his leave.

Several shifts later a woman who looked like Sappharon stepped in.

But it wasn't Sappharon. She didn't have the wings of a demon, for one thing. For another, her face was slightly different. Her nose was less delicate and her chin was squared.

Never mind that she had breasts which swelled large and ripe, drawing his eyes to them as a hungry grin played upon his lips. Sappharon's girlish tits were small and nearly non-existent.

It was as he was staring at her breasts that understanding seemed to dawn upon him. "Na'amah."

She grasped the tattered rags she wore as a skirt and gave him a clumsy curtsey. "My Lord."

"What are you thinking, child?" He asked her. "Have you been seen?"

"I do not believe so." She swallowed and raised her fiery gaze to meet his. "I seek your succor. Will you grant it to me?"

"Ta." No hesitation. "Damn it." He shook his head. "Of course I will, girl. Won't you sit?"

"I do not mean to trouble you, my Lord." Her tone was desperate as she found her seat. "But I am frightened. I haven't heard a single word from—or about—met Mome for many thousands of passes of the morning sun and—"

"She's well." Loki assured her. "She's with Lucias."

Her relief was palpable as her expression relaxed from fear to hope. "Thank every one of the Gods."

"You're a waif." This was said with some hesitation as his eyes flicked to the huge swell of her breasts. Her cheeks were sunken and her waistline thin, but there was no denying the natural figure she wore buried beneath the rags of her clothes. "Are you hungry?"

"Yes." She nodded, licking her lips. "I am famished."

He looked to the open library door and then returned his gaze to her. Given his house was currently full of unexpected company, this was not the safest place for her to be.

"Na'amah." He said, his tone gentle. "I will protect you. But I cannot do so while you wear your mother's face."

"No?" Her voice trembled slightly.

"May I suggest that, for now, you take on another form?" He offered. Her eyes flashed with offense. He raised his hands to her. "Only for now. Until I can ensure your safety."

She lowered her face as if she were looking at her feet. Then, almost hesitantly, she nodded. "If you tell me that this is the only way, then I shall agree to your command and form myself as a dog—as your pet."

"It is." He assured her. "There are others staying with me right now and—though I believe they are honorable and you will be safe—I cannot guarantee my protection over you if they learn what you are."

Granting him a doubtful smile, she complied.

-16-

Na'amah followed Lord Loki through his apartment to his kitchen. The demon who had opened the door to her sat at the table eating from a bowl and talking to a fairy. A third man sat at the table with his chin on his bent knuckles, his eyes shifting from one to the other of the other two as he listened, with an interested smile, to their bantering conversation.

His face was blindingly familiar to her.

But, then, why wouldn't it be?

It was Lord Regent Lucias' face to the smallest detail. The only reason she knew that it *wasn't* Lord Lucias was because the man wearing it had light brown hair and eyes.

"Is there any lamb left?" Lord Loki asked the room at large. "For the mutt?"

All three of them turned their eyes to Na'amah. She found herself scooting closer to Lord Loki's leg. She was grateful to him when he bent down and patted her head. It was the fairy who turned his gaze toward Lord Loki and gave him a smile. "No. But if she isn't picky then there's a leg bone in the cupboard she can gnaw on."

Lord Loki snorted. "Whose leg?"

"I had to execute a rapist." The fairy shrugged. "I saw no need to let the meat spoil."

"You are disturbed." Lord Loki muttered as he turned toward the cooling cupboard.

"Where did you get a dog?" The demon asked as he found his feet and lowered himself at Na'amah's side. His large black eyes were sparkling with pleasurable greed as he reached for her muzzle to stroke her, and his thick lips were split into a wide grin. "Did Dame Sappharon give her to us?"

"She asked us to look after her." Lord Loki agreed in amused tones as he pulled the leg out of the cupboard and threw it on the counter. I know that he views Samyael as more of a friend then a servant. That Na'amah's presence so obviously made the demon happy pleased him. "Aiken, for the love of all that's obscene. You chop this damn thing up for her. I can't bring myself to do it."

The fairy, shrugging again, stood. "You know, for such a masculine creature, you certainly do have a weak constitution."

The third man chuckled and shook his head. "You could have at least removed the foot."

"I intend to." Aiken replied to that. "But not until I'm ready to boil it."

The demon stuck his tongue out, disgusted, as he ran his hand upward so that he could scratch Na'amah between her ears. "What's your name, girl?"

"A good question." Lord Loki replied as he leaned against the wall and crossed his arms over his chest. "What do you think we should call her?"

"Ansibrius." The man who looked like Lord Regent Lucias muttered. "From the ancient text. It means my son's protector." He stood and walked toward her, lowering himself beside the demon so that he could look into her eyes. "Did my mother send you to watch over me?"

Lord Loki shifted uncomfortably at Na'amah's side. Without meaning to, she whined.

"I bet she did." The young God grinned at her and looked up at Lord Loki, a rare, and very greedy, expression brightening his features. "May I please keep her, Loki? Might I call her mine own? I've never had a pet before."

"I don't mind." Lord Loki replied as his eyes danced to Na'amah. "It would be better for her, to be certain. You can take her to see Sappharon when you visit your mother."

Na'amah barked her pleasure at that sentiment and began wagging her tail. This made the man who looked like Lucias smile.

And what a pleasing smile it is at that.

The handsome young God stood and reached for the meat that the fairy had cut up. Once it was in his hand, he began walking out of the room. She looked at Lord Loki, who indicated the young God with his chin, telling her she should follow him.

She barked at Lord Loki and then turned to chase after the younger one.

He led her to a bedchamber and sat on the bed. He patted the mattress beside himself and laid out the meat. Starving, she jumped upward and devoured every piece.

"Good girl." He said as he reached for her and scratched her between the ears. "Good Ansibrius."

She raised her snout and leaned toward him. He grinned at her and began stroking her muzzle. Comforted by his large hands, she reached toward him and licked his face. In an oddly childlike way he burst into laughter and threw his arms around her neck to pull her close.

"My name is Ishitar." He whispered. "And I will take the best of care of you for all of the rest of your days. It is my undying promise to you."

Understanding that he wouldn't be saying this if he knew what she was, she backed slightly away from him and barked.

It was a promise that she would never hold him to, because it was a promise that he would never be able to keep.

-17-

Corline buried her hands in the dirt and grinned. She found deep satisfaction in digging up the soil and planting the vegetables that she knew Lord Loki would crave with his meals.

Distracted by her task to please Lord Loki and Lady Lucias, she failed to sense the presence of danger.

She felt the sting of a bug's bite. She didn't know, of course, that this was no bug's bite at all, but a tranquilizing dart sent from the traditional blow dart gun of the bronzies, who had sought to claim her.

As the world spun around her, Corline shook her head, trying desperately to clear her mind.

Unable to, she fell forward.

No longer a threat, the bronzies took her for the sole purpose of adding her to the attractions of their carnival so that they could breed her.

-18-

Finding Lucias brooding in her library, Sappharon approached the Goddess very cautiously. "My Lady?"

Lucias flicked her dark brown eyes upward and gave Sappharon a frustrated frown. "What is it, brat?"

"Are you alright?" She asked.

Lucias sighed and shook her head. "No." She muttered. "Corline's pack appears to have moved on. She must have opted to migrate with it." Then, in frustrated tones, "And bearing Loki's child!"

Sappharon raised her hand to respond and then lowered it again. She thought it best not to say what was truly on her mind. Knowing the bitch was gone made her happy. Lucias wouldn't have wanted to know that. "I'm sorry for your pain."

"I knew when I took her for Loki that it would eventually happen." She's sighed. "She's mortal. And a true blooded benandanti werewolf. The packs must migrate with their prey. I only wish that she would have allowed me the courtesy of having told me that she was leaving us before she did so."

Sappharon nodded. "Perhaps it broke her heart to be forced to choose between you and Loki or her pack and she was unable bear the goodbye."

Lucias gave her a strange smile. She was surprised that the demon was being understanding of her feelings, rather than flippant or rude, because this was the manner in which Sappharon normally responded where Loki's mortal geese came to concern. "Perhaps you're right."

"Is there anything that I might do to ease your pain?"

Lucias' eyes danced over Sappharon's face. Sappharon felt a blush rise to her cheeks under her silent regard. Finally, Lucias said, "I beg you to promise me, right here and now, that you shall never leave me."

Sappharon started at that. She couldn't imagine a life that did not include her beloved Lady. Her hands, when she responded, were snappish with her offense at the mere thought that Lucias might believe she would. "Never in *life*."

Lucias nodded and held out her hand. "Come, brat. Sit with me."

Eager for any attention she might be granted, Sappharon stepped forward and grasped her Mistress' hand. Lucias raised it to her lips and kissed it as she guided Sappharon into the seat next to hers.

When she spoke, it was in cautious tones. "I have something I must tell you." She said. "And it is probably something that will anger you."

Sappharon steeled herself, ready for anything.

Or so she thought.

Though she should have seen it coming after Metatron's visit, nothing could have prepared her for Lucias' news.

"I've been with Loki." She said, her eyes assessing Sappharon's face so she might garner her reaction. "I wish to become pregnant with his child."

Sappharon flew the hand that was holding Lucias' away and glared at her. The very idea was madness.

"Please understand, Sappharon." Lucias beseeched her, "It isn't something that I am doing on a lark. I have my reasons."

"You always have your reasons for what you do." Sappharon signed desperately at her. "But this is madness. Noliminan will never stand for you bearing the fool's child!"

Lucias assessed Sappharon for a long, almost painful minute before looking swiftly away. When she spoke, her tone was resolved.

"He will not interfere." She assured Sappharon. "He will understand my game play for what it is."

"He will consider your bedding Loki a betrayal." Sappharon disagreed, "My Lady—"

"Sappharon." Lucias shook her head. "He won't. He'll see it for what it is. My nymph being set into play on the board."

Sappharon's brow furrowed at that. "Your pawn?"

Lucias gave her the barest ghost of a smile.

"Sappharon," she reached for Sappharon's cheek and set her palm against it. "Isn't that all he has ever been?"

Sappharon, turning her gaze to the kings' board, felt her lips curl at their corners into what became her first true smile in as many years as she could remember.

-19-

When Jeanir heard the bell start to ring in the village center, he lowered the book that he had been reading and scowled at his cottage door.

It was far too soon for any of the children in the village to even find the knife, let alone be put up for barter.

He uncrossed his long legs and stood, smoothing his skirt over his thighs as he rose and running his fingers through his long, braided hair in an effort to comb it. He gave his wings a quick shake to lose any loose feathers and then stormed through the room. He stepped onto the porch, pulled his door closed with no sense of delicacy and skipped down the stairs to the small path that led from his patio to the Great Road.

He was not the only one wandering the streets with an expression of confusion mixed with rage. When he reached the block in the village center, which had been built for the purpose of display and sale, he sought one of his closest companions and stood beside him with arms folded defensively over his chest. "Not one of yours, is it?"

"I guess we'll find out." Ach'tmeck replied with a frown. "I hope not. Even my oldest is far too young."

"As are my boys." Jeanir replied, shaking his wings again. "I thought we had a good ten years before Prince Iladrul made his first purchase."

"Ta." Ach'tmeck nodded. "Me too."

All of their nerves raw, they watched in silence as the guard who was on duty at the entrance of the village for the day—an angel named Nounak—stepped forward with a scroll in hand. He walked directly to the block, jumped upward, fluttering his wings to catch the air, and landed gracefully in the center. He unrolled the scroll, read it, and then looked swiftly around. His expression bore the same confusion that everyone in the courtyard, waiting to learn the fate of their children, was feeling.

"By order of King Wisterian, it is here, and thereafter, decreed that the doxy, Jeanir breken Thyman," to this, Jeanir started; that was his name and the other was his mortal father's, "relocate his belongings to the castle and report to King Wisterian in his permanent service."

"What?" The pure surprise that marked Ach'tmeck's features was chilling.

Jeanir set his hand on the block and leaned forward. "Are you certain these are my orders?"

"Sorry, Jeanir," Nounak replied with a nervous smile and a shrug. "Looks like your doxy is off the block."

"I didn't realize I was *on* the block!" Jeanir seethed under his breath.

He stopped himself as he looked around and saw all of the young faces who would soon receive similar messages. He forced himself to calm his emotions.

"My lot is my lot." He hoped his false smile appeared real to the young ones, who were looking up at him with wide, terrified eyes. "And to be a doxy bought and paid for is an elf's greatest honor. This is especially true when one is purchased by a King or Prince."

Maybe Wisterian knows what he's doing, he thought as he saw scared faces slightly relax beneath young eyes watching him with deep fascination. *Maybe it's better that it's one of us first. This way, we can set the tone regarding the appropriate fashion to accept one's fate.*

He decided his belongings, and his cutting, could wait. He would send one of the castle servants to gather them later and visit one of the physicians in the castle for his vasectomy. It was best, he knew, that he leave and that none of the younglings see him again until they joined him in the castle as doxies, themselves.

He walked swiftly out of the village but didn't bother walking the rest of the way. It would be faster if he used his wings and he wanted to find out just what in the name of Loki's Gods be damned beard this purchase of his flesh was all about.

He did find his feet when he made it to the courtyard, however. It had ever been courtesy, since Iladrul was born, not to use the gift of flight in the elves' presence. He walked swiftly through the castle to Wisterian's apartment, where he pounded, rather than knocked, on the door.

It was one of the castle servants who opened the door, but this didn't surprise Jeanir. "Is Wisterian available Mailak?"

"In his study." She replied. "Do you want me to announce you?"

"I am overly certain that he is expecting me." Jeanir replied tightly. "No need."

He stepped past her and made his way through the apartment to the library. The door was open. He had only to step into the door frame and knock on its wood. Wisterian looked upward, at first clearly irritated, and, then, wearing a tepid smile. "Good morn, Jeanir."

"Your Highness." Jeanir wasn't certain how he managed to hold his tone. He was furious with Wisterian. Yet, he also understood his place. "I've just learned I am to be your doxy."

"So it would seem." Wisterian's eyes trailed over his face as he tried to reconcile Jeanir's true response to what the angel believed to be an unforgivable insult. He pointed at one of the chairs on the other side of his large desk. "Take a seat. We'll talk."

"If it's all the same, your Highness," Jeanir frowned at him, "I'd prefer to stand."

"What is publicly done cannot be undone. So sit down." Wisterian's voice was somewhat commanding. Because of this,

67

Jeanir did as he was bid and took a seat. "I actually have a different arrangement between you and I planned than what you might expect."

"Oh?" Jeanir asked, his brow raising. "My heart is simply breaking. Shall I grab a hanky to catch the tears I'm apt to cry?"

Wisterian chuckled at that. "Balean came to see me yesterday."

Jeanir stiffened. "And?"

"And," Wisterian sighed, "my purchase of your doxy was his idea."

"Why would he suggest such a thing?" Jeanir, though furious with his brother, somehow managed to hold his affronted tone. "And why, your Highness, did you agree?"

"Because you trained under both Sir Michael and Sir Metatron." Wisterian replied, his brow furrowing. "You're the only one, aside Dame Sappharon, who can make that claim. Leastwise, without other pupils in your class."

"Sir Michael saw potential in me."

"Which makes you more valuable in the training yard than in a whore's bed." Wisterian spun away, finding his feet. "And it makes your children more valuable in the training yard as well."

Jeanir froze in his seat. When he spoke, his tone was dripping with discontentment. "What has your purchase of my flesh to do with my children, your Highness?"

"Gold has been passed, Jeanir." Wisterian walked around the desk and lowered himself to sit upon it at Jeanir's left side. "Your oldest boys have been sent to the knife. By Seventh Moon, the four of them, and your eldest daughter, will be gifted to Iladrul."

Jeanir flew to his feet. His hand balled into a fist and flew to the desk, pounding it. The purchase of his flesh had been one thing. He could bide that if he had to. Not, however, the sale of his children.

"They're too young!"

"That may be." Wisterian agreed in dead pan tones. "But the vampires have breached our borders. Titheron has been killed. Drastic measures must be taken."

"Then send *your* Gods be damned son to the knife." Jeanir growled through his teeth. "And your daughter, when you sire one, to whore herself in one of *my* sons' beds."

"You pulled the stone." Wisterian reminded him, his tone terse. "And made your vows."

"I made vows for *men*." Jeanir stormed. "Not children."

"Done is done." Wisterian snapped. "So make your peace with it."

Jeanir's lips pursed as he shook his head. There would be no making peace with this. "You've set the age, then."

"The age for what?"

"The knife is found for every boy my sons' age." Jeanir raised his hand and pointed a finger at Wisterian's chest. Though it was against all custom, he jabbed at his King. "Do you understand me, Wisterian? You've set the Gods be damned *age*."

Wisterian glared at him, horrified. "You can't mean to castrate every boy—"

"Castrating young boys was *your* decision." Jeanir growled. "All boys of the age. Do you hear me? I will not have my sons be soft and womanly unless every male doxy from here forth bears the same Gods be damned curse." He grit his teeth again. "I will not have them be ridiculed or thought of as fodder for a bronzie carnival."

Wisterian considered him with a dark expression for many shifts. Finally, his face pale, he looked, far too swiftly, away. Jeanir was glad to see that he had the sense to be embarrassed by what he had done.

"Very well." He muttered. "I've set the age."

Far from placated, Jeanir pulled his finger, which was still jabbed toward Wisterian's chest, away. "Have you told your son that he's to become a whore master?"

"Not yet." Wisterian muttered, returning his gaze to meet Jeanir's. "He won't be any more pleased by this than you are."

"How unfortunate for him."

Wisterian, understanding the position he had put Jeanir in, made no response.

-20-

Iladrul, who was sitting across the table from his mother playing a mindless game of storming stones, lifted his gaze to look upon the face of his father. As he did so, he shivered.

King Wisterian's expression was hard and unyielding. Even as he stepped behind Iladrul's mother and grasped her shoulders with his large hands, Iladrul knew that he wasn't here for pleasantries.

"Storming stones, eh?" He muttered.

Iladrul's mother, a copper haired angel named Helena, raised her gaze to smile at her husband. "Your son is a master."

Iladrul looked swiftly away lest either one of them see him roll his eyes. There was no skill required in the game of storming stones. It was a game of fate. The pulling of the stone directed the player's next move. Iladrul preferred the game of kings' castles. At the kings' board, strategy and forethought were the point.

"I would expect nothing less." Wisterian replied. "But I must steal him away from the stones."

"But it's Sixth Moon." Helena sighed. "You get him First through Fifth!"

"I understand, Mother." Wisterian leaned forward and kissed the crown of her head. "But politics call when they do."

"Very well." Helena sighed as she flicked her eyes to Iladrul. "You are dismissed, child."

"Thank you, Mother." Iladrul reached for her hand across the storming board, raised it to his lips and kissed the back of it. She smiled adoringly at him, pulling her hand away to allow him to follow Wisterian through the courtyard.

They didn't speak until they were in his father's apartment. Once there, Iladrul bowed his head and waited, respectfully, for Wisterian to share his news.

As Iladrul's father lowered himself into the chair behind the desk in his library, he gave his son a guarded smile. "How are you, boy?"

"Well." Iladrul swallowed. Wisterian watched him with appraising eyes from across the desk. "I'm at the top of all classes."

"So you are." Wisterian muttered.

His expression was drawn. Watching him, waiting, Iladrul suddenly felt extremely uncomfortable. He swallowed and asked, "How might I serve you, Pipa?"

The term of endearment made Wisterian smile. It was false, and it was tight, but it was a smile all the same. He was pleased with Iladrul because his son wanted to get right to the point.

"I've purchased your first round of doxies."

"Your Highness?" Iladrul started. "First round? I thought I was meant only one on the first draw."

"Necessity demands that you have five." He cleared his throat and looked swiftly away. "Four males. One female."

Iladrul's brow furrowed. He didn't understand why his father would purchase male doxies for him. It has always been his understanding that the males were reserved for the freewomen.

"The boys are to train with you." Wisterian, understanding his son's confusion, explained. "They are to become your personal guards." Iladrul looked swiftly away. He knew, now, that his father was aware that he had behaved like a coward when the demons had come for him. "As to the female, she will test everything that comes into contact with you."

Iladrul felt the blood rush out of his face. "She's to be my taster?"

"Ta." Wisterian agreed. "And she is to clothe you only after having worn the clothes on her own back for the full of a day."

"Please, your Highness." Shaking his head, Iladrul looked away. "I don't want them."

"The gold has passed hands." Wisterian snapped at him. "What you want is irrelevant. They are your property. And they are, from this day forward, your responsibility."

Iladrul lowered his gaze, knowing he would not sway his father. His voice was low and slightly cracked as he asked, "When do I meet them?"

"The boys are seeing to medical clearance." Wisterian muttered under his breath. Iladrul's brow furrowed, his expression mirroring his confusion. "Seventh Moon at latest."

"Are they ill?"

"They are seeing to medical clearance." Wisterian's tone was flat as he leveled his gaze irritably upon his son. "The tests of doxies are not your concern."

Infuriated by this response, Iladrul looked swiftly away. He was the Prince of his people. Of *all* of his people. And there were customs that he neither understood nor condoned. He didn't appreciate learning that there were also customs that were meant to be hidden from his scope of knowledge.

But he was just a boy, while his father was the King of his lands. A boy who had been taught from the cradle to know his place. "Yes, your Highness."

Satisfied, Wisterian nodded at him. "Tomorrow you will have a new Sword Master."

"What is wrong with Balean?" Iladrul asked, confused again.

"Nothing." Wisterian assured him. "But he is the General of your Kinsgard now. He has no time to train boys. You and your mates will be schooled by Jeanir."

"Jeanir, your Highness?" Iladrul blinked at him. He knew every one of the soldiers in his father's army, but he had never heard that particular name.

"You may know him not, but he is the finest warrior amongst us." Wisterian assured him. "He simply pulled the wrong stone."

"What are you telling me, Father?" Iladrul asked, confused.

"Balean might hold the title." Wisterian returned his gaze to meet Iladrul's own. "But it is Jeanir who is to become your true General of Arms."

Thinking of his dearest friend, a stable boy named Gregor who had been punished for class mixing after the pair of them had been caught playing together, the young Prince shivered at the hypocrisy.

-21-

Ishitar beamed at Zamyael as he slipped into the cottage that she and Zadkiel shared. She was sitting by the fire doing needlework, her long, shapely legs tucked under her bottom and her lips curled into a content smile. When she heard the door closing, she looked up at Ishitar and grinned, causing me to shiver.

"Where have you been, young man?"

"Staying with a friend." He walked toward her, bent over her chair and kissed her cheek. "Is Zad about?"

"He's in the kitchen." She replied. "Fair warning, Ishitar. He's in a mood regarding your absence."

"Azrael would have told him if I were in trouble."

She gave him a sideways glance that he understood at once. He sometimes forgets that no one but him can see or hear me.

"Alright." He conceded. "Fair point." He kissed her cheek again and pulled away. "I need to speak with all three of you."

"Sounds important." She said, putting her needlework into the small basket beside her chair and rising to her feet. "Does it involve a girl?"

Chuckling under his breath, he shook his head. "Now where would I ever find a woman who could even remotely compare with you? Be it in beauty or in grace?"

Pleased by his praise, she wrapped her arm around his and let him lead her to the kitchen. True to her word, Zadkiel stood over the table, rolling out dough. When he looked upward and saw Ishitar standing at Zamyael's side, he threw the hand not attached to the arm that was supporting his staff to his hip and glared at Ishitar.

"Where in the name of the Thirty Hells have you been, boy?" He seethed. "I've wasted two good pies."

Grinning at him, Ishitar released Zamyael's arm and pulled a chair out for her so that she could sit. "With a friend."

"A girl?" Zadkiel beamed at him.

"What is it with the pair of you and your obsession with my deflowering?" He asked as he pulled out his own chair to sit at Zamyael's side. "I was with Loki."

"Ware that one." Zadkiel raised his finger and began wagging it at Ishitar. "He's always getting himself into trouble. You would do best to keep your distance."

"Oh, come now, Zad." Zamyael flapped her hand at him. "Loki's born from a good egg."

"Yes." Zadkiel replied as he returned his attention to the dough on the table. "If you like a rotten yolk."

"He seems of good morals to me." Ishitar shrugged. Having played kings' castles with Zadkiel and Loki, we all knew that my brother didn't truly mean his admonishment of the oft times troublemaker. "By any road, I intend to stay with him whilst I take my lessons from the Hells bound Gods."

Zadkiel's golden eyes narrowed slightly. "Is that so?"

"Yes." Ishitar reached across the table to pull some of the dough off of the crust Zadkiel was building. This earned him a quick swat from the rolling pin, though he was too fast for Zadkiel to do any real damage. "That's what I've come to talk with the three of you about, actually."

Zadkiel snorted and hobbled back to lean against the counter behind him.

"I'll come for dinner every Seventh Moon." Ishitar promised.

"You raise them, you feed them and you clothe them and all of the thanks they are willing to give you is Seventh Moon dinner."

"This isn't funny, Zam." Zadkiel snapped at her before turning his golden eyes in Ishitar's direction. "Lord Loki has a target on his back. Have you thought of that? Your father loathes him."

"Living with Loki will allow me the affordability to see my mother." Ishitar shrugged. "Never mind that almost every God in the Hells bound Realms respects him."

"Utter madness." Zadkiel shook his head.

"Maybe." Ishitar grinned at him. "But the selection of my tutors is mine to direct. Not yours. And I'm dead set on my decision in this regard."

"If you believe that Loki is the one to best train you, then your Da and I will support you with that choice." Zamyael flashed Zadkiel a warning glance before turning and giving Ishitar an understanding one. "We worry overly much about you. That's all. We love you as if it were Zad who planted you and I who gave birth."

I felt a flash of jealousy ring through me with this statement. The thought of Zamyael with Zadkiel was infuriating to me. Especially given I knew that he had feelings for her.

"I know you do." Ishitar's eyes flew to me as a strange expression crossed his features. I understood that he must have sensed the sudden change in my mood. "And I appreciate everything the three of you have done for me."

I frowned at him. Given I had already attempted to talk him out of this madness, the boy knew that my displeasure with him, at this point, was more about the fact that Zadkiel and Zamyael were being wounded than it was about his selection of Loki as a mentor.

"We know." Zamyael smiled sweetly, motherly, at him. "We're just sad that it's time for you to leave our care."

"It was eventual."

"Perhaps." Zadkiel grumbled. "I just wish it were someone other than your father's greatest nemesis."

"It's because of Noliminan's enmity toward Loki that Loki is the perfect solution." I replied unnecessarily. "His enmity and your Gods be damned pies."

Ishitar, grinning, lowered his gaze. He gave me a slight nod and then returned his attention to Zadkiel. He repeated the first half of what I had said, making me smile. He knows I appreciate it when he repeats my sentiment to others. It is a reminder to me that, though no one else can see me, I am not, completely, alone.

And it is a reminder to others that I am not, truly, gone.

"Perhaps." Zamyael agreed, though hesitantly. "Just be careful, Ishy. Promise me."

"I promise." It was unnecessary but she didn't know that. "By the way, Azrael told me to tell you that you look beautiful today."

"Ishitar!" Rolling my eyes closed, I admonished him.

The last thing in all of the worlds that anyone needed to know was that I coveted Zamyael!

As for my Lady, she blushed. "I'm certain he looks handsome."

"He does." Ishitar grinned at her. "He's wearing a new set of robes that he procured just for you."

"Damn it boy!"

As my embarrassment flamed, her blush deepened. And, for the first time, her returned thoughts of desire for me were clear. I was both terrified and elated that she reciprocated my adoration.

"Perhaps I should wear a new skirt for him."

"When I have hands," I grumbled, belying my true joy, "I mean to throttle you with them."

"Perhaps you should." Ishitar, laughing under his breath, and responding to us both, stood. "I must go. But I shall see you on Seventh Moon."

"Don't be late." Zadkiel snarled.

"I wouldn't dream." Ishitar promised before leaning over and kissing Zamyael goodbye.

-22-

Wisterian, bent over his desk, started when he heard the cry of the falcon.

He turned toward the window and frowned. His discontentment grew as he marked the creature's face and realized, at once, who he belonged to.

"Come, Blackheart." He held his hand toward Jamiason's bird and forced himself to smile. He wished, desperately, he had a mouse to offer the creature, but he didn't. Not, he grinned, that it stopped the falcon from stepping toward him with his left leg, where the message was tied, held high. "There's a lad."

He reached for the scroll that was tied to the falcon's leg and flipped it open. As he read it, his lips pursed.

Jamiason, it would seem, was ready to palaver.

-23-

Jamiason heard Blackheart cry and turned toward the window more abruptly than he had intended to. The entire court was filled with vampires and demons asking for his aide. This moment was not the one where he could relieve the falcon of the burden of his message.

He turned his gaze to Marchand and willed the boy to see to the matter. Marchand, made wholly from Jamiason's blood, bowed and walked away.

Relieved, Jamiason returned his attention to the matters at hand.

-24-

Marchand felt Jamiason approaching his bedchamber long before his Maker knocked upon his door. He knew that the only reason that James was coming to him was to discuss the message from Wisterian.

He didn't care.

Any opportunity to be alone with the man that he considered to be his father brought him joy.

Before Paul, Marchand had been the favored among Jamiason's progeny. Not that there was much competition. The only other that Jamiason had ever turned was Louis. And Louis, though Marchand's twin brother, could be extremely difficult to manage.

Whereas Marchand had come to terms with his lot in life, Louis was furious with the circumstances that had come to pass which put them in their current, unnatural state of being. Louis' anger came mostly from the fact that Jamiason had promised them on the day that the gold had passed to their father that no harm would come to them.

He hadn't lied to them. He wasn't responsible for the fact that the demon who thought he should become Jamiason's heir had tried to kill Marchand to clear his ambitious path. And it had been Louis' idea, after Marchand had been mortally wounded, that Marchand be turned rather than allowed to bleed out and die.

Just as it had been Louis' pleading to Jamiason after Marchand had been turned not to leave him, still human, behind.

There was no question in Marchand's mind that Jamiason loved them both before he had become their Maker. But his love for Marchand became extremely protective and fatherly after the pair of them had been turned.

Until he found Paul, that was.

Once Jamiason found Paul, he had little and less use for either one of his twins.

At first, Marchand had been wounded by this betrayal. Over time, however, he came to understand that Jamiason had chosen Paul because neither Louis nor Marchand were fit to be his heir. Marchand was too shy and Louis was too volatile. Paul, however, was one of those men who could be groomed for to command.

When Jamiason reached Marchand's room, he didn't knock. Marchand was not offended by his rudeness. As his Maker, and his King, Jamiason knew he was welcome and that the invitation was not required.

"Unfavorable news?" Jamiason asked, though the question was pointless.

Marchand smiled at him and shook his head. "Wisterian has agreed to meet with you."

Jamiason sighed his relief and slipped into the room, closing the door behind him. "Thank all of the Gods."

"Will you tell him you mean to help him?" Marchand asked, truly curious.

"No." James shook his head. "It's best no one knows." His lips thinned as his cobalt blue eyes flew to Marchand. "I need to employ you."

"As my Maker, any command you give me is mine to obey." Marchand shrugged. Jamiason, still frowning, looked swiftly away. He rarely ever used the magic which would force either one of the twins to obey him as their Maker because he abhorred the idea that they could not refuse him. "Tell me what you will of me and I shall give it to you."

"I ask as your father." Jamiason muttered. "Not your Maker."

"Six and half of twelve, James." Marchand chastised him, though softly. "And you know it."

This made Jamiason smile.

"You will visit the Oakland Grove and tell Aiken that I request him to vacate so we can use the neutrality for our meeting with the elves."

"As you will." Marchand agreed. "Do you think he will comply?"

Jamiason pondered this for a long moment before giving Marchand a perfunctory nod. "His people litter the lands of Anticata. One tribe or another is bound to be caught up in any war that is waged."

Marchand lowered his gaze in understanding. "I shall leave at next sun fall."

"Thank you." Jamiason reached for his hand and squeezed it. "For never questioning my motives."

Marchand felt a tepid smile cross his lips at that sentiment.

Because, really, who was he to question a God about his motives?

-25-

Aiken sat on the opposite side of the kings' board from his youngest daughter, watching her with quiet fascination as she contemplated her move. She was a pretty thing with sky blue hair and his violet eyes, but she was the only one of his many children who bore the unfortunate mark of being the bastard that she was. She, like Aiken, was not born with the metallic scroll on her face which identified her fraternal lineage.

He often found it queer that his people would care. After all, he, himself, was a scroll lacking bastard. Never mind that he had never taken to wife and, thus, all of his children were bastards.

Yet, for whatever reasons, Triyana was the only one who had been ostracized for it.

Aiken had hoped that Prince Pialoron would have looked past her missing scroll. But he, like all the others, had rejected Triyana. Though his reasoning had nothing to do with her lack of a scroll, his daughter had taken the rejection poorly.

"How is Lord Loki?" She asked, her eyes turning swiftly away.

Aiken chuckled under his breath and gave her a cautious grin. "He bides."

She bit nervously on her bottom lip as she made her move on the board. "Will he come and visit soon, do you think?"

"He comes and goes as he pleases." He watched her with an unsettling sense of curiosity.

She licked her lips and raised her gaze. "Do you think he would walk through the meadow with me."

Aiken's eyes narrowed. Though he generally found Loki's ability to bed a woman at his whim amusing, he didn't care for the idea that Loki might consider adding one of his daughters to his ever growing gaggle of geese. "I think I would prefer that he doesn't."

"Fete." She snorted. "Really. What must you think of me?"

"That you're a peach that's nearly ripe for the picking." Aiken muttered. "Loki is my dearest friend." He felt his eyes narrow again. "But I don't trust him around my women."

"Oh, Fete." She batted her hand at him. "I can't stay honest forever."

"No." He agreed. "But you will do so until I've found you a proper husband."

"Then you mean me to become a spinster." She whined.

"No." He sighed. "Triyana, you're only just blossoming. You have plenty of time to find a husband before being considered a spinster." He shrugged. "Anyway, I believe that Prince Pialoron will come around. He just needs time to grieve his Shitva."

She glared at him for a moment and then turned her gaze away. "It isn't his Shitva that is keeping him from marriage."

"It is." Aiken assured her.

"No." She crossed her arms over her chest. "It's his eunuch. I've heard rumors that the water fairies have a penchant for their slaves."

"Unfounded." Aiken's lips pursed. He abhorred the practice that the water fairies had adopted of trading eunuchs as slaves. As for the rumors that they forced them to their beds, they were completely without merit. Never mind that the tribe that Prince Pialoron came from was mired in tradition and old world ways. "What have I told you about propagating gossip?"

She sighed and waved to the board. "It's your move."

Aiken considered her for a moment and then turned his attention to the board. He was just ready to slide his merman into place when his eldest daughter, whom he intended to abdicate his crown to so he could, finally, renounce his mortal veil, stepped into the room.

"Fete." He turned toward her, smiling as his eyes trailed with fatherly affection over her features. She was tall, like him, with long, dark blue hair and eyes and a beautiful blue scroll that matched that of her mother. She was the prettiest of his daughters. There was no denying it. "We have a visitor. He says he was sent by Lord Scrountentine."

Aiken felt a lump immediately rise to his throat. "Good news or ill?"

"He wouldn't say, my Lord." Karma replied.

"Vampire or demon?"

"Vampire." She was clearly confused by this question. "An extremely *young* vampire."

"A fledgling?" Aiken's brow rose. "Newly turned?"

"No." She shook her head. "I mean . . . He was clearly human." Aiken nodded. "No more than fourteen when he was made, I should think."

"Ah." Aiken fell back in his chair. "He's sent one of his twins."

"His twins?" Triyana asked.

Aiken ignored her question and turned to Karma. "Bring the child up, met paken."

"Yes, my Lord." She bowed to him and turned away.

He watched her go with an affectionate grin before turning to Triyana. "Leave me, girl."

She nodded her compliance, though she clearly didn't want to leave. She had never met a vampire, Aiken knew, and she was curious to meet a boy of any race that was near to her same age.

Never mind that he's nearly three hundred years old.

He passed her a thin smile as she, finally, stood. "Good night, Fete."

"Good night, met paken." He replied. "Lay your head down to dreams that are sweet."

She nodded and took her leave.

Some several minutes later, Karma returned with one of the twins at her side. Aiken had only ever seen them from a distance. As such, he wasn't sure which twin stood before him.

He rose and stepped toward the pair. As he did so, the youngish looking man lowered his doe like brown eyes, bent at the waist and gave Aiken a proper, respectful bow.

"Emissary Lord Darklief." His voice was strangely enchanting. It still held the melodic tones of the incredibly young. "Thank you for agreeing to hold palaver with me."

"I assume you come with a matter of import?" Aiken replied, trying to keep his tone level and kind.

The child gave him a wan smile and a curt nod. "I am Marchand Deboines."

"It is a pleasure to meet you, Marchand." This was truly meant. He was happy to have finally met one of Jamiason's twins. "I understand that Jami has sent you."

"Lord Scrountentine." He nodded, his brow slightly furrowed. "Yes."

Aiken nodded and flicked his gaze to Karma. "Leave us."

"Yes, my Lord." She gave the appropriate curtsey with false skirts and made her way out of the room.

When she was gone, Aiken turned his full attention to Marchand, who was very clearly trying not to follow her bare bottom out of the room with his eyes. Aiken was less than amused by this but chose to ignore it. "Please, Marchand Deboines. Won't you sit?"

"I shouldn't wish to take up too much of your time."

"It is no matter." Aiken assured him. "Any news from Jami is welcome news." He licked his lips, swallowed and then asked, "How does he fair?"

Marchand's smile grew tight. "Ill, I'm afraid."

"Ill?" Aiken leaned forward, suddenly concerned.

"I don't know if you know Iykva."

"I do." Aiken frowned. He had always been leery of Iykva.

"He has declared that he intends to strike war upon the elves." Marchand's dark brow was furrowed. "My Maker is extremely concerned because . . . Well."

Aiken waved a hand at him. He understood why Jamiason was concerned far better than this young man ever could. "Why does Iykva want to war on the elves?"

"I am uncertain, my Lord." Marchand's tone had a slight tremor to it. "My Maker believes that it has to do with the fact that the angels weren't granted the same burdens as we were. But what Iykva is saying is that he believes that if he gathers the elfin children together he can farm them as a food source."

"What on which moon that is good could come of that?" Aiken growled.

"Nothing, my Lord." Marchand swallowed. "But they believe that if they drink the blood of the elves, then we vampires will, ourselves, become elves."

Aiken's lips twitched. "It *is* a plausible theory."

"It is." Marchand agreed, raising his gaze as he braved to ask the burning question. "Would it work?"

"Who can say?" Aiken shrugged, thinking that it had certainly worked when Evan had bent his neck to Jami. "It's entirely possible."

"Even if it did," Marchand lowered his gaze again, "it's immoral."

"That it is." Aiken found himself smiling at the boy. He decided, as the child braved to look at him again, that he liked him. "What does Jami need from me?"

"Well," Marchand gave him a shy smile, "He wants to meet with Wisterian. He believes that Iykva owes it to him to lay down his demands before actually making his strike."

Aiken's lips thinned again, though he nodded, "Seems the reasonable thing to do."

"He's asked if they can meet here."

"In the Oakland Grove?" This request came as a profound surprise.

"Yes." What small bit of confidence he had seemed to have left him completely. "He understands it is an imposition on you as you would have to vacate. But he wants a place where Iykva wouldn't dare to make an attack on the young Prince."

Aiken sighed and leaned back in his chair. "What a mess."

Marchand nodded.

"Is Jami's goal really, at the end of the day, the protection of the elves?"

"I believe that it is." Marchand didn't hesitate in his response.

"Very well." Aiken muttered. "They may meet here."

"Thank you, my Lord." He seemed relieved.

"But tell Jami this." Aiken leaned forward, locking Marchand's gaze with his own. "If his goal is truly the protection of the elves, I will help him." Marchand nodded. "In order for me to do so, he must make one small sacrifice."

"Which is?" The boy was immediately concerned.

"I gave Paul Kinney a bauble." Aiken explained. "A very powerful bauble." Marchand lowered his gaze and bowed his head. "I did so when Jami asked me to look over the carrot top."

"The talisman." Marchand muttered. "The charm Prince Paul wears around his neck."

"Just so." Aiken nodded. "He must give that bauble to the elf."

"He must sacrifice Prince Paul for Prince Iladrul?" Marchand's already pale face went ashen.

"He must make his choice." Aiken corrected him. "If they are to go to war, I must ally my people with one race only. It is Jamiason who will decide which race that shall be."

-26-

Ishitar didn't bother to knock on the door to his mother's cottage. He had been here often enough that he knew she didn't care if he just walked in. The only rule she had ever voiced, where Ishitar was concerned, was that if the library or her bedroom door were shut, then he should knock. Otherwise, the cottage she and Sappharon shared was to be considered as much his home as it was theirs.

Na'amah, as Ansibrius, stood at his side, her mismatched eyes—one was blue and one was brown—surveying the room as she took in her surroundings. Her long, skinny, black and white legs danced slightly, because she was nervous. The air about the place leant to this. Lucias is often tightly strung and Sappharon is not known for being the gentlest of all souls.

85

I grinned at that thought and chuckled under my breath. Ishitar, turned his gaze toward me and gave me a guarded smile before stepping away from me to find his mother.

The door to the library was open so he poked his head in. Because Lucias was not there, he made his way down the hall to her bedchamber to find that door was closed. Shaking his head, he raised his hand to knock. It was the middle of the afternoon and, I suspect, the last place he expected to find her was lounging in bed.

When the door opened, it was Loki who stood on the other side. He wore an irritated expression which quickly turned into a mischievous grin. Ishitar, his lips thinning, bid Loki to tell his mother that he was there and would wait for her outside.

I followed Ishitar into the kitchen and watched as he poured himself a glass of wine before stepping into the afternoon sun. The day was warm and bright and the air was heavy with the scent and sounds of the forest surrounding us.

Once outside, Na'amah bounded forward, barking and jumping as she ran toward the garden. Ishitar seemed to realize, as his gaze followed her, that she was heading toward Sappharon, who sat on the edge of the garden area with eyes wide with fear because she was about to be attacked by her dog.

Laughing, Ishitar called after Na'amah and told her to calm down.

Not that it did any good.

She was on top of Sappharon, her pink tongue licking her mother's face, while Sappharon struggled beneath her and grunted her surprised irritation as she tried to push the dog off of her.

Still laughing, Ishitar ran forward and grasped the nape of Na'amah's neck to pull her off of the demon. Sappharon, waving her hands in exasperated curses, which made even *me* blush, found her feet and leaned forward to chastise the dog in throaty grunts.

"I'm sorry, Sappharon!" Ishitar, still laughing, apologized. "She's excited to see you again. That's all."

Sappharon's eyes narrowed and her lips pursed as she shook her head and flew her gaze to the dog. Na'amah, still jumping, though now under Ishitar's control, let out a long, low growl that was half bark and half whine. As the demon held the dog's gaze, her anger seemed to calm a bit until she fell on her knees and held her arms open. Ishitar let the dog go and began laughing again as Na'amah flew her front legs onto Sappharon's shoulders and began licking her mother's face again.

This time Sappharon joined in what laughter she could as she pulled the dog close to her and held her tight. Her thoughts screaming with her recognition that this was her child, she buried her face in Na'amah's neck and began sobbing.

"Sappharon?" Ishitar called, falling on his knees beside her so he could set his hand on her back to bring her comfort. "My Dame! She's being well taken care of, I assure you!"

Nodding, Sappharon raised her face from the safety of the dog's neck to meet Ishitar's gaze. Tears were coursing down her cheeks. Seemingly confused by Sappharon's uncharacteristic emotional reaction to seeing her dog, Ishitar pulled his hand violently away from her.

She made a funny little noise in her throat that, I knew, was an embarrassed laugh and raised her hand to wipe the tears from her eyes. Afterward, she reached for his face and patted his cheek, her lips curled at their corners in an oddly gruesome grin which would have been beautiful if her lips could have parted.

"I'm sorry, Ishitar." She signed. "I've had a very rough morning. Your visit today has taken me by surprise."

"Is there something I can do for you?" He asked, clearly confused; clearly concerned.

"No." She replied as she turned her attention back to the dog. "What did you say you named her?"

"Ansibrius." Ishitar grinned at her. "I know you meant for Loki to take care of her. But I've never had a pet and the moment I saw her I knew that I had to have her."

A strange sound escaped from her as she pulled the dog into her arms again. Her thoughts were ringing with gratitude. I hoped that it was not ill placed and that Ishitar would still love Na'amah when he realized she was deceiving him.

He was about to respond when he heard his mother's voice behind him.

"Ishitar?" He turned to look over his shoulder at her and smiled. "Is something the matter, met paken?"

"Net, Mima." He said as he found his feet and walked toward her. When he reached her, he leaned forward and kissed her cheek. "I have a free afternoon so I thought I'd stop by and say hello." He leaned to the side to look into the cottage. "Where's Loki?"

"He'll be out in a minute." She blushed. I find her very beautiful when she blushes. I suppose Lord Oedipus might have something to say to me about that if I were to ever admit it to him. "He wanted to wash up first."

Ishitar, his lips thinning again, reached forward to press his hand upon her belly. "So, am I to have a little brother or sister, then?"

"Yes." She looked worried suddenly. "Ishitar, please do not be angry. Your father—"

"Don't waste your breath." He warned her. Watching them, I felt my brow furrow. I knew that Ishitar was displeased that Loki and Lucias were now lovers. His curt treatment of Loki when the subject was raised was evidence enough of that. Still, I would have thought he would want to hear his mother's explanation. "Did Loki tell you that I've chosen to live with him?"

"He did." She gave him a guarded smile. "And that you are having Zuko teach you his tasks."

"They seem important to me."

"Yes, but . . ." She sighed. "Never mind. You're a grown man. You're old enough to make your own choices in regard to your schooling."

"Thank you."

Her lips drew thin.

"About my pregnancy—"

"Don't." Ishitar's eyes narrowed. He turned his gaze to me, his lips pursed with clear irritation, before returning his attention to his mother. When he spoke, his tone was guarded. "You should know that I made Loki another pie."

Her eyes narrowed slightly. "Are you certain you know what you're doing in regard to Noliminan's fruit? His anger in the past will be all flowers and fairies if he learns you are messing with his forbidden tree."

"No. I'm not." Ishitar sighed. As for me, I shifted uncomfortably at his side. "But he's had two pies now and he hasn't turned into Father yet."

"Perhaps not." She agreed. "But he *is* getting cocky."

"He always *was* cocky." Ishitar smiled thinly at her as the God in question stepped into the afternoon sun. "That's what makes him the perfect subject to test my theory on."

"If you say so." She muttered as Loki stepped forward and handed Ishitar a glass of wine.

Ishitar took the glass and announced, "I intend to steal Lady Lucias from your company for the afternoon. I'll bring her back by nightfall. I have some time on my hands before Zuko is home and I thought we could take a walk." He looked around himself. "It's such a beautiful afternoon. I hate to waste it."

"Of course." Loki replied. "Honestly, I wouldn't mind lounging on the hammock. I haven't been sleeping well lately and I could really use a nap."

"Perhaps it's all the late night reading." Ishitar, referring to Loki's attempts to translate one of my mother's Tomes, taunted.

Loki flushed and darted his strange, purple eyes to Lucias. When she didn't ask what he was reading he returned his gaze to Ishitar and shrugged. "The text is riveting."

"I'm certain." He gave Loki one of his contemplative glares as he raised his arm and held it out to Lucias. "Mima?"

-27-

Sappharon waited until she heard Loki snoring before turning toward Na'amah and indicating that she should follow her into the cottage. Once inside, she closed the door, peered out the window to verify that the noise of it closing hadn't woken Loki up, and fell to her hunkers before her daughter. Grinning, she reached forward and threw her arms around Na'amah's neck again.

She didn't know how to make the child understand her. Very few people knew the language she spoke with her hands and she doubted that her daughter had watched enough of her palaver with Ishitar to have picked up on the meaning of her gestures. So she did the only thing that she could do and pointed at her mouth while she shook her head. Fortunately, her daughter was intelligent enough to understand what she was trying to tell her.

"You can't speak?" Na'amah, still in the form of a dog, asked.

Sappharon shook her head again. As she did so, she held out her hands in a gesture that she hoped asked Na'amah to tell her everything.

Na'amah, however, frowned. She immediately took on her own form and opened the door to the cottage. She looked over her shoulder at her mother, who was panicking at this point because she didn't want her daughter—wearing not the first stitch of clothing, to make matters worse where Loki was concerned—to be seen by the God, and called out, "Lord Loki!"

Loki snorted, rolled onto his side and fell back to sleep.

"Lord Loki, please!" Na'amah tried again.

This time Loki groaned. "What do you want, woman?"

"I don't understand my mother." Na'amah said quickly. "Please come and translate for us. Then, I promise, we shall let you go back to sleep."

Loki let out an irritated growl. Sappharon was certain he was going to refuse, but he didn't. Rather, he rolled off of the hammock onto his feet and staggered, still clearly not entirely awake, toward the cottage.

When he stepped inside, he looked from one to the other of them and shook his head. "If you didn't have your father's chin, the pair of you could be sisters."

"You know Na'amah for who she is?" Sappharon signed desperately.

"You told me about her when I was in my sick bed." He groused at her. "Surely you remember that."

"I do." She nodded. "Of course I do. I'm just so surprised to see her! And with Ishitar!"

"Prince Ishitar thinks Lucias sent her to me as his pet." Loki grumbled as he pulled a chair from the table and fell gracelessly into it. He didn't seem to be interested in staring at Na'amah, for a wonder. Sappharon was relieved by this. "And best he goes on thinking that way. Hopefully he doesn't raise the issue with his mother."

"Even if she tells him that she didn't send me to him," Na'amah said quickly, "he wouldn't turn me away. He likes having me around, I think." And then, in a timid voice. "You know who my father is?"

Loki sighed and looked from one to the other of them. Finally, his eyes landed on Sappharon. "You haven't told her?"

"No." Sappharon signed. "I do not want to place Metatron into any more trouble than he is already in." She blushed and lowered her gaze. Despite everything that had passed between them, she still, desperately, loved Metatron. And, despite her disdain for him, she had come to reluctantly regard Loki as a member of her small family. She found that she didn't want to raise this sore subject up to throw in his face. "If Noliminan had proof that we consummated our love, what he forced you and Metatron to do in front of the Council would seem like child's play."

Loki's lips thinned and his cheeks blazed red. His eyes darted swiftly away.

"Mrilk treckt." He muttered the unthinkable words. Sappharon's eyes grew wide upon hearing them. Even she would never dare spill that particular curse at Noliminan. It was the most foul of any terms you could call another body. "I loathe him for that."

"It wasn't Metatron's fault." Sappharon, swallowing her surprise at Loki's brazenness, softened the motions of her hands.

"I speak not of Metatron and you know it." He spat. As he did so, Na'amah's eyes flew to her mother. They were full of questions. Then, low and under his breath, "Though neither one of us can bear to look at the other now. Even when Council meets we avoid one another's gaze."

"Neither he nor I will ever be able to repay you for what you did to prevent my humiliation." Sappharon, grateful to Loki for his protection over her, softened her motions. "Loki, you didn't lose anyone's respect. If anything, you gained it."

"Regardless," Loki groused. Then he waved his hand at her. "Past is past." He forced himself to meet Sappharon's gaze. "Na'amah came looking for me because she was frightened that she had not heard from you. I promised her my succor. So she's staying with me for the time being. I asked her to turn into the dog because she happened to come on the same night Price Ishtar asked to move in with me." He looked slightly irritated, then, as his eyes flicked to her bare breasts before returning—far too swiftly to belie his desire to continue staring—to Sappharon's gaze. Sappharon, nobody's fool, narrowed her eyes at this action. "Her timing was not at all convenient."

"I do not mind being Prince Ishtar's pet." Na'amah said, her tone soft. "I've never lived in anyone's company before. Not even as an animal. And he is so kind to me."

"He's a good boy." Sappharon agreed, her eyes still narrowed.

"He's a good lad." Loki translated for her, grinning playfully to himself for having been so clearly read and pointing at Sappharon to indicate these were her words and not Loki's.

"Actually," he lowered his hand, "I'm becoming attached to him."

"He is fond of you as well." Na'amah grinned. "He watches you, you know. When he thinks you aren't paying attention. He finds you very curious."

Loki's brow furrowed at that. His purple eyes danced with strange interest over her face. Sappharon was curious as to what thoughts were swimming in his mind but, wisely, did not voice her suppositions.

"That's queer." He finally said. "I wasn't aware that Prince Ishitar held a fascination for men."

"He doesn't." Na'amah shrugged. "He's merely studying you. Trying to puzzle you out in his mind. Sometimes, when he's alone he talks to himself. Almost as if he's talking to someone else that I can't see, actually. He goes on and on about how you remind him of his father."

Loki snorted. "Insulting."

"He doesn't mean it that way." Na'amah assured him. "Who is he talking to, do you think? Or is it that he's insane?"

"Azrael, is my guess." Sappharon signed. "He could see him when he was a boy. Even when Azrael wasn't formed. It's entirely possible he can see him still."

Loki turned his gaze upon her. A strange expression darkened his masculine features. "You believe that Azrael is still around?"

I rolled my eyes and shook my head. Generally, Lord Loki wasn't this simple minded.

"Of course he's still around." Sappharon frowned at him. "He's still responsible for depositing the damned ones into your basement, isn't he?"

"Of course." He actually sounded relieved. He smiled slightly. "That makes more sense than my thought that Zadkiel had expired his soul and some new system had been worked out."

"No." Sappharon sighed. "Zamyael told me that he was punished for letting loose his tongue." Then frowning. "I'd like to know what was so Gods be damned important that it was worth the price he paid."

"So would I." Loki muttered as he raised his hand to his lips to toy with them. As for me, I shivered. "She didn't tell you?"

"No." Sappharon signed to him. "She would never betray him. She has been in love with him since time out of mind." She shrugged. Despite my better sense, I felt my heart take flight at that sentiment. "She only told me that whatever it was is the reason she's now living with Zadkiel. Raziel was, apparently, less than happy with Zam over what she learned."

"Curious." Loki muttered. Then he grinned. "What is it with you female demons and your obsession with the members of the Quorum?"

"They *are* pretty to look at." Sappharon grinned playfully at him.

"If you say so." Loki shrugged and gave her a brotherly roll of the eyes. He turned his gaze to Na'amah. "You called me in here to translate."

"Yes." Na'amah smiled eagerly at him. "Please."

They talked well into the afternoon, Na'amah sharing her travels as she sought Sappharon and Sappharon sharing what detail she could about her life in exile with Lucias. Loki was patient with both of them until they fell into a lull and merely sat across the table from one another holding hands. After ten shifts of the shadows without a word between them, he reached for their clasped hands, patted them and asked, "Are the pair of you finished with me? May I, please, go back to nap?"

"Yes, Apprentice Lord Loki." Na'amah said, reaching for his hand and squeezing it. "I should revert to my other form in case the little Lord comes home."

"The little Lord." Loki snorted as he found his feet. "Best you not let him hear you calling that. He might take it as a slight on his manhood."

"Oh, no. I'm certain that would be the last thing he would be thinking." She grinned. "He's extremely well endowed if you must know."

"Not really something I needed to hear about." Loki scoffed and began walking toward the door. "Could have gone my entire life without that little tidbit of information." It was said in jest, making Sappharon smile. "If you will please excuse me, Ladies, I believe I am now about to lose my lunch."

As the door slammed closed behind him, the women looked at one another and burst into gales of laughter. Sappharon, grateful to once again have her daughter, vowed to never to lose contact with the girl again.

-28-

Laying a bouquet of red roses beside Queen Raguel's headstone, Michael lowered himself to his knees and began to pull away the unwanted weeds that surrounded the earth within which she lay. Though he had made it a point to visit her at least once per sun cycle since he had buried her, his tasks had prevented him from doing so for far too long.

"I'm sorry, your Grace." He muttered as he wiped the dirt from her epitaph with the hem of his robes. "I've been remiss with my duties. But, I assure you, my absence was unavoidable."

Satisfied that the headstone was clean, he fell back on his heels and forced himself to smile.

"Nothing is the same without you." He sighed. "His Grace has been taking Raziel to wife again; he made her Lady Regent in Lucias' stead." His brow furrowed as he wondered how his father fared in exile. "Poor Raphael is still afraid of his own damn shadow." He toyed with the stem of one of the roses he brought her which was littered with too many leaves, stripping it clean. "Camael and Uriel shared vows." He smiled and flicked his eyes to where he remembered her head to lay. "Though I must ask that you keep this as our secret lest the King of Lords punish them both." He chuckled and returned his attention to his task. "As for Gabriel, he is thriving in the Guf. I know that you would be proud of him."

A pang of sadness overwhelmed him, suddenly, as he spoke to her. He realized, in that moment, that the details of her beautiful face were beginning to fade from his memory.

How could this be? He thought as he bit his bottom lip lest it begin to tremble. *I spent the better part of my life dreaming of your face . . . How can its lines be leaving my mind's eye now?*

A sob threatened to rise to his throat. He swallowed it down and blinked away the tears that were beginning to burn his eyes.

"I miss you." He whispered. "I think of you every day. Even if my visits are becoming scarce as the suns fly their cycles. There isn't a moon which rises when you aren't living within me and my heart."

And there wouldn't, he knew as one of those damn tears he was fighting fell, ever be a single moon in which he lived that he forgot about her for even the barest shift of Lord Countenance's shadow.

-29-

"How did he seem?" James swallowed his discontentment as he raised his gaze to meet Marchand's.

The boy looked at him with quiet concern. "He's a strangely beautiful creature for a man."

"Yes." James agreed, his mind casting to the God that he had once loved above all other beings in any one of the cruel, cold worlds. "He is."

"His women wear no clothes." Marchand's cheeks flamed red. "Did you know that?"

"I did." Jamiason forced himself to smile. "Nor do the men. It's not a custom that the mischief fairies have adopted."

"I wish you would have warned me." Marchand lowered his gaze.

"You wouldn't have gone if I had." Jamiason sighed and sat backward. "And I couldn't trust Louis to hold his tongue." He felt the beginnings of impatience stirring in his mind as Marchand's covetous thoughts for Karma bounced off of him in James' direction. "What did he say?"

"He agreed." Marchand raised his gaze. "On a condition."

"Of course there's a Gods be damned condition." Jamiason threw the quill he was holding at his desk. With Aiken, there was always a condition. "What does he want from me?"

Marchand hesitated for a moment and then, in a voice that was low, yet traced with clear curiosity, "He said that you're to decide which race he is to protect. Vampire or elf."

Jamiason started. "Why would he—?"

"He said that, given this is a mortal war, he can only ally his people with one race." Marchand muttered. "You're to decide who is to wear his Talisman. Prince Paul or Prince Iladrul."

Jamiason bit his tongue. Hard.

He hadn't been prepared for this eventuality. Though, he supposed, he should have been.

"He said that, after the war, he can give one or the other of them a new Talisman." Marchand's voice trembled. "If they both survive and can come to a truce, that is."

"They *must* both survive." Jamiason's vision was beginning to stain red with the blood of his tears. He blinked these tears back, not wanting Marchand to sense his weakness. "All four of you must survive."

"There's a very real possibility that—"

"I know this!" Jamiason snapped at him. "Don't you think I understand the danger I am putting you in?"

Marchand made no verbal response. He merely nodded.

"Come back in sixty shifts." Jamiason commanded him. "I'll have a letter that I will need you to give to Blackheart to deliver."

"Yes, my Lord." Marchand stood and turned to leave. "As you will me."

"Marchand?" He turned to face his Maker. "Tell Paul I must speak with him."

"Yes, my Lord."

"But not tonight." Jamiason turned away from him. "Tonight I must think. He must come to me on the morrow."

Granting Jamiason a weak smile, Marchand nodded and left Jamiason to do as he was bid.

-30-

Macentyx, the oldest of the brothers by a matter of minutes, stood behind Jeavlin, the youngest, brushing his brother's hair. Jeavlin, out of the four of them, had required the most prodding to take care in how he looked on this morning when they were to meet their Master.

"What if he doesn't like me?" Jeavlin raised his gaze in the mirror to meet Macentyx's.

"What if *you* don't like *him*?"

"It doesn't matter if I like him or not." Jeavlin reminded his brother.

"Nor does it matter if he likes you." Macentyx sighed. "Just keep quiet, serve him well and give him no reason to punish you." Jeavlin paled as he nodded. Macentyx forced himself to give his brother a smile. "As Father tells us, it is an honor to be the first bought doxies of a Prince."

"It's an honor I'd as soon do without." Haidar, the second born, scoffed. "Where is Osete?"

"With Sezja." Macentyx muttered. Sezja was their younger sister. That she was also being gifted to the young Prince this morning infuriated the four brothers to no end. "She needed encouragement."

Haidar snorted. As he did so, the door opened and their father stepped into the room. His eyes darted from one to the other of them as he forced himself to smile. "You lads look fine."

"Thank you, Sir." Jeavlin swallowed. "What is he like?"

Jeanir's brow furrowed. "A boy. Same as you. And terrified."

"What does he have to be frightened of?" Haidar scoffed.

"Much and more." Jeanir rounded on his son. "He's being forced to grow up far too early." His eyes darted around the room. "As are you." He sighed. "Never mind that he's on the verge of leading an army off to war. It would do you all well to remember that."

"Yes, Sir." Macentyx answered for his brothers. "We will."

"Good." Jeanir gave them another forced smile. "Come. It's time to meet Prince Iladrul."

Sighing, Macentyx stepped away from Jeavlin, setting the brush aside. He waited for his brothers to steel themselves and then encouraged them both to follow their father out of the small bedroom they shared and into the main room.

Their mother waited for them there, her eyes red rimmed and her face puffy from crying. As were Osete and Sezja, whose faces were as ashen as were Jeavlin and Haidar's.

"Don't you boys look handsome?" Macentyx forced himself to smile at his mother for her lie. They *were* handsome boys. But not today. All of them were primped with powder, paint and skirts. They looked more like women than men. As they would from that day forward. "What a glorious day for you!"

Haidar somehow managed to hold his wagging, acid tongue. Macentyx was grateful for this small miracle. Out of all of them, he prophesized that it would be Haidar who first felt the sting of Prince Iladrul's whip on his back.

"It is an honor to be purchased by a Prince." Osete said in dead panned tones. "And, even more so, the first ever born of our race."

"Yes." Their mother grinned at him. It was such a horrific and false grin that Macentyx had to look away lest he, himself, cry. "Such an honor."

"I must take them." Jeanir muttered in low tones. "Kiss your mother goodbye."

They each did in turns; Macentyx, being the oldest, going last. As his mother pulled him toward her she bent her lips to his ears and whispered, "Watch over them Mac. I beg you. Especially Haidar. Don't let him mouth off to the young Prince."

Knowing this was meant to be their secret, he merely nodded against her lips. Though it was an impossibility to control Haidar, or his tongue, he would promise his mother all five moons of Anticata if that is what she required of him. "Goodbye, Mother."

She let him go, raising her hand to her mouth to hide her pain. She crossed her other arm over her chest and merely nodded at them. Jeanir gave her a weak, apologetic smile and then herded his children out of the small cottage that they shared with their mother.

Every elf and angel residing within the Doxy Village seemed to be waiting for them. Seeing them, Macentyx forced himself to stand tall and proud. When he noticed that Jeavlin failed to match his mood, he reached for his brother's hand, tugged on it and gave him a nod intended to direct Jeavlin to toe the mark.

To Mac's great relief, Jeavlin did.

He rose to his full height, stuck his chin out and mimicked his brothers; in action, if not in thought. Macentyx allowed his youngest brother a smile that he hoped revealed his pride in him before turning his gaze to his father's back. It would be best to walk through the Village in this manner lest he see the faces of the friends that he would sorely miss.

Having never stepped foot outside of the Doxy Village, Macentyx was unable to hold this form once they'd crossed the bridge to the other side of the river. He was too overwhelmed by the beauty of the forest that they had ever forbidden from entering.

Jeanir didn't admonish or try to temper the boys or Sezja from their wide eyed fascination. Not, that was, until they reached the edge of the Courtyard where the angels and elves made merry. Before they crossed the tree line, he turned to his children and gave them a final piece of advice.

"Keep your eyes averted. Do not let them land on any elf or angel that you come across. You are Prince Iladrul's property, now, and you are to show no affection or emotion of any kind to any elf but him."

Swallowing the lump that rose in his throat, Macentyx nodded. His brothers and sister, he marked, were doing the same.

"Good." Jeanir turned away, stepping past the tree line and into the Courtyard.

As they followed him, it took everything in Macentyx not to let out a gasp.

The Courtyard was a bustle of activity with elves and angels sitting at their breakfast. Laughter and chatter rang around them, but then came to an abrupt halt as the five of them stepped into the light.

Macentyx swallowed again and forced his chin to remain high and his eyes focused on the tops of his father's great, white wings. There would be time, he told himself, to drink in the bustle of the Courtyard in quiet subservience as he saw to Prince Iladrul's needs.

He somehow managed to keep his eyes glued to his father's wings as they made their way out of the Courtyard and through the castle. Given his state of mind, and his keen intent to stare at his father's wing, he saw nothing that he would later remember until they reached the door separating the living quarters of the Royal Family from the rest of the castle.

Standing outside the door was an angel that Macentyx recognized. It was the man his mother truly loved. A servant of the castle, who only visited the Doxy Village when he was able to sneak in without being seen because he was neither freeman nor noble and, thus, not allowed a doxy of his own.

Mac managed to stay his surprise and was grateful to see that his brothers and sister had done the same.

"Andrel." Jeanir held his hand out, grinning. He wore an expression upon his face that Macentyx could only associate with pride. "I don't believe you've met my eldest children."

Andrel turned his eyes to Macentyx and gave him a guarded, tired smile. His dark brown, gold rimmed eyes—so alike to Macentyx's own, the boy realized being up close to him for the first time—danced over Macentyx's face before darting to each of the other children in turn. "I cannot say that I have."

This was not a lie. Macentyx and his brothers and sisters had spied upon this angel and their mother on many occasions. That wasn't to say that they had ever been seen by him or spoken with him.

101

"They have been gifted to Prince Iladrul." Jeanir's pride was overwhelming.

"An honor." Macentyx heard the click coming from the angel's throat as he swallowed. "One that shouldn't wait for pleasantries."

Jeanir, laughing, raised his hand and clapped the angel on the back. This earned him another guarded smile as Andrel turned toward the door to unlock it for the small group. Macentyx, who was the last through the door, did not miss the profound sorrow that laced Andrel's features as he passed him.

Mac turned, unable to take his eyes off the angel after having seen that expression. Andrel, gave him a final, guarded smile before closing the door behind them and locking them within.

"Mac!" Osete whispered urgently.

Macentyx shook the questions from his mind and turned to follow his brothers and sister. He gave Osete, who also bore those strange, gold rimmed, brown eyes, a swift smile, nodded and followed.

Though his mind should have been on his fate, and his fate alone, Macentyx's thoughts were focused on the puzzle of Andrel's strange, far too familiar, eyes.

-31-

"They have arrived." Iladrul turned toward the door, where his mother hovered wearing a smile. "Are you ready to meet them?"

"Does it matter if I am?" Iladrul inquired.

"Iladrul." Helena sighed. "This is a big day for you!"

"It's a day I am not prepared for." He could say these things to his mother. She understood them. And he needed to say them to someone. "I do not even know what to *do* with a doxy!"

Helena's green eyes trailed over her son's face for a moment. Finally, she said, "You don't have to do anything that you aren't ready to do."

"That isn't what Father says."

"Father wants you to be protected." She reminded him. "Which is why he chose these boys and that girl." She shook her head. "The rest of it can wait."

Iladrul, frowning, looked away. "What will they think of me if I do not break one of them tonight?"

"I imagine that they would be relieved." She walked toward him and sat upon the sofa beside him. She grabbed his hand and squeezed it. "They are, all of them, even younger than you. If you are not ready, then how must they feel?"

"Terrified?" Iladrul conjectured.

"Terrified." Helena agreed. "Iladrul, they are yours. There is no law regarding how you must treat them or when—or even *if*—you must break them. These relationships are yours to navigate."

"You don't believe they will think me an inept fool?" He could hear the tremor in his voice and he loathed himself for it.

"I think that they will believe you to be a kind master." She shrugged. Then she stood and held out her hand to him. "Come, child. Let us meet your new charges."

He stood, realizing that his knees were shaking as he did so. But he followed his mother, forcing a brave face for her benefit.

When he stepped into the sitting room, where his new property were gathered, he found himself stopping short.

These elves were, each one of them, breathtaking.

The boys all looked the same. From head to toe. Long, dark brown hair. Dark brown eyes that were rimmed with gold. Full lips, thick noses and strong bodies for their age.

As for the girl . . . Iladrul was barely able to look at her. She was just that beautiful.

He stepped forward so he might stand before them. As he did so, the four boys cornered themselves around the girl, almost as if they were protecting her.

They are *protecting her.* He realized. *From me.*

He forced himself to smile. "Welcome into my care."

One of the boys, who stood at the front, stepped forward. His expression was taut as he bowed. "We are proud to serve you."

Iladrul turned to this one. Obviously, he spoke for them all. "May you and I have a word?"

The boy paled, then forced a smile. "Of course, my Prince."

Iladrul nodded at him and led him out of the sitting room and into his bedchamber. Once there, he turned toward the boy and gave him a guarded smile. "I'm told you and your brothers have been trained at battle."

"Yes." The boy swallowed. "By our father."

Iladrul nodded. "What are your names?"

"I am Macentyx."

"And your skill?" Iladrul asked. "At war?"

"I favor the split sword." He replied, his gaze lowered.

"And your brothers?" Iladrul asked. "Their names and their skills."

"Haidar." The doxy muttered. "He's keen with the dagger." Iladrul nodded. "Osete is a fair hand at bow. And Jeavlin is quicker with his wit."

"We can use an elf quick with his wit." Iladrul sighed under his breath, granting him a nod. "Will they be loyal to me? Or should I fear any plans I share with them."

"Loyal." Macentyx's tone was laced with surprise. "We have been born and bred to be so. You are our Master."

"Gold paid doesn't drive out the desire for freedom." Iladrul reminded him. Macentyx pulled back from him, not trusting that answer. "The girl?"

"Sezja." His tone had a bite now. "Our sister."

"She's good at . . . ?"

"Needlework and cooking." He smiled tightly at Iladrul. "As a woman should be."

Iladrul frowned, his lips growing taut as he did so. "That's your one and only lie to me that shall ever be forgiven."

Macentyx lowered his gaze and nodded.

"What is your sister proficient at?"

"Poisons." He muttered. "She knows them all. And their antidote."

"Good." Iladrul sighed. He turned away from the doxy. "I would prefer to get to know the five of you before I call you to your baser duties." Macentyx didn't reply. After a few moments, Iladrul looked over his shoulder. He saw the doxy's silence was born out of curiosity. "And I don't favor men."

Macentyx lowered his gaze and nodded. "You want my sister."

"She is beautiful." Iladrul looked away. "But I will not find her bed if I am unwanted there."

"My Prince?" This was said in a whisper. "You don't mean to force—?"

"No." Iladrul cleared his throat. "You are dismissed."

The doxy, his expression slack with uncertainty, bowed to Iladrul. He said not a single word before leaving the room.

-32-

"You asked to speak with me, my Lord?"

Paul wasn't used to being called to the throne room to speak with Jamiason. Generally, when James wanted to speak with him, he did so in the privacy of their apartment.

The heavy expression on Jamiason's face as he raised his brooding eyes to greet Paul did nothing to bolster the vampire's confidence.

"Yes." Jamiason remained seated upon his throne with his elbow on the arm and his hand raised. His pinky was stretched outward and his thumb was toying with the tips of his first and second fingers. "Come."

Paul heard footsteps behind him and turned slightly to look over his shoulders. The twins were coming together at the door, closing it behind themselves. Paul felt an innate sense of dread as they clicked closed, locking Paul in the throne room alone with their King.

He returned his attention to Jamiason and gave his king a tight lipped smile. "How may I serve you?"

Jamiason assessed him for a long moment before lowering his hand and letting out a tired sigh. When he spoke, his tone was guarded. "Emissary Lord Darklief has agreed to allow us to meet with the elves in the Oakland Grove."

Paul blinked at him, surprised. "You spoke with him?"

"No." Jamiason shook his head. "I sent Marchand."

"Marchand?" Had he not been overwhelmed with his surprise that Jamiason had contacted Emissary Lord Darklief, he would have been offended. Visiting other lands on Jamiason's behalf had always been his duty. That James would send one of the twins in his place was almost insulting. "On a mission of politics?"

"I needed you here." He leveled his eyes on Paul. "Danger lurks within our own borders. Not in the lands of the Oakland Grove."

"Of course, but—"

Jamiason raised his hand to silence him. Paul lowered his gaze and swallowed his anger. It wasn't his place to argue with Jamiason about the manner in which James protected his borders.

"Aiken never grants a favor without a favor repaid." Jamiason's tone was tight. "His concession to allow our meeting with the elves to take place at his Grove is no exception."

Paul raised his gaze and asked, "What has he asked you for, my Lord?"

"He hasn't asked me." Jamiason replied, holding Paul's gaze. "As Prince of our lands, his request is being made of you."

"What must I offer him?" Paul, who would be nothing without Jamiason's backing, was more confused than ever. He had been a poor farmer before being turned. There was nothing he possessed that could possibly be of any worth to a God. "What has he asked for?"

"We are to choose which side his people will align with." Jamiason lowered his gaze slightly. Paul's brow furrowed as he watched this. "If you keep the talisman he has given you, he will align the fairies with the vampires." Paul, knowing, now, the direction in which this conversation was going, swallowed. "If you give the talisman back to him, he shall align himself with the elves."

"You wish me to give it back to him." Paul whispered.

"You were given a gift from a God, Paul." Jamiason shook his head. "In this one instance, I cannot interfere with your decision. You must do what you think is right."

Paul, frowning, turned away from him. As he did so, he raised his hand and fingered the ball attached to the chain that hung around his neck. The moment his finger touched its surface, it began pulsating with a brilliant pink light.

He had worn the talisman for long enough that this did not surprise him.

Letting go of the bauble, he returned his attention to Jamiason. His King was watching him with intent curiosity; clearly he was uncertain regarding Paul's choice. Seeing him so, assessing Paul, ready to judge him for his decision, Paul shivered.

If Paul gave up the bauble, he would lose Emissary Lord Darklief's protection. If he didn't, he would disappoint his King. His challenge, now, was to determine which he could live without and which he could not.

"My Lord, I'm . . ." He swallowed and lowered his gaze. "I would like to consider my position."

"Very well." The meaning behind Jamiason's tone was indecipherable. As was his expression when Paul braved to raise his gaze. "I ask, however, that you do not ponder your decision overly long."

"Of course not, my Lord." Paul swallowed and lowered his gaze again. "I understand the stakes."

"Keep in mind, of course, that if your decision is to keep your bauble," Jamiason advised him, "I expect you to present me with an alternative as to where we may meet with the elves." Paul raised his eyes again to look upon his King. "Remembering, of course, that neutrality is not an easy gem to find in the ever shifting sands of these times."

Paul, realizing, finally, that he was being manipulated to obey the wishes of his King, bowed low, turned away from Jamiason and took his leave.

-33-

Aiken turned the cup over and frowned up at his youngest son, Boltric. "Not this one?"

"No." Boltric, who thought he was a master of this particular game, looked up at his father and grinned. "Shall we try again?"

"No, boy. You've bested me." Aiken, chuckling, shook his head. "And it's getting late. Your mother will be by to pick you up shortly."

"Can't I stay, Fete?" He asked, his pink eyes shimmering. "I promise to behave."

Aiken considered him for a long moment. He had been remiss with this child, as he was with all of his sons. And it was, after all, the boy's sixth years summer day. He supposed that Boltric deserved spoiling.

"Very well." He smiled at the child. "You can stay. So long as you promise to teach me the magic of your trick on the morrow."

Boltric stood and ran around the table. He flew his arms around Aiken's neck and kissed his cheek. Smiling, Aiken, very tentatively, patted his back.

"It's a promise, Fete!" Boltric declared before releasing Aiken and running out of the room to find the bedchamber where Aiken's children slept when they spent the night in his hut.

Chuckling, Aiken shook his head and reached for the twelfth cup, which stood among sixteen. He raised it, reached forward for the prize that he had known would be hiding beneath it, and dropped the nut into his mouth. As it popped beneath his teeth, Karma stepped into the room.

"Fete." She gave him a guarded smile. "You've another visitor sent by Lord Scrountentine."

"Do I?" Aiken assessed her with a sly smile. "Is it the carrot top?"

"It is." She replied, smiling in response. "Would you palaver with him?"

"I suppose that custom suggests that I must given I've made my demands of him." Aiken shrugged. He waved his hand at her. "Bring him in."

"Yes, my Lord." Her smile grew as she lowered her gaze. His antics had always amused her. Perhaps this, above all other things, was what gave him confidence that she, out of all of his many children, was his rightful heir. "Right away."

He watched her leave the room with fatherly affection and returned to the cups lined in front of him. He began turning them over, one by one, knowing it was best that the boy believe that he found the hidden nut by random intention rather than that he had known where it had been placed all along.

The child, though not close to Aiken, deserved to believe his father's word when he had been told Aiken had been bested by his wit.

Some six shifts later, Karma returned with Paul Kinney at her side.

"My Lord." Karma gave him the appropriate curtsey with pretend skirts. "Prince Paul, come to palaver."

Aiken raised his gaze slowly, knowing that his feigned disinterest would cause Paul Kinney discomfort. As he met the carrot top's gaze, he gave him a tight smile. This was not the first time that they had met and Aiken knew, very well, how to play him.

"Paul Kinney." He swept his hand to the seat where Boltric had recently been sitting. Paul followed the movement of his hand and stepped toward the chair to lower himself within. "How very nice of you to pay me a visit."

Paul's lips thinned slightly as he looked to the rows of overturned cups. He reached for one that had not yet been disturbed and placed it to its rights. As Aiken had suspected, a second nut had been hidden beneath it.

"You've missed this one, my Lord." Paul replied as he raised the nut upward and held it toward Aiken. "There are two in the game. Your son would prefer to believe that you sought them both when you overturned the cups."

Aiken chuckled under his breath at that and shook his head as he took the nut from Paul's fingers. Like the first one, he placed it in his mouth and savored the taste of it as it popped between his teeth before returning his attention to Paul.

"I'd intended to leave it for him." Aiken smiled. "But you've made a fair point." He leaned forward. "How might I assist you, Paul Kinney?"

Now, Paul lowered his gaze and fidgeted. He reached for the silk of the tapestry that Aiken had spread over his table to protect the wood in the event of spills and ran his fingers over it. When he looked upward, it was with a guarded, very hesitant, smile.

"Lord Scrountentine has advised me that he has asked you to allow us a meeting with the elves within your grove." Paul's tone was tight. "And that your price for the meeting was the return of the talisman you have given me."

"Is that what he has told you?" Aiken replied, raising his hand and staring, as though bored, upon his fingernails. "That the talisman was to be returned in exchange for the meeting?"

Paul's brow furrowed. "Yes, he said—"

"The child progeny must have been confused." Aiken replied, lowering his hand and shrugging. He understood why Jami had lied to the vampire Prince, but he didn't condone it. Paul had to give up the talisman of his own free will or the gesture would be pointless. "What I said was that I can only align my people with one race. And it shall be that race who will keep the talisman."

Paul shook his head. His expression was dark with confusion.

"My peoples are a mortal race, Paul Kinney." Aiken explained. "They must side with vampire or they must side with elf. They cannot fight a war in which their loyalties are divided."

"I understand." His tone reflected that he did. "And you have asked Jamiason to make that choice for you."

"You never have been simple." Aiken smiled tightly at him. "Regardless of what we say about you."

Paul's eyes flashed before he looked swiftly away. Wisely, he did not respond to Aiken's insult.

"Now that you know the truth of my intent," Aiken asked, suppressing the amusement from his tone, "do you mean to change your mind in regard to returning the talisman to me?"

Paul, still not looking at Aiken, shook his head. When he spoke, his tone was tight.

"No, my Lord." He muttered. "I serve Jamiason. My fealty belongs to him. If what my Maker wants is for the elves to have your protection, then, clearly, as far as James is concerned, my life is forfeit."

"I do not believe that is the case." Aiken's lips pursed. "Jami merely wishes to do what is right."

"Perhaps, my Lord." Paul raised his gaze and met Aiken's. The fire within them surprised the fairy God. Even though he knew that Paul was made of tougher stuff than he was often given credit for, the vampire had never braved to stand tall before him. "But is anything about this right?"

"No, Paul Kinney." Aiken smiled at him. He decided, in that moment, that he liked him. "Nothing, at all about this is right."

Paul, reaching for the chain around his neck, nodded. When he no longer wore it, he stared at it for a long moment before stretching his arm in Aiken's direction. Aiken took the talisman from Paul and gave him a tight, understanding smile.

Paul, finished with their palaver, stood and bowed.

Aiken, still holding the talisman in his hand, found himself pondering what had passed between them long after he was gone.

-34-

Seven moons after Wisterian received word that Jamiason wished to meet with him, a small band of elves and angels arrived at the Oakland Grove. As they rode in, Iladrul's eyes were wide. Here, there were trees so tall that Iladrul wondered where the branches ended and the sky began. He saw huts built within each of them and long, vine ladders that fell from the branches to the ground.

"It's dizzying, isn't it?" Balean asked him, smiling.

The young Prince started at the sound of the General's voice and forced himself to smile in return. He didn't feel much like smiling these days.

"It's beautiful." Jeanir, who rode on the other side of Balean muttered.

"It *is* breathtaking landscape." Iladrul finally agreed, his eyes flicking to Sezja, who rode beside him. Though the landscape was more than merely beautiful—it was magical.

It was as though the Gods had kissed the very trees.

They came to a stop and his father flew from his horse to land deftly upon his feet. It was a graceful thing to watch and Iladrul, though he bore no wings, tried to match it. He thought he'd managed well enough, though he didn't care for the amused smiles on Balean and Jeanir's faces.

Iladrul stepped next to his father and looked up at him, trying not to show the fear that was coursing through his veins. His father reached for him, squeezed his shoulder and guided him through the strange village.

"Don't be afraid of Jamiason." His father smiled down at him. "He wants to meet you."

Iladrul, unable to meet his father's gaze, lowered his. "Yes, your Highness."

Wisterian ran his hand over the back of Iladrul's head. Iladrul felt lost in the size of it. "He's a good man, Iladrul. He will be a strong ally after all of this ends."

"As you say." Iladrul placated him.

"I speak truth." Wisterian assured him. "When this is over, he will be your friend. No matter what else passes between his race and yours during this war."

"Yes, Sir." Iladrul shivered.

"Good." Wisterian smiled at Iladrul and kissed his son's forehead "Come. We must meet and thank Emissary Lord Darklief."

"I thought he would be gone . . . " Iladrul's tone was weak.

He had no desire to meet Jamiason. But, having never actually met a God, he was terrified.

"He will be." Wisterian's tone was tight. "Before Jamiason comes."

"Must I meet him?"

"Yes." Wisterian nodded. "He is doing us a great favor by allowing us the neutrality of his Grove."

"Yes, your Highness." Iladrul whispered and followed his father into the cusp of trees.

As they walked deeper within the Oakland Grove, Iladrul's sense of dread lifted. The people they passed were extremely tall and seemed—on the surface—to be hospitable to the elves presence.

None of them wore any clothing, which made Iladrul extremely uncomfortable. He was unable to stop himself from gawking at the women, who seemed to be oblivious to the leering stares of the angels that had travelled with Iladrul to protect him. His father elbowed him slightly when he realized that Iladrul was staring, forcing the young boy to lower his gaze to focus on his own, booted feet.

When they reached a great tree in the center of the strange village, Iladrul's father stopped, bowed low to a male fairy standing at the foot of the tree and gave him a warm smile. "We have come for an audience with Emissary Lord Darklief."

The fairy's strange, buttercup yellow eyes flicked to Iladrul. When he smiled, Iladrul realized that his canine teeth were sharp and pointed. He shivered slightly as the memory of the demon with his murderous teeth came to mind and then forced himself to smile in return. "He's been expecting you Lord Wisterian."

Iladrul's father bowed and started climbing up the vine ladder that went to the very top of the tree. Iladrul followed with Balean and Jeanir at his heels.

At the top of the ladder was a trap door that led into the hut. Wisterian pushed this open and pulled himself through. Once there, he bent over, reached his hand down to Iladrul and pulled him the rest of the way up. He left the angels to their own devices as he stepped to a closed door and knocked.

A deep voice on the other side bid them to enter. Wisterian pushed the door open and stepped in, waiting for Iladrul to step beside him before facing the room.

As Iladrul found his purchase, his mouth fell open.

The hut had been made around and out of the tree. On each of the walls were delicately threaded tapestries which were more beautiful and detailed than any oil or water color painting Iladrul had ever seen.

"So this is the famous elf."

The deep voice forced Iladrul out of his reverie. He turned his gaze toward its owner and stared with open mouthed surprise. The creature was commanding. Very tall and very slender, he had long white hair that fell below his hip, which was littered with wildflowers. His thick lips were curved into a tight smile and his eyes—a vivid, and almost disturbing, shade of violet— were trailing with great curiosity over Iladrul's face.

"Awfully small to be causing such a ballyhoo."

Wisterian bowed low to him. "He won't always be small, Emissary Lord Darklief."

"No." The fairy agreed with a crooked smile. "He certainly is well made."

"He favors his mother." Wisterian replied, still smiling tightly. "How fare thee, Emissary Lord Darklief?"

"I bide." He shrugged and turned his attention to Wisterian. Iladrul was relieved to be out from under the scrutiny of his gaze. "And you?"

"We do the best that we can with what we have left." Wisterian smiled dryly at him.

"I suppose that is all any of us can do." Emissary Lord Darklief replied. "Jeanir. I am pleased to see you once again."

"My Lord." Jeanir bowed very low to him.

"We appreciate your allowance of our use of your Grove." Wisterian said swiftly. Iladrul marked that Emissary Lord Darklief's eyes narrowed slightly. "We must be a terrible inconvenience to you."

"I'm certain I can find something other to do with myself." Emissary Lord Darklief's mouth became drawn in a taut frown. "In the meantime, I'm told you come to meet Jami in truce."

"We do, my Lord." Wisterian assured him.

"Good." Emissary Lord Darklief replied. "I expect you to remember this. While you are here, I want no trouble to reign between you and Jamiason's people."

"We shall respect your rules and your borders." Wisterian lowered his gaze. "I assure you that the peace you broker will not be broken by me or mine."

"Very well." The God nodded to him. "Then you are most welcome guests." He granted Wisterian another one of his taut smiles. "I have just a few tasks to complete, and then I can vacate and leave you in peace."

"At your leisure, my Lord." Wisterian bowed his head. "We are, as you have said, your humble guests."

-35-

Aiken didn't really have anything pressing to do which wouldn't wait for his return to the Grove. Anything, that was, aside giving Prince Iladrul the bauble that Paul Kinney had delivered to him.

He watched Wisterian by way of his peripheral vision as the angel hovered over his son, almost as though guarding him. Aiken wasn't offended that Wisterian didn't trust him not to manipulate the situation should he manage to get the princeling alone.

After all, that was exactly what he intended to do.

A crooked smile played at the left corner of Aiken's lips as Jeanir and Balean cautiously approached Wisterian to beg a word with him. He watched guardedly and with curious interest as the pair of them led the angel away from the elf, taking him to the corner of the room so that they could speak with him in low whispers. The boy, no longer under the scrutiny of his father's gaze, walked languidly through Aiken's hut, passing out the back door and onto the balcony. Aiken, knowing he wouldn't get a second chance to palaver with the child without the Wisterian overhearing, stood and followed.

He felt the cold glare of Wisterian's eyes upon his back, but he ignored this. He cared little and less if he offended the angel. It wasn't Wisterian that his people would, eventually, be beholden to.

The child stood at the edge of the balcony, his hand gripping the branch of the tree that Aiken's hut was made from, leaning forward and looking downward with wide eyed wonder. The tree was the tallest in the grove and Aiken's hut was built at the very top of it.

The fall, should the elf tumble, would break the child's body and bring about his death.

"Careful, my Prince." Aiken kept his voice low lest he startle the child. He didn't want to have to fly after him to catch him should he let go of the branch. "It's a long way down."

"Forgive me, my Lord." The boy swallowed as he turned to face Aiken. His gaze was slightly lowered. Whether from fear or respect, Aiken neither knew nor cared. "Your lands are amazing to me."

Aiken smiled at that and nodded. His lands were beautiful, there was no doubt. Yet, he had once visited the castle where the elves resided and knew that, breath taking as his lands were, they didn't compare to the wonder of those that Iladrul would, one day, command. Those lands consisted of the first castle built in the first forest ever, in the history of all time, created.

And by Noliminan and Lucias' hands.

As he stepped toward the boy, Aiken was pleased to see that the elf did not cower. He was trembling; frightened. But he stood his ground. Aiken found himself admiring the child for his courage.

He flicked his hand, conjuring the talisman. Very slowly, he held it toward the boy.

"Take this child." He commanded. "And wear it about your neck. Never take it off." He smiled around the next words which were, for all intents and purposes, a pretty little lie. "You will not die so long as you keep it close to your skin. And you will find the courage you require to take action when you must so long as you trust in its magic. Your fear, you will find, shall leave you."

Iladrul looked at the bauble, his eyes wide as they drank in the pink of the dancing light that pulsed from within it. He swallowed and, with a small trembling hand, reached for the talisman. He took it gingerly from the palm of Aiken's hand, looked upward with his dark, emerald eyes and licked the right side of his upper lip with a nervous, pink tongue.

When he spoke, his tone was low and reverent.

"Will it really keep me alive?"

"Did I tell you that it would?" Aiken was unable to suppress his smile.

"Yes."

Aiken shrugged at him as if to say, "well there you have it", and the boy lowered his gaze.

"Thank you." Iladrul whispered as he slipped the chain over his neck and hid the bauble beneath his shirt. "I shall wear it always."

"Very good." Aiken said as he turned to face Wisterian, whom he had just heard step into the corner of the door, "my business here is done, Wisterian."

"Yes, my Lord." Wisterian's eyes narrowed as they darted between Aiken and Iladrul. He wanted, very much, to know what Aiken had said to his son.

"Remember." Aiken raised his finger and pointed to Wisterian, "you are here for peace. Stay away from the vampires' camp. And raise no rabbles which shall cause trouble for my peoples."

He didn't wait for confirmation that Wisterian would take his command seriously. There was no need. To raise the enmity of a

God when one was merely an angel would bring about damnation.

-36-

Paul pulled his teeth from the neck of the pretty female fairy, swallowing the last gush of blood with greedy hunger as it flowed into his mouth. He bit his tongue and ran it, tenderly, over the wounds he had made before raising his face slightly to kiss her just beneath the lobe of her ear.

She moaned and pressed her body toward him, tempting him to bury his teeth into her vein once again.

He resisted the urge.

He had taken all of the blood from her that he dared. To take any more would put her life at risk.

"Must you go, Paul?" Her throaty tones made him shiver with a different kind of hunger; the kind he could no longer sate.

"I must." He pulled away and met her gaze. Her eyes, like her hair, were the color of wheat. Looking into them, he desperately missed his father's farm. "If we are still here on the morrow, may I visit your tree again?"

"You are ever welcome, dear." She replied, blushing prettily with the little bit of blood left within her. "Though it would be best if we take our courtship slow."

Paul gave her a weary smile.

He hadn't been aware that this was meant to be a courtship.

"As you wish."

He kissed her cheek one last time and bid her goodbye. He wouldn't, he decided, be visiting her before he and his party departed.

He had no interest in finding another wife and he didn't want to risk that she would follow after him when he left the Oakland Grove.

He wandered through the village, stopping short when he turned a corner and saw five young elves standing at the base of one of the trees. Four of them stood in box formation around the fifth who, judging by his coloring, Paul assumed was the young Prince.

The boy had a very young, rather girlish look about him. The dark blue, ankle length skirt he wore did nothing to dissuade this image. Nor did the delicately made, bronze crown, which twisted into a teardrop of pulsing white light over his forehead.

Paul didn't believe that the elf would always look so damn womanly, however. His chin was square and strong and his nose, while slender and delicate, had the potential of growing straight and rigid. Never mind the manner in which he carried himself, shoulders back and head held high.

He would be commanding, Paul suspected, given a century or so to age.

It was as this thought crossed his mind that the boy in the back to the elf's left turned his gaze in Paul's direction. Upon seeing Paul, he stiffened and muttered something under his breath which made the other boys, including the Prince, turn to look at Paul. Forcing a smile, Paul stepped out of the trees to walk toward them. As he did so, the four boys surrounding Prince Iladrul tightened their box around him.

"Prince Iladrul." Paul nodded respectfully toward the boy. The elf nodded in response but said nothing. "I am Paul Kinney. I am Lord Scrountantine's companion."

"Of course." The boy's lips thinned. He raised his hand, holding it out to Paul. "It's a pleasure to meet you."

Stepping forward, Paul took the child's hand and gave it a good, firm shake. The moment he let go, Prince Iladrul flew his hand to his hip to wipe it against his skirt. The blood sweat that had come from Paul's recent feeding trailed a line in the dark blue material of his skirt that would, more than likely, never come clean.

"The pleasure is mine." Paul continued to hold his forced smile. He didn't like the contemptuous glean in the young elf's eyes. Nor did he like the set of his smile. "I hope I am not late."

"No." The boy said, his eyes holding Paul's gaze. "My father and your Maker are holding palaver." His lips twitched slightly.

"It would seem my father trusts Lord Jamiason. Balean tells me that they fell asleep whilst chatting."

Paul's eyes flicked upward to the base of the hut. That Jamiason had spent the day there, rather than the lair, was disconcerting at best. Emissary Lord Darklief's hut was open, exposing James to the rays of the sun.

No one was supposed to know that his veins ran with the blood of a God. Especially not someone who they were about to declare as their enemy.

"They are old friends." He admitted to the boy.

"Perhaps." The child's eyes narrowed. "Shall we awaken them?"

Paul smiled wryly at that. "The first rule where vampires are concerned—even demon vampires—is that, when they are sleeping, it's best to let them lie. We are far less than pleasant when we are disturbed from our deaths."

The elf paled. The other four boys, who had been still as statues until that moment in time, began exchanging glances. The young Prince was clearly about to respond when the trap door above them opened and Aiken's oldest daughter, Karma, leaned through.

"Lords Wisterian and Jamiason are ready to receive you." She said. "The doxies are to stay on ground to advise Balean and Iykva that this palaver will be held only between the Princes."

Iykva isn't going to like that. Paul rightly prophesized.

Too bad for him. Jamiason's thoughts bounced around Paul's mind. Paul shivered and forced a smile. *Bring the child up.*

"After you." He indicated the ladder to Prince Iladrul.

Granting Paul a mistrustful smile, Prince Iladrul reached for the ladder and began climbing.

Prepared for anything, Paul, reluctantly, followed.

-37-

When Iladrul reached the top of the ladder and stood before the door of the hut, he raised his hand and pressed it against his chest. His fingers curled around the bauble that Emissary Lord Darklief had given him, bringing him an unexpected sense of comfort.

He looked over his shoulder and shuddered as his gaze met Prince Paul's. He couldn't shake the disgust that he felt as he thought of the touch of the Prince's slimy, blood stained hand. His nose curling, he turned to the door and knocked.

It was his father that bid him to enter.

He stepped through the door, not believing that anything else could surprise him in this strange, otherworldly place, and stopped short as his eyes fell upon an all too familiar face.

When his gaze met that of the blonde haired demon, his lips fell slack and his eyes grew wide. Of all of the demons in all of the worlds, this man—this creature—was the last he expected to see sitting at his father's side.

"Iladrul." Wisterian stood and swept his hand to the other side of the table. "Prince Paul. Please. Won't you sit so that we might hold palaver?"

The demon's thick lips curled slightly at the corners as he continued to hold Iladrul's gaze. He said nothing, however. Rather, he merely watched Iladrul and waited for him to gain his senses.

Swallowing, Iladrul flicked his gaze to his father. He was shaking his finger, almost irritably, toward the seat that he meant for Iladrul to take. Iladrul nodded at him and returned his gaze to the demon, his fear intensifying as he met those cold, detached, cobalt blue eyes.

"Iladrul, this is Jamiason Scrountentine." Wisterian flicked his eyes to the demon and then back to Iladrul. "James, my son, Iladrul."

Jamiason Scrountentine bowed his chin slightly and the raised it. His eyes closed, and then opened, with the gesture. The corners of his mouth twitched slightly as his eyes flicked to Iladrul's chest. They hovered on the bauble for a moment before raising again and meeting Iladrul's gaze.

"Lord Wisterian." The vampire, who had followed Iladrul, nodded to Iladrul's father. "It is an honor to finally meet you."

"And you, Prince Paul." Wisterian's lips thinned. "I do wish it had been under better circumstances."

"As do I." Paul muttered as he found his seat.

The demon's eyes flicked to the seat that Iladrul stood before and then back to meet Iladrul's gaze. Iladrul swallowed again, nodded at him and lowered himself clumsily into the chair.

As he did so, Wisterian turned his gaze toward his son.

"Jamiason has presented me with his demands." He flicked his eyes to the demon, who sat motionless and staring at Iladrul with those terrifying blue eyes. "In order to avoid war with his people, I must hand him the keys to the gates of our city. The vampires and the demons are to be free to come and go at their whim and drink from whom they please."

Iladrul snapped his gaze to his father. "Father, you cannot mean to actually—"

"I do not." Wisterian shook his head. "However, I have negotiated us some time." His lips thinned as he turned his gaze to Prince Paul. "You are to give my son fifteen summers to age and train an army."

Paul's eyes flicked to Jamiason, found whatever confirmation he required and returned his gaze to Wisterian. "A reasonable request."

"In exchange," Wisterian's lips thinned, "we are to agree that, once war has been struck, we will only fight your people during the hours of the moons."

Iladrul frowned at that. The only advantage that they had over the demons and vampires was the burning light of day. They could destroy an entire village in one strike if they were allowed to breach their borders when the sun crested the sky.

He swallowed, however, and looked away from his father to meet Lord Scrountantine's cold gaze. When he spoke, he somehow managed to keep the tremble from his tone. "Also a reasonable request."

Paul made a strange sound from his chest, which Iladrul assumed would have been a snort if the vampire had been able to breathe, and turned to face the young Prince. Iladrul literally ripped his gaze from that of the demon and turned toward Paul. He realized, as he did so, that Paul had extended his hand toward him.

Iladrul looked at the hand, shivered, and then clasped it. This time it wasn't wet, but it also was no longer warm. In fact, shaking the man's hand was like shaking the hand of a corpse.

He forced himself to smile, however, when he saw Paul's nostrils flare slightly and his chest rise as though he were catching Iladrul's scent. He didn't care for the hungry gleam in Paul's eyes or the surprised slack of his lips as he leaned forward to sniff a second time.

It was as he was leaning forward that Lord Jamiason stood and slammed his hand upon the table. The sight of his movement and the thunderous crash of his hand upon the wood made Paul spin and Iladrul cry out.

"Sit back." He seethed, his gaze frozen on Paul. "Make no threats toward Prince Iladrul whilst in Aiken's lands."

"I'm . . ." Paul swallowed and leaned swiftly backward. His voice had a throaty, hungry quality to it that Iladrul didn't care for. "Forgive me, my Lord. Something came over me. I don't—"

"Silence." Jamiason replied as he lowered himself back to his seat. He turned his gaze to Iladrul, his eyes flicking to the bauble around Iladrul's neck and then upward to meet Iladrul's gaze. "Ware Emissary Lord Darklief and his penchant to make mischief." He cautioned. "But keep the talisman that he gave to you on tight chains around your neck." He flicked his eyes to Paul and then back to Iladrul. "When the time comes, Aiken's treachery will mean the difference between your life and your death."

He stood again and held his arm out to Paul.

"Come, child." He commanded. Paul stood, without question, and took his arm. "The time for our departure is long overdue."

Unable to tear his gaze away from the demon, Iladrul watched him as he wrapped his arm around Paul's waist and, for the second time, jumped upon a balcony, scanned his surroundings, spread his wings and took flight.

-38-

Iykva was furious when he reached the base of the tree and was barred entry by General Balean. His very purpose for having made this trip with Paul and Jamiason was to attend the meeting.

The war was, after all, entirely his to win.

As the red moon crossed the sky with the pink moon close on her heels, he became more and more agitated. Finally, he could take it no longer.

He stormed away from the tree to the lair that Emissary Lord Darklief had made for the travelers to stay in during the daylight hours. Once there, he found his bag, scavenged thorough his trikla and found a small scrap of paper and a small bit of lead.

As far as Iykva was concerned, if he wasn't part of the negotiations, there was no requirement that he abide by the agreed upon terms.

After scribbling his message, he tied the scrap of paper to one of three falcons that had been following him from a distance and shooed the bird away. As its shadow crossed the silver moon above him, Iykva found a tight, yet extremely satisfied, smile.

-39-

When Aiken entered Loki's apartment, he was wearing a tired scowl. After having met Jamiason's elf for the first time, he finally understood Jamiason's draw to Paul.

Not that Aiken, himself, hadn't always been drawn to Paul. He was an extremely handsome man.

For a speaking ape, that was.

But his personality and Jamiason's personality were extreme polar opposites. While Jami, since his exile, was very serious in his nature, Paul was what many people considered to be a laughing fool. He was always cracking wise, especially when it was inappropriate to do so.

In many ways, Paul reminded Aiken of the Loki of old. Loki before he'd lost his head the King of Lords' scythe, that was. Though he would never admit this to anyone, that reminder was why Aiken had always been leery of the man.

"Oh." Aiken started at the sound of Ishitar's voice. "Aiken. I wasn't expecting anyone home today."

Aiken turned toward the young Prince of Providence and forced himself to smile. He stood in the door frame of Loki's library, his shoulder leaning against one side and his long legs crossed at the ankle. He looked extraordinarily casual to Aiken in that pose.

"I doubt Loki is expecting me either." He winked at Ishitar. "The vampires demanded an audience with the elves and, given I have a fondness for both races, I offered them the Oakland Grove."

Ishitar's brow rose over his contemplative eye. "Is that so?"

"Ta." Aiken forced his smile to grow. "Perhaps they can come to a truce."

Ishitar continued to assess him with his brow high over his eye. "And, perhaps, the planet Kramalta will soon see its first snow."

Aiken's smile became true at that sentiment. It was a world that the King of Lords was trying to destroy because its people had offended him in their refusal to worship their Gods. To punish them, King Noliminan was depriving the planet of all fresh water supplies. The place had become all but a barren desert where only the most hardy of souls, a lizard like race of mortals known as grops, had adapted to survive.

"Which race is the one striking for war?"

"The vampires." Aiken, reluctantly, admitted. "Or, rather, the demons."

"Jamiason Scrountentine?" His tone was strangely gentle. Aiken suspected that this was because Ishitar understood the relationship between Aiken and the man who had once been his demon.

"A demon named Iykva." Aiken shrugged. "As their King, Jami will be forced to lead them."

As Ishitar nodded, Aiken noted that his eyes narrowed slightly. They darted over Aiken's face, almost as if assessing him. Finally, he looked away. When he spoke, his voice was a low growl. "Gods . . . I grow weary of these four walls."

"I'm going to the Courtyard on the Twenty Third Level to meet a friend." Aiken offered. "I'm sure she won't mind if you join us."

"She, is it?" He returned his gaze to Aiken and smiled.

"Is a friend." Aiken winked at him. "And one I think you know: Lady Zamyael."

"Zamyael?" He started. "She braves a Hells bound courtyard?"

"She does." Aiken nodded. "It's a rather barren level where your father never tarries. And the Lady Regent thinks far too much of herself, these days, to sully her space with we commoners." Ishitar chuckled at that and shook his head. "You should join us."

"I really don't want to draw attention to Zamyael if she's braved visiting these lands." Ishitar sighed. "I wish I could join you, but—"

"Really, your Royal Highness." Aiken scoffed. "You're one of the three most powerful Gods in either realm or exile. You can't devise a spell to cloak your face?"

"I suppose I could make myself look like Loki." He muttered. Then with a tight lipped frown, "He's staying with my mother tonight."

"There you go."

"He drinks harder spirits than I." Ishitar complained. "What if they go to my head?"

"Then I'll see you safely home and to your bed." Aiken, not caring much for Ishitar's dark expression, shrugged.

"What if one of his gaggle would see me to theirs?"

Ishitar forced himself to smile. Aiken, not caring much for his sense of humor, forced himself to smile in response.

"Then, your Royal Highness," Aiken winked at him again, "I'm afraid you're on your own. Though, for your safety's sake, I do hope that you understand well and true how Loki has managed to become so famous for his Gods be damned beard."

For the first time since Aiken had met the young Prince, Ishitar threw back his head to grant him a good, honest laugh.

-40-

The air was still. And eerily quiet.

Shivering, Iladrul felt his grip tighten around the reins in his hands.

"Jeavlin?"

He leaned toward the boy on his left flank, swallowing back his fear. Something about their surroundings did not sit well with him.

"Yes, my Prince?" Jeavlin blinked his unsettling, gold rimmed eyes. Clearly he was surprised to be the one to be addressed. Generally, Iladrul only passed words with Macentyx. He thought it best not to engage the others until he was ready for the responsibility of owning them which had been thrust upon him against his will.

"What do you see?" Iladrul asked, trying desperately to hold his voice at a low whisper. It was time to see if the doxy was as perceptive as Macentyx had touted him to be. And, perhaps, the young Prince would learn a thing or two about trails and tracking in the process. "What do you hear?"

"No birds." He blinked again as he raised his gaze to the sky. "And no stars."

Iladrul's lips thinned as he gave the boy a barely perceptible nod. "Anything else?"

Jeavlin lowered his gaze, his brow furrowing. As he raised it to the side of the road, his own lips thinned. "Too many hoof prints. A hoard has ridden this road."

"A hoard?" Iladrul's voice trembled slightly.

"And recently. I smell soot and ash." The boy shuddered. "Vampires, do you think?"

"If I had to guess." Iladrul, now seeing and smelling these things for himself, agreed. He pulled the reigns in his hands, tightly, bringing his horse to an abrupt stop. As he did so, he called, "Jeanir!"

Jeanir looked over his shoulder, realized that Iladrul and his doxies had come to a stop and pulled his horse around to face the young Prince. "What is it? What's the matter?"

"Something isn't right." Iladrul shook his head. "The road is rough shod and the vegetation seems disturbed." He flicked his eyes upward. "I smell smoke. And I see no stars."

Jeanir's jaw clenched as his nostrils flared and he took in a deep, long breath. "Loki's beard . . ."

He spun his horse in the other direction and drove it with breakneck speed to the front of the line. The relief that overwhelmed Iladrul as the party of angels surrounding him came to an abrupt halt was welcomed with quiet desperation.

"I thought the vampires meant to give us time to prepare." This was said by the one called Haidar. Iladrul flicked his eyes in his direction, frowning at him. "Didn't Prince Paul tell you that he would give you time?"

"Obviously, he lied." Iladrul rounded on the boy. "Draw your weapons." He turned his attention to Sezja, who rode at his side. "I want you to duck into the trees and make haste for the castle the barest moment it appears we are to face a scuffle."

"I can hold my own." She replied to this, turning her dark eyes in his direction. Unlike her brothers, her brown eyes weren't ringed with gold. They were ringed with blue. This made them, in Iladrul's estimation, the most beautiful eyes he had ever seen. "My father trained me. Same as my brothers."

"Girls aren't meant to battle." Osete grumbled.

Iladrul barely marked the movement of her hand flying to her hip to pull out a dagger she carried there and chuck it at her brother. It struck the leather strap of his quiver, which was slung over his shoulder, and shivered there. Osete, let out a gasp of fear as he reached for the grip and pulled it off of his shoulder.

"Something more to say?" His sister asked him.

Osete, swallowing, shook his head. As he did so, Sezja leaned forward and swiped the dagger from his hand. Iladrul, trying to hide his impressed smile, looked swiftly away.

"The sun will be up soon." Haidar, who rode at his right flank, muttered. "The dirty beasts won't have anywhere to hide."

"If they're still about." Macentyx agreed. "My guess is they've done what damage they intended and went underground."

"If they are underground," Iladrul reminded them, "we can dig them up." He frowned as he realized that their party was on the move again. "Come." He advised his doxies. "But stay at the ready."

They fell into step with the angels, their path set on the Great Road. Until, that was, they came to the branch of the road that shot toward the Doxy Village. Iladrul, who had been watching the smoke in the sky, came to an abrupt stop as the rest of his party continued toward the castle.

"What is it, my Prince?" Macentyx licked his lips.

It was a question that required no answer. He knew what Iladrul knew. The smoke was coming from the direction of Macentyx's people. Not from the castle.

Iladrul shook his head and raised his hand to cover his lips. "Why are we heading toward the castle?"

Macentyx raised his arm to cover his mouth as if he meant to cough. "Your safety comes first."

"If the vampires have gone to ground," Iladrul lowered his head and began toying with an imperfect stitch on his saddle, "then my safety is not in question."

"With us at your side, your safety is not in question." Osete corrected him, almost imperceptibly.

Iladrul raised his gaze and met the eyes of each one of his doxies in turn. He didn't need to voice his intentions. These boys, and their sister, were perceptive and intelligent in the arts of war.

Upon receiving a near to undetectable nod from all five of them, Iladrul pulled roughly at the reigns of his horse and urged it into a violent run toward the Village.

The angels meant to protect him began crying their protests and chasing after him. But his horse, and the horses he had gifted to his doxies, were well bred; sired from the horse God, Pegasus. Though they had no wings, when they were at a run they may as well have taken flight. Even those angels who took wing had no hope of catching Iladrul or his doxies on the backs of *these* horses.

What he found at the end of that road forever changed him.

Every cottage had been set to fire. Screams were coming from some of them as the occupants within them burned. The smell of burning flesh permeated the air. As did the bitter taste of death associated with it.

It was with great horror that he looked around himself. Angels lay dead everywhere. As did the bodies of the young doxy children.

There was one small body in particular from which he was unable to pull his gaze.

The child couldn't have been more than three moons old. It's head—he couldn't tell if it were male or female given its state—had been caved in by the heel of someone's boot. One of its arms and one of its legs had been ripped from its body and flung away as whatever beast had taken it had greedily fed from its lifeblood.

"Dear Gods." Sezja's voice was quavering. Her dismay pulled Iladrul's attention in another direction and away from the horror that was the remains of the babe. "Is that . . . ?"

"Mother!" Haidar screamed and flung himself from his horse. Iladrul watched in horror as he ran toward the body of his mother, bloody and beaten yet, somehow, gray and withering.

"Mother . . . ?" Jeavlin's voice was small.

"Don't look." Macentyx warned them all. "Remember what father has always told us. Don't look at the faces of the fallen you have loved lest they opt to stay to comfort you."

Iladrul felt a chill rush over him with those words. With it, his senses returned to him.

In the distance came a cry that was familiar to him. It was a cry that was akin to that which the demon who had attacked him—who Lord Scrountentine had protected him from—had made.

"A vampire." He muttered. "And not gone to ground."

He flew off of his horse and went running in the direction of the creature. Sezja ran behind him, close on his heels. As they came upon it, stumbling violently into the sunlight, the flames exploding around it, the girl pushed the being off of the road and into the river. The flames were immediately extinguished by the rushing water, though the creature was clearly still fighting for its life as it gripped desperately at a rock on the side of the river that was shaded by the trees above it.

Iladrul rushed toward Sezja, who was grasping the creature by its hand. Sloughs of skin slid off of the meat of its arms as Sezja pulled it out of the river to lay, writhing, on the cool grass at the young Prince's feet.

"I couldn't . . ." It was a woman's voice that came from this creature. "The babes . . . Dear Gods . . . They were only children!"

Biting back the urge to kick the bitch, Iladrul clutched at the talisman around his neck to give him courage and fell to his hunkers, reaching toward her to smooth back the hair that covered her face. As he looked into her wide, haunted eyes, he actually felt pity for the creature.

He loathed himself for this.

131

"What have you *done*?" He asked, his voice far more distant and adult than he had ever imagined it could be. "What has happened to the children of this village?"

"They murdered them all." She whispered, her eyes dancing over Iladrul's face in terror and revulsion. "Every single one not of breeding age." Her tone took on an angry property then. It was probably the one thing, in the end, that saved her. "They drained them dry and discarded their bodies like useless fodder."

Iladrul shuddered and turned his face away to hide it into his shoulder. This creature did not deserve to witness any weakness he might be unable to hold at bay.

When he recovered himself he turned to face her again. He could hear the angels approaching him—his father screaming his name—but he ignored this. "What did they do with the others? Those old enough to breed?"

"Took . . . them." She swallowed. "They mean to . . ."

She didn't finish, but Iladrul didn't need for her to do so. His father had told him what the vampires meant to do with the elves should they win their bloody war.

"Where did they take them?"

She shook her head. She was growing weak from the wounds she had sustained when she had been set afire by the light of the sun. "They took them to . . ."

Before she could finish, she succumbed. Iladrul, frustrated and angry, flew to his feet and spun away. When he saw that Haidar stood directly behind him, he commanded, "Find a blanket and wrap her up. She can stay in the cellar in one of the cages."

"Yes, my Prince." He spun on his heel and ran in the direction of where they had abandoned their horses.

When he was gone, Iladrul turned back to face the demon and saw that Sezja had lowered herself to her hunkers and pulled her dagger from her belt. He didn't realize his own intent until he found himself pouncing toward her and pushing her out of the way.

"No!" He cried her, snatching the dagger from her and running it across his own flesh. "I won't let you!"

He stared with sick surprise at his wounded wrist as the blood began first bubbling, then pouring down his arm. Knowing there was no time to waste, he thrust his arm toward the creature's mouth and let her drink it in large, hungry gulps.

As she fed from him, he understood what Sezja had known when she had pushed the creature into the water: if he meant to find the doxy elves still living, he had to keep this unintended ally alive.

No matter the personal cost.

-41-

Iykva smiled greedily as he read the message.

Their mission had been successful. Though the castle, itself, had been secure and guarded, the foolish angels had failed to build the same defenses around the slaves' quarters. As a result, the demons and vampires had managed to capture over three hundred and fifty elves of breeding age.

"What are you smiling about?"

Iykva started. He hadn't heard Paul returning from the forest. "A message from the West."

"Oh?" Paul's tone was thick and guarded. "What news?"

"Our army's leaders have asked us to meet them at their camp." Iykva lied. He raised his gaze and met Paul's. The Prince's green eyes were surveying him with mistrust and loathing. "It will mean a slight detour. Though, not one that will take us too far off course."

"Jamiason wants to get home to the twins." Paul replied to this.

"The twins will wait." Iykva's eyes narrowed as he tried to tame the bite to his tone. "Your army needs to see you. To be bolstered by an appearance from you." His lips curled at the left corner in a sardonic grin. "Unless you don't mean to stand beside them should war erupt. As a real Prince would do."

Paul's eyes flashed with unmasked loathing. They trailed over Iykva's face before he looked swiftly away. "Of course I mean to stand beside them."

"Then tell Jamiason that it is important that you visit them." Iykva advised him. "And that his penchant for young boys can wait another day."

Paul was on him in a flash. His hands were around Iykva's neck and his green eyes were blazing. Iykva, who hadn't been expecting any kind of attack from the laughing fool, had been unprepared to defend himself. As a result, Paul was able to pin him to a tree.

Paul leaned forward, his lips mere inches from Iykva's own. When he spoke, his tone was laced with venom.

"Never let such blasphemy escape your lips again." He seethed.

Iykva raised his hands to those at his throat and began clawing at them. It was useless. Though he was a demon and Paul was a mere vampire, the child had fed from Jamiason's neck. He had drunk of the Gods blood that Evanbourough had given James. Even if diluted, such blood as ran through Jamiason's veins was more powerful than that which ran through Iykva's.

"You will respect your King and keep your opinions about him to yourself." Paul seethed as he flung Iykva around by the neck and threw him to the ground. "Do you understand me?"

Swallowing, and scooting away from Paul, using his hands for leverage, Iykva nodded. He would do well, he knew, to hold his tongue.

At least, he thought, *for now.*

-42-

"What is he playing at?" Jamiason groused.

"I know not." Paul muttered. "Something doesn't sit well with me over this."

"Nor with me." James admitted.

Turning away from Paul, he reached for a scrap of paper and a quill. Though he wasn't certain what mess Iykva was leading him into, he knew that he must be at the ready. The only way to be so was to make certain that the people that he trusted were also at the ready.

He scrawled a note to Marchand and Louis, then reached forward to hand it to Paul. "Send Blackheart home."

"Iykva will notice if—"

"I doubt it." Jamiason shook his head. "The falcon comes and goes at his whim. It is unlikely that Iykva is paying enough attention to even recognize that I've made him a pet."

"Then he's an unobservant fool."

"No." Jamiason corrected him, shaking his head. "A self-preserving fool." His lips thinned. "And that type of fool is the most dangerous kind."

Paul, nodding his agreement, took Jamiason's note from the grip of the demon's hand.

-43-

Once secured within his library, Wisterian began pacing furiously.

Jamiason had gone back on his word.

"And to my son." He seethed, his eyes leveling upon Jeanir.

"It makes no sense." Jeanir agreed. "Jamiason is not one to make false promises."

"This time he did."

"He can't have known that—" Jeanir shook his head. It didn't matter if he had known or if he hadn't and Jeanir understood that. "He can't have condoned the attack, my Lord. Even if he must now defend it."

"That's twice, that we are aware of, that his people have fallen out of his control." Wisterian seethed at him. "*Twice* that his people have attacked mine!" His fists flew, pounding the wood of his desk. "I could *destroy* Iykva! And with my bare hands!"

Jeanir didn't dispute that Iykva had to be responsible for this fracas and Wisterian was glad of it. Though, not surprised. Iykva had made no bones about the fact that he was displeased with Paul's promise to Iladrul that war would wait until his people were adults.

Or that he had been barred from the negotiations, for that matter.

"How do you mean to order me to respond?"

Wisterian raised his gaze and met Jeanir's own. He felt his blood run cold as he thought to the image burned within his mind of his son bent over the vampire with his wrist bleeding into her mouth.

"My son sacrificed his own life's blood to keep that cunt of a vampire alive." He hissed. "Find out what she knows. No matter what means it might take."

Jeanir, who had been schooled in the art of war by two Master swordsmen, paled.

He did not hesitate, however, in his agreement.

-44-

They travelled miles out of their way to reach the camp where the demons and vampires had settled in preparation of war. When they crested the hill that overlooked the camp, both Jamiason and Paul found great relief to see the rows upon rows of campfire's glittering in the distance. Enough so that they did not question the many red tent roofs which separated one row of fires from the other.

"So many . . ." Paul muttered.

"Ta." Iykva grinned at him. "We've been breeding sons and daughters as we travel across the lands."

"In anticipation of war?" Jamiason asked, a chill running through him as he did so.

"In anticipation of our salvation, your Highness." Iykva corrected him. The smile that he suddenly wore was telling and troubling. As he raised his hand and swept it toward the rows of tents in the valley beneath them, Jamiason suddenly understood way. "In anticipation of our redemption."

"The tents!" Paul voiced the thought that James was unable to.

"My Lord," Iykva's strange smile spread across his handsome face, making his features ugly, as he turned his gaze to meet Jamiason's own. "Welcome to the Feast of Light."

Realizing that Iykva had damned them all, Jamiason turned his gaze to Paul, saw the horrified expression upon his features, and swallowed.

PART TWO:
FALLEN HEROES

-1-

"What is this nonsense?" King Noliminan, who was sitting behind his desk, sat back in his chair, crossing his arms over his chest. "Lucias would never sully herself to bear that fool's child."

"I have come to understand she intends to, your Grace." Raphael muttered under his breath. "Lucias is building a Quorum of archangels."

"Who told you this?" He snapped.

"Your Grace," Raphael swallowed, "a reliable source."

"What *reliable* source?" He growled. "I'm in no mood for your damn games this morning."

"Your Grace, I'm not playing games." Raphael shook his head.

"Then tell me who is brokering these rumors."

"Your Grace . . ." Raphael muttered under his breath. He hadn't wanted to share this news with King Noliminan. Yet, he knew that if he didn't, and King Noliminan learned that he had known and hadn't told him, every debt promised to the Hells bound Kingdoms would become Raphael's, alone, to pay. "Zamyael."

"Damn her black heart." The King of Lords' fist flew, slamming against his desk. Raphael, who was still terrified of everything and anything since he had been Lucias' prisoner during the first rebellion, flinched backward, crossing his arms over his chest as if that would protect him. "Where is she hiding?"

"I know not, your Grace." Raphael muttered. "I was visiting one of the Hells bound courtyards and I happened across her, Emissary Lord Darklief and Prince Ishitar. The trio of them were sharing cups."

"Ishitar was *seen*?" His eyes grew wide. He flew to his feet. "Aiken took him to a public courtyard?"

"No one realized who he was, your Grace." Raphael swallowed the lump that immediately rose in his throat. "He cloaked himself with the face of another."

"Find Michael." King Noliminan seethed. "Tell him that I must speak with him immediately to deal with Aiken and his constant mischief making."

"Your Grace, no one recognized the fact that—"

"Bring him to me now!" He roared. "This is unforgivable on the heels of his ill begot creation of a new race!"

"But, your Grace," Raphael tried, "the dragon men will be just the thing to—"

Raphael didn't see the blow coming. King Noliminan, already standing, leaned across the desk so swiftly that his movements made him little more than a blur. One moment Raphael was standing in front of him; the next he was sitting upon the ground staring up at him after having tripped over one of King Noliminan's chairs.

"No more of your delay!" King Noliminan barked at him. "Find Michael and order him to appear before me! *Now!*"

-2-

Marchand wasn't good at telling lies. Because of this, he let Louis spread the tale. "We've been ordered by Lord Jamiason to leave the castle to join him and Prince Paul on the field."

"Jamiason would never order you from the castle." Stephen was one of James' most loyal followers. He saw to every order that was made of him to the barest detail. The last order that he had received was to protect the twins at all cost. "What madness do you speak?"

Louis, who had stayed up well into the day to draft a forgery of Jamiason's orders in their Maker's hand—James, himself, had forgotten about this particular detail—thrust his letter toward the demon. "This comes from Lord James, himself."

Stephen looked doubtful as he flicked the parchment and raised it to his face. Louis was cunning, however. He had pulled the paper from a desk drawer in Jamiason's apartment. Thus, it permeated with Jamiason's essence of an orange grove at harvest time.

Stephen read 'Jamiason's' orders and, wearing a weary expression, lowered the paper. His tone, when he spoke, was heavy with doubt. "Without escort?"

"Those are the orders." Louis shrugged. He raised his hand and pointed to the parchment. "So he's scribed."

"Madness." The demon shook his head. "Especially in these times."

"Yet, I cannot deny him." Louis turned his gaze to Marchand, who forced himself to bite his tongue. "Nor can Marchand." He returned his attention to Stephen. "As he is our Maker, we must obey his every command. We must go at once. Or we shan't make any miles before it's time to go to ground for the day."

The demon raised his brows, assessed Marchand and gave him a reluctant nod. "Very well. If this is Lord Jamiason's order then I must comply."

"Grea—"

"But with a condition." Marchand and Louis exchanged a furtive glance before returning their attention to the demon. "You'll go with my prodigy."

"She's—"

"Young." He agreed. "But she was a Princess, and a warrior, before I turned her." He flicked his gaze to Marchand, who hadn't spoken a word during this conversation. "And fond of you."

"Of *me*?" Marchand started.

"Ta." He nodded. Though his lips thinned.

Marchand blinked at that. He had no idea how he was supposed to respond. Given the years he had lived, he thought of himself as a man. Yet, he had never dared to hope that anyone would look past his face to see his nature.

Never mind that he couldn't remember ever having met the girl.

"This is my condition." The demon returned his attention to Louis. "Do you accept? Or must I write to Lord Jamiason?"

"We accept." Louis answered for them both.

Marchand wanted to strike him.

"Good." The demon nodded at Marchand. "Go to ground come morning. And, come evening, Melody will be ready to join you."

Melody? Marchand shivered. It was a lovely name.

Does she have a lovely face?

Truly, though, even if, by some miracle, a woman found him attractive, it didn't matter. There wasn't time for such nonsense. There was, he understood, only time for war.

-3-

"The King of Lords is most displeased with you." Michael snapped at Emissary Lord Darklief.

What King Noliminan was most displeased with Emissary Lord Darklief about was his having arranged for a flight of female dragons and a travelling band of human merchants to drink from a spring that had been spelled—after bartering with Lord Eros. "What were you thinking?"

"I was thinking that Moira has stolen more than her pound of flesh from me." Emissary Lord Darklief shrugged at him. He wasn't taking the matter very seriously. It was almost as though he found great humor in the fact that he was meant to be punished. "And I found an opportunity to repay her when the speaking ape made a deal with me. I held up my end of the bargain. He didn't hold up his. Therefore, I got my price by other means."

"Humans and dragons are not meant to interbreed." Michael seethed, ignoring Emissary Lord Darklief's reference to the human as a 'speaking ape'. That had ever been Lucias' quip. And, though Michael had never admitted it to a single living soul, the joke of it amused him beyond telling. "Of all the asinine . . ." He shook his head as he forced himself to bite the inside of his cheek lest he smile. "And, now, the King of Lords must figure out who is to lord over this new race of beasts."

"Not my problem." Emissary Lord Darklief shrugged again.

As he did so, Lord Loki and Prince Ishitar stepped into Lord Loki's apartment. Michael was helpless but to smile at the younger of the two Gods as Ishitar called out his name and sprang forward. Michael took Ishitar into his arms, granting him the fatherly affection that the lad had always craved from him, and kissed him lightly on the forehead before pushing him gently away. He didn't miss the amused exchange between Apprentice Lord Loki and Emissary Lord Darklief that this small bit of affection created.

Clearing his throat, he turned to Emissary Lord Darklief and frowned. "Don't make him wait."

"I wouldn't dream." Emissary Lord Darklief drawled, his lips curled into a self-satisfied smirk.

Michael turned to Lord Loki and Prince Ishitar and gave them both a perfunctory bow. "My Lord; your Royal Highness."

"Brother." Prince Ishitar replied, granting Michael a bow in return.

As Michael left Apprentice Lord Loki's apartment, he heard Lord Loki chuckle and ask, "What, by the name of my goatee, have you done *now*?"

With no one around to see him, Michael allowed himself a rare smile.

- 4 -

Iladrul sat outside of the cell where the vampire had been imprisoned with his head bowed into the knuckles of his hand. He had been trying for days to extract information from her, but she was still grappling with her conscience and uncertain that she should tell him where her people had taken his elves.

Though he was ill equipped to be the one to interrogate her, he was the only one she would talk to. He had, after all, saved her life.

"I'm running out of time." Iladrul sighed. "My people are going to be slaughtered if I don't find them."

"They won't be." Her voice quavered. "The vampires need them alive if they are to feed from them."

Iladrul rolled his eyes and shook his head. "They only have so much blood."

"Their children—"

"They can't *have* children." Iladrul snapped, raising his gaze to meet hers. "The boys of the breeding age were all castrated!"

She paled. Her eyes grew wide. "They weren't."

Iladrul, who had only learned this because he had asked Macentyx about the medical clearance he and his brother had gone through, shook his head in frustration. "They have."

"But they were intact!"

"Only the seed was stopped." Iladrul groused. "They were left with their stones and pillars."

"How can that be?" She asked. "They aren't eunuchs?"

"No." He stormed. "Just . . . altered." He felt his lips twitch. He loathed the practice and was angry that his forefathers had put it into place. "By killing those who had not yet found the knife, your people have damned their own cause."

"The children . . ."

"The children that you *murdered*." He was getting tired of her self-pitying ways. "Where did they take the others?"

"Across . . ." She swallowed. "They are taking them to the sea."

"Which sea?" Iladrul demanded.

"The Northern Sea." Her voice was trembling. "They mean to cross to the Isle of Nononia."

Iladrul flew through the room and up the stairs. As he ran across the courtyard he was forced to roughly push elves and angels out of his path. He had to speak with his father and there was no time to dally. If the vampires went to sea then all would be lost until Iladrul, himself, could procure a fleet of ships to follow.

Which could take months, if not years, to achieve.

144

"Father!" He called when he saw Wisterian, seated on his throne and watching the bustle of the courtyard before him.

Upon hearing his son call his name, Wisterian stood. Helena, Iladrul marked, remained seated.

He rushed before them and gave them both a bow before telling his father what he knew. "The vampire tells me they are to travel to Nononia!"

"Dear Gods." Jeanir, who was standing behind Wisterian's throne, as was his place as a doxy, intoned.

Wisterian spun toward him. "You must take your army and you must make haste."

"What if they double back to get the rest of the elves?"

"Then I shall be here to deflect them." Wisterian advised. "We shall move every elf and angel into the castle, which is the one place on our lands with the least entries which can be breached." He turned his gaze to Iladrul. "You must go with the men in my stead."

"Of course, Father." Iladrul would have gone even if his father had forbade it. He suspected that Wisterian knew this, given it had been him who had found the Village in the state that it was.

"Good." He turned to Jeanir again. "Rally the men, Jeanir. You'll leave tomorrow at first light."

Jeanir bowed to him and took his leave. When he was gone, Wisterian turned to Iladrul.

"My son," he said, "now is the time to prove your quality."

"I won't let you down, Father." Iladrul promised as he toyed with the talisman.

"No." He sighed. "I don't believe that you will." He turned to his wife then. Iladrul realized, as he did so, that she had been weeping. "Go to the Temple of the Charbala. Pray with the Priestesses there. Beg Lady Theasis that your son will be returned safe unto your bosom."

She rose, stepped toward Iladrul as if to take him in her arms, thought better of it, and did as she was bid.

Iladrul knew, as he watched her go, that she would remain in Charbala prayer until the war was over and he was safely home.

-5-

Raphael was reading one of the King of Lords books aloud to him when Michael knocked on the door. He rose to answer, but King Noliminan flicked his hand at him and told him to sit down. He barked his order to Michael through the door that he should enter. Michael did and, irritated with his warrior, King Noliminan raised his gaze to meet Michael's own. "You're tardy."

"Forgive me, your Grace. I was delayed by Emissary Lord Darklief." Michael advised him as he stepped forward and found his knee. King Noliminan flicked his hand upward and toward the chair beside Raphael. As obedient as he ever, Michael rose and took his seat. "He's extremely satisfied with himself."

"So I assumed that he would be." Raphael watched with keen fear as the King of Lords glared at Michael. Though Raphael didn't understand why, he had been angry with the archangel ever since the war between himself and Lucias. Raphael had asked Michael more than once what he had done, but Michael had ever refused to divulge what had crossed the King of Lords. "I told you very recently that we live in a time of peace."

"You did, your Grace." Michael's brow rose slightly.

"That being said, I can spare the General of my army to other tasks." Michael's eyes flicked to Raphael. Raphael swiftly lowered his. "For the time being, that is."

"Your Grace?" Michael's voice shook slightly.

"This new race . . . these . . . *things*," King Noliminan's nose curled slightly in distaste, "are going to need someone to look after them until such time as a God can be bred among them."

"I agree, your Grace." Michael replied, his tone now guarded and curious.

"It comes to my mind, given the benandanti are disappearing in vast numbers, that despite Aiken's mischief, this race couldn't have come about at a better time." He sighed and sat back in his chair. "We could invoke in this race a sense of duty and protection." His eyes trailed over Michael's face for a moment before proceeding. "I want you to live among these creatures as their King so that you might teach them all things that you know."

"Your Grace, I . . ." Michael shook his head. His expression was that of both surprise and, though such was so rare since the end of the war that Raphael scarcely recognized it for what it was, expectant hope. "I am to be their *God*?"

The King of Lords narrowed his eyes slightly. "Why on which moon would I make *you,* of all people, a God?"

Raphael felt the verbal sting as if it had been a physical slap. He sensed that Michael did too. Though, Michael was obviously better able to stay his immediate reaction than Raphael, who let out a nearly inarticulate groan of pain on his brother's behalf.

"No. You shouldn't. I misunderstood and thought that—"

"Your betrayal against me with Raguel is unforgivable." He barked. "And you are well overdue your punishment."

Raphael snapped his gaze to Michael.

The Queen of Ladies? What had he done?

"Your Grace, I swear to you that nothing passed between myself and the Queen!" Michael pleaded with our Lord and Master as he found his feet. "I merely mourned her when she died! That was my only sin! And someone had to! Since you were angry with her, I—!"

It was Michael's turn to be struck now. And harder than Raphael had ever been. Unlike Raphael, he was able to plant his feet to the floor and stand his ground. When the pair of them had recovered from the moment, he merely swallowed and lowered his gaze.

"*Temporarily*," King Noliminan was literally growling at Raphael's brother, though he ignored Michael's denial completely. "I will give you the powers of a God. After you have propagated an appropriate heir you are to return to me and we are never to speak of your betrayal against me again."

147

"Your Grace?" Michael's eyes were dark and brooding. "What betrayal?"

"I did order that you be chaste." King Noliminan's eyes narrowed. Raphael realized at once that Michael had just been baited.

"Yes, your Grace. And I have been—"

"Yet, you cannot remain chaste whilst breeding a proper son with these disgusting creatures." King Noliminan growled at him. "Now *can* you?"

"You mean for me to . . . to *breed* with them?" Michael looked so affronted that to look upon his features was almost painful. How he managed to keep his tone respectful, Raphael would never know. "And then you mean to consider my following your orders to do so to be a betrayal against you?"

"I do." King Noliminan nodded and tented his hands at his chest. "The twelve of you are always complaining that I bind your hands idle."

Raphael, understanding that Michael had the right of things, wanted to scream on his brother's behalf. The King of Lords was ordering Michael to do something that he did not want to do and was then going to punish Michael for having done it.

"Your Grace, we only ever begged to find love with—"

"My *wife?*" King Noliminan raged his question.

Michael's reaction was far calmer than Raphael's would have been trapped in the same conversation.

"This is not a request, Michael." King Noliminan glowered at him. "It is an order. So make peace with it in whatever manner you think best."

Michael's skin was as pale as parchment. His black eyes were swimming with discontentment.

"Of course, your Grace." He finally managed. "When do you wish that I leave you?"

"Now." King Noliminan replied, his expression one of pure irritation. "Remove the eggs from their mothers and then guard them until they hatch."

"How many are there, your Grace?" Raphael braved, in shaking tones.

"A little over four thousand." King Noliminan muttered, ignoring Raphael's obvious discontentment all together. "Plenty to give a good start to a new race."

"I am to guard four thousand eggs?" Michael asked. His tone was so tight that Raphael felt that he might come unstrung at any moment. "By my*self*?"

"Of course by yourself." King Noliminan sighed his irritation. "I cannot afford to lose all *twelve* of my Quorum."

"Of course not, your Grace. But—"

"Do you intend to fail me, Michael?"

"Never in *life*, but—"

"Then why are you arguing with me about this?"

"I am not arguing with you, your Grace." Michael shook his head. "I assure you." His voice took on a trembling property that was entirely out of character. Raphael could feel the rage pounding off of him in the King of Lords' direction. "I have never argued with you. But, if I could borrower even one of Lady Martiam's angels, then my chances of succeeding will improve by a thousand fold."

King Noliminan seemed to consider this for a moment. Finally he said, "Very well." He reached for a piece of parchment and his quill. He dipped the pointed end of the quill in ink and scrawled a letter to Lady Martiam, which he quickly handed to Michael. "Give the Lady my instructions. And then no more of your petty delay, Michael. I want this task seen to straight away."

Michael took the parchment deftly between his fingers, standing as he did so. When he spoke, his tone was tight and his words were forced through his teeth. "As I ever do, your *Grace*."

He spun away, stormed out of the room and slammed the door behind him.

Raphael was left to stare upon King Noliminan with a wide eyed, puzzled and—he would never admit this last to anyone but himself—disappointed glare.

-6-

Thamores walked between two rows of tents, his lips pursed and his eyes glued to the ground. The sight of the children, huddled together in their tents wearing haunted expressions, was more than he could bear. He wondered how, exactly, he had given into Iykva's pressure to set his wolves on guard duty during the daylight hours.

For filthy vampires, no less.

When he reached the end of the row, he turned so that he could take a pass down the next one. As he did so, he raised his gaze and smiled at the wolf who served as his second in command. "Nala."

"Thamores." She returned.

"Anything to report?"

"No." She shook her head. Her long blonde hair danced over her shoulders like spun gold. He felt a pull for her, as he watched this, which he couldn't deny. He sensed by the smell of her, as she stepped toward him, that she was coming into heat. "The kiddies are extremely quiet."

"They *are* quiet." He felt his lips purse as he looked toward one of the tents.

There was a boy and a girl sitting within; just as there were in every one of the tents. Iykva had arranged them in pairs with the intention that they do what boys and girls of their age do when put in the same sleeping quarters.

The boy held the girl tightly and stared back at Thamores with cold detachment. As for the girl, the moment the benandanti looked her way, she turned her face into the boy's chest so that she wouldn't be forced to look at him. He gave the boy a tight smile and returned his attention to Nala.

"Any activity?"

"No." Her brow furrowed. "Not in a single tent."

"Queer." Thamores muttered as he ran his arm across his nose to block the smell of her from his senses. It was damn distracting. "And, somewhat, unnatural."

"Do you think they are still too young?" She asked. "I've never seen an elf before."

"These are the oldest of them." Thamores shrugged. "Could be that they aren't interested yet."

"But Iykva said that the Prince has a set of them." She sighed. "And he's the same age."

Thamores let out a breath through his teeth and stepped toward the tent where the boy was still glaring at him. He lowered himself to his hunkers and forced himself to smile.

"I must ask you something, boy." The young elf's jaw clenched and his chin thrust forward. He was strangely delicate. Strangely fair. "Answer me true."

"Mreck tat prewst." The boy replied in harsh tones before his lips thinned.

Thamores felt his brow furrow. "Don't you speak the common?"

"Mreck tat prewst!" He repeated angrily.

"I don't speak elfish." Thamores returned, frustrated.

"Go fuck your mother!" The boy replied in the common before leaning forward and spitting into Thamores' eye.

Thamores recoiled, though he had to admit that he admired the boy's fire. He raised his hand to wipe the spittle from his face and then flicked it away. As he did so, he was unable to stay his amused chuckle.

"Alright, then." He grinned. "We've established our hostilities."

The girl began to whimper. She raised her head and admonished the boy in elfish. Though Thamores didn't understand her words, he had a fair idea that she was telling him to give Thamores what he wanted so that he would leave them without harming them.

The boy, clearly irritated, pushed her away.

"Why are none of you doing what you have been put together to do?" Thamores asked the boy.

He glared in response.

"Answer me, elf." Thamores raised his hand as if he meant to strike the child. He never would have. He just needed to scare an answer out of the lad.

The boy flicked his eyes up to Thamores' hand, saw that Thamores had pushed his wolf's claws from his nails, swallowed and licked his upper lip with a swift, pink tongue.

"We are doxies." He said, his voice now shaking with fear. "We are not allowed to do our dirty business with one another."

"Dirty business?" Thamores' brow furrowed. He was amused by the lad's statement, though, given the elf's heavy tones, he would never admit this. "Regardless, nature must eventually take its course."

The boy looked swiftly away. "Any man who would allow his nature to put a woman at risk of damnation has no right to call himself a man."

"You believe that all of the boys in this camp feel the same way?"

"They had best." He seethed, returning his gaze to meet Thamores' own. "And you'd best tell your wolves to keep their dirty paws off as well."

"My wolves already have these orders." Thamores growled.

"Yet," the boy's eyes narrowed, "as you say, nature must, eventually, take its course."

Thamores gave him a perfunctory nod and found his feet. He turned toward Nala, who had been watching the conversation with unguarded interest, and shook his head. He grabbed her by the arm and pulled her well away from the tents.

Damn it . . . Now is not the time for you to come into heat.

"Is there something that I need to know about the behavior of the pack?" He asked.

"Not that I'm aware of." She sighed. "Although, the child has a point. Our people aren't exactly known for our soft nature. It's only a matter of time before one of them takes matters into his own hands." She looked swiftly away. "Although the sun still has to rise over thirty mountains, the golden moon shall wax before we reach the Northern Sea. Those of us who were made rather than born have no control over our curse when she becomes fat and full. You know this."

Thamores let out a deep breath through his teeth. "This is a bad idea all the way around."

"Why did you agree to it, then?" She asked, not exactly snappishly but neither was she coy. She was a wolf, after all. And second in command of her pack.

He shook his head in frustration and turned away from her.

"He reminded me that we are brothers." He explained. "What was I to do? My father was an exiled demon. As was my mother. That their curse was different from his makes him no less my kindred."

"It's wrong, Tham." She stepped toward him and set her hand on his shoulder. Now her tone was calming. Soothing. "You know it is."

He felt his lips thin as he nodded his agreement. "Tell the men if I learn that even one of these young girls has lost her innocence to one of them, she will be the last girl that he claims of any race."

"Such a threat won't stop them." She warned. "You know it won't."

"Perhaps not the first one." He agreed as he returned his gaze to her. "But I guarantee, after they see what I do to him, there won't be a second." This was followed by words which had the potential to damn him. "If any one of them has a problem with that then they can meet me at moonlight."

She swallowed and looked swiftly away. She didn't want him fighting with any one of the other male wolves because it meant that if he lost she was the victor's to claim. She, in her own way, loved Thamores. Even if she had been thrust into his bed when he had taken over the pack when he had slain her prior alpha.

He leaned forward, laced his hand around her neck and pulled her toward him to plant a kiss on her forehead.

Loving her, in his own way, he had no intention of ever losing such a challenge.

-7-

Loki looked up from the tome he had no business reading when he heard the slam of his door. Then came the guttural roar.

I watched his brow furrow as he began biting on the left side of his lower lip. No longer being able to read his thoughts, I could only wonder what was going through his mind.

Until, that was, Michael stepped through his library door. His expression of surprise could not be denied.

"Tell me how on which moon I am to remain a virgin whilst breeding with one of Aiken's Gods be damned, ill *begot* creations!"

Loki, shaking his head swallowed.

Aiken had told him about his mischief. Being Aiken's closest companion, this was a given. But the rest of Michael's diatribe seemed to confuse him.

"I don't . . ." He sighed and pointed to Lucias' favorite chair. "I wasn't part of Aiken's misbehavior. What has this to do with you?"

"I must live amongst them as a God would." Here Michael's expression darkened. "Though, I am not to *be* their God! Just to *breed* their God!"

This part, Loki clearly understood.

Michael was finally being punished for having the audacity to grieve over the Queen of Ladies' death. Loki, who was the only man that Raguel had ever taken to her bed aside from Noliminan, had been told by Raguel that she was in love with Michael.

I know that he suspected, by what Raguel had shared with him, that Michael was equally in love with her.

"Then to be punished for returning to him as spoiled goods." Michael turned his dark—and generally unreadable eyes—to Loki. His pain was palpable in his expression. "I am to adhere to one order whilst betraying another." He grumbled. "Or to be considered as having betrayed another!"

"What is he playing at?" Loki growled, his anger toward Noliminan palpable on every line of his face.

Michael rolled his eyes closed and shook his head. "I know not." Opening his eyes, he forced himself to meet Loki's gaze, "My Lord Loki, please . . ."

"You were never here." Loki assured him. Then, licking his lips, he said, "There is a way to beat his trap."

Michael glared at him. This was followed by a disbelieving, almost mad, laugh. "How?"

"Are you willing to disobey him?"

"*Never.*" This was a horrified whisper, which only served to make Loki grin.

"The seed doesn't die immediately, Michael."

"My Lord?" He asked, confused.

"Lady Anemoi is a member of my gaggle." He continued to grin. "And I have a most convincing tongue." Michael blushed at the reference and looked swiftly away. "I can charm her into helping you."

Embarrassed, he muttered, "I fail to see how the Lady of Winter—"

"Can freeze your seed?" Loki asked, brow rising. "Until there is a female ready for breeding in which we can—very innocently—insert it?"

Michael seemed to crumple. "Piss on the Gods . . ."

"You would be able to obey both orders at once." Loki assured him. "And whatever fuck-a-ding Noliminan is up to would be completely thwarted."

"He never bid that I must literally have sex with them." Michael swallowed, raised his gaze and then smiled. He ignored Loki's misstep by actually saying Noliminan's name aloud. Given my respect for Loki, I was relieved by this. Such was strictly forbidden by one of his stature. "Only that the children are mine. I will have obeyed both orders."

"And," Loki sighed, "more importantly, you will have saved your innocence for whatever soul you believe deserves it now that Queen Raguel is no longer an option for you."

Michael let out a tired, almost painful gasp. He hadn't been aware that anyone knew about his deep love for the Queen of Ladies. "My Lord Loki."

Loki smiled wearily in response.

-8-

Prince Ishitar was in his bedroom when he heard the low, growling scream. Na'amah, watching him, became extremely interested as he lowered the wood that he had been whittling into a fairy. He stood, his brow furrowed, and slipped out of his bedroom.

Na'amah, also curious, followed him.

When Prince Ishitar stopped just outside of the library and began listening to Lord Loki and Sir Michael's conversation, Na'amah was more than a little surprised. Though she had known the young prince for only a short amount of time, she felt that she understood his fundamental nature. As such, she wouldn't have expected him to snoop or spy. Yet, he clearly found this conversation one that he couldn't tear himself away from.

Until that was, Sir Michael's voice calmed and it became a conversation between two men who seemed to be friends rather than one man seeking counsel from a better.

It was at that point in the conversation between Sir Michael and Lord Loki that Prince Ishitar turned away from the library door and returned to his bedchamber.

He sat on the bed, his brow furrowed and his lips curled into a frown. Na'amah, who wanted to gain his trust and confidence, stepped toward him, laid her head upon his knee and turned her mismatched eyes up to him after giving him what she hoped was—for a dog—an understanding sigh.

"Why would my father issue such conflicting orders?" Prince Ishitar asked her—or so she thought; he was actually asking me—as he laid his hand between her ears and began to rub her there. "Of all people to play kings' castles with? Why would he set Michael up to lose his hillocks?"

She marked that he seemed to be listening to someone, as if they were speaking to him, and that he, then, sighed. After which, he nodded and said, "Zadkiel has always told me that Noliminan is unforgiving."

He smiled tightly, listening again.

"Didn't I see that for myself where Camael is concerned?" She whined. She hadn't heard that story. "Yet, it makes no sense. Michael is one of the most loyal to Noliminan of the entire Quorum. He has never, in his life, acted against Noliminan's orders."

What was Na'amah to do but whine at this sentiment as he seemed to listen again? So she did.

"Why would he punish Michael for doing exactly what he had been told to do?" Prince Ishitar shook his head. "Why would he want to put Michael—out of all of his servants—in his place? He already *knows* his place! This makes no sense."

Na'amah, who agreed with that sentiment, barked. His constant conversations with himself agitated her.

"Hush." He warned, though he was smiling down at her, his eyes full of his love for her. "I'm getting one of my damned headaches." He raised his thumb and index finger to his nose to rub the bridge of it, almost as if to prove the point. "Michael will weather this storm. He shall find the perfect angel to serve him; to help him."

Na'amah, knowing that making Prince Ishitar's headache worse would anger him, licked his hand and then fell still. He snorted at that and rubbed her head again.

"I miss Zadkiel." He muttered under his breath. Na'amah raised her gaze to meet his. "Don't look at me that way." He smiled. "He was a good father to me." He laughed then and shook his head. "For a brother."

Na'amah, who didn't know how to respond to that, barked.

"I wish that I could see him right now." Prince Ishitar muttered. "I wish that I could speak with him." Another chuckle; another shake of the head. "Because I can't always turn to him for help. I have to learn to navigate these situations on my own."

Na'amah barked again.

"Stop it!" Prince Ishitar laughed. "I told you that I'm getting a headache!"

To this she did a combo whine, bark. This made him laugh all the more.

"Alright." He said, standing. "You're hungry." And then with a shake of his head. "And from what I understand, Aiken has another body in the cooling cupboard. This time a human I think."

He laughed again as his nose curled in distaste.

"I don't get his taste for it." He leaned down and rubbed her head. "Or yours." Then with another laugh. "But I'm not a fairy. Am I?" His smile grew. Na'amah found herself puzzled by her covetous feelings for that smile, given he was beyond her reach. "Nor a dog! So eat what you will, and I shall broker no judgment upon you."

Na'amah had no other response than to, once again, whine her agreement.

-9-

Zamyael heard the ringing of the bells, which were secured to the chain forged around Zadkiel's ankle, and panicked. She raised her gaze to meet his and swallowed the bile that rose in her throat. His golden eyes were haunted and round. His equally golden lips were thin and drawn.

"What does he want?" She whispered.

"I know not." He muttered as he used his staff to assist himself to his feet. "Whatever it is, best I don't keep him waiting."

Terrified for her dear friend, she nodded.

She had no words to comfort him. She knew what Noliminan was capable of and that if he was calling Zadkiel after all of these years of silence, it could only be because he was angry with him. Given she had paid the heavy costs that she had when Noliminan set out to play his games, she understood well enough that whatever price there was to pay would be levied upon Zadkiel's head.

"Don't wait up." He muttered as he hobbled to the door of the cottage that they shared. "I may be in for a very long night."

Though she nodded at him, she had no intention of going to bed until he returned. Zadkiel, though not her lover, had become her dearest friend. She would be here for him when he returned, no matter the state in which he arrived.

"Oh, Azrael . . ." She sighed. "If Zad's in trouble . . . I wish I could see you tonight."

There was no answer, though she had not expected there to be one. In her mind, I was as gone to her as was Lasterian.

She returned to her needlework, trying to ignore her growing dismay. Realizing, after twenty shifts of Lord Countenance's shadow of trying to clear her vision from the tears that were burning her eyes, that her task was useless, she set her craft aside.

When she did so, she heard a knock on the door.

Surprised, she stood and walked with great apprehension toward it. When she opened it, she froze.

Standing on the stoop was a human she did not recognize. He had long brown hair, which he wore bound behind him with a leather strap, and dark green eyes. Which were, she noted, dancing over her face with what could only be described as deep devotion and admiration.

As for his clothes, they were strange to her. Dark blue, cotton pants that were far too tight and a shirt that appeared to be chambray but was clearly made of much finer stuff. It was open to the middle of his torso, revealing a strangely hairless chest for a human man. His boots were those meant for trail riding and his belt was slender and seemed to be meant more for decoration than function.

She swallowed and raised her hand to the door, ready to close it on him when she sent him away. "Yes?"

The man shook his head and pointed to his throat. He looked around himself quickly, then raised his hands. In the gestures which only Sappharon had ever used with her, he signed with lightening quickness, "You asked me to come to you, Zam. Here I am. I cannot speak to you and you cannot see my true face. But I am Azrael." She blinked at me, as if confused. "May I, please, come in?"

She stumbled backward, her hands flying to her chest. "Azrael?"

"Wearing the face of a human who lives ages in the future on another, very distant world." I signed. "I can take on the form of others. Just not mine own. This is a man that no one will pay any mind to for long and long, as he has not yet been born. May I, please, come in?"

Swallowing, Zamyael looked around herself. She licked her lips and asked in a choked whisper, "Zadkiel?"

"Noliminan has asked Metatron to whip him raw." I signed, lowering my gaze. "Until Zadkiel reveals where Ishitar is hiding."

"Dear Gods . . ."

"May I, please, come in?"

"Yes." She whispered, stepping back and pulling the door open. "I'm sorry. Yes. Of course you may come in."

Wearing a haunted smile that matched the terror in my heart, I returned to the cottage that I had long ago come to consider as my one true home.

-10-

Ishitar stepped into his bedchamber and froze. Aiken stood within, folding his clothes into two neat stacks, separating Ishitar's shendyts from his small clothes. He had raised a pair of the latter upward and was staring at it with such unguarded curiosity that Ishitar actually blinked.

"Taking your liberties?" He asked.

Aiken, starting, spun to face him. His cheeks blazed pink as he let out an embarrassed chortle. "No—I—It's not what you think."

"No?" Ishitar asked, his lips curling into a puzzled smile.

"No." Aiken tittered again. "Forgive me. Clothes fascinate me."

"One would never be able to suppose such a thing of you." Ishitar teased as he flicked his gaze to Aiken's loincloth.

"I don't understand wearing one set of trousers." Blushing again, Aiken looked swiftly away. "Let alone two."

"They're actually quite comfortable." Ishitar shrugged. "But, then again, I don't much care for the feeling of—"

The first crack of the whip fell across Zadkiel's back at that moment. Unable to stay my horror of being forced to witness this, every form of me screamed and turned abruptly in an unsuccessful attempt to look away. My movement was so sudden and unexpected that Ishitar, himself, let out a cry and turned violently toward me. As he watched me, I fell to my knees, raised my hands to my face and began to tremble.

"My Gods!" Ishitar cried.

"What?" Aiken, wearing a confused expression, asked.

"What in the name of Loki's beard is the matter with you?" Ishitar ignored the fairy. "What did you just see?"

"Zadkiel!" I cried.

"Da?" Ishtar flew toward me so that he could kneel beside me and set his hands upon my shoulders, forcing me to turn to face him. "What—how do you mean?"

"He's in your father's library." I swallowed and tried to blink away the blood that made up my tears. "Your father is . . ."

Ishitar's nostrils flared. He flew to his feet and bolted out the door, ignoring Aiken's plea to tell him what was going on. He was in the hallway outside of Loki's apartment before he, seemingly, remembered to use his Godly powers to will himself into his father's library.

It was there that he found Metatron standing over Zadkiel with a whip at the ready to flail another lash.

"Stop!" He cried, pushing Metatron out of the way.

He swung around to face his father, who was looking up at him with a self-satisfied smirk. Beside him sat Raziel, her full lips curled into a slightly amused smile. Looking upon the pair, I wanted to jump forward and strangle them both.

"What is the meaning of this?"

"These are the lengths I must apparently go to in order to garner a word with you." Noliminan replied with a bored shrug, flicking his eyes to Metatron and Zadkiel. "The pair of you have outlived your usefulness to me this evening. You may go."

Metatron, who wore an expression of pure horror, sprang forward to take an unconscious Zadkiel in his arms. Ishitar, spinning toward him, commanded him to wait. He, himself, flew to the end of the desk upon which Zadkiel was strapped and placed his hand upon Zadkiel's brow. As he did so, he saw the extent of the damage that had been done. Zadkiel's entire body—but for his face—was covered in gaping wounds from his heavy scourging.

"No pain, Da." Ishitar whispered as he leaned forward to kiss Zadkiel's brow. "No more pain from these wounds." He raised his gaze to meet Metatron's. I know that he would have loathed Metatron if not for the expression of distaste and horror he wore. And, if not for the fact that Metatron had had no choice. "Take him home, Met."

"Yes, your Royal Highness." Metatron's deep voice trembled. He stepped forward and gathered Zadkiel into his arms so he might use his own powerful magic to transport them to Zadkiel's cottage.

When they were gone, Ishitar spun around to face his father and Raziel. He glared at Raziel and seethed, "Leave us. This conversation is between my father and me."

She appeared to be ready to protest, but she stopped herself as Noliminan turned his light brown eyes toward her and gave her a curt nod. Though she clearly didn't like being dismissed, at his command she obeyed. As she was walking out of the room, Ishitar turned toward the desk and waved his hand toward it to clear it of Zadkiel's golden blood. When it was returned to its rights, his attention flew back to his father.

His initial question bore repeating. "What is the meaning of this?"

"What is the meaning of you sitting in an open courtyard with that Gods be damned Aiken of the Oakland Grove and that strecktla of a demon, Zamyael!" His father seethed.

Ishitar's lips thinned at the insult toward the woman who he thought of more as his mother than the woman who had birthed him. Now, however, when Noliminan was playing at kings' castles with Ishitar, was not the time to raise his love for Zamyael to his father's attention. Clearly, his message had been that he could destroy everything that Ishitar cared about if it would further his advance in their game.

"How is it that I learn that you are no longer living with Zadkiel through rumor and word of mouth rather than direct from your own lips?"

"You haven't exactly been available when I've come to call." Ishitar seethed as his eyes narrowed. "You and Raziel have been up to games of your own, if I am not mistaken. Were you to make time for me when I paid you a visit, perhaps, you wouldn't be forced to learn the move of my mermaid out of Raphael's supplicated fear of you."

"Where, exactly," his father seethed, "are you living now?"

"With Lord Loki." Noliminan snarled upon hearing this news. Ishitar smiled. "You and Mother did bid that I learn from both worlds so that I might bring them together in peace." He shrugged. "I'm only doing as you require."

"Loki," Noliminan growled, "is an unfit selection."

"While this may be," Ishitar grinned, "he is well respected by both realms. You cannot deny that he is the perfect solution."

He couldn't. And it, very obviously, maddened him.

Noliminan looked swiftly away and seethed, "What is this I hear about your mother being pregnant with Loki's child?"

"She's building a Quorum." Ishitar's eyes narrowed. "As you well know." His eyes narrowed even further as he glared at his father. "Unless your plans have changed now that you've taken Raziel to wife."

"They haven't." Noliminan snorted. "You know Raziel will never match the place your mother holds in my heart."

"Then allow Lucias to play her own game." Ishitar suggested. "She has to prove her own power. She'll never garner the respect of the Council if she doesn't. She needs twelve pillows on her side of the thrones to prove she is your equal and your rightful match."

Noliminan sat back in his chair, his eyes crawling over Ishitar as if assessing him. Finally he asked, "That's what this is all about?"

"Of course that's what this is all about!" Ishitar snapped. "You can't possibly believe she'd choose Loki over you."

Noliminan's features relaxed slightly. I didn't believe for a minute that his emotions matched his now calm expression. He loathed Lord Loki. Never mind that he would never stand for the woman that he loved above all others to lie abed with another man. His response to Ishitar, in that moment, was merely part of his overall game.

"Who is Loki in the grand scheme of things?" Ishitar asked him, his eyes darting to me and then back to Noliminan. I felt my brow furrow over the expression on his face at that moment but passed it off as irritation that yet another private conversation was being overheard by me. "Other than a nymph who was—by your own decree—turned into a very base and self-serving God."

"Very well." Noliminan leveled his gaze upon Ishitar. His light brown eyes flashed, confirming my supposition that he was lying to his son about the true depths of the anger that resided in his heart. "You may live with Loki. And you may learn what you can from him." Ishitar began to smile. I wanted nothing more than but to warn him that he was being played, although, I suspected, my warning was unnecessary.

"For now," Ishitar, who was playing a game of his own, agreed.

-11-

Zadkiel recognized me at once, even though I didn't wear my true face. It was the horror he saw in my eyes, the insanity that had been brewing within me as Lord Countenance's shadow waxed and waned, which identified me for who I was. Never mind the gentle manner in which I led him from Metatron's arms to the kitchen so that I could apply the salves that I had at the ready.

"Oh Zad." Zamyael began to weep when she saw him. "Oh, my love."

"I held his secret." Zadkiel gave her an impatient scowl. He wasn't her love and he knew it. No matter that he had grown to care for her as he would were she his wife. He had come to terms with the fact that she would never be his long ago. "I didn't tell him where our boy is living."

"I know." She reached for his face—the only part of him that hadn't been whipped—and ran her fingers over his cheek. "Azrael told me."

"You must not use my name." I shook my head and signed. "Or I'll be forced to find another face."

"I'm sorry." She sobbed. "I'm just . . . Oh, Zadkiel!"

"It's alright." Zadkiel placated her, flinching as I reached for his shirt to pull it off of his back.

Some of the blood was starting to clot and the cloth had stuck to it. As a result, I had to rip it, and his skirt, off of him until he stood before us both in nothing more than his small clothes. Which were, Zadkiel realized as he looked down to his thighs and genitals, equally as bloody.

Good thing I have no need to ever sire any children.

He was so disjointed from himself that he actually laughed at the thought.

"I'm glad that you find this funny." Zamyael snapped.

I raised my hand and shook my head. I meant to calm her, not to belittle Zadkiel.

It quieted her. She looked swiftly away, her black eyes blazing with anger and her clear hatred toward Noliminan, after having seen Zadkiel in this state.

"I'm sorry." I signed. "The removing of your small clothes will hurt worse than the rest. But I must apply the salve to all of your wounds lest they fester."

Zadkiel flicked his eyes to Zamyael. No woman had seen him undressed in the full of his life.

"Zam?" He muttered, clearly embarrassed. "Do you mind giving me some privacy?"

"Of course." She blushed. "I'll be . . . I'll see to my needlework."

"Thanks." He forced himself to smile at her.

When I pulled the cloth that had sealed itself to the skin of his manhood he was, this time, unable to bite back his screaming cries.

-12-

Jeanir slid into the chair at the table opposite from Iladrul. As he did so, his daughter stepped forward and handed him a plate of food. He smiled distractedly at her and focused his full attention on the young Prince.

"We're keeping a good pace." Jeanir advised the youngling.

"Not a good enough pace." Iladrul replied, spinning away from the table and finding his feet. He paced across the tent to the tactical map. "We need to send a scout ahead. We need to see if we can't mark the vampires' travels."

"They can't be moving as fast as we are." Jeanir sighed as he took his first bite of food in days. "Their movement is limited to the night and they are herding a vast hoard of children."

"And doing Azrael only knows what to them." The girl stepped past the boy as he said this. Jeanir marked, with guarded interest, that Iladrul's eyes landed on her, even hovering for a long moment on her rump before returning to the map. "How much further to Devonshire?"

"A day." Jeanir shrugged. "Less if a small deploy rides ahead."

"Then we ride ahead." Iladrul turned to face him. "But just you and I." He flicked his gaze to Sezja and then back to Jeanir. "And your children."

Jeanir nodded his agreement to that sentiment. He didn't know what allies the demons and vampires had employed, so he would feel better having reinforcements. "We'll leave at first light."

"Best get some sleep then." Iladrul muttered, flicking his eyes to Sezja and then back to Jeanir. Jeanir gave him a tight smile as he stood. "Good night."

"Good night, my Prince." He walked toward his daughter, pulled her in his arms and kissed her forehead. "Sezja."

"Goodnight, Pipa." She replied looking up at him, wearing a tight smile. She had never known how to behave around him. Nor he her. It was easier for him, somehow, with sons rather than daughters. "I'll have him up and dressed by the time you're ready to leave."

Now his smile was easy. She was nothing if not obedient.

He gave her a nod and took his leave, granting Prince Iladrul a final smile before exiting the tent.

His daughter could do worse, he thought, than having the young Prince as her master.

-13-

Two days after being forced to whip Zadkiel on Noliminan's order, Metatron found himself glaring at the plate before him long after the three Gods who had been sitting at the table next to him had taken their leave.

He wasn't one to eavesdrop, but these Gods had been boasting so loudly about their request to Raziel to raise a vote to return the ability of the Gods to turn their servants to the sex they preferred at a whim that his attempts to ignore them proved to be utterly in vain.

Listening to them, the anger in his soul began to brew.

He had asked Lucias to grant him succor and she had ordered him to bide. Which he had, against his better sense, done.

But this?

It was too much to bear.

Swallowing his anger, Metatron stood.

He'd lost all appetite for lunch.

He decided, as he began storming through the Courtyard, that what he really needed to quell his anger was to speak with Lucias. To ask her if she would, please, after what he had been forced to do to Zadkiel, grant him succor.

Though he knew that Lucias was not currently at home, he did know what she was up to. It was commonly known that "Lord" Lucias still held meetings with the Gods, angels and demons that served Noliminan in order to gain a broader scope of support. The meetings were always held on the afternoon three days prior to the silver moon rising fat and full on the world known as Anticata. Today's meeting would be in full swing by now, which would afford Metatron the opportunity to slip in without being noticed.

He stopped at his small cottage and donned a cloak that would cover him from head to toe; being made of flames, he was difficult to overlook when not hidden beneath his cowl. Then he made his way to the large structure where, rumor held, these meetings took place.

As he slipped within, Metatron was relieved to find the place both crowded and dark. The angels and demons here were those that were either in service to the Gods or those that worked the kitchens, wash rooms and brothels. As for the Gods, though there were less of them, they ranged in all functions from critical members of the Council to secondary replacements, apprentices and, in some cases, Gods who were too young to have yet been given their assignment.

The overwhelming smell of their anger was palpable. It gave rise to a stink that Metatron immediately associated with the sweat of a hard battle. These desperate, angry people were on the verge of a new revolution.

As Metatron looked around the room, he realized that not a one of them were sitting in their seats. In fact, Metatron marked, many were so caught up in Lucias' rally that they were actually standing on their chairs.

As for Lucias, Metatron couldn't even hear her—or, he supposed given she spelled herself to appear male for these meetings, *his*—voice over the roar of the crowd.

Curious as to what Lucias was saying that would evoke such angry passion, Metatron fought his way through the crowd in the shadows at the side of the hall until he was close to the makeshift stage.

And then he heard her words . . .

They were eloquent and to the point, sweeping Metatron into even greater anger until, half way through her pretty speech, he realized that he, too, was screaming her name.

"Now is the time to denounce the atrocities that the Council would thrust upon you!" She cried, "Will you let a small handful of Gods decry the sacrifices that we all have made? Would you let them betray those children brave enough to join us in our cause, those too loyal to you to put you at risk or those too frightened to find their own voices?"

"No!" The crowd raged backed at her before their voice became a jumbled mass of words that were indistinct from one another.

"My sons!" She cried, "My *daughters*!" Here she pounded upon her chest. "Two members of the very Quorum who serve and protect you in all things that they do! Are we now to have no say over the fate of *them*?" She shook her head as if offended by the mere thought of it. "Noliminan would take away their femininity for the simple joy of putting me in my place. I will not sit idly by and let them be, once again, forced into their male forms!"

The crowd began screaming at her, each of them calling out Uriel and Mihr's names. Metatron, standing amongst them, was stunned to find himself publically crying out on behalf of his sisters.

And for Michael who was—for all intents and purposes— exiled from the Quorum to see to the dragon men that Emissary Lord Darklief's mischief had wrought.

Simply because he had been the only one in all of the worlds to have actually been unfortunate enough to have loved Noliminan's ill-fated wife.

"All twelve of the Quorum have always supported us!" Lucias enflamed the crowd. "They have always sacrificed their own happiness for *us*! Now it is our turn! *We* must support *them*!"

The audience, Metatron included, howled its agreement.

"They will never join us." Her tone softened to a note that verged on sadness. "They will not thank us for fighting for their rights or in their names." She seemed to be meeting each pair of eyes that made up her audience in turn. "Some of them may even be forced to see to our punishments."

Metatron listened to the crowd screaming his and Michael's names at that particular truism.

"That does not make them love us any less." Lucias assured them. "It makes them love us *more*! Because they know that what we do we do for them this time! For them," she screamed, "and for their hundreds upon hundreds of brothers and sisters, be their wings white *or* black!"

The roar of response was deafening. Metatron's voice, loudest amongst them, was failing him. Yet he was helpless but to cheer her on to the bitterest of ends.

When the meeting was over, he pressed himself into the shadows and watched the crowd disburse. Lucias remained, talking to each and every one of the members of the audience who dared to approach her. Metatron listened to her issue her gratitude time and again that they supported her cause until the only three left in the auditorium were himself, Lucias and Sappharon.

When they three were alone, Lucias turned her eyes in Metatron's direction and smiled.

"What are you doing here, boy?" She asked as she waved her hand and found her true face. He was glad. He had come to prefer seeing her as a woman now that he knew this to be her true nature. "I told you before—"

"I cannot bide it anymore." He seethed through his teeth, looking around before lowering the hood of his cowl. "Has anyone told you what I was forced to do to Zadkiel? As Zad refused to share with your husband where your son lately lives?"

"No . . ." Lucias stammered, clearly surprised. Her eyes narrowed and she shook her head. "What has happened to Zadkiel?"

"I was forced to whip him back and front." Metatron admitted, biting his cheek with his distaste over the memory. "And I was forced to—" He shook his head and looked away. He couldn't look at her when he said this. "If Prince Ishitar hadn't interrupted I would have been forced to do much worse."

"Dear Gods." She whispered. "Metatron! You didn't!"

"What choice?" He growled. "At your order that I serve him whilst you play your games?"

"Yes, but—"

"Will you grant me your Gods be damned succor now?" Metatron snapped his gaze back to her. "Is this, finally, enough for you to no longer force me to bide?"

"Metatron—"

"It isn't." He growled. "Is it?"

"You must understand that—"

"That you love your mortal born angels and demons more than you love your true sons and daughters." He growled, pointing to the coliseum where the rally had taken place. "That you will protect them? But not me? Not Zad? And not Az? Or Michael, who has been all but exiled, for that matter?"

"I have a plan to—"

"You always have a Gods be damned plan, *Father.*" He seethed and forced his cowl back over his head. "Let us hope that, one day, you love the twelve of us enough to actually put your ill wrought actions into play. Lest he destroys us one and all!" Though he loathed disobedience, he was unable to stop himself today. He flicked his eyes to Lucias' swelling belly and sneered. "Especially given you mean to force more of us to live in this wretched and unforgiving world."

Unable to look upon her another moment, Metatron turned away and stormed out of the hall to, reluctantly, return to his duties.

And the Gods damn her, *at this point, for whatever Noliminan forces me to do.*

-14-

Iladrul's eyes grew wide as he looked around the throne room of the castle belonging to the human tribe who called themselves the Devonshires. It was barren and cold. There were no tapestries or paintings, as graced his own halls. Rather, these people seemed to live a cold existence geared toward survival alone.

"These people are to be our allies?"

"They already *are* your allies, my Prince." Jeanir reminded him. "You only need convince them to stand beside you in this particular war."

"Why would they?" He shivered and turned his gaze to meet Jeanir's. "When they clearly have no means by which to protect their own walls?"

"We stood with them when their people were under attack." Jeanir reminded the boy. "On several occasions. It is their turn to stand with us."

Iladrul reluctantly nodded his agreement. What choice did he have but to do so? He had no other allies that he was aware of and he couldn't win this war with broken angels and elves of ages that were far too young.

He took a step to the side, putting himself closer to Sezja, who, he was grateful to find, did not step away. He didn't reach for her hand or show her any kind of affection because he wasn't certain how he felt about her yet. Let alone how she felt about him. Still, he was comforted by her soft, windswept scent and the warmth that radiated from her small frame.

It was several long minutes before the door opened and an entourage of human men streamed into the throne room. At the center, looking as if he were no more than one of the many knights that surrounded him, stood their King.

Iladrul had only seen King Jon Devonshire once before. That had been many years ago, when the King was in the prime of his youth. Now, twenty years later, his thick black hair was graying at the temples and his brilliant blue eyes were deeper set, yet somehow wiser.

"Jon." Balean stood forward with his hand extended, "It has been too many years, my old friend."

"Aye." The human's serious expression broke. His thick lips split into a welcoming grin. "And your face has not changed a bit."

"Yours has become wizened." Jeanir's tone was low and respectful.

The human King turned toward Jeanir upon hearing these words. As he did so, his eyes landed upon Iladrul. "Dear Gods. Is this that mewling child who hid behind his mother's skirts?"

"The same." Balean chuckled. "Near to grown now, and here for your counsel."

"What counsel I have to give is surly yours." King Jon swept his hand toward the thrones. "Shall we sit? And hold palaver?"

Iladrul bowed his head respectfully and followed the human and his many knights to the head of the room. When the King and a man, young but clearly bearing King Jon's face, found their comfort, the knights that had escorted them found seats in the audience as well. Iladrul and his men remained standing.

He was here to beg arms. As such, he owed the human King the respect that such a request warranted.

"How may I help you, Prince Iladrul?" He asked, his bright eyes drinking in the lines of Iladrul's face.

"My people have long stood beside yours." Iladrul swallowed and swept his hand toward Balean. "When an enemy has breached your gates, my forefathers have come quickly to call."

"And we are grateful for your aide." His eyes narrowed. Iladrul understood at once that the King of Devonshire knew why he was there.

"We, now," Iladrul swept his hand toward Balean again, "find ourselves in need of the favor returned."

King Jon let out a long, low sigh. He turned his attention away from Iladrul's party and toward his son. They conferred in low whispers for a moment before he returned his attention to Iladrul.

"What army I have to offer you is small." He was clearly regretful. "Our own walls are breached violently and often." Iladrul opened his mouth to protest, but the human raised his hand to silence him. "My son will lead what men we can spare. I only mean to warn you that our troop will be small."

"As, you can see," Iladrul licked his top lip, "is ours."

"My sister and her husband may have more men to spare." The young Prince at King Jon's side suggested. "Rumor has it that we will be passing through her lands in pursuit of the vampires and demons."

"You know, then, that Lord Scrountentine and his people head for the Sea?" Balean asked.

"We do." King Jon nodded. As he did so, he stood. "As we know you must make haste." His smile was thin. "Trevor and his men will be ready to join your party by sunrise." His eyes flicked to Iladrul. "Will it suit?"

"It does." Iladrul bowed low to him. "I assure you, Jon of Devonshire, that your aide to me now will long be remembered."

"As your aide, many years ago, is being remembered today." He bowed to Iladrul—actually bowed—and then turned away.

His final words before he left Iladrul to stare after him were, "I only wish that there was more that I could offer."

-15-

Na'amah sat at Prince Ishitar's feet with her nose resting over her crossed paws and her eyes drinking in the features of her mother's face. Ishitar often came to visit with his mother and, when he did, Na'amah was always allowed to join him.

"Damn it." Ishitar muttered under his breath.

Na'amah, curious as to what had upset him, raised her gaze and released a tired whine. As she did so, she watched Lady Lucias deftly pluck the fairy from the kings' board and raise it before her eyes to contemplate it for a long moment.

"I didn't see it coming."

"Take heart." Lady Lucias gave him a guarded smile as she sat the fairy down with the other pieces that Ishitar had lost to her own pawns. "You're miles improved from our first game together." She sat back and crossed her arms over her chest, her eyes flicking down to Na'amah and then back up to her son. "Your problem is that—like your father—you are more concerned with what is taking place on the kings' board than you are with what is taking place in my head."

"How in the name of Loki's Gods be damned goatee am I supposed to know what's taking place in your head?" Ishitar groused. "You didn't give me the barest clue that you intended your pirate to visit the fairies' grove."

"Do you believe that a real pirate would give a real fairy any type of warning that he meant to visit the grove?" Lady Lucias asked. "Look at every one of my pieces. I'm within a move of every one of yours. They may not be looking your way. That doesn't mean that they are not watching you."

Na'amah whined over that particular sentiment.

She felt the tips of Ishitar's fingers on the top of her head and she immediately quieted down. She sensed that playing kings' castles with Lady Lucias was just one of the triggers that set the pain of his many violent headaches ablaze in his mind.

"I know that it is frustrating." Lady Lucias sighed, her eyes returning to Na'amah. "But you must be prepared for every eventuality."

Na'amah wanted to whine again as she held the Lady's gaze, but she managed to keep her discontentment in her throat. Lady Lucias was looking at her more and more often lately, and always with a quietly curious expression that both terrified and troubled her.

It was as this thought was crossing her mind that a hesitant knock played at the main door of the cottage. She jumped to her feet, ready to trail after her mother to answer, when she heard Lady Lucias command that she stay and that Ishitar see who came to call. She howled at that, causing Ishitar to laugh and pat her head as he made his way past her.

When Ishitar was out of the room, Lady Lucias cloaked herself with a male face and turned her gaze away from Na'amah and toward Sappharon. Her hand, however, rose with one long finger pointing in Na'amah's direction. "That isn't a dog. I've known it from the start but I haven't understood, exactly, whose child it is until today."

"My Lady?" Sappharon signed, her eyes wide. Na'amah's own heart began to thrum.

"Whose child, Sappharon?" She asked. "And don't lie to me."

"I don't know what—"

"I know by the smell of it that it is yours." Lady Lucias muttered. "Who is the father?"

Sappharon's eyes darted to Na'amah. She swallowed and then returned her gaze to Lucias. "Does it matter, my Lady? I swear that he was my only indiscretion. Though I once loved her father, I have always known, in my heart, that it was a mistake. As has he. Besides, it was long, long ago."

Lady Lucias' eyes narrowed and then returned to their rights.

"No." She finally conceded. "You and I have never been lovers. You are right in telling me that it doesn't matter who you *did* love. Never mind that Noliminan would damn you and the child for it. I just have grave concerns over a dathanorna propagating lies to my son about what it is."

Na'amah, let out another howling whine.

"She won't hurt Ishitar." Sappharon's hand movements softened. "I promise you."

Na'amah was grateful that her mother didn't share with Lady Lucias that she had confessed to coming to love Ishitar. It would anger the Goddess to know that she was in a position to manipulate her son into loving her in return.

Lady Lucias sighed and returned her gaze to Na'amah. Finally, she granted her a tight—and very tired—smile.

"If you trust her then I suppose that there is no harm in having an extra pair of eyes upon him. But you must be careful that no one else discovers what you are. Your existence can only mean the death of both yourself and your mother."

"We both understand this truth, my Lady." Na'amah replied, lowering her gaze.

Lady Lucias, amused that she had spoken to her—and in her own female voice—let out a string of quiet laughter.

"Yes." She said as the door opened and Ishitar stepped in with two young male vampires and one female vampire at his heels. "I suppose that you do."

"Lucias." Ishitar's quiet, kind voice seemed hesitant to interrupt them. Na'amah knew that he had not heard their conversation. He seemed more taken aback by his mother's male form than he was by her words with Sappharon, truth be told. It was the first time that he had seen the Lady cloaked in her male face since Na'amah had been with him. "These are Louis, Melody and Marchand. They are—"

"Jamiason's twins." Lady Lucias said, her tone that of surprise, as she found her feet. She held her hand toward the twins, each of whom shook it in turns. This made the Lady's smile grow. "Or, his prodigy, to be more exact."

177

"Yes, my Lord." One of the twins said as he released her hand and bowed to her. "Forgive us for imposing on you so late in the day."

"Not at all." Lady Lucias seemed to beam at him. "Given your limitations, a late night visit is only to be expected." Then with a smile. "How is the brat King?"

The twin who had not spoken laughed, causing Na'amah to shiver. It was a melodic, beautiful sound. Yet, it was also cold and terrifying. As for the woman, she remained still.

"I'm afraid that we've never seen that side of him, my Lord." The one who had not laughed replied as his lips thinned. "He's always been the model of seriousness and propriety when in our presence."

"Yes." Lady Lucias replied, indicating the sofa and biding the vampires to take a seat. "I'm afraid that he is a victim of his own disenchantment." She lowered herself at the kings' board, watching Ishitar return to his seat as she did so. Passing Na'amah, Ishitar reached between her ears and scratched the top of her head. Lady Lucias watched this as well, her smile once again becoming guarded as she appraised her. "It's unfortunate because he was once so spirited."

"So I understand." The vampire said, taking his seat. "What a beautiful dog."

"He belongs to my son." Lady Lucias tore her eyes away from Na'amah and turned them toward the vampires. When she was no longer looking at her, Na'amah walked toward Ishitar and laid her head upon his thigh. Smiling, Ishitar wrapped his large, comforting hands around her muzzle and lovingly began to stroke her. "Her name is Ansibrius."

"Ansibrius." The one who had laughed muttered. "Interesting."

"Quite." Lady Lucias replied, bemused. "How might I help you, my children of the night?"

The smile immediately fled the laughing one's face and his expression became dire. It was, again, the other who spoke.

"Lord Jamiason has asked if we might borrower three of your winged horses."

"Of course you may." Lady Lucias shrugged. "To what purpose?"

"We must deliver a message to King Wisterian." The vampire child replied, his brow furrowed. "Our Maker said it was urgent that Wisterian receives it before news of some eminent disaster reaches the ears of the demons with which we keep our company."

Lady Lucias let out a long, low whistle through her teeth. Na'amah had heard that whistle before. "I'd completely forgotten about the exiled angels and demons of the subsequent revolts." She muttered. "Did Jamiason tell you what the Council means to do?"

"No." The vampire shook his head.

"They mean to, once again, allow the Gods to change the sex of their servants at their whim."

"They mean to do *what*?" Ishitar asked, lifting his gaze from Na'amah to look at his mother.

"You heard me, child." Lady Lucias replied. Her dark brown eyes returned to young vampires. "If you think Iykva and the others are angry now, just you wait until this particular vote is passed."

"They can't do that!" Ishitar cried, standing. "Mima, you can't let them!"

"Ishitar!" Lady Lucias snapped. "I am not your Gods be damned *mother*!"

Her eyes were darting nervously between each of the vampires. It was all too clear to everyone in the room that the moment that Ishitar had called Lady Lucias by the endearing term of 'mother' that all three of them knew exactly who Ishitar was.

It was even more clear—at least to Na'amah—that Lady Lucias' surprised denouncement of Ishitar, as his mother, had wounded the young God in a manner that was irreparable.

Ishitar's anger was palpable when he spoke. "The Quorum will be devastated!"

"To the Hells with the Quorum." Lady Lucias snapped. "Quiet, you, and sit yourself down!"

Na'amah watched in fascination as Ishitar glared at Lady Lucias. His eyes flicked to the chair where he had been sitting and then back to his mother. When he spoke, his tone was hard and cold.

"To the Hells with the Quorum?" He demanded. "No, my *Lord*." Lady Lucias' eyes grew wide. This was the first time that Ishitar had ever addressed her in the male vernacular. "To the Hells with *you*. For your failure to protect the Quorum; your sons and daughters." He growled. "But more so for your denouncement of *me!*" He looked away and seethed. "I have come to love you. To believe that you love me, too. But you really are no better than my father at the end of it. And you never loved me any more than he has ever done after all."

"Ishitar, that's not—!"

Ishitar waved his hand at Lady Lucias, silencing her, and then stormed out of the room. Na'amah found herself looking from her mother to Lady Lucias with wide eyed surprise for a moment before, knowing her place, she followed him.

-16-

Ishitar was miles down the path that led up the mountain to Zadkiel's cottage before he seemed to realize where it was that he was headed.

When he understood his intent, he abruptly stopped.

"Damn it." He spat before letting out a hard and irritated sigh. "I cannot go to Zadkiel." He shook his head and turned his gaze to Na'amah, who had caught up with him and who, now, sat at his feet, looking quizzically up at him. "He will be furious about this. All that I will succeed in doing is getting him into trouble if my father learns I have been visiting him now."

Na'amah merely continued to stare at him with her strange, mismatched eyes.

"Why do you have to be a Gods be damned dog?" Ishitar screamed at her. "I need a friend today! A real one!" He flicked his eyes to me and then back to Na'amah. "Not a brother that no one can see and certainly not a fucking *dog*!"

Na'amah flinched. Ishitar watched in what appeared to be surprise as his dog disappeared completely and then reappeared as the strikingly beautiful women that Na'amah was when she took on her mother's face and form.

"What?" He looked around himself, seeming to panic. "Where is my dog? What did you do with her? I want my dog back."

And, just as suddenly as the woman had stood there, now there was the dog.

Ishitar stared at her and then closed his eyes and shook his head. He was getting another one of his headaches. The change in face of his dog only served to compound it.

"Nritclkic." He muttered an ancient word as he stepped toward the dog and opened his eyes. "This has been a terrible day."

Na'amah, staring up at him, whined.

Ishitar, clearly overwhelmed with pain and anger, lowered himself to his hunkers. Na'amah stepped hesitantly forward. When she did so, Ishitar wrapped his arms around her neck and buried his face in her coat.

As for me, I merely watched the pair with silent fascination.

"All I want in all of the worlds right now is to disappear out of everyone's line of sight."

-17-

"And he did."

I grant Charlie a guarded smile. Charlie, who has been listening to me retell this tale in surprising silence, turns toward me with a furrowed brow.

"He did?" Charlie asks, sensing my pause.

"He did." I sigh. "I couldn't find him anywhere. And, as you can imagine, this caused me to panic."

"Because . . . ?"

"Because he was the only one who could see or hear me." I whisper. "I knew he was safe. Having watched him throughout the entirety of his life, I knew his true power better than he, himself, knew it. No one could harm him. Other than, perhaps, his mother and father. But what of me? What was to become of me if I were to lose the last visage of my corporeal self which was left to me?"

Charlie, despite the warmth of the day, shivers. Even though he believes I am spinning him a yarn of fiction, he has come to care for me and the other characters in my story. He has come to understand the true nature of my insanity in that moment and time when Ishitar was no longer standing before me.

"Did you find him?"

"I did." I smile. "Through Na'amah's eyes."

Grinning, Charlie bows his head and reaches for Rocky, who sits at his side, to pet him. Every time I have mentioned Na'amah in Ansibrius' form he has reached for him. He understands, more than most, the love that a man feels for his dog.

"After several hours of searching for Ishitar, I heard Loki's voice through Na'amah's ears, speaking to my boy within the confines of his bedchamber." The memory warms me and makes me smile. "He was asking Ishitar to translate one of the images in the damned tome he was reading."

"The tome he *shouldn't* have been reading."

"Just so." I laugh. "And Ishitar, though irritated with Loki over the constant questions regarding the tome, gave him the translation for the very purpose of enticing him to leave the room."

"Did he come back to you?" Charlie asks this question hesitantly. "Ishitar, I mean?"

Even more hesitantly, I respond. "Eventually."

182

-18-

The challenge came far more swiftly than Thamores had anticipated. It also came, as Nala had prophesized, on the heels of him pulling one of the wolves off one of the young elfish girls who had ventured away from the camp to see to her necessaries.

Fortunately for the girl, Thamores had been on patrol that night. Even more fortunately for her, he happened to be walking down her row when he saw one of his wolves shifting his gaze around himself before darting out of the line of tents and into the forest.

He had dragged the wolf off of the girl—too late to spare her innocence—and slain him with a single bite to the neck. His brothers, who had never truly accepted Thamores as their alpha, had circled Thamores' tent that very night and marked it in the manner in which wolves do when they mean to claim ownership over their territory.

Now he stood, wearing his human face, over the slain bodies of the three wolves, blood dripping down his chin and his mouth curled into a snarl. He growled low in his throat, daring anyone else who would challenge him to show their faces.

None did.

These three were the strongest of the pack aside the wolf he had slain for raping the young elfish girl. If Thamores could slay them, he could slay them all.

"Tham." Her voice was low and respectful. Her scent, which was musky and sensual, permeated the air. He would take her, as was his right, when he came to his senses. "It's done. It's over. Come bed me now."

He first felt, and then heard, the growl that rumbled low in his chest. It wasn't her place to tell him when his show of strength was over. It was even less her place to tell him when he could have her.

Seeming to understand, she stepped swiftly away. As she did so, he felt himself calming.

He was grateful for this small wonder. With the golden moon waxing, and the smell of blood permeating the air, he needed to reign in his senses.

As he gained control over himself, he realized that he was famished. And, to his chagrin, that the smell of elf all around him was enticing. He wondered, desperately, if the meat tasted as sweet as the vampires claimed the blood to be.

Damn you. They're only children.

He swallowed the saliva that rushed into his mouth and rolled his eyes closed. As he did so, he turned toward the forest, hoping to catch the smell of game.

A deer. And not far away.

"Thank the Gods." He muttered.

"Thamores?"

"Nothing." He forced himself to smile. "I'm hungry. And, I smell meat."

"So do I." She said, her eyes darting to the nearest tent. She was thinking, he knew, the same thing that he had been. The smell of the elves was enticing. "Tham . . . ?"

"I know, Nala." He sighed. "But I smell deer."

The lines that had furrowed her forehead smoothed as a small, relieved smile played at the corners of her lips. "Enough for two?"

"Enough for two." He agreed as he bent forward to kiss her forehead. The smell of her enticed him almost to the point where he forgot about his hunger for food. "And, then, I will take you."

Turning toward the forest, Thamores leapt forward. By the time he reached the ground, he wore his wolf's form on the run. Nala, who could only change with the waxing of the golden moon, smiled after him before following on her worthless, human's legs.

-19-

"Thank you." Iladrul smiled at Sezja as she sat his plate of food before him on the table.

She didn't smile in response. She never smiled in response. She served him because it was her duty to do so. As she would have served whatever boy whose father had purchased her for his pleasure.

When she turned away from him, he sighed. Jeanir, who had been watching the exchange between the pair of them, lowered his face to hide his grin.

As angry as he had been when Wisterian had told him that his daughter would be gifted to Iladrul, he was, now, extremely pleased with the pairing. He thought, given the way Iladrul looked at the child, that the young Prince might be falling in love with her.

Her disinterest in him, Jeanir believed, only served to fan that flame.

Iladrul was a boy who was used to getting what he wanted. Though Jeanir suspected the child was still innocent, this included pretty girls. That a doxy—his doxy, bought and paid for—held no fascination for him was probably extremely frustrating and confusing to the lad.

Prince Trevor, who had also witnessed the exchange, put his fork in his mouth and smiled around it. As he did so, he met Jeanir's gaze and gave him a friendly wink.

"Excuse me." Jeanir smiled in return as he found his feet. "General Balean? If you don't need anything else from me, I think I'll retire for the evening."

"No." Balean, who had seemed distracted for the majority of the day, muttered. "Nothing."

"Very well." Jeanir bent his neck to Iladrul. "My Prince."

"Good night, Jeanir." Iladrul replied with a thin smile.

Slipping out of the tent, Jeanir felt his smile return as his gaze fell upon his five children. The boys, as they ever did, surrounded the girl, asking her questions about the manner in which Iladrul had treated her during the dinner service.

"You shouldn't gossip about your Master." Jeanir used his gruffest voice so that they would believe he was admonishing them. "It might be he who slips out of the tent."

"Forgive us, Father." Macentyx bit at his bottom lip. "It's just that, we've seen the way he looks at her and—"

"And it is his right to look at her that way." Jeanir reminded him before turning to Sezja. "Would it ruin you to pass him a kind word or a smile?"

"I don't wish to encourage him." She lowered her gaze.

"It's your *duty* to encourage him." Jeanir sighed. "Honestly, Sezja. You could do worse than earning the love of a prince."

"There are plenty of free girls who want him to do his dirty business with them." Jeavlin muttered under his breath. "Let one of them deflower him."

Jeanir frowned at that. "You stay out of it."

"But he's right, Father." Sezja replied with a pleading quality to her tone. "I don't even find him fair."

"Then you're a fool." Osete spat. Jeanir started. He raised his gaze to see that his son was now wearing a horrified expression on his face and that his cheeks were blazing red. "I mean . . ."

"We all know what you mean." Macentyx's lips thinned as his expression hardened into a disgusted scowl.

Jeanir could only shake his head. He'd had no idea that any one of his sons had a bending for males. Though, given Osete seemed more at ease with his mother than with Jeanir, he supposed he shouldn't be surprised.

"Fair or not, he's your only option for ever finding someone to love you." Jeanir reminded them. "All five of you." He flicked his eyes over his sons' faces, marking the discomfort that they found at that statement. "Give him the opportunity to do so."

"We'll try." Haidar crossed his arms over his chest. He always had been the brazen one. "But no promises that we shall love him in return."

"You will." Jeanir, who had once served a God who, by all accounts, was a monster, understood the truth of those words. He understood them far too well. "You'll find you don't have a choice if you mean to survive."

The children all lowered their gazes. He'd spared none of them any details as to his own plight so that when the day came that they were to serve masters of their own they would be ready to deal with the hand life had dealt them.

"Yes, Father." Macentyx promised him on all of their accounts. "We'll do our best."

"Good." He raised his hand and ran his finger along Sezja's cheek. "You don't have to bed him given he isn't going to force you to do so. But can you not, at the very least, be kind?"

Though it clearly pained her to do so, Sezja gave Jeanir a nearly imperceptible nod. It was the best that he would get from her and he knew that.

"Good." He leaned forward and kissed her forehead. "Now, all of you, off to bed. We have many miles to trek tomorrow, and on swift feet."

"Yes, Father." They all said in unison.

"Osete." He flicked his eyes to his son. "Go to Iladrul. Serve him this night and well. If you do so, who knows what friendship may blossom between you?"

Osete swiftly lowered his gaze. The other three boys exchanged a distasteful glare with one another. "Yes, Father."

Knowing he had done everything that he could for his children, for the nonce, Jeanir left them to find his tent.

-20-

Zamyael had just been readying herself for bed when she heard the knock on the door. Frowning, she pulled a robe over her shoulders and made her way to answer it. When she opened it, she did so with an irritated frown.

Until, that was, she saw Ishitar, and his dog, standing on the other side.

Her frown immediately turned into a grin. "Ishy. Your Da isn't home."

"That's alright, my Lady." He replied, smiling softly before leaning forward to kiss her cheek. "I've come to speak with you, if you don't mind the company."

"Not a wit." Her smile grew. She stepped back, pulling the door with her. "Please. Come in. Let me fix you something to drink."

"I'd like scotch if you have any." He replied to that as he slipped into the door. The dog looked up at her with its strange, mismatched eyes before following him in. "Make it a double."

"A trying day?"

"A *very* trying day." He smiled at her as he watched her close the door and walk toward the bar. "Will you speak candidly with me about something, my dear Lady?"

"Always." Zamyael replied, looking over her shoulder and giving him a very open smile. "You know that."

"Loki told me that you were my wet nurse when I was a baby."

She swiftly looked back to the glasses and poured two generous servings of scotch. When she turned to face him it was with guarded curiosity. As she handed him his glass she said, in a tight voice, "That's correct."

"Why?" He asked. "And why, really, were you forced to live as a male before your trickery with Parsiphany occurred?"

Sighing she indicated Ishitar's favorite chair. "Please. If we must talk about this, I should feel better doing so sitting down." Ishitar smiled at her and took a seat. She followed, taking a delicate sip of her scotch before asking, "Why is this important to you? After all of these many moons?"

"Because I know nothing about either one of my parents." Ishitar replied. "Noliminan hardly acknowledges my existence, and Lucias abandoned me to Da and Azy to be raised. I want to understand why neither one of them wanted me when I was a babe."

"If you believe that Lucias didn't want you to raise on her own then you are sadly mistaken." Zamyael replied softly. "Giving you away to Zadkiel was the hardest decision that she has ever

188

had to make in her overly long life. You out of all of her children . . . You're the only one that she was allowed to birth." She looked swiftly away. "Until now."

Ishitar shook his head, choosing not to respond to the majority of that pretty little speech. His lips, as they always did when Loki and the babe in Lucias' belly was mentioned, thinned. "Yet she *did* choose to give me away."

Zamyael couldn't refute that. She lowered her gaze and sighed.

"Yes, Ishitar. For her war against your father's beliefs and orders. And, it must be said, to protect the army of angels and demons that had run to her for succor from the cruelty dealt them at the hands of their Gods."

Ishitar took a drink and said, "Lucias is cunning."

"Ta." Zamyael agreed. "She is."

"And Noliminan?" Zamyael felt her brow furrow. "Is he insane?"

Zamyael frowned at the question. He had asked her for honesty and she had promised to give it to him. "Perhaps, if he were, then his actions would be forgivable."

Ishitar's expression softened slightly as his eyes danced over her face. She raised her gaze to meet his.

"No, Ishitar. Your father is not insane." She began toying with one of her braids. "I believe that he is simply paranoid."

"What does *he* have to be paranoid about?" Ishitar asked. "Everything that exists that would stand against him does so by his creation and treatment of it."

"I honestly have no idea." Zamyael admitted. "But it's always been so." She shrugged. "I suppose that he's paranoid that Lucias will realize just how powerful a Goddess she is and overtake him."

"If the two were to war," Ishitar asked, "and I mean really at war, not just playing at kings' castles with one another," Zamyael nodded, "could she best him?"

"I believe that you have just posed the ultimate question." Zamyael smiled at him.

His eyes began tracing the lines of her face again. She felt herself swallow under his regard. She wasn't entirely sure what he was trying to discover. She knew him well enough, however, to know that his questions were not innocently posed.

"Why were you, really, forced to live as a male?"

"There are some things, Ishitar," she warned him, "that you might not want to truly know about."

"Perhaps I need to know them." Ishitar replied. "I have a choice, Zam. I can become my father. I can become my mother. Or I can simply become me." She smiled at that. "I'd prefer to become the third person and I can't do that if I repeat the mistakes of my parents."

Maybe so, Zamyael thought, *But that statement alone proves that you are very much your mother's son.*

"I was forced to become a male because your father has a penchant for raping woman." She told him candidly. "You've seen that for yourself." He nodded. "Which is why I must now hide from him." She shook her head. "I was born a Goddess." He nodded. Loki must have shared this with him too because he didn't seem surprised. "I was meant to be Lucias' wife."

"Lucias was living as a male by then." Ishitar muttered.

"She was. Yes." She agreed, though hesitantly. "What spurred her to live as a man, according to what Lucias told me, was that the pair of them tried to have a baby amongst themselves for many ages but were seemingly unable to. So they created Raziel and me to take on that burden because they had no choice."

"Then you weren't really born."

"No." Zamyael replied. "I was created from Lucias and Raziel was created from Noliminan."

"I understand." He nodded.

"Lucias, newly forced to live as a male, still lived very much in her feminine energy when I was young." She lowered her gaze. "And so, she was patient with me. She waited for me to fall in love with her before she attempted to . . ."

He reached for her hand and squeezed it. He didn't let it go. She loved him for that.

"Before she would, as a man, take you to her bed."

"Ta." She smiled at him. The smile faded fast. "Noliminan was not so patient. He took Lucias' empathy for little more than feminine weakness."

"Because you weren't doing what he had created you to do and he took it as defiance."

"That's right." She couldn't bear to look at him. "And he decided that if Lucias wouldn't force me to do what he had created me to do than he, himself, would."

"He forced your virginity to him."

"He did." She nodded at him. "Lucias was furious. They fought. I'll spare you the details of what came next because it is ugly and because it all amounts to the same thing. Noliminan finally decided that the best way to put me in my place so that he could continue to have at me without Lucias' interference was to turn me into a demon." She flapped her wings to make a point. "Lucias, in response, made me male so that Noliminan would no longer covet me."

Ishitar's eyes narrowed slightly and his brow furrowed. "I know that you love Lucias."

"I do." She smiled at him.

"But don't you think that her turning you into a male for the sole purpose of cock blocking Noliminan is just as horrible as Noliminan turning you into a demon to punish her?"

Zamyael started at that. She had never looked at her plight in quite that manner. She had always believed that what Lucias had done to her had been borne by Lucias' love for her. She couldn't—wouldn't—believe otherwise now. "Lucias didn't—"

Ishitar sighed. "Perhaps I have the wrong of things, my Lady."

Zamyael swallowed and nodded. She lowered her gaze. *What if he's right?*

"Thank you for talking with me, Zamy." His tone was gentle.

191

"Of course." She replied, meeting his gaze again. She realized, as she did so, that he still held her hand. She squeezed his. "The day that Azrael pulled you from my arms was the second worst day of my life."

The first, of course, being the day that Lucias had taken Zamyael's ill begot dathanorna from her in order to protect her and the child.

"Well, I'm here now." Ishitar replied. "And I will let no one come between us again."

Knowing Ishitar's parents far better than Ishitar did, Zamyael doubted that he would have much say should he be ordered not to see her any more.

Still, looking upon his handsome face, his expression stern and hard, she took comfort in the fact that he intended to fight for her should it come to that.

-21-

Iladrul lowered himself at the makeshift vanity to remove the delicately made crown from his brow.

It was a pretty thing, made of solid bronze and looped in delicate filigree patterns. At the center of his forehead it swooped downward and curled into a tear drop. Within the tear drop of brilliant white light pulsed whenever it touched his brow.

Once, when Iladrul was young, he had asked his friend, Gregor, to wear the crown to see if the light would pulse. It hadn't. Nor had it when he had asked Faunus to don the bauble.

Looking at himself in the reflecting glass, Iladrul found himself longing for his friendship of old.

Gregor had been one of the few boys who had ever treated Iladrul as just another boy. With Gregor, Iladrul could romp and play rather than practice at swords or politics. They would wrestle in the hay together or ride horses, bare back, through the forest.

Even though their friendship was forbidden, Gregor's father, a joyful angel named Zander, always welcomed Iladrul into the stables on the rare occasions when Iladrul was able to escape his duties to visit his friend.

Until, that was, about ten suns past.

On a very lazy summer afternoon, Iladrul had left the other lads to their play in search of more lighthearted fun. He had gone to the stables to visit Gregor and Zander had eagerly let him in.

Earlier that day, Gregor had convinced Zander to tie a swinging rope to the rafters of the barn. While he had been doing so, Gregor gathered the unbound straw that was kept in the cellar and piled a goodly amount of it together so he could fly from the rafters and fall, safely, to the ground below.

When Iladrul arrived, Zander was very stern that the young Prince should not put himself at risk by engaging in this kind of play. So, Iladrul contented himself to sit on the edge of the rafters, cheering Gregor on as he took many a running leap to the rope, swung wildly through the air, up into the sky, where he would let go and then fall, laughing, into the soft mound of straw below.

Being a young boy, Iladrul, of course, could bear the watching of such frivolity for only so long before taking Gregor's lead. It had been as he was hoisted as high in the air as gravity could possibly allow him to go, with his limbs flailing as he fell, that one of Titheron's soldiers had come to stable his horse.

In the typical, over reactive fashion of Iladrul's father, Zander—who hadn't even realized that Iladrul had disobeyed his order not to play on the rope—had been dragged to the throne room to be berated for allowing Iladrul his moment of unprincely play. As his punishment, Zander's wings had been severed from his body and nailed to the entry of the stable wall. The bones of them still hang there as a grisly reminder to all what may happen to those who disobey the set social boundaries between the classes.

"Bygone days." Iladrul told his reflection as he curled a lock of his copper hair around his finger.

Behind him, a shadow shifted. He raised his gaze slightly to find Osete watching him intently. He blushed slightly and offered the doxy a stiff smile.

"I was thinking of an old friend." He explained.

"Yes, my Prince." Osete replied, his tone gentle.

"The blonde elf who cares for our horses." Iladrul sighed. "He and I used to play together."

The confused expression that crossed Osete's features could not be denied, though he didn't voice the obvious question. He, better than anyone, knew that the social classes did not mix.

"But that was many sun cycles gone by." Iladrul muttered. "I haven't spoken with him in ages."

"Shall I fetch him for you?"

Iladrul started at the question. His lips thinned as he shook his head. "I'm not allowed."

"Forgive me, my Prince," Osete lowered his gaze slightly, "but no one would be any the wiser."

Iladrul cocked his head slightly and turned on his chair to face the doxy. "Excuse me?"

"It's late." Osete replied, still not raising his gaze to look at Iladrul. "No one of any consequence is awake. And, should anyone happen to see him, is it unreasonable that a prince would command his stable boy special allowances for his horse?"

Iladrul shook his head. "I do not wish for him to be punished."

"He wouldn't be if I were in the room with you." He finally raised his gaze. As he did so, his cheeks grew slightly pink. Iladrul found himself oddly drawn to the boy in that moment because his embarrassment gave his features a girlish quality that reminded Iladrul of Sezja. "No one would believe you'd share my services with a stable boy."

Iladrul looked swiftly away. He didn't like the flare of emotion that rose up in him at that statement. "What nonsense are you speaking of?"

"Only that, if you were to pass me about, you wouldn't dirty me with his lowly hands." Osete swallowed. "Forgive me, my Prince. I didn't mean to step out of line with the offer."

Iladrul returned his gaze to the boy. He studied Osete's features for a long, uncertain moment before lowering his gaze. "I'm sorry, Osete."

"My Prince?" The surprise in his tone was palpable.

"You didn't step out of line." He forced himself to meet the other boy's gaze. "I *would* like to see Gregor."

Osete smiled. "I'll go fetch him."

"Thank you." Iladrul smiled in response. "Keep in mind we didn't part well. Don't force him to come if he doesn't wish to see me."

Osete's smile grew as he found his feet. Iladrul watched him with great curiosity as he strode away. He wondered why, unlike Osete's brothers and sister, the boy was always so kind to him.

Shaking his head, he returned his gaze to the mirror.

It didn't matter why Osete was being kind. The fact that he was, Iladrul supposed, was enough. Whatever motivation the boy had in befriending Iladrul was his own business.

As he was toying with his crown, debating whether he should put it back on or not, the flap of the tent opened. The moment that it did so, the air was permeated with the smell of hay and horses.

Iladrul flew to his feet and flung himself toward Gregor. As he took him in his arms, he felt the other boy first stiffen and then raise his right arm to hug him back.

"My friend." Iladrul turned his face to kiss Gregor's cheek before releasing him. Gregor wore a sloppy, dumbfounded smile that brought his heart joy. "I've missed you."

"Yet, it took you long enough to realize that, with neither your father here nor mine, we might hold palaver with one another." Gregor chuckled as his eyes flicked to Osete, who was now entering the tent behind him, and then back to Iladrul. "I thought you hated me now."

"No." Iladrul shook his head. "I didn't want to get you in trouble. Who knows what Balean would tell my father if he saw us together."

"That I'm a better swordsman than his son." Gregor shrugged. "You can't seriously be thinking of making that boy your General."

"It's his right as Balean's heir." Iladrul sighed. "You still practice, then?"

"Not with anyone that's worthy." He shrugged again. "My little brother."

"Then, perhaps, it's time you fight against a real warrior." Iladrul grinned and turned to Osete. "Fetch my split sword."

"Yes, my Prince." Osete beamed as he spun away to do as he was bid.

When he was gone, Gregor leaned toward Iladrul and asked, "How was it?"

"How was what?"

Gregor snorted and elbowed him. "Your first time, you dolt!"

"No." Iladrul laughed and shook his head. "I haven't broken any of them yet."

Gregor blinked and let out a whistle through his teeth. "Not even the girl?"

Iladrul blushed as he shook his head.

"I always knew you were a fool." Gregor winked at him and then let out one of his large, jolly laughs. "I'd have pinned her down the first night I owned her."

"I'm trying to be a kinder master." Iladrul replied tersely. "If she wants to come to my bed, she will."

Gregor shook his head. "I bet there are plenty of doxies back home who wish their masters were half as kind."

"There are plenty of doxies back home who lay as ashes on the wind." Iladrul snapped. "And plenty more ahead of us who are, more than likely, going to follow them."

Gregor flinched at the reminder of what had happened in the Doxy Village. Being a stable boy, rather than a freeman or noble, Gregor had been schooled with the doxy children. Some of them that were now dead were his friends. Never mind that he was in love with one of the girls that had been taken. It was this, more than anything else, which had encouraged him to volunteer to travel with Iladrul in his father's place.

"Do you think she's well?" He asked, his voice shaking. He understood that Iladrul could drive out his heart for asking such a question of a doxy. He had no right. "Is she still alive?"

"I don't . . ." Iladrul sighed. His eyes flicked to the tent flap, which was opening, as Osete entered. He debated not finishing his sentence and then decided that, at some point, he had to start trusting the boy. He gave Osete a tight smile and returned his attention to Gregor. "I believe she is alive. But, no, Gregor. I do not believe she fares overly well. Lord Jamiason was very clear that he meant to force them to breed with one another."

Both boys paled. Iladrul instantly regretted his honesty.

"I'm sorry." He sighed. "But if they don't, then their lives will be forfeit."

"If they do their lives are forfeit!" Gregor snapped indignantly.

"I won't let them be punished for something that isn't their fault." Iladrul assured Gregor.

"The boys have all been cut." Osete reminded Iladrul, his face pallid and his tone one of fear. "They can't breed. What will happen to them when the vampires realize that?"

"We'll just have to retrieve them before they can." Iladrul advised them both. "Anyway, what they really want is their blood. Not their babies."

"How are they keeping them prisoner during the day?" Gregor wondered aloud. "Do we know?"

"They must have allies." Iladrul muttered a supposition he had held since the doxies had first been taken. "Someone who guards them when the sun is out."

"Who would do that?" Osete's tone was heavy with venom.

Iladrul shook his head. He didn't know.

"Come." Iladrul said as he reached for the split sword still held in Osete's hand. "Let's do something useful with our time."

He raised his gaze to meet Gregor's. "Osete and I must train my future General of Arms."

-22-

"Morning." Aiken, whose mind was on the mess that Jamiason had gotten himself into with the elves, grunted at Loki when he stepped into the kitchen.

He was furious with Iykva and the other demons for having attacked the elves after promising a truce while visiting his Oakland Grove. When he'd seen the devastation for himself, after the pixy souls he kept in the bauble around Iladrul's neck had called to him, he'd wanted nothing more than to stake the damn demon to the ground to face the morning sun.

"Is there anything in the cooling cupboard for the dog?"

"Not much." Aiken replied. "I think there might be some pork." Loki nodded and bent over to see for himself. As he did so, Aiken shared the news that he had been dreading. "Metatron visited me yesterday."

Loki looked at him over the door of the cupboard. After Aiken had met with the King of Lords in regard to his mischief with the humans and the dragons, they had both been expecting a visit from Metatron with the King of Lords' determination as to how Aiken would be punished. Neither one of them had been eager for such a visit to occur. "Oh?"

Aiken, frowning, said, "I'm to have Karma assist Michael with the minding of the eggs and, subsequently, the new race."

"Michael isn't going to like that very much." Loki said as he pulled the meat out of the cupboard and threw it on the floor to the dog.

"No." Aiken shook his head. Karma was responsible for causing quite a lot of mischief through the years that Michael had been forced to correct. Michael made no bones about the fact that he didn't much care for the girl. "And nor is Karma." He sighed. "I was just about ready to hand her my crown and retire from my mortality in the Grove. This will delay that eventuality indefinitely."

"That's more than likely the point." Loki replied as he leaned against the counter and crossed his arms over his chest. "To keep you too busy to cause any further mischief."

"As if it's stopped me before." Aiken snorted.

"You really did step out of line this time." Loki admonished him. Aiken took it in good stride. Loki didn't give a wit about Aiken's mischief with the humans and the dragons. He was upset over the fate which had befallen upon Michael.

"I know." He admitted. He was just as angry over Michael's lot as Loki was. "Yet, in the end, it served the Kind of Lords' needs. Didn't it? These creatures will be a powerful race."

"I agree." Loki interrupted him. "But it isn't your place—or mine—to muck about with the creation of new races." A strange expression crossed his handsome face. Aiken smiled despite Loki's displeasure with him. "Speaking of which, Lucias ought to be dropping whatever abomination she's carrying any day now."

"Maybe it won't be—"

"It will." Loki sighed. He uncrossed his arms and walked to the table, lowering himself into a chair across from Aiken. "She told me that she is specifically *not* breeding archangels for the Quorum this time."

Aiken's brow furrowed at that. "Why not?"

"Because of the way that her sons and daughters of the Quorum are treated." Loki shrugged. "She doesn't want Noliminan to have any command over them." Aiken started at the sound of the King of Lords' name coming from Loki's mouth. "If they're mortals, he cannot interfere with them."

Aiken grinned in response. "Forced into his own damn trap."

"I think that was Luci's intention." Loki smiled.

"Well then." Aiken said, raising his glass of juice in Loki's direction. "Let our betters place our demons where they may on our board."

-23-

Michael was more than merely angry when the damn mischief fairy showed up at his door. He was furious. He and Karma had a long—and very tumultuous—past.

Nor did she seem any happier to see him. She nearly threw the paper which spelled out her orders from King Noliminan in his face as she sashayed through the door and—unwanted—into Michael's life.

"At the very least," He seethed at her, "you shall don some clothes."

"No." She snapped at him as her eyes fell upon the angel Michael had selected to assist him. Maxium was one of Adam's descendants who looked strikingly like Lucias. "I shan't. I may only be a fairy, but I'm still mortal. So you can't tell me what to do."

Michael growled under his breath at that as his eyes danced, as if with their own will, to her full, ripe breasts. They were covered with her long, wavy, dark blue hair, but the nipples of them poked through. Something other of Michael's danced under its own will, infuriating him.

"I have plans of my own with which this has interfered." She groused as her eyes flicked, once again, to Maxium before returning to Michael. "I was to marry a desert fairy next cross of the moon. We were to join our tribes by politic."

"La de da." Michael snapped at her. "You must feel ever so put out that your rouge father's politics have been delayed."

"As a matter of fact." She rounded on Max. "Stop staring at me!"

"Then don some clothes." Michael seethed. "You cannot expect to live with two grown men prancing about unclad and not have us stare."

Her lips pursed. Her blue eyes danced from Michael to Max.

"Fine." She snapped. "I'll don a smock. But I shall loathe every minute."

"Too bad for you." Michael replied to that. He flicked his eyes to Max again. "Come, Max. Let's see to the turning of the eggs."

Max tilted his head to the side, raised his brows and shrugged. "If you insist, my Lord. Although, I'd rather keep the fairy company."

"She's not your friend." Michael growled at him. "Or your pretty." He looked away from her in irritation and disdain. "So do as I bid and come with me."

Max, grinning at Karma, gave her a bow. "My Lady."

"At least one of you has found his manners." She hissed.

Michael, less than pleased with either of them, let out a guttural growl and stormed out the door.

-24-

Thamores watched with unguarded interest as a falcon flew from the trees and into the sky. His brow furrowed as he slipped his arm out from under Nala's neck and propped himself up to look in the direction of the forest.

As his gaze landed on a face that should not be standing in a patch of sunlight in the middle of the afternoon, his puzzlement became even more acute.

Slowly, he rose to his feet. As silently as possible, he stepped into the forest and snaked his way around the demon until he stood directly behind him. Only then did he whisper his name.

"Jamiason Scrountentine."

James jumped and spun around. His blue eyes were wide and wild. As if by instinct, he jumped backward so that he was standing in the shadows, the fact that he had been seen standing in the direct sunlight registering with him at once.

"Thamores. I . . . I must have been sleep walking."

Thamores' eyes narrowed. "We've known each other for too many cycles of the sun, James. Don't start lying to me now." Jamiason lowered his gaze slightly. "How is it that you were standing in the sun?"

"I . . ." He shook his head as he raised his gaze to meet Thamores'. "Tham. You have to understand. I was the first vampire."

"Which means, eventually, you will be their Emissary God." Thamores crossed his arms over his chest. "I know that. As will I be for my people. But not until I die my mortal death." His brow furrowed. "Are you telling me that you already have?"

"I died my mortal death when I lived as a nymph in Aiken's grove." He sighed. "As an exile, if I were to die, now, I would cease to be." Thamores frowned at that sentiment. "You can't tell anyone, Tham. You have to promise me."

"You know I won't betray you." Thamores was offended by the accusation.

"I do." Jamiason nodded. "If you give me your word."

"Fine." Thamores, not in the mood to play games, narrowed his eyes. "You have my word."

"I am already a God." His voice was so low that Thamores could barely hear him. "Evanbourough allowed me at his neck." He lowered his gaze again. "Without the King of Lords' accord."

"Piss on the Gods, James!" Thamores cried. His sudden exclamation startled a flock of birds roosting above them. They all cried out and took wing at the same time, momentarily darkening the sky. "You and Evanbourough will both be expired if—"

"Which is why you can't say anything." Jamiason stepped forward and grasped his arm. "He thought he was helping me and I didn't realize what drinking his blood would do to me." His brow furrowed slightly. "I'd like to believe that he didn't either, but he's a self-serving mouk who always has an agenda."

"Does anyone else know about this?"

"Paul." He nodded. "And I'm certain Aiken knows, though he's never come right out and told me that he does."

Thamores began violently shaking his head. "Madness."

"Madness is that you are standing at Iykva's side, guarding these children." Jamiason raised his hand and pointed to the rows of tents. "Why would you agree to such a thing?"

"Why would you allow such a thing?" Thamores snapped his response to this question.

"Because I have no choice." Jamiason answered, his tone flat. "You, however, do."

"No." He shook his head. "I don't. It's what this pack wants and I'm not yet part of them enough to make unreasonable demands."

"It's what the pack wants because a blood bath is coming when the gold moon grows fat." Jamiason spat. "How do you mean to control them?"

"I don't . . ." Thamores let out a low sigh that was almost a growl. "I'm uncertain."

"Then, perhaps, you understand my position." Jamiason's tone softened.

"I . . . do." Thamores reluctantly admitted. "Where were you sending the falcon?"

"To my twins." Jamiason said, his voice low again. "With a message about what is going on here. I intend to find a way to free these elves before it's too late."

"It's already too late." Thamores groused.

"It's not." Jamiason sighed. "I've advised my twins to contact a herd of centaurs that owe me a favor. They're going to be here before the gold moon is fat so that you and your pack can hunt the forest while they protect the elves. Iykva will think I'm protecting his people from your wolves. In truth, the centaurs will work with me to find a way to clean up this damn mess and get these children to whatever is left of their home."

"This herd can be trusted?" Thamores asked. "To remain on your side and protect the elves rather than join the vampires?"

"Yes." Jamiason nodded. "They've wanted an alliance with the exiled angels for years. Specifically with Raystlyn. But if they can get in good with Wisterian—"

"They're half way there." Thamores muttered. "Damn." He shook his head. "I forgot about Raystlyn's loyalty to Helena."

Jamiason pursed his lips over his sharp teeth and nodded. "Hopefully Wisterian has, as well."

Thamores chuckled under his breath at that. It was a doubtful supposition that Wisterian had forgotten anything of the kind. Helena and Raystlyn's affair had been a serious scandal as far as the exiled angels were concerned.

"When your wolves return from rutting," Jamiason asked, "which side will your pack serve?"

"Yours." Thamores assured him. "And it won't be just my pack." He hoped he wouldn't regret the next promise. "I'll call a council of the benandanti."

"Those that you can find." Jamiason reminded him. "Any idea where they are disappearing to?"

"None." Thamores admitted. "It's why I've decided to run with werewolves instead of my own kind. Hopefully, I'll be over looked."

"That, my friend," Jamiason raised his hand and clapped Thamores on the bicep, "is an unlikely supposition."

Thamores, not comfortable with compliments when they came from other males, responded with a cold, thin lipped smile.

-25-

Loki grinned at the babe in his arms.

He was a disturbingly ugly creature. Yet, at the same time, I believe Loki viewed him as the most beautiful baby that he had ever seen.

The child's body was covered in light grey scales. There were darker scales that spiraled from the base of his hairline—which was made out of snakes rather than actual hair—at his right temple around his left eye and mouth to curl back to the right around his neck. This spiral continued through the entire breadth of his body to end at the heel of his left foot. As for his yellow eyes, they ran vertically along his face. His nose was little more than a small bump with two vertical slits on either side.

"What is he?" Loki raised his gaze and grinned at Lucias, who lay upon the birthing bed, watching him with guarded interest. "What can he do?"

"Other than you, Nol and I," she smiled coyly, "anyone else who looks in his eyes will see their greatest fear." Loki's brow furrowed. I wondered how much will it took him not to admonish her for raising her husband's name in that particular moment. "When they do so, if they are mortal, exiled or damned, they will turn to stone. If they are immortal, and still walk in Noliminan's light, there is a potential they shall run mad."

"Turn to stone?" Loki frowned at her. "And their soul?"

"Trapped in the statute of their body until someone chisels out their heart." She chuckled. She was clearly amused by her antics. Loki, clearly, was not. "Then they can re-grow themselves to the fate that they would have been given by the manner of their lives."

"Lucias." Loki shook his head in disdain as he returned his gaze to the child in his arms. "What thoughts possess you to come up with such a creature?"

"As he breeds with other races the blood will dilute." She replied to this as she reached for the baby's hand. He cooed. As he did so, one of the serpents that made up his hair curled itself around her finger and began licking the tip of it with its black, forked tongue. "He will, of course, be the most powerful of his people. Necessarily, given once his mortal veil is lifted he will become a God."

"Who, exactly," Loki wondered aloud, "would breed with him?"

"He can rape his women if he must." She shrugged.

Loki's lips pursed and his nostrils flared.

"Not my son." He groused at her. "This child will grow up knowing the difference between right and wrong."

Her eyes narrowed slightly. It was as if she were assessing him, wondering if he were judging her for her own behavior when she took what she wanted against another soul's will.

"He will know from the cradle that, where a woman is concerned, a soft hand will ever be offered."

"As you say, Loki." She placated him. "He is, after all, *your* son." She looked away as she said this. Loki didn't mark this, but I, standing at the baby's cradle, felt a sudden chill by this sudden coyness. "He has powerful blood running through his veins. He will have the ability to seduce that which he craves."

Loki chuckled under his breath at that and shook his head. As he did so, he raised the babe to his lips and kissed the scales where his brow should have been. When he lowered the child, he turned his gaze to Lucias again and asked, "What shall we name him?"

"Gorgon." She grinned.

"That's a dragon's name." He scoffed.

"He has dragon in him." She replied to that. "Mostly serpent. But aren't dragons little more than giant serpents?"

"Depends on the type." Loki corrected her.

"Gorgon." She insisted. "It's decided."

"Thank you for allowing me to have my say on the matter."

I doubt that he was angry. Gorgon is a strong, masculine name. In fact, this is the name of the very first dragon ever hatched. He was loved by all races until he fought in Lucias' war. Then he, like all the other Gods who stood against Noliminan, was exiled to one world or the other and never heard from again.

The child could do with far worse a legacy.

"Gorgon it is." Loki agreed.

"There is something that I must tell you."

Loki looked up at her with abrupt swiftness as if he didn't like her guarded tone. "What would that be?"

"Noliminan has demanded that Gorgon replaces Michael in the Quorum." She said this so swiftly that I was uncertain I had heard her words as they had been meant to be said. "We're to have Countenance come and see to his aging. My condition was that you and I raise him to manhood so we can influence him."

"You *agreed* to this madness?" The anger within him was uncontainable. Had he not been holding the child in his hand, he would have exploded with it. As it was, he tempered himself long enough to stride across the room and set the babe in his cradle. When he no longer held Gorgon he rounded on her. "You agreed to gift my son to that *monster*?"

"He's not a monster." Lucias snapped, her eyes glowing with her displeasure that he would disparage her husband's name. "I did it for Michael. We get him in exchange."

"In ex*change*?" Loki ignored the fact that she had defended Noliminan. After everything that the King of Lords had done to him, personally, I suspect that was an extremely difficult thing for him to manage. "My son for Raziel's?" His teeth clamped shut as he began violently shaking his head. "No. I will not gift him to that carvetek mouk."

"I had no choice." She leaned forward. "We can raise him. Noliminan has no use for him until he's an adult." Then, almost as if this were an afterthought, "And then we get Michael."

"I don't *want* Michael!" Loki roared at her. "I want my *own* son!"

"I had no choice!" She snapped at him. "Do you think I would have agreed if I had?"

He chose not to respond to that question.

"Michael is in trouble *now*." She explained. "Today. We can interfere where Gorgon is concerned when you sit upon my throne."

"*If* I sit upon your throne!" He cried. "Breeding a Quorum isn't an assurance that I will be accepted as a King!"

"People love you, Loki!" She countered. "Everyone loves you. No one will challenge your claim!"

"Raziel will." He reminded her. "As will your husband."

She rolled her eyes and looked away. "I think of you as my husband as well."

"Do you?" He seethed. "Because it seems to me that, if that were the case, this would have been a conversation rather than an order. Am I *still* nothing more to you than your servant? To bide your desires in *your* time? Is this what you are telling me?"

"You know that isn't the case." She frowned at him. "Loki, we can save Gorgon later. We need to save Michael now!"

"We need to save *Metatron* now!" He flared. "Or Azrael! Or Zadkiel! Or even Camael, for that matter!" He was infuriated with her for the first time since he had met her. "Michael is exiled, yes. And in a bad situation to be certain! But I've taken care of him and given him my protection already! If you had to trade my son for any one of your other children, Michael was *not* the one who needed your immediate aide!"

"He was the only one that Noliminan would trade for." She sighed. "Loki—this can be corrected once you are on my throne! You have to trust me."

"Isn't that all that I have ever done?" He seethed as he turned away from her and pulled his babe into his arms. "Trust you?"

He clearly needed to get as far from her as he could in that moment lest he do or say something he regretted. Though, he wasn't about to leave his newborn child in her care given she had already traded him as a pawn.

Though I suspected he would come to understand, in his own time, he couldn't bear to look on her traitorous face for a moment longer in that particular moment.

-26-

"Thank you." Iladrul smiled at Sezja. As he did so, she flicked her eyes to her father.

He gave her an encouraging nod. Seeing this, she forced her own smile.

"You're welcome, my Prince."

Iladrul started. His eyes, which had, moments ago, been hopeful, were now sparkling with pleasure. His lips, which had worn a smile, now split into a toothy grin. Seeing him so, Sezja was helpless but to finally see the draw that Osete felt for the young prince.

"Will there be anything else?" She asked.

"Not tonight." He smiled gently at her. "Unless you'd be interested in joining Osete and I at the kings' board."

Her brow furrowed slightly. "I'm not expert at the game."

"Osete is." His smile grew. "You can play as a team."

Her eyes darted to her father. He was leaning slightly forward, biting his lips to suppress a smile. He gave her another encouraging nod.

Knowing that her father wanted this pairing, she forced herself to grant Prince Iladrul another smile. "Very well, my Prince. As long as the game is played fair."

"Swear." He raised his hand, kissed the tips of his fingers and held them toward her. It was a childish elfin gesture, given when a promise was made between friends, but it made her smile grow true.

"I'll have Osete set up the board." She said, before turning away from him and walking swiftly out of the tent.

As they ever were, her four brothers stood in a pack, waiting for her. Seeing them, she felt at peace. "Osete!"

He looked toward her, wearing a weary smile. She knew that he was jealous of the attention that Prince Iladrul gave her.

"He wants you to step up his kings' board." She told her brother. "You and I are to play as a team against him."

"Sezja . . ." Macentyx began.

"It's what Father wants." She sighed.

"Father isn't the one who'll be pinned to the table." Haidar spat. "Don't put yourself in that situation!"

"I won't let him rape her." Osete snapped at his brothers. "Anyway, he wouldn't. He's not like that."

"What do you know about what he's like?" Haidar asked. "He's clearly not interested in *you*."

Osete flinched as if he'd been slapped.

"It's my decision. And you all know that I can hold my own." She reached for her hip and patted the dagger she kept there. Her brothers, all of them but for Osete, who stood glowering at his boots, grinned. "I'll be safe enough."

"Still," Haidar mumbled, "we'll be standing outside the tent. You need only call my name and I'll be on him in a flash."

"He won't hurt her!" Osete snapped before spinning on his heel and storming away.

Sezja turned to Haidar and glared, "When are you going to learn not to berate his love interests?"

"Iladrul shouldn't *be* his love interest." Haidar seethed. "It's unnatural and it's disgusting."

"He doesn't know any better." Macentyx shook his head. "Give it a rest, Haidar. He's only falling back on a life's worth of training."

"That isn't what this is about." Javelin, who rarely ever commented on this particular subject, interjected with a soft tone. "He really does prefer . . . that. And, as his brothers," he smiled apologetically at Sezja, "and sister," she smiled in response, "instead of judging him, we need to see him through this. He truly seems to love Prince Iladrul and Prince Iladrul is never going to love him in return."

Sezja sighed. Javelin was right. Prince Iladrul clearly had no bending toward other males. Not that she had seen, by any road.

"I'll see to Osete." She told her brothers. She turned away from them and waved over her back. "I'll see you in the morning."

"Call our names!" Haidar cried after her.

Raising her hand and waving it at him again, she followed after the brother who needed her.

-27-

Aiken started as Loki stormed into the apartment and toward the library. Rarely, in all of the years that he had been Loki's friend, had he seen the God as angry as he seemed to be in that moment. Concerned, he rose to his feet and followed Loki, not bothering to knock given Loki hadn't shut the door.

"I am little more than a stallion she means to stud." He stormed at Ishitar, who was sitting by the fire reading. Ishitar looked up at him with an expression of guarded curiosity. "She gave my son to your father in exchange for Michael to serve on my Quorum!"

"For Michael?" Ishitar blinked.

He lowered the book and put it on the empty chair at his side.

"How many times has Metatron come to her and begged her succor?" Loki seethed. "But, yes. She chose Michael to trade."

"What an odd move to have made." Ishitar's tone was thick with his discontentment. "He needs him. He can't win a war without Michael."

"This isn't a war." Loki growled. "It's a Gods be damned game of kings' castles!"

"And you are little more than a pawn." Aiken braved. "The nymph set on the Oakland hillock for the purpose of taking out the Lady Regent and her followers."

Loki rounded on him, glaring. He said nothing, however. There was nothing for him *to* say. Aiken had the right of things and all three of them knew it.

Instead, he turned to Ishitar. "I'm to give up my first rightful heir; my first child born out of a lover's embrace." He shook his head. "I can't bear it."

"You won't have to give him up." Ishitar muttered, his lips thinning. "We can fight for him later."

"Your Gods be damned mother's words!" Loki seethed.

"She was wrong." Ishitar agreed. "But you know as well as I that once barter is sealed only a God of equal power to the God of greater strength can break the vow." His light brown eyes danced over Loki's face with curious interest. "Are you powerful enough to face my father? Or to force the breaking of this vow against Lucias' wishes? Because if you are I will support you in doing so."

Loki's expression danced through many shifts as he contemplated this question. They rode the waves from certainty to defeat. Finally, he rolled his eyes closed and shook his head. "I want to. But no. I will lose any fight I raise with your father."

"You're certain?" Ishitar asked. His tone was guarded, yet, he wore a smile. A small, curious smile that Aiken didn't understand.

Or trust, for that matter.

"I'm . . . certain." Loki nodded. "I want to defy him. But something in my heart is telling me that to do so will create more consequences than have already been wrought." He sighed and shook his head in exasperation. "I can't beat him."

"Then you have your answer." Ishitar replied, still wearing that contemplative smile.

What in the name of the Sixty Realms has you so Gods be damned pleased?

"We let my father take the child." His eyes flicked to Aiken before directing them back to Loki. Aiken cared even less for the acute curiosity that he saw in the youngling's light brown eyes as they landed upon him than he had for the contemplative smile directed at Loki. "For now. We move Michael into your care. Once there, Lucias can raise him to be the God over the race of dragon men."

Loki, clearly frustrated, let out a harsh breath through his teeth.

"And," Ishitar continued as if Loki had made no reaction, "when you are ready to face my father, we force the issue of the boy and bring him back to your side of the thrones."

"Madness." Aiken spat.

Loki, shaking his head, agreed to what he interpreted Aiken's outburst to mean. Aiken opted not to correct his friend's misconception.

"I'll never be ready to face your father."

"Perhaps." Prince Ishitar agreed with a disinterested shrug as he reached for the book he had discarded. "But, then again, perhaps not."

-28-

"What can I tell you about what happened next?" I ask Charlie. "But to say that Ishitar made another Gods be damned pie."

"Another pie?" Charlie asks.

I turn toward him. His tone brokers my attention.

"Azrael." His brow is furrowed and his lips are drawn. "I have to ask you. Given your love for this child, were you not afraid that Noliminan is going to find out that Ishitar has been raiding his tree?"

"I am concerned." I tell him. "As I've told you before."

"Then why do you let him keep making these pies?"

I consider my answer for a long moment.

"Because I have come to understand a fundamental truth regarding this situation."

"Which is?"

"That I have no power to sway him."

He considers me for a long moment, wanting to press me further but uncertain that this is a wise course to take.

I am not surprised when he nods, raises his hand and twirls his finger impatiently to entice me to go on.

-29-

Iykva stormed down the aisle of tents, his eyes flicking to each pair of elves in turn.

What was wrong with these damn creatures? They had been on the trail to the Northern Sea for many moons now. Why had they not yet allowed nature to take its Gods be damned course?

He felt his lips thin as his eyes darted to Thamores. He had just told Iykva that he intended not to march with the vampires this night as, come tomorrow, the golden moon would be fat. He feared that his wolves would destroy the elves that Iykva meant for them to guard and protect.

The one small consolation, Iykva supposed, was that a centaur herd that resided slightly north of their current location had agreed to take up arms for Iykva's cause. They would guard the elves in Thamores' stead until Thamores, and his pack, returned to their duty once the golden moon had once again waned.

His pack and what benandanti needed protection from whatever threat was disseminating their numbers.

Iykva smiled wryly at that thought.

With the benandanti fearing the loss of their true blood race, they would be easy to control. So long, Iykva knew, as false promises were made to protect them.

Never mind the humans who had joined his cause after learning that the clan of Devonshire, who was their sworn enemy, stood with the elves. Allies, it seemed, were more abundant than Iykva could have hoped for.

Still, he was frustrated. He had promised his people the blood of elves and there simply wasn't enough to go around.

"Force them together." He seethed, turning his gaze to Thamores. "Or I will."

"You can't force them together." Thamores stopped walking and turned to glare at Iykva. He crossed his arms over his chest in a manner of defiance that Iykva didn't much care for.

This mortal fancies himself stronger than me. Perhaps after the moon wanes, it will be time to teach him better. And before his pack.

"Find a way." Iykva seethed.

Tired of Thamores and his ever growing list of excuses, he stormed away.

-30-

Iladrul was surprised when Osete excused himself, leaving him alone with Sezja. It was the first time any of the brothers had allowed him any sort of privacy with the girl.

"You don't have to stay." He told her as he packed the pieces of the kings' board into their carrier.

"I'd like to stay." She replied, her tone gentle. "If you don't mind my company."

"Not at all." Iladrul swallowed. "But it's getting late and I must bed down for the night."

She looked swiftly away. When she spoke, her voice was shaking slightly. "I thought, tonight, I might stay with you."

Iladrul's entire body thrummed with those words. He licked his lips and swallowed the lump that had suddenly risen in his throat. "You aren't required to."

"I know." She still wouldn't look at him. "You've been patient with me."

"I'll continue being patient with you." His words belied his desires. "You don't have to—"

"I'm ready." Still not looking at him. "Just . . . be tender with me."

He reached for her hand. When she allowed him to take it, he pulled her to him. She looked up at him with wide, expectant eyes. Her generally hard expression was soft with fear. Her vulnerability tugged at his heart.

"I promise you." He whispered before leaning forward and taking her lips with his. As he kissed her, his entire body exploded with his desire for her. He pulled away and raised his hand to set it upon her cheek. "This hand will never harm you."

She let out a nervous little laugh and reached for his other hand. "What about this one?"

"The other shall cut it off before it has the chance." He smiled down at her.

It was her turn to lean into him, hiding a coy smile in his shoulder before she reached up for him. As she kissed him, she let her tongue run across his upper lip.

The sensation was exquisite.

"Come to bed." She whispered when she pulled away. "And let me ease your troubled day."

Terrified, yet exhilarated, he allowed her to lead him to his cot.

-31-

"Something unexpected happened to me that same night." I flick my gaze to Charlie.

"Oh?" He asks.

"Oh." I agree with a slight laugh.

"And what might that be?"

"Zamyael and I . . ."

I am no longer smiling. My memory of that night is precious to me and I have shared it with no one.

"You saw earlier in the story that we were falling in love."

"I did." Charlie nods.

"I had been staying with Zad and Zam, wearing the mortal face I had chosen." He nodded again. "That night, she and I . . ."

"You gave into your desire for one another?" He asks, not certain if he should smile.

"We did." My lips thin.

Sensing my discomfort, he turns slowly toward me. His brow is furrowed. "Why do you sound regretful?"

I look swiftly away. His regard—and his obvious concern—burn me. "The answer to that question lies at the end of this tale."

"Then perhaps it's best that you continue telling it." He encourages me gently. "Perhaps it is your need to speak about this, above all else, that has brought you to my side this afternoon.

I have no room in my heart to disagree.

-32-

Chiron approached Thamores with extreme caution. Though he and his herd were loyal to Jamiason, he had always been leery of Thamores Blackpaw and his kindred.

Benandanti not being creatures that are easy to sneak up on, Thamores first smelled and then heard the centaur approaching. When he turned to face Chiron, his wolfish, yellow eyes flashed with what the centaur could only assume was hunger.

Especially when he licked his lips, leaving an undeniable trail of spittle along the top and a thick pool of drool at the right corner.

Chiron took two steps back, preparing himself to run if the necessity presented itself. "Thamores Blackpaw?"

"Ta." His tongue caught the pool of spittle before it could drip as his eyes trailed over Chiron's flank. The centaur took two more steps back. "You must be Chiron Dilthrop."

"The same." Chiron agreed. "I understand that you have instructions for me."

He flicked his long ear at a fly. This time, when Thamores licked his chops, Chiron stomped his front foot. It was a silent warning that, if Thamores made any moves toward him, he was in for a trampling.

This earned him a guarded smile. "Mostly just make sure the elf pups don't run."

"Is that a large concern?"

"Oddly enough, no." Thamores shook his head. "They don't seem to understand that it's even an option. They're extremely obedient to almost every request Iykva has made of them."

"Almost?" Chiron flicked his ear at another fly.

This time it was Thamores that took two steps back. Chiron bowed his head in a silent acknowledgement of their truce. It earned him another guarded smile.

"You'll notice that Iykva has paired them boy on girl." Chiron nodded and flicked his eyes toward one of the nearby tents. "For the purposes of breeding them."

"A never ending supply of sustenance." Chiron's lips thinned with distaste.

"This is the one order that they are refusing to obey." Thamores chuckled.

"Nature isn't taking its course?" Chiron asked, his brow rising.

"Not in a single tent." The benandanti's chuckle became an amused laugh.

"That's . . ." Chiron shook his head. "Bizarre."

"Bizarre is one word for it." Thamores shrugged. "I asked one of the boys about it and he prattled on about the girls and their honor."

Chiron shook his head. Though he understood that, under most circumstances, a man wouldn't force himself on a woman, he failed to see how that could be the case with every single one of these adolescent elves. He, himself, had trampled many a stallion with a penchant for rape.

Never mind the fact that not a single pair of them had come together out of loneliness, fear or love.

Scratching his head in confusion, he returned his attention to Thamores. "What is Iykva planning to do about it?"

"I'm uncertain." Thamores sighed. "Fortunately the vampires are unable to spread their seed, so raping them isn't an option."

"He hasn't asked you to set one of your wolves upon them?" It was a disgusting thought, given that these creatures were still children, but it wasn't above the realm of possibility.

"I made it clear to him that this is not something I will condone." Thamores growled. "I killed one of my wolves for attempting to do just that. And three of his brothers when they came after me."

"Yet," Chiron grinned at him, "I'm here. Which means you know you can't control the pack when the golden moon rises with a full belly."

"I'd as soon not take the chance." Thamores agreed. As he did so, he raised his hand to the sky. "And it's best I get them out of here and as close to hoofed game as possible before she does."

"We'll have the elves pack up and start the march." Chiron sighed.

"They've been marching all night." Thamores shook his head. "They need to rest so their blood replaces itself before the vampires crawl out of their caves and bend their necks."

Chiron frowned at that. When he spoke, his voice was seething. "Why does Jamiason not put an end to this atrocity?"

"He will when he can." This was said in low tones and only after Thamores looked around them to make certain no one would over hear him. "Bide your time, Chiron Dilthrop. When the opportunity is ripe, Emissary Lord Scrountentine will show his quality."

"Or damn us all for not showing ours." Chiron replied.

Though he made no response, Chiron understood by the shift of his eyes that Thamores wholeheartedly agreed.

-33-

"We're gaining on them." Jeavlin muttered as the earth that he had raised to his face to catch a scent of who had recently passed sifted through his outstretched fingers. "A day's ride at most if we keep up this pace."

"Perhaps we can afford two." Iladrul muttered.

"My Prince?" Faunus, who was less than thrilled that Iladrul had taken his doxies into service as his personal squires, inquired.

"How fit are you?" He ignored Faunus and posed the question to Gregor.

"If I were a fiddle," the lad grinned, "I'd be strung and ready to play."

Iladrul repressed the smile that came easily to his lips.

"Can you catch them?" He inquired. "Scout them out and tell us their strengths and weaknesses?"

"Without this lot holding me back?" Gregor's grin split his handsome face. "I'll catch them by noon tomorrow."

"Good." Iladrul turned to Faunus. "Set camp for the night. And tell your father and Jeanir that we have plans that must be made."

"Is it really a good idea to be sending a stable boy on such an important mission?" Faunus scowled at him. "Really, my Prince—"

Iladrul shook his head. He wasn't interested in Faunus' complaints. He turned his gaze to Haidar. "Go with Gregor, Haidar. He can use a fine hand like you."

"My Prince?" Haidar blinked at him, surprised. "You'd send your doxy—?"

"I'd send my friend." Iladrul stopped him. "And one of the best trained soldiers in my army."

"I am . . ." He swallowed and shook his head. "I am honored by both sentiments."

"Mac." Iladrul ignored the doxy and turned to the lad's brother. "You and Osete come with me." He flicked his eyes to Jeavlin. "And you and Sezja must seek out Prince Trevor. Tell him what I have done and see what advice he might share."

"Yes, my Prince." Jeavlin didn't waste a moment. He turned on his heel to find his sister and do his Master's bidding.

Jeavlin's willingness to obey without question pleased Iladrul. It was good to know he had at least one obedient servant who would never question his motives.

When they were gone, Faunus glowered at him.

"This is a mistake, Iladrul." He scoffed. This caused Iladrul's eyes to narrow at his failure to show his respect and his familiarity. "Doxies and stable boys? As scouts?"

"No." Iladrul turned away from him and began walking to his tent. He didn't have time to soothe the wound that tore at his friend's ego. "But if you insist on pressing the issue, then go with them."

"Maybe I should." He snapped.

"Then do so!" Iladrul rounded on him. "I don't have time for infighting." He growled. "Though I wouldn't expect Gregor, or Haidar, for that matter, to watch your back if I were you. Their job is to spy without drawing attention to themselves and come back quick." He shook his head as if the last of it should be obvious to the bastard babe of a kitchen wench, "It's a job *made* for stable boys and doxies!"

Faunus' lips thinned as he looked swiftly away. After angry consideration, he stormed after the Haidar and Gregor.

"Will he cause us trouble, my Prince?" Osete asked, his tone low and respectful.

"If he does," Iladrul's eyes flicked to Macentyx, "I expect you to see to him."

Macentyx's strange eyes narrowed as his lips thinned. He didn't respond. Rather, he gave Iladrul a tight, almost imperceptible, smile.

"Stand guard, Mac." Iladrul muttered before reaching for Osete's hand. "Watch over the pair of us whilst we pray."

Macentyx's eyes flicked from one to the other of them, dark shadows crossing his features. "As you will me."

Iladrul ignored his discomfort and led Osete away from the camp and deep into the woods. When they found the river, he turned to the other boy and begged, "Watch over me?"

"Until my dying day, if that is what you require."

Iladrul nodded, turned toward the river and fell to his knees.

Lady Theasis . . . I beg it of you . . . Lend me your strength.

On his knees, in prayer to his Goddess, Iladrul was unaware that the bauble around his neck had begun to glow.

-34-

Aiken looked up, surprised, as a pixie landed upon the table before him. The creature's small wings began to buzz in the pattern which made up his words as he made his bow.

Having expected news eventually, the fairy rolled his eyes closed as he let out a long, tired sigh.

It's time then.

The buzzing of the pixie's wings confirmed this.

As Aiken stood, his eyes flew to Prince Ishitar, who was sitting on one of Loki's high back leather chairs with a book in his hand, seemingly oblivious to his surroundings. As he did so, the pixie flew upward, landing in Aiken's hair, just above the point of his right ear.

"I believe I'll go to bed." Aiken announced.

Ishitar raised his gaze, studied Aiken for a moment and then nodded. "I'll follow shortly."

Aiken gave him a false smile then made his way to Loki's bedchamber. Once the door was securely closed, he tilted his head to listen to the buzzing of the pixie's wings. When he had a beat on Iladrul's location, he nodded and willed himself out of the Hells' Realms and into the meadow where the young elfin boy knelt at prayer.

Behind him, another boy let out a surprised gasp, though, oddly enough, he didn't scream. Aiken looked over his shoulder to see that the boy—younger than Iladrul, if only by a year or so—was staring at him with wide eyes. His expression was a mixture of both fear and awe, causing Aiken to give him a patient, reassuring smile.

The boy nodded, swallowed, and, respectfully, lowered his gaze. When he did so, Aiken returned his attention to the young Prince.

"I may not be the lovely Lady." He said, his tone gentle. "But I've come at the call of your prayers all the same."

Iladrul spun swiftly toward him, his hand on the hilt of his dagger, as he gracefully found his feet. Aiken froze—not afraid of any damage the boy could do him—with his hands raised, palms toward the child.

"You go to war tomorrow." Aiken suggested, his tone respectful and low. "Or, if not, very soon."

"Emissary Lord Darklief . . ." The boy managed, his hand leaving the hilt of his split sword. He wore an expression which told Aiken that he held no trust for the fairy God.

That was alright.

Aiken might have changed his mind about helping the boy if he had stood before him a lamb rather than a lion.

"You frightened me."

"In these days," Aiken gave him a slight nod, "it is wise to be on your guard."

The boy nodded and lowered his gaze. "How might I serve you, my Lord?"

Aiken smiled at that; he was helpless not to. "You prayed for courage; you prayed for aide." He said. "I cannot give you the one, but my people can most definitely provide you with the other."

Iladrul looked confused as he raised his gaze. He studied Aiken's face for a moment—Aiken supposed he was measuring the God's intent—and then swallowed. "You're aligned with Lord Scrountentine."

"No." Aiken sighed. "Once." He forced a tight smile in the boy's direction. "No more."

"I don't understand."

"My people are mortal people." Aiken crossed his arms over his bare chest, knowing that the boy would take this gesture for vulnerability.

He wasn't vulnerable—not by any means—but he understood all too well how to play at politics with mortals. It was best, he had long ago learned, to allow those you wanted something from to believe that they had the slight advantage.

"With magic running through their veins, the same as yours. I cannot take the risk that, should your race be destroyed, Jamiason and his army will not set their sights on the weaker tribes of my fairies next. This is why I gave you my protection." He indicated Iladrul's chest with his chin. "My talisman."

Consideration crossed the elf's copper brow. As it did so, a flash of recognition shot like an arrow through Aiken's mind. The boy before him had features that were extremely familiar to him. Features that belonged to neither the boy's father nor the boy's mother.

Perhaps the rumors are true. Perhaps this is Raystlyn's child after all.

It didn't matter.

If the elf was Raystlyn's child, rather than Wisterian's, that was none of Aiken's concern. Though he would do well to remember that the blood coursing through this creature might be more powerful than any of them suspected. The mixture of the blood of an elf and the blood of a mage was, possibly, an enigmatic combination.

"*Would* Lord Scrountentine attack your people?" He finally asked.

"I wouldn't have thought, after promising your people a temporary truce, that he would have attacked *yours*." Aiken shrugged. "The survival of his race is at stake. There is no telling what lengths to which he might go to protect them."

The boy nodded. What choice did he have? Aiken was offering him an army. Right now, he had only a rag tag team of angels and elves and a thrice beaten army of thin and ill trained humans.

"You would ally your people with mine?"

"I would." Aiken agreed. "With the understanding that, should I ever have need of you, a favor would be returned."

The boy considered, for a moment, then nodded. "Of course. It would be understood."

Aiken turned his face slightly away lest the boy see his lips twitch. The fool of a child hadn't asked what the favor would be, which left the barter open ended. This was a position that suited Aiken just fine.

"Very well." He raised his hand, palm to the sky, returning his gaze to Iladrul. As he did so, the pixie souls embedded upon his flesh rose up to dance upon light feet to hear his command. He brought them to his face and blew, giving their wings the slight puff of air that they required to bolster their flight. "Seek the river fairies nearby and instruct them to come to Prince Iladrul's aide." He told them. "I, myself, must travel farther."

"Where do you go?" Iladrul asked, his eyes wide with fascination as the pixies scattered in all directions around them.

"There is a tribe of water fairies in the direction in which you currently travel." Aiken replied. "I must put them on the march this way. Otherwise, Jami and his warriors will, most assuredly, destroy them to clear their path."

There was another stop that he had to make first, however. Though, he didn't share this with the elf in case there were spies about. When it comes to war, nothing is a more powerful weapon than the element of surprise.

-35-

Pialoron stood against the far wall of his bedchamber, next to one of the great glass windows. His arm was raised above his head and his forehead was set against it. His eyes danced over the gardens below him and a soft smile played upon his thick, silver lips.

Under the hood of his modest robes, he had long silver hair, braided so that his plait danced between his iridescent wings. He was tall, even for a fairy, at eight branch and nine twigs. His body was long and lithe, though hard and muscular. His skin was pale white, though it shimmered slightly with a rainbow of color when he was in the sun. His eyes were vibrant and a penetrating silver in color. Running over the left side of his face from his hairline to his chin, curling around his left eye, was a shimmering plate of silver filigree.

At another wall, and to Pialoron's back, stood another fairy of the same age. He was of average height, at seven branch and two twig, and was emerald green in color by way of his hair, eyes and filigree.

"He's not going to be happy with you." Aminar said softly as he looked at his emerald fingernails, which he had buffed to a shine. "You were supposed to come home betrothed to Lord Aiken's daughter."

"She was unfitting." Pialoron muttered softly as he turned his silver eyes toward one of the females, who was darting across the garden lawns with a basket under her arms. "Not at all my type."

Aminar let out a soft snort of laughter and lowered his hand to his side. "And what was wrong with this one, my Prince?"

"She isn't Aminas." Prince Pialoron said softly, shrugging his shoulders and pushing himself away from the window to turn and face Aminar.

His silver eyes glowed with grief, breaking Aminar's heart.

Three years earlier, Aminar's twin sister had drowned at sea trying to save three young ones who had gone fishing during a brutal storm. Pialoron, who had intended to marry Aminas, had been devastated. "Perhaps I'm just not ready."

"Perhaps you never will be." Aminar voiced his frustration. "But if you do not marry—and soon—the rumors regarding you and I will bury us both."

Pialoron sighed at that. "Maybe you're right."

"I love you as a brother, my Prince." Aminar told him now as he stepped forward and toward the man that he served. "You know that I do. And I will bear the rumors and their consequences if it is what you require of me." Pialoron gave him a painful smile at that. "But consider this: all that your father wants is an alignment with a stronger tribe. Lord Aiken's daughter could provide that to him. If you were to marry Princess Triyana, you and I could live in peace."

"This I know." Pialoron said as he reached forward and took a lock of Aminar's long green hair, which tonight was unbound for Pialoron and hanging in loose waves over his bare shoulder. He let it slip between the tips of his fingers and Aminar could not stop himself from shivering as he watched Pialoron's eyes trail it. "But it isn't the ideal thought of marriage, is it? One would think that if one bound himself to another for the full of a lifetime that it might be for love rather than convenience."

"Neither princes nor eunuchs have such luxury as to believe in love in lieu of convenience." Aminar replied gently. "Especially not when the Prince has developed the unnatural habit of slipping into his eunuch's bed."

A frown crossed Pialoron's fair silver lips and Aminar immediately regretted his words.

"Do not mimic my father, Amin." He said coolly as he released the hair that he had been so lovingly caressing. "Or I'm likely to put you in your place."

"Of course, my Prince." Aminar muttered, lowering his gaze. "Please forgive me."

He felt Pialoron's silver eyes as they roamed the contours of his face. "No, Amin." Pialoron replied before turning and walking soundlessly away upon his bare feet. "It is I that must beg your forgiveness."

"You have every call, my Prince." Aminar replied softly, still looking downward. "I take advantage of your kindness where I am concerned."

"At times." Pialoron replied as he found his place back at the window overlooking the gardens. "Yet, I made you my friend when you and I were but boys. As such, I come by calling you so now in honest nature."

Aminar raised his gaze slowly and allowed it to wander over the curves of Pialoron's back to the sliver of profile that he could see of his Prince's face beneath the silk hood of his robe. Pialoron seemed to be watching something through the window that gave him peace. His expression was one of serenity.

"I come by calling you so now in honest nature as well."

"I know that you do." Pialoron said softly. "It is quite possibly why I love you, my dearest friend."

Aminar lowered his gaze, frustrated with his lot in life. "Thank you, my Prince."

Pialoron nodded but said nothing further. Whatever it was in the garden now had the full of his attention.

-36-

Michael glared at Karma's back, hating himself for the lustful thoughts that enveloped him as his eyes trailed downward to her well-made bottom. She might have donned a frock, but it scarcely covered her backside. The round muscle of her fleshy buttocks was far too visible beneath the hem of the dress for Michael's tastes.

"You've turned enough of them." He barked irritably.

"Not those two." She returned, not granting him the courtesy to turn toward him. "And they're all growing cold. We could do with more straw to cover them."

He didn't want to be touched by her motherly concern for what he was coming to consider to be *his* eggs, but he was helpless to feel otherwise. She might have been thrust unwillingly upon him and this task, but she had taken to it with a gusto that Michael never would have expected from a mischief fairy.

Never mind the fact that she was Emissary Lord Darklief's daughter to the very core of her soul.

"I'll tell Max to bring some in." He muttered.

She nodded, almost dismissively, and then turned toward him. Her face—he had to admit that she was pretty in the patches of sunlight that streamed from the thatched roof above them—bore a resolved expression that made her seem stronger and wiser than her years. "The nights are getting colder."

"They are." He admitted with a sigh. "Autumn is coming. Followed by winter."

"Does it snow here?" She asked, clearly surprised.

"Here?" He nodded. "Yes."

"I've never . . ." A childish quality washed over her features which made her even more beautiful still. "I've never seen snow."

He smiled, despite his better judgment. "It's very pretty." He reached forward and flicked at the scant sleeve of her garment. "And very cold. This will never do."

She snorted. "We'll see about that."

He chuckled under his breath and shook his head.

Yes, he thought as he watched her bound away and out of the rookery, *we shall, indeed, most definitely see about that.*

-37-

Aiken heard the door to his hut open, but he didn't turn that way. What he was telling his son was far too important for distractions. By any road, the moment that the air permeated with the scent of cloves and old spices, he knew immediately that the intruder was Prince Ishitar.

"As many men as we can spare, Xylon." He advised his son. "Do you understand?"

"Yes, Fete." Xylon nodded, his long white hair—so alike to Aiken's own; if any of them bore a resemblance to Aiken it had to be this boy—dancing around his face. "I understand."

"See to it." He replied, somewhat doubtfully.

Gods how I miss Karma! I need her here for this task! Not prancing about the forest seeing to the hatching of eggs.

He didn't voice this thought aloud because, honestly, there was no point. Xylon's feelings would be hurt and Ishitar would remind him that his daughter was being punished for his own sins.

He waited for the door to close behind Xylon before turning to face Ishitar. As he did so, he gave the young Prince a guarded smile. Seeing it, Ishitar smiled in response. "I'm unable to find Loki and Zuko is on task."

"Loki is probably with your mother." Aiken replied. This must have annoyed Ishitar, because his lips thinned. Pleased by Ishitar's reaction, he threw in another jab meant to wound. "And their new son."

"Have you seen him yet?" Ishitar snapped. "The babo, I mean?"

"Not yet." Aiken admitted.

He had asked Loki if he might visit Lucias and take a peek at the child, but Loki had advised him that he would prefer that Aiken wait. That he didn't want Aiken to see his first legitimately born heir had hurt the fairy God's feelings. But he was too prideful to tell Loki this and he had learned, through far too many hard trials, to at least try to mind his place.

"Nor have I." Ishitar sighed. "I really should visit the child soon. But I'm still angry with Lucias."

Aiken's brow furrowed at that sentiment. He had overheard Ishitar telling Loki that Lucias had denied that she was his mother. He supposed why, initially, that sentiment would have stung.

Now, however, Aiken thought that the entire argument was being overblown. Ishitar was, after all, supposed to be an unknown secret. Lucias couldn't admit to being Ishitar's mother without the rumors of his existence being confirmed.

"I suppose when you're ready, you'll take a look at him." Is how he responded. "I've got business to attend to. You're more than welcome to join me."

Having Ishitar join him wasn't something that Aiken truly wanted. He liked to keep his secrets and he wasn't certain, just lately, that he trusted the youngling. It wasn't fair of him to hold grudges against his Prince simply because of an unguarded smile of amusement at Loki's misery, but he held them all the same. Something about Ishitar just didn't sit well with him.

Today, he couldn't afford the distraction of having to watch his back.

"Something troubling you?" Ishitar asked, his caramel eyes assessing Aiken's features.

"Not really." Aiken shrugged away the lie. "It's just that these are a modest people. It's one thing for me to traipse into their home as I am." His eyes flicked the length of Ishitar and grinned. "Would you be offended if I asked you to don their smocks? To pretend that you are my man servant?"

Ishitar first started, then smiled.

"No, Aiken." His tone held a note of respect that I rarely have ever heard him command for others. "I would be honored."

Aiken nodded and reached toward Ishitar. One moment, he was wearing his famous shendyt, and the next he was swaddled head to toe in silken finery with only his face bared. He smiled and looked down, admiring his new garments.

"You did say modest." He chuckled.

"They hold to their traditions." Aiken shrugged. "In fact, they don't even believe in the Gods." Ishitar appeared to be surprised by this, so Aiken decided to explain. "Well. That's not entirely true. They believe in *a* God." He shrugged. "Tristan, in fact, as he was originally their God. But they have no concept of who or what the Heavens or the Hells are really made to be."

"Who, then, do they think *you* are?" Ishitar asked, clearly he was genuinely curious.

"Lord Aiken Briar Darklief of the Oakland Grove." Aiken smiled. "A barbaric halfling who shames his people by forcing them to walk about without clothing whilst I allow myself the courtesy of my loincloth." He pointed to his face. "And a bastard, at that, given my face lacks a scroll. But the most powerful fairy King of them all, so they hold their gossip to themselves when they know I am about."

"And you don't correct them?" Ishitar asked, clearly perplexed. "You don't show yourself as their God to them?"

"They live as they do and they are happy as they live." He shrugged. "They worship their God and love him. They don't need to know that their God is me."

"That's . . . an interesting notion." Ishitar muttered, clearly contemplating Aiken's willingness to not demand his people's supplication to him.

"It works for the fairies of this particular tribe." Aiken felt profoundly unsettled by this line of questioning from one who could use the knowledge against him. "Besides, the mischief fairies, who are my true kindred, know the truth of what I am."

Ishitar could only nod.

"Now as for you," Aiken smiled, because he liked the idea of this next sentiment, "you must lower your gaze and stand three feet behind me and to the left at all times."

"Why?" Ishitar blinked at him.

"This particular tribe of fairies trades in eunuchs." His tone held a note of distaste. "They wouldn't accept me bringing a human man with me and treating him as my equal. So, you must be my manservant. They'll be offended that you aren't a fairy, but—"

"If I must don wings then I shall." Ishitar offered.

"No, your Royal Highness." Aiken shook his head. "Unless hiding from your father, yours is a face that should never be masked."

Ishitar cocked his head at that. I understood the boy well enough to know that he found this to be a kind thing to say and that he believed that it came from Aiken's heart.

Which, to Aiken's credit, it did.

Though his motive for saying so had little to do with flattery.

"Thank you, Aiken."

He shrugged. As he did so, he reached forward and toyed with the mantle that he had placed around Ishitar's shoulders.

"Why *do* they clothe themselves so?"

"At this point?" Aiken's brow furrowed slightly. He hadn't expected this question. "Simple tradition and religion. Though it didn't start out that way. The custom had, originally, been born out of practicality." His smile became thin. "When Tristan was the God of we fairies, the water tribes were at war with the sea dragons. He taught the tribes how to make a silk that is fire retardant. They donned as much of themselves in this silk as they were able when anywhere but in the privacy of their own homes because they never knew when a sea dragon would attack." He chuckled to himself. "Most tribes of water fairies have been content to leave it at that. But this particular tribe is never seen without their silken robes by even other members of their family."

"Must I cover even my hair?" Ishitar asked, curious.

Aiken nodded, pulling the mantle over the silk of Ishitar's cowl. "Here, you wouldn't show your hair to any but your wife."

Ishitar smiled at that. "I intend to take no wife."

Aiken gave him a false smile. "A man after my own heart."

Ishitar's smile grew. "Yes. But I intend, even less, that I would ever take a husband."

"A pity." Aiken flicked his violet eyes upward and met and held Ishitar's gaze. He wasn't offended by Ishitar's joke; he had heard much worse, and often, about his affinity to bed either sex. "But I suppose that I must bide your rejection."

He stepped back and let his eyes trail over Ishitar's well clad figure.

"Good." He muttered. "The shadows of your mantle will hide your face. They don't believe in Lord Lucias. Yet, one doesn't need to believe in Lord Lucias to know the moment that they lay eyes upon you that you are his kindred."

"Unless their name happens to *be* Lucias." Ishitar muttered.

"Znit, znit." Aiken forced himself to give Ishitar a patient smile.

His eyes were still darting over Ishitar with studious interest. As they did so, something burned within Ishitar's eyes that I rarely, if ever, saw.

He very clearly admired Aiken.

He seemed to understand, as Aiken was examining him, that Aiken either didn't trust him or didn't like him. And that, whichever it was that Aiken felt about him, the fairy would never supplicate to him.

"Alright, your Highness." Aiken's eyes flashed as they met and held Ishitar's gaze. "Let us see if we can pass off the very Prince of all peoples as nothing more significant than a eunuch and a slave."

-38-

Though fully dressed in his silks when Pialoron heard the knock on the door, he ordered Aminar into the closet lest he be found immodestly attired and in intimate company. Upon learning that it was his father that had knocked upon his door—and that he was in a perfect rage over the fact that, not only had Pialoron rejected the daughter of Lord Aiken Darklief of the Oakland Grove as his wife, but that Lord Darklief was now here to dress Pialoron down for the insult—he was grateful that Aminar had minded him.

"Papa," Pialoron implored, "the fairies of the Oakland Grove worship every one of the pagan Gods! And they walk freely amongst one and another wearing not even their small clothes!"

"That may be." Lord Elric snapped as they walked together down the hall toward the throne room. The anger pounding from Lord Elric was palpable. "But his is the most powerful tribe of fairy in all of Anticata. We could have established ourselves with an army that would rid us of the menace of the sea dragons for good. As for the girl, you could beat her into submission if she refused to obey our customs and laws!"

"I do not wish to marry a woman I must beat into submission." Pialoron complained, unintentionally.

"Every woman needs a reminder as to her place from time to time." Lord Elric replied haughtily to this. They had reached the Audience Room by now.

"Yet every man in the Oakland Grove has laid his eyes upon her!" Pialoron snarled, crossing his arms over his chest.

Why couldn't his father just give him time to grieve Aminas? Why did he insist on marrying him off so soon after her death?

"She's probably been had by every one of them!"

"Lord Aiken has assured me that her maiden wall has not yet been breached." He turned to his son and gave him a heavy warning. "And I believe him. So if he offers you Princess Triyana's hand again you *will* take it. Do you understand me?" Then, under his breath, "There are enough whispers and accusations regarding the reasons that you refuse to marry as it is."

"You have no worries." Pialoron spat. "I've told you! And you complain out of the other side of your mouth that I did not save myself for marriage by laying with Animas before she died. So which is it that you want of me, father? To be chaste with the women? Or to behave like a man?"

Elric ignored that last part because he couldn't deny the truth in it. Instead, his eyes scoured Pialoron's face, blazing with accusation.

"It's that damned eunuch that concerns me." He grumbled. "Your kindness toward him is unnatural!"

"Our time is innocently enough passed." Pialoron raged, his eyes darting away from his father. "What evil thoughts invade your mind? What must you think of me to voice them aloud?"

Elric's eyes narrowed. "I see the manner in which his gaze trails over you."

"No more than the adoration of a slave for his master." Though Pialoron had the better sense to be frightened. "Or a subject for his Prince. Or a brother for the man who was to marry his sister for that matter!"

"Perhaps." Lord Elric turned away and reached for the door to the Throne Room. "But, perhaps not. So mind your manners with Lord Aiken. And be gracious toward him regardless of your opinion of his bloodline or lack of small clothes."

Sighing, Pialoron forced himself to shove his anger and fear deep into his stomach. Elric was right about one thing: Lord Aiken *was* the most powerful fairy of any tribe in all of Anticata.

The mischief fairies of the Oakland Grove even touted Lord Aiken as the son of one of the pagan Gods that they worshiped.

Pialoron didn't believe this to be true. Nor did he believe that Lord Aiken, or his children, believed such nonsense. Yet, he was familiar enough with politics not to disavow this belief to any member of Lord Aiken's heathen tribe.

As they stepped inside, Pialoron's eyes fell on the strong curve of Lord Aiken's back. The silken tie of the loincloth that was twisted in a bow at the small of his back only served to draw attention to his bare buttocks. Pialoron had the good sense to look swiftly away before his father marked where his eyes had fallen and, incorrectly, assume the worst.

"Lord Aiken." Elric made his tone light and airy as he tried to belie the importance to him of a union between the Oakland Grove and the Sea of Vladtomy. "Here he is. Here is my son."

Lord Aiken—who was taller, even, then Pialoron—turned away from the tapestry that he had been admiring and toward Pialoron and Lord Elric. As he did so, the manservant at his side did the same. Pialoron noted that Lord Aiken had ordered his manservant to obey the custom of Elric's people by donning himself in silks, covering even his hair and darkening the features of his face with shadows.

After having walked among Aiken's people this surprised him.

"Well. If it isn't the boy who finds himself higher in station than a woman born of the bloodline of the Gods." Lord Aiken said. Though Pialoron was quick to note that his smile was light and that his tone was teasing. "Prince Pialoron. I am grieved that I missed your visit to my Oakland Grove. Perhaps I wouldn't have needed to follow you to the Sea of Vladtomy had I made myself available to offer you the gifts that I will bestow upon the man who seeks my daughter's hand."

"My Lord." He bowed low to Lord Aiken and forced his eyes to stay averted to his face, despite his distaste and desire to look away. "I merely found myself unworthy of a beauty such as her upon seeing her fair face."

"Her reputation *does* proceed her, my Lord." Lord Elric remarked in floating tones. "A real beauty so I'm told."

Lord Aiken chuckled under his breath. He had crossed one arm over his well-made chest and raised the hand of the other to his mouth to tug upon his lower lip. "Her face *is* rather blinding."

Pialoron found himself looking upon Lord Aiken with wide eyed surprise. *Has he just insulted his own daughter?*

Aiken turned languidly and held his hand out to the manservant beside him. "This is my eunuch. I call him Joshua."

Pialoron noted that the eunuch raised his face. When he did so, the shadows danced away as the light of the torches touched his strong, well-made features. He gave Pialoron a quiet, almost contemplative smile. Pialoron realized, as he looked upon the man, that the only race that he might possibly be was human.

Human!

Pialoron had never in his life seen a human. Most of the human clans kept well away from those not of their own races because they considered themselves to be superior to all. In fact, he had heard of one town which had a sign on all entry roads that warned those of other races that if they entered the village they would be persecuted—not prosecuted—to the full extent of the law.

How has Lord Aiken actually purchased one to make him his own? Beyond that, how has he convinced the human to obey him enough to adhere to a custom that was not Lord Aiken's?

His mind was teaming with curiosity. He bowed his head to the manservant but allowed himself to pass him no words as they were not appropriate given he was another man's property.

And, he could admit this to himself, given that he was flustered by the actual presence of the human, lest they be jumbled and incomprehensible.

"Lord Elric," Lord Aiken turned to Pialoron's father. "I wonder if you wouldn't be so kind as to give me a moment alone with your son. Perhaps a bit of consideration—aside my daughter's unfortunate face—will give him to change his mind to marry her for the other gifts that she—or I—might bestow."

Pialoron lowered his gaze, embarrassed that he had played the girl's misfortune against her. Truly, he hadn't found her to be that unattractive. She *wasn't*, precisely, unattractive.

Rather, she was just . . .

Not Aminas.

He was suddenly sorry that he might have hurt her feelings by rejecting her.

"I would so like to see hoards of grandchildren blessed of your line and mine." Aiken finished.

"As would I." Lord Elric puffed out his chest and turned, his eyes narrowed, in Pialoron's direction. "I shall draw up the terms of our treaty to aide you against the vampires and the marriage contract once my son has acknowledged the honor that you bestow upon him." Then in seething tones. "I know that he shan't disappoint either one of us a second time."

"I'm certain that he won't." Lord Aiken replied, still holding those teasing, bemused tones. "Given the overly large dowry that her maidenhead carries and the protection that my people can afford you from the menace marching your way."

"Father."

Pialoron gave Lord Elric the appropriate bow as he made his way out of the room. It was Lord Elric that was interested in the dowry. Not Pialoron. Yet, he *was* concerned about the rumors that he had heard regarding demons and vampires making their way to the Sea to cross to the Island of Nononia.

He suspected that Lord Aiken knew both of these things.

He watched his father with keen interest until the door shut and then turned his attention back toward Lord Aiken. As he did so, he marked that Lord Aiken was removing the hood of the mantle from his manservant's head onto his shoulders. His long, delicate fingers began plucking at the human's light brown hair, fluffing it out and arranging it so that it would please him to look upon.

"Pretty." Lord Aiken muttered, grinning at the man he called Joshua, who was looking at Lord Aiken with quiet patience. Aside that, the eunuch's expression was unreadable. "Don't you think so, Pialoron?"

"I wouldn't know to judge another man by his beauty." He muttered, looking away. "Especially not a human man."

Lord Aiken chuckled at that and turned to give him a narrow smile. "Of course you wouldn't."

"I did not mean to insult you, my Lord." Pialoron decided to get right to the point. "Or Princess Triyana. It is merely that I found your daughter—"

"Unpleasing." Lord Aiken shrugged. "She isn't the prettiest of my daughters, to be certain." Pialoron blushed again at the lie of his rejection. He lowered his eyes to his feet. As he did so, Lord Aiken turned to give him his full attention. "But really, Pialoron, you only need bed her when the time comes for propagating the line. And you can mount her from behind so as not to see her offensive face." He chuckled. "The rest of the time—should you live in the Oakland Grove with me—you are free to rut with my women as you please."

"My Lord," Pialoron frowned at him. He was offended on the Lady's behalf. "That is not how we do things at the Sea of Vladtomy. We mate with whom we pair and pair only with those whom we have chosen."

"Is that so?" Lord Aiken asked. His tone had that amused quality to it again and his violet eyes were burning with warm understanding. "But, then, how are you to make little princes when the woman that you've *chosen* to marry has died? And when you, now, do not wish to marry a woman at all?"

"I don't . . ." He shook his head. "It isn't that I do not wish to marry. I merely found your daughter not to my taste."

"Given her lack of a scroll?" Lord Aiken dared to ask.

Pialoron, hating himself for the lie that he would care who the girl's mother was, nodded.

Lord Aiken chuckled under his breath again. The human was watching him with vague curiosity and amusement. "From what

I hear, you shall never, again, find any woman enough to your taste to marry. Scroll or no scroll. From what I understand, your taste now runs to eunuchs."

"My *Lord*!" Pialoron, blushing profusely, cried out, "That is simply untrue! Lies meant to—!"

"Aiken," Joshua said, his tone soft and, to Pialoron's great curiosity, affronted, "this is unproductive and your accusations border on rude."

"Is it?" Lord Aiken grinned. His manservant cocked his head and gave him a strange, commanding gaze. Aiken flapped his hand, almost irritably, at the human. "Oh, very well."

Pialoron would have found this exchange queer, but he had little and less time to focus on the strange relationship between Lord Aiken and his eunuch. Lord Aiken walked to Lord Elric's throne and threw himself within it.

The gesture was so rude as to be offensive! No man ever sat upon the throne of another without the invitation of it! No matter if that man was, by his right, a more powerful tribe's King!

"Triyana doesn't please you because she is a bastard. As are all of my sons and daughters, given I've never married any one of their mothers. And Triyana," this he said regretfully, sadly, "was the only one of my children thus far born with my face and, so, no scroll."

He trailed his finger through the air over his own face as he said this. Pialoron almost believed, by this gesture, that his daughter's plight actually pained him.

Does it? Is he more than a pagan heathen who rapes his women, men and children in equal measure as the rumors suggest he is wont to do?

"I shall not press the point as to the true reasons why you refuse to bind another woman to your side."

"I care not who you are." Pialoron said, ready to spin away because he loathed his own judgments and the fact that this fairy—this *King*—had heard the rumors regarding his odd relationship with Aminar. "I will not bear your insults."

"I do not mean to insult you, boy." Aiken's tone was soft and—damn it—fatherly. "Please. Sit. Palaver with me." Pialoron watched as his eyes flicked to the manservant. Joshua's expression was still soft; still contemplative. "Because you know a fundamental truth in your heart that you cannot deny to me."

"What truth?" He asked, though he did turn to face Lord Aiken.

"Your love for Aminar is innocent and stems only from your love of Aminas." He sighed. "You never would have looked at Aminar twice had he not the feminine qualities of a eunuch who had been made so as a child rather than as a man." He shook his head. "He is pretty and he is childlike. Like a woman. And he reminds you, in his softness, of his sister."

Pialoron lowered his gaze.

"That may be how it started." Lord Aiken's voice was gentle. "But that is not how it is today. You *do* love your eunuch, if only as a brother or a friend." Pialoron raised his gaze, though he couldn't meet Lord Aiken's own. "And you love him now because you love *him*. Not because you love his twin sister."

"I still love Aminas."

"You always shall." Lord Aiken sighed. His tone was heavy. "She was your Shitva. She will always be your Shitva. I have mine own that I have lost. And that one, too, cannot be replaced."

"Is that why you never married?" Pialoron asked, his eyes wide with understanding.

Lord Aiken nodded.

"But never mind about my Shitva. And never mind about yours. You have Aminar today. In the here and now. And Aminar makes you happy. It also helps that Aminar loves you."

"He has to."

Lord Aiken's lips narrowed.

"No he doesn't." He looked away. "Your father bought and paid for him as a babe by selling the flesh between his legs to the dark magi. So, yes, he is bound to serve you. That does not mean he is required to love you."

Pialoron shook his head.

"What is important here, boy, is that if you remain here—unwed—your pretty little eunuch will find himself staked and bound at low tide." Pialoron flinched. "Whereas," he continued, "should you marry my daughter, you are free to live in the Oakland Grove with me and my kindred. Remember that it is Aminar that will be the one to pay for the supposed sins that others believe rest in your heart."

"Aminar is an innocent." Pialoron insisted, not missing at all that Lord Aiken understood everything. "Untouched by anyone. Including me."

"I care not if he is an innocent or if he is not." Lord Aiken smiled kindly upon him. "No more than I care about your innocence where Aminar is concerned." He shrugged. "Pagan Gods that may or may not exist my people *do* worship. Yet, we love our kindred regardless of the internal struggles that they face with their own, very real, demons."

Pialoron raised his gaze to meet Lord Aiken's own.

"If you are to become my kindred—my handsome and much beloved son by marriage—then you will find the ability that you need under my care to protect Aminar in whatever manner that you believe you must." Then with another of his strange laughs. "And all that I ask of you is that you marry my scroll lacking bastardess of a daughter just long enough to make her feel beautiful. To give her the courtesy of your seed but enough times so that she might grant you many sons and daughters. Children who will be very powerful and much loved," he chuckled again, "at least by their pagan God of a grandfather."

"My Lord." Pialoron swallowed, his voice now a whisper. As he did so, his gaze turned to Joshua, who was still watching Aiken with guarded curiosity and quiet surprise. "What you offer me for the price of my seed is all well and good. I fail to see how that protects Aminar."

"Aminar will live as a freeman in my Grove once you marry into my tribe." Aiken shrugged. Then his nose curled in disgust. "I have little and less taste for slavery." He flicked his eyes to

Pialoron. "You and Triyana are free to return here with not the first rumor to follow you. Aminar, however, must, by necessity, stay with me. If he does, then I promise to take him under my protection."

Pialoron was about to question why Aminar must stay and why Lord Aiken would take over the care of him when Lord Aiken whispered, to Pialoron's terror, "You haven't violated him. Nor will you. But the rumors that surround you will damn him." Aiken's violet eyes met Pialoron's silver gaze. "No one, here, is going to forgive him for allowing you to crawl behind him and into his bed. Or for hiding in your closet, waiting for you to return from this conversation to advise him that it is safe for him to return to his own chamber."

Which was only half of it, Pialoron knew. Only what this strange, Oracle King, understood.

"I *haven't* touched him." He whispered. "I am not . . . Aside with my trespasses with Aminas, I *am* worthy to marry your daughter."

"I know that you are, child." Lord Aiken reached for him. He slid his hand beneath the silk that Pialoron wore and wrapped it around the back of Pialoron's head. His strong fingers entwined into Pialoron's long, silver braid. Pialoron, despite his fear of the strange King, found comfort in this gesture. "I told you that I know. And Triyana is also pure and able to marry you intact. Which makes me proud to marry you to her and call you my son." Pialoron melted beneath his smile. "Come to my home, my boy. Marry my daughter to appease the politics of your people." He gave Pialoron another warm, very pointed smile. "Knowing, of course, in your heart, that I will protect your friend once I am looking upon the face of my first grandchild."

Pialoron, who knew well and good the protection that had been afforded him and his friend, smiled.

He would give Lord Aiken all of the grandchildren that the strange King desired as long as the rumors which might damn Aminar would be buried in the sand that troubled his people and the rain that seemed to never stop, often times ruining their crops.

The rains that drown our children whist fishing for their dinner. And our Shitvas, who swim after those children to save them.

He would be happy to raise heathen children in a peaceful world where no one would judge them for the fact that a servant as loyal and true as Aminar stood faithfully at their father's side.

-39-

Iykva stood at the end of the meadow, a grin crossing his handsome face as he reflected on the camp made on the other side.

I am near to enough to claim defeat!

He almost felt sorry for the damn baby Prince.

Almost.

Too much was at stake to find tender feelings now. He had his prize sitting in tents behind him. Even if, so far, their blood had afforded him only an hour in the rising sun, he meant to keep them for his own.

An hour, after all, was better than nothing.

Better than you've known in over three hundred of her cycles.

Distracted as he was, he didn't see the young elf with the long brown hair rise with his bow, threaded with a silver tipped arrow, leveled at his heart.

Nor did he see the blonde elf reaching for the other and pulling him violently into the line of the trees.

Gregor, it would seem, had just saved Iykva's life.

Which was a good thing for the elves and angels camping on the other side of the meadow.

If Iykva would have fallen in that moment, the band of demons surrounding the elves' camp, who had just fed and could withstand that one hour within the light of the rising morning sun, would have destroyed them all.

-40-

"Centaurs." Iladrul raised his gaze to meet Gregor's. "And werewolves, just returned from rutting under the golden moon. Packs and packs of them. I believe that a benandanti leads them. And that even more benandanti have fallen in line."

"How can you possibly *know* that?" Faunus growled. He had been in foul temper since he, Gregor and Haidar had returned from scouting the demon's camp that morning while the elves and angels set up their own.

Iladrul, not having time for his complaints, ignored him.

"How many packs?" Is what he asked.

"Twenty?" Gregor turned to Haidar for confirmation.

"Twenty two." Haidar shook his head. "If I have to guess. They don't interact amongst one another, which is the only way I can tell. That the benandanti was able to bring so many packs to work together—and for vampires, no less—is unsettling."

"Unsettling." Iladrul agreed, absentmindedly. "Any word from the fairies?"

"None." Gregor replied. "At least that we have heard. But that can be a good thing. If they are marching our way and the vampires don't know about that—"

"The element of surprise." Iladrul nodded. Though he wondered, secretly, if he had been duped. Did Emissary Lord Darklief truly intend to align his people with Iladrul's? If so, where *were* they? "Keep your ear to the ground."

"Yes, my Prince." Gregor nodded.

Iladrul turned to Osete, who had been sitting in the shadows, waiting. "Get your father. We need to palaver."

"Yes, my Prince." Osete stood, bowed, and, as ever, then did as he was bid.

"What about my—?"

"I sent him to find more allies." Iladrul waved a hand impatiently at Faunus. Balean had the better sense to know that Jeanir was the stronger of the pair of them. Why couldn't Faunus make the same admission about Gregor? "He'll be back by nightfall."

"You've left the camp unguarded?"

"He's left the camp in the hands of my father." Haidar spat. Iladrul felt his brow raise as he looked up at his doxy. Generally he found himself impatient with Haidar's constant arguments, but, today, he was grateful for them. "And my father runs his commands based on strategy rather than impulse."

"Haidar . . ." Gregor muttered, shaking his head.

"What?" Iladrul snapped. "What aren't you telling me?"

"It's nothing." Gregor sighed. Iladrul didn't believe him. "We're all tired. That's all." He gave Faunus a guarded smile that Iladrul didn't quite trust. "And hungry." He turned his attention to Haidar. "Where's your sister? Can she bring us something to eat?"

Haidar nodded and left the tent. It was then that Gregor looked at Faunus and then back to Iladrul. He bit his lip and then said, "Faunus nearly cost the whole damn war."

"I did not!"

"There were demons and vampires surrounding your camp." Gregor snapped, impatiently. "And he was ready to take out Iykva in front of them all!"

"Faunus." Iladrul turned to him. "Is this true?"

"I had a perfect shot!" Faunus cried. "I could have ended the war!"

"With Prince Iladrul and the rest of our party dead." Gregor seethed. "It was a childish, impulsive move."

"Damn it." Iladrul stood and spun around. Gregor was right. It was a childish move. He glared at Faunus. "You know better, Faun! You don't take out one target when there are twenty threats!"

"There weren't any threats!"

"Do you not have the nose the Gods planted on your face?" Gregor growled at him. "Or is it simply a bauble that is useless?"

"I don't think—!"

"He's right." Iladrul snapped. "I can scent vampires all around us." He shook his head and raised his finger to point at Faunus. "This isn't about your ego. This is about saving the doxies."

"I know that." He pouted.

"Good." Iladrul nodded at him. He returned his attention to Gregor. "What about the men? Are they ready?"

Gregor, his lips thinned, said only, "They'd sure as Loki's beard better be."

-41-

"Chaos." I tell Charlie. "That's what came next. To the point where there is no linear way for me to continue the story. All that I can do is to direct your attention here or there as the battle ensued and hope to make some semblance of sense from it."

"If you believe Stephen King, this is, after all, the manner in which all battles, eventually, play out."

I nod, understanding at once that he is speaking of the strike that Roland Deschaine and his Ka-Tet fought in the final battle to save the beams in King's Dark Tower series.

"In this instance," I advise Charlie, "and for once, Stephen King has the right of things."

-42-

Iykva rose, found an elf and drained the child near to dry as the female that he had paired the boy with stared on in horror. Though he left enough of the would be corpse alive that he would regenerate more blood.

He did, after all, need these bags of bones.

Grinning at that thought, the demon stepped toward Thamores, who was leaning against a tree which gave him a clear view of the meadow. "Good moon, Tham."

Thamores turned his wolfish eyes to Iykva, granting him the very slightest of grins. "Good moon."

"I'm glad your back." Iykva admitted. "And in time for the battle."

"You mean to wage war tonight, then?"

"Yes." Iykva agreed. "They're close. And less than aware that we know that they follow us."

-43-

At the same time, Faunus was storming out of the tent toward his father. He meant to put an end to this foolish business of stable boys and doxies running Prince Iladrul and the war. It was not how things were meant to be done. His father, he knew, would agree with him.

This was his thought as the arrow shot over his left shoulder. He had time to mark its whistle and turn his gaze toward it. He watched, in horror, as the thing flew with nightmare precision to land in the center of Balean's forehead.

His father took two steps back, his arms raising to pull the arrow from his brow, and then fell in a useless heap to the ground.

-44-

Chiron's throat felt as if it were being ripped open as the tattered pain of his cry called his men to arms. They stormed across the meadow, toward the elves and angels, with their bows taut and arrows flying in the wind.

It was his arrow, he would later reflect, that hit the mark to fall General Balean.

-45-

Jeanir heard Balean cry, stumbled out of his tent, screaming after his brother, and fell to his knees. Had he bent his head but a moment sooner, things might have turned out differently.

As it was, the second arrow from Chiron's quiver flew, hitting its mark in complete mimicry as the one that had felled Balean.

Jeanir unmindful of the arrow, twisted violently at his waist, screaming at his daughter to retreat into the tent.

Sezja obeyed without question, tears blinding her eyes and blocking out the horrific vision of her father's face, which was streaming with rivers of blood.

Obeying her father saved her life. Which, in turn, saved the child growing within her womb.

-46-

The battle waged well into the night. Many men, on both sides, fell. It seemed, to Iladrul, who at this point was covered in blood and stumbling blindly with exhaustion, that he was losing this battle.

Which, I understood, all too well, he was.

With Haidar at his side, Iladrul stumbled forward, ready to take out a demon as she crossed his path. His swing was wide and off its mark. Enough so that, as the sword fell at his right hip, he knew that it was his time to die.

"Die proud." He muttered to himself. "This time . . . die proud."

An unnecessary prayer, as it turned out.

-47-

Pialoron saw the young elf fall to his knees. It bolstered him to kick the flanks of his horse to urge her forward into a mad run.

He didn't have arrows—not like the centaurs—and he couldn't change forms to become a wolf.

What he did have was fresh men who hadn't been fighting all night in battle. And now, as both sides were ready to collapse, this small advantage meant much and more.

He saw Xylon and his men on the other side of the meadow and he smiled. To the right of the meadow came the desert tribes. And to the left came those of the northern snows. The fairies, for the first time in thousands upon thousands of cycles of the sun, were, in that moment, united as a single, solid tribe.

The demons, realizing that they were surrounded, didn't stand a chance.

It was no surprise to Pialoron that the final cry he heard rising from the demons and vampires was one of bitter retreat.

-48-

Aiken stepped toward his son, raised his hand and set it, proudly, upon Xylon's shoulder. Xylon, who had never before fought in battle, let alone led an army, turned toward him and smiled. "You came."

"I came." Aiken nodded. "I'm proud of you, child. You fought brave and you fought *well*."

"Nonsense." Xylon's cheeks flushed with heat.

He wasn't used to praise from his father. As such, he coveted these words.

Yet, he understood, the demons and vampires had taken one look at the fairy tribes surrounding them and retreated. Xylon, himself, had had little to do with winning this particular battle of the war.

"Not." Aiken shook his head. "None of your men died needlessly. Nor did those of your enemy or ally. Which makes your attack as successful as it gets."

"Thank you, Fete." Xylon felt his cheeks blaze again. "I see Prince Pialoron. Does this mean that there will be a wedding soon?"

"Soon enough." Aiken's lips twitched at their corners. Xylon wondered what thoughts caused him either his amusement or displeasure. "But today is your day. So let us leave weddings and grandchildren to the side."

Xylon's lips thinned. There it was then. His father was displeased that Xylon, himself, had yet to marry and propagate. "As you say."

It wasn't that he didn't want to take to wife. He did. But he had no interest in any of the fairies from his own tribe and his father seemed more intent on pairing his daughters than in pairing his sons.

"Perhaps you're meant to take a different path." Aiken sighed and looked swiftly away. "No one would judge you."

"I'm not on a different path." Xylon assured him, somewhat irritably. "I seek the softness of a woman. Same as you."

"Same as me." Aiken replied, his sudden smile oddly warm. "Well. Then. That's settled."

"Forgive me." Xylon turned toward the voice and smiled as he realized he had to look up to see the face of the female centaur. "Emissary Lord Darklief, I come at Emissary Lord Dilthrop's command."

Aiken nodded. "I'm surprised he'd bring a mare."

Her thick, equine lips thinned. "Against his better judgment, I can assure you."

Aiken laughed at that. "Yet, smart." He pointed to the ground, indicating the soft grass. "Rest yourself, Lady. If you please."

She did as she was bid. As she did so, Xylon's eyes were drawn to the large blossoms which she used to cover her small breasts. He found it odd that other races insisted upon covering themselves. Yet, as he looked upon her, he also found it intriguing. There was a curiosity that dawned within his mind which never existed when looking at the females of his own people.

"How fares Lord Loki." She asked, her tones thickening. This caused an unwanted stab of jealousy to run through Xylon's veins. No one ever asked his father how *he* fared.

"Loki fares well." Aiken replied, chuckling slightly. "Shall I tell him you asked after him?"

"If you please." She nearly purred, causing another flush of jealousy to run through Xylon's veins. "Shall I make my report?"

"Ta." Aiken replied. His eyes, Xylon noted, flicked swiftly to his son before returning to the centaur. This only served to further embarrass the boy. "If you please."

"Emissary Lord Dilthrop believes that the benandanti, Thamores, can be trusted." She said, her eyes following Aiken's before returning to meet the God's gaze. Xylon felt his cheeks flush, once again, with heat. She was a damn pretty thing to look at. Especially when she was looking at him. "But not his pack."

"Does Tham feel the same?"

"He does, my Lord." She replied, nodding. "He's aligned with Jamiason, from what I understand."

"Good." Lord Aiken muttered, somewhat distractedly.

"My people fought the elves because it was what was expected." Her brow, which was chestnut, like her hair and coat, rose. "Yet, we want our alliance to be with Raystlyn and his people." Her tone was guarded. "Not with Iykva."

"Let me speak with Raystlyn." He advised her. "And explain to him the meaning of your stand."

Rising, she grinned. "Thank you, my Lord." She said. "Chiron will appreciate the assistance."

"As I appreciate his." Aiken stood as well and held out his hand. She took it, raised it to her lips and kissed his knuckles. He pulled hers back and repeated the gesture. Xylon, watching all of this with quiet fascination, smiled. "Please tell him that I shall pass his tidings to his two legged son."

"I will." She replied, lowering her gaze. "Good Sun, my Lord."

"And to you."

-49-

Iladrul lowered himself beside Osete, laying his hand upon his shoulder.

Jeanir was laid out before him on the ground, wrapped from head to toe in white, cotton cloth. Osete had a sponge in his hand which he had been repeatedly dipping into a bowl of water so that he might wipe his father's brow.

"Are you alright?" Iladrul asked, almost hesitantly.

The other boy nodded, but made no response other than this.

Iladrul, understanding, squeezed his shoulder. "May I bring comfort to you?"

Osete shook his head, sat upright and settled his buttocks on his heels. "But, thank you."

Iladrul nodded, leaned toward him and kissed his cheek. He felt Osete's skin grow hot against his lips, causing him to smile slightly as he pulled away. "He was a good man."

"Thank you." Osete whispered.

"I'll find your brothers and sister." Iladrul rose, sat his hand upon the crown of Osete's head and ran it downward over his soft, brown hair. "Tell them to come help you build his pyre."

Osete nodded and turned his gold ringed eyes toward Iladrul. "Faunus needs help as well."

Iladrul's brow furrowed. He raised his gaze, saw Faunus bent over his father, weeping, and let out a tired sigh. He was still too young and unfamiliar with real grief to know how to deal with it.

Forcing a smile, he gave Osete another kiss on his crown and then made his way to his friend. When he reached Faunus, he did not reach for him. This relationship was much different than that he shared with Osete. He did, however, lower himself to Faunus' side.

"Faunus." He said, trying desperately to keep his own grief from the tone of his voice.

Faunus raised his hand and wiped both of his eyes; he was embarrassed by his tears. "My Prince."

"I loved your father, too." It was the only thing that Iladrul could think to say. "I grieve for your loss."

"Thank you." This was a whisper, cracked with boyish tears.

"May I help you wrap him?"

Faunus turned his haunted brown eyes to Iladrul and let out a grateful sob. "You would do so?"

"I would consider your allowance of me to do so an honor." Iladrul nodded as he forced another smile. "I must find the doxies, first, however. They must help Osete grieve their own father."

"Of course." The relief in Faunus' expression was painful to bear witness to. "I'll procure a basin of water so that we might wash him."

Iladrul reached for him and clapped him lightly on the back. After doing so, he rose to his feet and made his way toward his tent. He knew that the other three boys were there, with Sezja, comforting her.

As he slipped in, the air of sorrow surrounded him, very nearly suffocating him. He, once again, forced a smile as he stepped toward Sezja. He took his beloved in his arms and kissed her forehead. She buried her face against his shoulder and wept. As she did so, he raised his gaze to meet Macentyx'.

"Osete needs the four of you to help him." He tried to sound calm and kind. "And I must assist Faunus with General Balean."

Sezja let out another hitching sob. He found his hand raising upward so that he could cup the back of her head in his palm and tangle her hair in his fingers.

"Will he be alright?" Haidar asked, shifting uncomfortably at Macentyx's side. "Faunus, I should mean."

Iladrul gave him a perfunctory nod. "Once his father is washed, clothed and set to a proper pyre."

"Did you see Faunus during battle?" Macentyx asked. "He cowered like a mewling puppy. And he's meant to lead your army? It seems he begs the vampires to win."

"Now is not the time." Iladrul flared at his doxy.

Yes. He had seen Faunus duck behind the trees when the battle had begun. And, yes, he had seen Gregor rise up and lead Balean's men. The only reason more of them hadn't been slaughtered had been by the good grace of Emissary Lord Darklief's assistance and by Gregor's wit and bravery.

The conversation would be required. He understood that.

But not today.

Not while Balean lay cold and dead and covered in his own blood. Not before the fallen were put to pyre.

"Come." He finally said, kissing Sezja on the forehead once more. "There are men who must be honored. Our own tears—and scheming—must wait."

$\mathcal{P}$ART $\mathcal{T}$HREE: $\mathcal{W}$ORDS $\mathcal{M}$ISSPOKEN

-1-

When Loki demanded that Ishitar visit Lucias so that he might meet our half-brother, Ishitar, though pleased that Loki was beginning to show his fire, was less than anxious to go. He was still angry with Lucias for having denied being his mother.

He made his excuses and the visit was delayed.

Loki, at first, seemed not to care. His mind was buried in the tome that he so desperately wanted to translate and his own anger toward Lucias for having promised little Gorgon's services to Noliminan in exchange for Michael's.

As for the obsession over the book, this was something that Zadkiel, who had become impatient over missed Seventh Day dinners and so now made them at Loki's, was greatly amused by.

Loki had fallen asleep at his desk, slumped over his notes. Zadkiel, who couldn't read the damn book any more than Loki could, stole some of his papers. He then copied the majority of it onto another page, changing Loki's interpretation of them just enough to lead him astray, yet not enough that Loki would notice.

It was nothing overt and I could tell that Ishitar found great amusement with our brother's childish prank as he watched Zadkiel slip the copies onto Loki's desk in the exact position from which he had stolen the original prints. He then gave Loki a good firm shake to wake him up before using his magic to return to the chair at Ishitar's side.

Loki flew upward at his desk, his eyes darting around the room as he searched for whomever it was that had shaken him. Ishitar made it a point to keep his attention diverted to his own weighty tome, though he was watching Loki very intently from the periphery of his vision and biting his cheek to keep himself from smiling.

"Did either of you say something?" Loki asked them, his brow furrowed and his dark purple eyes still darting around the room as he sought out the person who had awoken him.

Ishitar turned a bored gaze toward Loki, swallowing back the laugh that rose in his chest as he watched Zadkiel begin to toy with the hem of his skirt. "I'm sorry?"

"I asked if one or the other of you said anything." Loki replied.

"No." Ishitar muttered before biting his cheek again.

Loki sighed, pushed his chair back and stood. "I guess I'm done in." Ishitar, still biting his cheek, could only nod at him. "I'll see you in the morning."

"Good night."

Loki walked toward the door, stopping when he reached it. He turned, almost hesitantly, in Ishitar's direction. "I know that you're still angry with your mother, but—"

"I am in no mood for a lecture, Loki." Ishitar groused, his good humor suddenly drained away.

"I don't mean to give you a lecture, Ishitar." Loki yawned around his words. "But you have to go and see the babe tomorrow. Lucias has promised your father to have Countenance see to his aging. She's waiting for you to take a peek before she allows this and Noliminan is losing patience with her."

"And by the next time I see Lucias she'll be surrounded by sons and daughters." Ishitar snapped at him. "I don't care, Loki. Tell her to go ahead and—"

"No." Loki's tone had a hard bite to it. "Whatever animosities you have toward your mother are your own and I won't try to sway you against them."

Ishitar, seemingly surprised by Loki's irritated regard, raised his gaze to meet Loki's. After the fifth pie, which had been eaten earlier that day, Loki, it would seem, had finally found his fire.

"But none of that is little Gorgon's fault. Nor mine. It isn't fair that you let your hurt feelings get in the way of what's right where we are concerned. I must make my demands upon you that you go."

Ishitar sighed at that. Though Loki would never be able to demand anything of him—he wasn't about to give the God that many pies—Loki was behaving exactly how Ishitar needed him to behave to play out what ever game he was playing.

As for the baby, he was right. Gorgon was Ishitar's half-brother. No matter that he was jealous of the boy for his ability to be raised by their mother, he owed it to the child to at least try and love him.

Zadkiel, reached for Ishitar's hand and squeezed it. "He's right, Ishitar."

"I know." He replied to both of them. "Very well, Loki. First thing in the morning."

Loki gave him a doubtful nod and took his leave.

-2-

Gregor sat in the corner of the tent and watched as Iladrul began pacing back and forth in front of Faunus, who sat with his head lowered into his cupped hands. Prince Trevor watched the younger Prince, his dark eyes marking each step that Iladrul took. Prince Pialoron sat on Prince Trevor's left and Prince Xylon on his right.

It was Prince Pialoron who broke the silence. "My father will block their path to Port Town at the Sea of Vladtomy."

Iladrul stopped pacing and turned to give him a weary smile. As he did so, Xylon said, "And my father set fire to their fleet. They have no choice but to go inland."

"Handy having a God on your side." Iladrul muttered as he threw himself into the remaining empty chair. As he said this, Prince Pialoron gave him a strange, guarded frown. "We could use more of them."

Xylon shook his head. "He isn't allowed to utilize his immortal powers in a mortal war."

"Convenient." Prince Pialoron snorted. Gregor found himself turning his gaze in the fairy's direction. "Where would they go?"

"To their castle." Every pair of eyes turned toward Gregor but those belonging to Faunus. He shrugged under the scrutiny of their gazes. "It's what I would do."

"It is certainly fortified." Prince Trevor muttered his agreement. "They walled the windows so that sun cannot get through. There are virtually no openings aside the front and back entry."

"What are the chances we can impregnate it?" Prince Pialoron asked.

"Slim." Prince Xylon sighed.

"They'll try to get to their ships first." Gregor stood and walked toward the tactical map. "They don't know they've been destroyed yet." Looking down at the map, he pointed his finger to the village that Prince Pialoron's people came from. "Your father's men will stop them here."

"Yes." Prince Pialoron agreed, turning toward the map and cocking his head slightly so that he could get a better view of it. "That's right."

"If they happen to skirt around your village," he trailed his finger along the tract of land that led in the direction of Port Town, which was the harbor from which any fleet wishing to cross the Northern Sea must depart. He pounded his finger on the map again, then trailed it southward, to the edge of the forest. "Our best bet is to cut through these woods and wait for them here."

"Cut through . . ." Prince Trevor's brow furrowed as he leaned toward the map. "The Forest of *Spirits*?"

"Yes."

"We can't . . ." Faunus' voice trembled. "It's haunted."

Gregor flashed him an irritated scowl. "What of it?"

"It's rumored that no one who goes in ever comes out." Prince Xylon muttered.

"Maybe. But it *is* the last place they'd ever suspect we would go." Prince Pialoron offered as he leaned in closer. "Though it's a long march."

"No matter which way we go," Iladrul sighed, "it's a long march." He raised his hand and set it on Gregor's shoulder. "And we elves are running low on supplies. At least, in the

259

forest, there will be food on the hoof. Enough to feed my men and women."

"It's risky." Prince Xylon sat back and met Gregor's gaze. "But you're right. It's our best course."

"Are you certain about this?" Iladrul asked Gregor.

"I've always wanted to see a ghost." Gregor shrugged.

This earned him a small smile. Iladrul nodded at him as he turned to the others in the group. It was Faunus who he addressed. "And you?"

Faunus looked at each face in turn, swallowed and then gave a curt nod. Gregor was pleased that he seemed to have the better sense to realize that he was out numbered. That his vote, in the end, would come to nothing.

"So be it." Iladrul, looking somewhat relieved, raised his hand and clapped Gregor on the back. "Let's go and find ourselves some ghosts."

-3-

Returned to his cottage, Zadkiel pulled the sheet of paper that Loki had translated from the pocket of his robes. He had feigned ignorance when Ishitar had asked him if he understood any of Loki's ramblings. He didn't believe that he had lied, exactly. The symbols that Loki had copied were as foreign to him as they were, apparently, to Loki.

All of them, that was, except one.

King Noliminan's symbol. The symbol that he pressed into hot wax when he wanted to seal his letters.

And right after that symbol was one that Loki had—Zadkiel knew this in his soul, though how he wasn't sure—rightly translated.

The symbol meant father.

Noliminan's father . . . ?

Zadkiel pondered this for long and long after he lowered himself awkwardly into one of the chairs at his table.

"Noliminan's father." Zadkiel said the words aloud and shivered.

Perhaps it's a riddle. Perhaps it means nothing more than the void from which he was created.

That seemed logical.

It was common knowledge that before Noliminan there was nothing at all. He was the first. *The* father.

Perhaps the riddle is Noliminan fathered. Or, sired. Or, for that matter, created.

"That must be it. It's a verb in this context. Not a noun." He muttered to himself as he pulled on his bottom lip. "Noliminan fathered Lucias."

He knew within his heart that if he were to look at the order of things in the book that Loki always carried around that he would see the three symbols in succession. Noliminan's, then the one that stands for father, and then Lucias'.

Relieved that he had solved that puzzle, he pushed himself to his feet and shuffled on his crippled leg toward his bed.

- 4 -

Paul followed Iykva down the rows of tents, his lips pursed and his eyes narrowed. It took every ounce of strength in him not to lunge forward and strangle the demon. Knowing that dispatching Iykva would do little to resolve his problem, however, he forced himself to stay his hand.

"It makes no earthly sense!" Iykva growled as he leaned forward and pulled open the flap of one of the tents. As with every other tent, the occupants, sitting on opposite sides, merely looked back at them with wide, haunted eyes. "What is *wrong* with you?"

"Perhaps they're frightened." Paul suggested, glaring at Iykva. "Or perhaps they're still too young."

Iykva threw the flap of the tent closed and spun on Paul. "If we don't get fresh crops, then this has all been for naught. We can't keep feeding from them at the rate that we are and expect them to be able to continue to replenish themselves."

"No." Paul agreed. "We can't."

Iykva glared at him for a long moment. Finally, he spun away. "Bring me Thamores."

"To what purpose?"

"Until I see the swell of a belly," Iykva growled as he began storming away, "not one more neck is to be bent. Not by me, not by you, not by *anyone!*"

Watching Iykva's back as he stormed away, Paul felt his lips curl into a satisfied smile. Whether the demon recognized it to be true or not, Iykva had just granted Paul and Jamiason the precious gift of time.

-5-

Raphael watched the King of Lords as he leaned over his Crect'antee, which is a large bowl with a golden liquid that brews within it. Noliminan uses it to watch a particular mortal when he hasn't a desire to send Metatron to pay visitation upon them. To Raphael, he had, lately, seemed to be more and more interested in the first born elf. Raphael wondered why this should be so, but he had learned long ago not to question the King of Lords when he took a peculiar interest in one mortal over all of the others.

What troubled Raphael about this particular interest was that King Noliminan's general obsessions were over those mortals of the female persuasion. He thought nothing at all of pretending to be a member of their race and either seducing or raping them. It was something that Raphael had long found distasteful, but about which he always held his tongue.

"He is a pretty thing." King Noliminan muttered.

"Yes." Raphael agreed that he was. As he would be a very handsome man, once he grew out of his boyishness. "He is, your Grace."

"The politics that his forefathers have insisted upon puzzle me to no end."

They puzzled Raphael as well. The angels had revolted against the Heavens because they had felt as if they were oppressed as slaves. Yet, the moment that they had the opportunity to set up a social system where equality reigned for all, they instead mimicked the class racing of the Sixty Realms.

"Yes, your Grace."

"These doxies." He chuckled under his breath and shook his head. "I should want to own one of mine own."

Raphael chose not to respond. The King of Lords owned not only one doxy, but twelve. Baser raced angels the Quorum may not be, but they were—as Haniel's friend Raystlyn had once so adequately pointed out—little more than higher priced slaves.

Pondering this, Raphael had been ill prepared for the knock on the door. He jumped slightly and then let out an embarrassed giggle as King Noliminan looked at him with an expression that was a mixture of both annoyance and amusement.

"It's just Raziel, Raph." He said as his gaze returned to the Crect'antee. "She has an appointment, if you'll recall."

Raphael, who didn't recall that, gave him a flustered smile. He knew every minute of King Noliminan's schedule better than the King of Lords, himself, did. As such, he was certain that this visit was either impromptu or illicit.

"Yes, your Grace." Is what he said as he found his feet and made his way out of the library to the front door. When he saw the Lady Regent standing on the other side he understood that he had the right of things. "Good evening, Raziel."

"Raph." Raziel stepped in, leaned forward and kissed Raphael's forehead. Raphael bore this with guarded patience. Raziel was, after all, his mother. "Is he about?"

"In the library." Raphael nodded as he stepped away. "Shall I serve you drinks?"

"Not tonight." Raziel stepped past him. "In fact, why don't you make yourself scarce?"

Raphael, unsurprised by this request, rolled his eyes. He had wanted nothing more than to just turn in. But he gave Raziel an assenting nod. "Of course."

"He isn't entertaining another woman, is he?" Raziel asked with flat tones and her nose curled.

Would you have been invited to his bed if he were?

"No." He muttered. "He's merely watching the elf."

Her smile was sly and catlike. Raphael shivered under the coldness of it. "He does lately seem obsessed by that foul creature."

"Yes, my Lady." Raphael replied, trying not to glower at her. "If his Grace needs me, please have him ring my bell."

"I shall, Raphael." Raziel replied, turning away and dismissing Raphael entirely.

Without even realizing that he was doing so, Raphael stared at Raziel's back and shook his head in dismay.

-6-

"Where, exactly, have you been?" Karma snapped as she swung the little lizard creature that she was tending from one hip to the other.

Michael turned to her and glared. "None of your concern."

"You've been gone for three morning suns!" She groused. "And left Max and I alone with these little monsters."

After a full moon of taking care of the little beasts, she was tired and frustrated. Of the four thousand eggs originally laid, a little less than fifty of them had survived the incubation period. And half of those that had were now ill with a virus that was spreading among them swifter than a fire amongst dry kindling.

The Gods only knew how they would have managed had all of the eggs survived.

"There was somewhere I was meant to be." He growled at her. As he did so, he turned his head away from her. When he spoke, his voice held a distant quality. "It couldn't be avoided."

"You could have at least told us that you were leaving!"

"I tried." He muttered, turning his head so that he was looking at her again. As he did so, she felt her brow furrow. His black eyes were moist and puffy. And his lips were set in such a way as to suggest that he was biting the inside of his cheek to stay his words.

Is he about to cry?

She found herself blinking at him. She didn't want to feel any type of regard for him, but if something had upset this particular man enough that he would cry over it then the world had most definitely come to dire straits.

Michael wasn't they crying type. He was gruff and mean and with never a kind or understanding word.

"What's the matter?"

"You wouldn't understand." He snapped, reaching for the babe in her arms and bringing it to his lips so he could bury his face in its thick, black hair. "He has a fever."

"You don't say?" Her lips pursed. "They *all* have fevers."

Sighing, he lowered the babe so that she could see his face and gave her a snappish nod.

"If we don't do something soon—"

"I know." He replied, frowning at her. As he did so, he handed the baby back to her. "Here. I'll be back."

"Where are you going *now*?!" She was infuriated with him!

"To visit my father." He replied turning away from her. She forced herself not to start. Lord Lucias had been exiled. If it were learned that Michael had gone to visit him, Michael could be severely punished. "He'll know what to do."

"Are you certain that's wise?"

He glowered at her.

"Do you have any better ideas?" She shook her head. "Didn't think so."

"But, if the King of Lords—"

"Oh." Micheal replied, his expression drawn and tight. "Haven't you heard?"

"Heard?" She didn't like the fire that suddenly lit his eyes.

"I no longer serve Noliminan."

"What?" She started; as much from his disrespect from saying the King of Lord's name without adding fealty as from his angry words. "Why do you blather?"

"You heard me right." He muttered as he turned away. "I'm an Exile."

"But—" Despite her personal feelings about Michael, she felt a tug of unwanted pity for him in that moment. "What—Why?!"

He turned to face her again. The tears that she had seen earlier had sprung back into his eyes. "For breaking the one rule that would most bruise Noliminan's pride."

She shook her head violently.

Michael? Breaking a rule?

"I made the fool mistake of falling in love with his wife."

The ground seemed to open up around her. She couldn't comprehend his words to possibly mean what they must. "Michael . . . Surely, not with Raziel?"

His lips pursed and he looked swiftly away.

When he spoke, it was in a low whisper.

"I fell in love with Queen Raguel."

"Raguel?" Her nostrils flared in anger at the stupidity of the idea.

"That's where I went." He growled at her. "When I received my orders." He looked away from her again, infuriating her. She deserved his attention in that moment. "To her grave."

Karma felt the anger within her soul explode around her.

She and Max had been busting their humps taking care of Michael's charges and the archangel had been wasting his time mourning over the grave of a long dead woman that he had no business having ever loved in the first place.

"I should make haste."

She glared at him, watching his back as he walked away. Long after he was gone, she found that she was still staring at the spot where he had stood.

She knew she would eventually cross words with him over this.

266

-7-

Jamiason watched with deep intensity as Evanbourough paced back and forth across the tent that had been constructed for James' use. He had been expecting this lecture since the moment that Iykva had stepped out of line. And, he understood that, given the rest of the Council believed Evanbourough to still be the reigning God of his race, he had no choice but to allow his old friend to rant.

"Theasis is livid." Evanbourough snorted as he made another turn, followed by another pass. "She says that if you don't put an end to this madness—and soon—there will be the Hells' fire to pay."

"What can she do?" Jamiason asked, standing and spreading his hands. "Anyway, she isn't angry with me and mine. She's nattered with you and the manner in which you left things with her."

Evanbourough's thick lips thinned as he spun to face Jamiason. Though James had only recently earned his black wings at the end of the first revolution, he understood the price that many had paid when their ability to shift in and out of their essence had been stripped away from them. Theasis and Evanbourough's affair had been only one of many which had been violently ended on that fateful day.

"She isn't the only member of Council who has noticed the goings on between your people and the elves."

"I'm doing what I can." Jamiason forced himself to sigh. "I've engaged the wolves—"

"Madness." Evanbourough snorted.

"Thamores will be loyal."

"Perhaps." Evanbourough shook his head. As he did so, his long black hair danced over his shoulders, catching the flicking light of the candles which surrounded them. To Jamiason, with his preternatural vision, it seemed as if Evan's hair had literally caught fire.

He thought fondly, for a moment, of the archangel, Metatron, and repressed a smile.

"But he has no control over his wolves." Evan's lips thinned again. "No more than you do over your vampires."

Jamiason's lips pursed. "What would you have me do?"

"Set those damn elves free!" Evanbourough stormed at him. "Before irreparable damage is done!"

"It's already *been* done." Jamiason started at the sound of Paul's voice. Distracted by Evanbourough's presence, he hadn't realized that the lad had slipped into the tent. "Aiken's people will never back down. You do realize that."

Evan growled under his breath. "And then there's *that* one."

"Aiken's people are siding with Thea." James countered. "Isn't that what you wanted? An out for the elves."

"In the form of the Gods be damned mischief fairies?"

"It's all fairies, my Lord." Paul corrected Evan. "From all tribes."

This only served to annoy Lord Evanbourough. "Regardless." He snorted. "I know how to placate Thea." His nostrils flared. "But there are others, more powerful than I, who will ignore all attempts."

"No one of any import gives a damn about the elves." Jamiason groused.

"Not so." Evanbourough stormed. "Raphael tells me that the King of Lords has taken an interest in the first one."

"The King of Lords?" Paul started. "Why would he care about an insignificant elf?"

"Who knows why the King of Lords ever takes an interest in what he does?" Evanbourough complained. "The point is that he has. So you'd best be wary."

Wary, Jamiason thought, *and weary.*

His back already bore a target where the King of Lords was concerned due to an outburst that he had once had at Council. When it had been determined that James would be exiled without so much as the benefit of a trial, Jamiason had stormed toward his Ruler and demanded to know the reasons why. The one who had paid for that outburst had been Aiken. The King of Lords had turned his anger toward the fairy God for his failure to keep his property in line.

"I'll take care of it." He assured Evanbourough as his eyes flicked to Paul. "*We'll* take care of it."

"See that you do." Evanbourough admonished before he was, quite simply, gone.

-8-

Michael stood before the door to his father's cottage with his heart in his throat. The letter from the King of Lords, which gave him his orders and outlined the terms of his exile, burned in his hand.

How was he to face his father and admit his failure to him? What would Lord Lucias' reaction be when he learned that Michael was now permanently in service to him rather than Noliminan?

Knowing there was nothing else for it, he raised his hand and knocked on the door. When he did so, he heard the barking of a dog on the other side and his brow furrowed. He recognized that bark. It belonged to the Prince of Providence's lately come by pet.

When the door opened, Michael was less than surprised to see Sappharon on the other side. Her strangely beautiful face was drawn in its scowl of general irritation as she crossed her arms over her small breasts. Her hands began flapping wildly at him, but he did not understand their gestures. As such, he forced himself to straighten his back and respond with false brevity.

"I must see Lord Lucias." He muttered. "Under orders of the King of Lords."

She snorted, rolled her eyes and turned away from him. Terrified of what would come to pass, he swallowed the bile in his throat and followed her.

She led him down the hall to a closed door. Before knocking, she turned to him and made the odd flapping gestures with her hand again. When his brow furrowed in confusion, she let out another irritated snort and then knocked on the door.

It was Prince Ishitar's voice that responded, "Come."

Confused, Michael pushed past Sappharon and opened the door. As he did so, his breath caught in his chest.

The woman on the bed, holding the swaddled bundle, was more than beautiful. She was exquisite. Her features, chiseled to perfection, were set in an expression that was warm and content. Her full lips, pink as any rose petal that Michael had ever seen, were curled into a smile. And her eyes—dark brown eyes that were as familiar to Michael as his own mother's—were soft as they caressed his features.

"Michael." She said, her smile broadening. "My son."

"My . . ." He swallowed and shook his head. "Lucias?"

"Ta." Her smile softened. "And I have been expecting you." She pressed the bundle toward Prince Ishitar, who sat on the bed at her side. He took it rather reluctantly as he gave Michael a grave, almost foreboding, smile. "Come, child. Meet your half-brother."

Michael's eyes flicked to Prince Ishitar, who was holding the bundle close to his chest. His brow furrowed with confusion as he took a step forward and reached for the edge of the blanket. As he pulled it away, his heart screamed with discontentment. As he looked deep into the baby's vertical, yellow green eyes, every fiber of his being cried out in horror.

"What the . . . ?" He shivered and stepped swiftly away as one of the snakes that made up the baby's hair entwined itself around Prince Ishitar's wrist. "It's a monster!"

"It's a Gorgon." She purred. "He's my son."

Shaking his head, Michael raised his gaze to glare at her. "The King of Lords' . . . ?"

"No." Her smile was tender and warm. "Loki's."

"Loki's!" He cried out. Ishitar, he noticed, pursed his lips as if irritated. "What madness do you speak of?!"

"It isn't madness." Her smile widened. "It's genius. This lad is the first of twelve."

"Twelve . . . ?"

"Ta." She reached for the babe and lovingly caressed the snake around Prince Ishitar's wrist. "A Quorum of mine own." Her eyes flicked up to meet Michael's. "And you are to be the first member."

"Madness." He hissed again.

"Not at all." She shrugged. "Surely, you didn't believe I'd allow Raziel to warm my throne forever."

"Well, no, but—"

"I don't intend to return as Lord Regent." She leveled her gaze on him. Her smile had fled her lips. She sat before him as he had always known her: all business. "I shall be the Queen of Ladies. And Loki," her grin returned, "shall be my beloved Lord Regent."

"Madness!" He repeated.

"Madness or not," she shrugged, "you'd best come to terms with my plans. Because you, Michael, shall be the warrior to seat me on my throne."

Clarity struck Michael in that moment. A clarity so vivid as to tear his sanity asunder.

She had been responsible for Queen Raguel's death. She had been the one to take his Lady from him.

Now, looking upon her, he understood all too well her true motivation for having done so.

And, oh, dear Gods . . .

How he *loathed* her for this.

-9-

When Raphael opened the door to the King of Lords' apartment to find Lord Loki standing on the other side, he couldn't have been more surprised. Generally, the pair avoided one another like a well spread plague.

"Lord Loki!" He gave the young God a welcoming smile. Despite King Noliminan's feelings for Loki, Raphael had always admired the man. "How might I help you?"

"I've been summoned." He muttered, his lips drawing thin beneath his ever so famous beard. "Is he in?"

"Yes." Raphael's brow furrowed. "Please. Come in. I'll announce you at once."

"I have the feeling that I am more than expected." He crossed his strong arms over his chest and cocked his head slightly to the side. "Didn't tell you what he wanted me for, I take it."

"No." Raphael shook his head. "I had no idea that you'd even been requested."

Loki snorted and waved his hand at Raphael. "I can find my own way."

"I'd best follow." Raphael granted him a thin smile. His presence in the room wouldn't prevent the King of Lords from berating Lord Loki if that was his intent. But it may temper him enough to hold Raphael's Master at bay. "He may need me to keep a history of the meeting."

Loki looked over his shoulder at Raphael and gave him a strange, tight smile. "For prosperity's sake?"

Raphael laughed in spite of himself. "Just so."

Shrugging, Loki turned away from Raphael and continued to the library. Once there, he knocked on the open door and leaned in. "You summoned me?"

King Noliminan's light brown eyes blazed as they scanned the length of Lord Loki before flicking to one of the chairs on the other side of his desk. "Sit."

Raphael was relieved when Lord Loki complied without argument or comment.

"While you see to the aging of that monster you call a child--"

"Careful, you're Grace." Lord Loki's eyes narrowed. Raphael flinched. "You speak of a member of your Quorum." His lips thinned. "And of your wife's son."

The King of Lord's nostrils flared as his own eyes narrowed. "What do you intend to do with your demon?"

"He'll bide the damned ones." Lord Loki shrugged and sat back in his chair. "By any road, I'll only be gone for three waxing moons by your shadows."

"But several cycles of the sun by yours." The displeasure on his features as he made this statement caused Raphael to shiver. "Breeding more monsters, if my wife has her way."

To this, Lord Loki only shrugged.

"Your demon cannot be free to wander about." He snapped. "You will put him in Raphael's care until such time as you return."

"Prince Ishitar is more than capable of—"

"Ishitar has his own responsibilities to tend to." The King of Lords grunted. "Your demon stays here. With me."

Raphael watched Lord Loki stiffen. "I don't think—"

"That is your greatest problem," King Noliminan spat. "You don't think." He flicked his eyes to Raphael. Raphael swallowed back his fear and waited. "See that he's moved, Raphael. And at once."

"Yes, your Grace." Raphael's voice quavered as his eyes turned to Lord Loki. "I'll see that he's comfortable, my Lord."

"You'll see that he behaves." King Noliminan corrected Raphael. "His comfort means little and less to me. His obedience, however, I demand."

"You can't expect Sam—" Lord Loki tried.

"I can,' King Noliminan seethed, his eyes narrowing even further, "and I do."

Raphael watched in silence as Lord Loki shifted in his chair. He appeared to be battling some internal demon that only he could see; grappling for the proper response that would convince the King of Lords to change his mind about Samyael.

"Very well." He finally replied. "I will speak with Sam and I will order him to obey you."

The self-satisfied smirk that crossed King Noliminan's face was chilling.

Raphael, once again, shivered.

"See that you do."

-10-

Wisterian bit the inside of his cheek as he raised his hand to knock on the door to Raystlyn's library. This was the last place in any one of the inhabited worlds that he had any desire to be. Yet, after receiving Jamiason's letter explaining the battle that had ensued between the elves and the vampires, he knew he had no choice.

Especially given that Iladrul's letter had followed shortly thereafter, detailing his losses.

Were it not for Emissary Lord Darklief, Iladrul's party would have been completely obliterated. As it was, the fairy tribes had arrived in time to protect Wisterian's son. And the only thing that Aiken had asked from Wisterian, in return, was to seek Raystlyn's aide and send him to join the fray.

He knocked; then he waited.

When the door opened, he wasn't as surprised to see the archangel Haniel as he knew that common sense warned him that he should be. There had been rumors abound before the first revolution that Haniel and Raystlyn were friends. Still, given Haniel served the King of Lords directly, his disobedience, and his willingness to risk the wrath of his Master, was duly noted.

"Sir Haniel." Wisterian gave him the proper bow. "Is Raystlyn available?"

Haniel gave him a wary look, nodded, and then slipped past him. When he was outside the door, he turned toward Wisterian and asked, "Does it need to be said that you didn't see me here?"

"Of course not." Wisterian gave him what he hoped was an assuring smile.

"I'm grateful." Haniel nodded his head to Wisterian, jumped upward and took wing.

Wisterian watched him until he was out of sight, marking that he was flying in the direction of where it was rumored that Michael and the dragon eggs resided. He pondered for the briefest of moments that, if this is where Haniel was headed, the archangel had twice broken the rules of exile.

Wisterian decided that this matter of his better was one best put out of his mind.

When he found the arch mage, it was in the kitchen, dishing out a bowl of stew. Probably it was one of the brews that Haniel was known for making. It certainly smelled divine.

"Wisterian." Raystlyn frowned at him from where he stood at the fire pit. "What a . . . surprise."

Wisterian gave him a wintery smile. "I need your help."

"*My* help?"

"Surely word regarding the war that my people have been dragged into has reached even these dark halls." Wisterian teased him wearily. Given the bad blood between them, he wasn't in the mood for pleasantries.

"It has." Raystlyn stood to his full height then. As he did so, a shadow of concern darkened his features. "Iladrul is . . . ?"

"He has survived the heavy battles." Wisterian crossed his arms over his chest. "Actually, it is Iladrul that I've come to discuss with you."

"Oh?" His tone was cautious and curious.

"Tell me true, Raystlyn." Wisterian felt his eyes narrow. "Who is the boy's father?"

Raystlyn shifted uncomfortably by the fire before grabbing his bowl and stepping to the table. "Does it matter who sired him?"

"It could save his life."

Raystlyn raised his gaze to meet Wisterian's. "In what way?"

"If he has your blood in him . . ." Wisterian flinched at the very thought that this might be true. "You could teach him to harness your magic."

Raystlyn considered him for a minute before looking swiftly away.

"Raystlyn," Wisterian heard the pleading in his tone. He didn't much care for it so he bit it back. "If that lad is your son—"

"Why unbury the past?" Raystlyn frowned as he returned his gaze to Wisterian. "What good can come from it? Even if he did inherit my magic, he's too old, now, to properly harness it."

"What if he isn't?" The pleading was back in his tone. But, now, Wisterian didn't care. Even if he was not Iladrul's biological father, the boy was every inch his son. "Raystlyn, please. If there is even the slightest possibility that you can teach him to defend himself, you owe it to the lad to do so."

"Don't you mean that I owe it to *you*?" Raystlyn asked.

"It would be a debt repaid." Wisterian offered. "The issue would be forever buried between us."

Raystlyn considered Wisterian with his strange silver eyes before looking swiftly away. Finally, after what seemed an eternity to Wisterian, he said, "Fine."

Wisterian was overcome with relief.

"But know this, Wisterian," he warned, "The child will not know how the magic came to be in his blood. I have no intention of drawing any more attention to myself to the eyes of the Gods than I already have."

Wisterian felt his lips purse at that. It was true that, as the first angel to publically admit to standing at Lord Lucias' side during the first rebellion, Raystlyn had taken the brunt of the anger from the Gods who had stood on the side of the King of Lords. Though, he failed to see how admitting that Iladrul was his child could harm Raystlyn. The affair between the arch mage and Wisterian's wife was, in no way, a secret.

Still, rather than antagonizing him, he nodded his head in agreement.

"Very well." Raystlyn muttered. "I'll take wing after I finish my supper."

"Your kindness," Wisterian assured him, "will not be forgotten."

Raystlyn, not quite taking Wisterian at his word, gave the angel a tight smile and returned his attention to his evening meal.

-11-

Haniel was well aware of the risks that he was taking by visiting Raystlyn and Michael. Yet, after receiving a letter from Lord Lucias explaining Michael's current plight, he felt compelled to do so. Michael, it would seem, was in need of his brews. And, given he was already breaking the rules of exile, what harm would there be in stopping in to visit an old friend before making his way to the grove where the lizard men had hatched?

He understood that his justification would not serve him were the King of Lords to discover that he had betrayed his orders. Yet, given his brother's fate, he was less than concerned for his own skin. If Michael could be exiled for the mere turn of his thoughts then not a one of the members of the Quorum was safe.

So why continue to play by misguided rules?

Knowing Michael as he did, Haniel should have expected his brother's reaction upon opening the door to find him standing on the other side. Fierce, loyal Michael was livid with him for putting himself at risk. He lectured Haniel for his constant insistence upon defying King Noliminan's orders and breaking the King of Lords' rules.

"You have always been far too defiant." Michael seethed as Haniel, who had merely shrugged off his admonition, stepped past him into the small cottage that he shared with another angel and Emissary Lord Darklief's eldest daughter. "One of these days it will land you in trouble."

"And you have always been far too level headed." Haniel retorted as he passed a smile to the mischief fairy, who was watching them both in quiet fascination. "What has your constant obedience gained you?"

Michael's lips thinned and his black eyes flashed with indignation. "Why are you here?"

"Lord Lucias sent me word that your children are ill." Haniel shrugged. "I've come to brew them a stew."

"Will it help them?"

Haniel turned in the direction of the fairy, who stood at the doorway to the kitchen with one of the strange looking creatures on her hip, and smiled. Michael, it would seem, had convinced her of the benefits of donning a smock.

"By Moira's will," he nodded, "they will not be beyond the skill of my magic."

"You patched Zadkiel." Michael grumbled, his black eyes flashing. "You can patch my gargoyles."

"Gargoyles?" Haniel's lips pursed with his amusement. "Is that what you're calling the little creatures?"

"It's a stupid name." The fairy agreed in irritated tones as she swung the babe from one hip to another. "Maxium came up with it when one of them tried to suckle from me."

Haniel chuckled under his breath at the pun. "From your gargouilles?"

"Inappropriate." Michael growled his agreement. "But they respond to it." His lips twitched slightly at their corners, suggesting that he was fighting back a grin. "So it's stuck."

"Crude." The fairy snorted.

Yet, just as with Michael, Haniel could not mistake the turn of her lips as anything but a repressed smile.

"My point is," Michael ignored her, "you brought our brother back from the dead after Lucias stole his powers."

"What do you mean?" Haniel's brow furrowed. "Stole his powers?"

"For the sole purpose of extinguishing Raguel." Michael growled.

"Dear Gods above and below." The fairy groused. "Let's not brabble about *this* again!"

"What are you talking about?"

"Do you know what our father is up to, dear brother?" Michael asked, his nostrils flaring

"How would I have the slightest inkling?" Haniel frowned at him. "He's always up to something."

"*She.*" He seethed through his teeth. "*She* is always up to something!"

"What are you stammering about now?" The fairy stormed.

Michael glared at her, grabbed Haniel by the bicep and pulled him out of the room into the kitchen. He slammed the door behind him, lest the fairy follow, and flung Haniel away from him. "Do you want to know her plans?"

"I'm certain you intend to share them."

Haniel attempted to keep a light hearted note in his tone. It was a difficult thing for him to do. Seeing Michael in such a state, he certainly didn't feel light hearted.

"Sit upon Raguel's throne." Michael seethed. "With Lord Loki to replace our mother."

Haniel blinked. It was the only response he could muster.

"They're breeding, Haniel." Michael stormed at him. "Twelve little monsters with which to replace us all." He slammed his hands against his chest. "Beginning with me!"

"What are you saying?"

"The Quorum is being disbanded." He seethed through his teeth. "She intends to replace each one of us with the mortal monsters that she is breeding and then align our pillows on her side of the throne."

A nervous laugh escaped Haniel's throat. Michael was upset about *this*? After all the ill deeds that had been done against every member of the Quorum at the King of Lords' hands?

"Don't you see?" Michael's eyes flashed once more. "Your turn is coming! You'll join me in exile by the wax of the next golden moon!"

Haniel took a deep breath and then stepped toward him.

"Michael." Had Michael been any one of his other brothers, even the mighty Metatron, Haniel would have reached for his arm to console him. "If what you say is true, then Lucias is trying to save us."

"Save us?" He spat. "*Save* us?"

"You know he—"

"You know she has never looked out for anyone but herself!" He stormed. "Zadkiel being flung from the Heavens was *her* doing!"

"Zadkiel expired a Goddess without the King of Lords' say." Haniel corrected him.

"Upon *her* orders!" Michael reminded him. "And Azrael is gone to us all because she convinced him to speak words he was never meant to share!"

"To protect Prince—"

"Do you honestly believe that Ishitar needs protecting?" Michael seethed. "From *any*one?"

"Michael." Haniel swallowed. "You're speaking irrationally now. The King of Lords could destroy Prince Ishitar with a turn of his thoughts."

"But he can't destroy her." Michael screamed at him. "Now can he?"

Haniel shook his head. He didn't know the answer to that question. None of them did. Lucias had withstood arguments against the King of Lords that other's would have been expired for.

"Ware her, Haniel." Michael warned him, his fists balled at his sides. "And mark me well." Haniel swallowed the fear he suddenly had the better sense to feel under his brother's rage. "For if she climbs upon my Lady's throne, she will become Queen of us all." His lips thinned. "And when she does, every one of us shall be damned."

He turned on his heel then and stormed across the kitchen and out of the cottage. Once on the other side, he slammed the door behind him. As he did so, the one behind Haniel opened and the room exploded with the permeation of wild flowers.

"He's gone mad!" The fairy whispered.

Haniel shook his head and turned his gaze upon her. He offered her a kind smile that she didn't, necessarily, return.

"No, my dear." He assured her. Michael hadn't gone mad. Not in Haniel's estimation. "Michael has merely, *finally,* come to his Gods be damned senses."

-12-

"Lord Loki has already left?" Samyael asked, nervously shifting his weight from one foot to the other. He liked Emissary Lord Darklief well enough. But the behavior of the mischief fairy was, oft times, unpredictable.

"Several days ago." Emissary Lord Darklief's pale white brow furrowed. "Sam. You're white as a winter storm. What's troubles darken your heart?"

Sam shook his head and lowered his gaze. As he did so, he began wringing his hands. "Nothing, my Lord."

"Nothing." Emissary Lord Darklief snorted. "How long have we been friends, Sam?"

"Ages." He swallowed.

"Then I think that I'd know when you're lying to me." He stepped out of the doorframe. "Come in. Share your worries with me."

Samyael raised his gaze and looked into Emissary Lord Darklief's brilliant, violet eyes. He saw nothing within them but concern. "It's . . ."

"Out with it." The fairy God replied as he closed the door behind Sam. "What's troubling you?"

"I've lurked in the King of Lords' shadows for many days now."

"So you have." Emissary Lord Darklief muttered, almost under his breath and clearly with great irritation.

"I've seen many a queer passing."

"I'm certain." This time the fairy God's tone was guarded.

"None so queer as the time he spends pondering over Jamiason's elf." He said it quickly lest he change his mind. "He watches the creature night and day. And he speaks old words that I neither recognize nor understand."

A strange light crossed Emissary Lord Darklief's fair features. His nostrils flared slightly as his hands made their way to his hips. His feet, which were as bare as the day he had been born, seemed to plant themselves into the stone tile beneath him.

"It's troublesome to me, my Lord."

"What does Raphael have to say about all of this?"

"That it's been going on for many moons, my Lord." Sam swallowed. He didn't like the fire he saw burning within Emissary Lord Darklief's eyes. "And that I should mind my own, lest I get caught in the line of whatever game the King of Lords is playing."

"Yet you intended to speak with Loki about this?"

"Jamiason . . ." Samyael swallowed again. "He's my dearest friend. If the King of Lords means to harm that elf . . ."

"Settle down, child." Emissary Lord Darklief frowned at him. It was almost as if he sensed Samyael's fear about speaking of the elf's existence to him. "I don't wish to see Jami's heart come to harm any more than you do."

He raised his hand and began to stroke his chin. He looked every bit the man in deep thought and careful consideration.

"Raphael says this has been going on for some time, you say?"

"Many passings of the Golden Moon, my Lord." Samyael agreed.

"Grant me a favor."

"Anything, my Lord." Sam felt the relief of knowing that he had not angered Emissary Lord Darklief wash over him.

"Watch him." He said as he turned away and began walking toward the door that Samyael had just entered. "Talk with Raphael over what you find queer and keep me abreast of all of it."

"My Lord?"

"Just do as I ask of you, Sam." Emissary Lord Darklief paused and looked over his shoulder at the demon. "Do everything that Noliminan asks of you." Samyael flinched at the sound of the King of Lords' name. "Be as obedient as a rain in summer. And as observant as the smallest pixie on the wind."

"You wish that I should spy on him?"

"On him." Emissary Lord Darklief nodded. "And on his son."

"Prince Ishitar?!"

"Ta."

"But Prince Ishitar is—"

"If you love Lord Loki, you will do this for me without question Sam." Emissary Lord Darklief opened the door and stepped through it. As he did so, he turned to face Samyael a final time. "And you will do it well."

-13-

When the hand wrapped around Iladrul's shoulder, he started. He hadn't heard the footsteps of whomever stood behind him approaching and so hadn't been expecting the company.

He spun around, reaching for his dagger as he did so, and felt his mouth go slack.

Although he had heard of the beauty of the Silver Mage, he had been less than prepared to have his eyes actually fall upon the creature.

"Settle child." The angel instructed him, raising his long finger to his lips to place it upon them in a manner which suggested that Iladrul should remain silent. "I am here at the behest of your father."

"Forgive me, my Lord." Iladrul flew to his feet and gave the Silver Mage a proper bow. "Your presence is most welcome!"

The strange creature's silver eyes danced over Iladrul's face before scanning the length of him and then returning to meet his gaze. Iladrul swallowed, hard, under his scrutiny.

"You are as fair as rumor would have me believe." The angel said as he raised his hand upward and pulled the locks of his long, flaxen hair over his shoulder so that they fell down his back is a shimmering river. "You've the look of your mother about you."

"So I've been told, my Lord." Iladrul swallowed and raised himself from his bow. "And of my father."

"Well." The Silver Mage chuckled under his breath. "That's debatable." He stuck the finger that had been on his lips beneath Iladrul's chin to raise his face. Once done, he grasped at Iladrul and turned his head from side to side as if to get a good look at him. "Perhaps his nose."

"Yes, my Lord."

"Wisterian believes that you have the blood of a mage running through you." His silver eyes narrowed. "What are your beliefs?"

"That I . . ." Iladrul felt himself tremble. He had heard the rumors that his mother had bedded this creature. And he had scoffed at those who had suggested he might be the Silver Mage's son. " . . . do."

The angel smiled at him and gave him a curt nod.

"Especially wearing this bauble." Iladrul swallowed again and grasped at the talisman that Emissary Lord Darklief had given him. Though he wasn't certain why, he was hesitant to actually show it to the Silver Mage. "Do you know what it is?"

The Silver Mage's eyes narrowed as he reached for the thing. When he touched it, he pulled his hand away as though it burned him.

"Powerful magic." He muttered, his eyes widening and then narrowing again. "A gift from the Gods."

Iladrul swallowed before granting the Silver Mage a small nod.

The Silver Mage's eyes flicked upward again, meeting Iladrul's gaze. "You may survive Lady Moira yet."

"Yes, my Lord." He heard the tremble which laced his tone. "You say my father sent you?"

"He did." The Silver Mage sighed and turned away from him. It was a fluid, graceful movement that brought a tingle within Iladrul from his neck all the way down his spine. "He believes that I can teach you to use the powers that you hold within you."

"Do you believe this?" Iladrul whispered.

When those damn silver eyes fell upon him again, Iladrul wished that the earth would open beneath him and swallow him. The Silver Mage assessed him for a long, torturous moment.

Then, he smiled.

"Oddly enough," the angel said as he flicked his white wings behind him, "I do."

"Then I am your humble child." Iladrul fell to his knee, raised his hand to his forehead and gave the angel the fealty he deserved.

"That, my son," the Silver Mage replied, his eyes flashing, "remains to be seen."

-14-

Aiken approached the lands where Jamiason and his demons had made their camp very warily. He understood, all too well, that his was a presence which was not welcome here.

In fact, his eyes hadn't scanned the contours of Jamiason's face since the day that he had watched Jamiason being dragged into exile by Michael and Metatron.

Still. If he were to protect Jami's elf, he had no choice but to go through with this encounter.

As for the demons who would brand him a traitor, he cared little and less about them. They had lost his favor by their own behavior.

As he walked down the rows of tents, searching for Jami, his nose curled in disgust. Each one of them, as had been reported, housed two elves, one boy and one girl.

And, not a pair of them were getting up to what they had been forced together to do.

"Asinine demons." Aiken muttered under his breath as he passed one of the tents, flinging the flaps of it closed to give the couple within their unnecessary privacy. "Castrated boys and girls only lately come into their menses."

Seeing their faces, Aiken was suddenly furious with Iykva. He knew, without a doubt, that Jami had cast Aiken's people into the roles of the right side.

He continued on, his anger growing, until he came to a dark shape in the night. The shape bore no wings and smelled acutely canine.

"Thamores?"

The creature spun to face him. His yellow eyes flashed. As they did so, his lips curled into an unwanted smile. "Emissary Lord Darklief."

"That isn't necessary and we both know it." Aiken's lips pursed. "What is the meaning of your presence here?"

"Jamiason asked me to aide him in watching over these prisoners."

"These children." Aiken hissed. "And Jamiason had nothing to do with any of it."

"Perhaps not." Thamores' yellow eyes flashed as they slid from side to side. "But would you speak these words too loudly?"

"Of course not." Aiken sighed. "Where is he?"

Thamores' lips thinned. "You're the last person he wants to see."

"I'm overly aware of the details of the argument between myself and my Shitva." Aiken snapped. "Where *is* he?"

Thamores glared at him for a moment, sighed and then pointed at Jamiason's tent.

"But you won't be welcome."

"Welcome or not," Aiken grumbled as he passed the benandanti, "I *will* be received."

Though Aiken didn't see it, Thamores, who had always admired the God of the fairies, smiled faintly as he shook his head and returned to his post.

-15-

Paul felt the hairs on the back of his neck raise as the flaps to the tent opened and the smell of summer flowers permeated the room. He knew, the barest moment that he heard the flutter of wings, who it was that had come into their presence.

As, it would seem, did James.

His Maker flew around with his blue eyes wide, his lips pulled thin, and his nostrils flaring. "What in the name of the Thirty Hells are you doing here?"

"I've come to warn you." Emissary Lord Darklief replied as his eyes flew from Jamiason to Paul. "You're looking well, child."

"Thanks." Paul muttered, knowing that small talk was the least of things that was required if Emissary Lord Darklief had actually broken the long bout of silence between himself and Jamiason. "As are you."

"Answer me!" Jamiason seethed. "You know you're not welcome."

"Calm down." Emissary Lord Darklief groused as he flung himself into the closest chair. "I come on a mission of peace."

"What peace?" Jamiason asked, his eyes wide and troubled with shadows.

"You asked me to protect your elf?" Emissary Lord Darklief spat. "I'm here to do just that."

"What are you blathering about?"

"Noliminan has taken an interest in him." Paul swallowed the bile that had risen to his throat. Jamiason and his Gods be damned elf! "And is watching him very intently, by all accounts."

"Whose accounts?" Jamiason's voice was trembling.

"It doesn't matter." Emissary Lord Darklief snapped. As he did so, his eyes flicked to Paul. "You can be trusted?"

"With my life." James assured the God.

287

"Very well." His violet eyes returned to Jamiason. "If you don't finish this, and soon, this will no longer be a mortal war. It will be a war amongst the Gods. You do understand this?"

"The Gods never insert themselves into—"

"A battle for the thrones has ensued." Emissary Lord Darklief stopped him. "A battle between Gods far more powerful than I."

"How do you know that?"

"It matters not." Emissary Lord Darklief's eyes fell upon Paul again, causing him to shiver.

"Dear Gods, Aiken." Jamiason whispered. "Do you mean to suggest that you have spies?" Emissary Lord Darklief chose not to respond. "That's treason!"

"And just who are *you*?" The fairy asked as he found his feet. "To talk of treason? When you set your most powerful ally against your own people to protect that elf child from war?"

"That's different!" Jamiason cried. "The stakes are much higher where your meddling is concerned."

"Meddling which I do on your behalf." Emissary Lord Darklief reminded him. "Take heed, Jami." He said as he walked toward the opening of the tent to take his leave. "That's all I've come to say."

-16-

"Michael's been exiled!" Uriel ran toward her husband, her green eyes wide and her nostrils flaring with anger. "Did you hear?"

"What are you raging about, woman?" Metatron asked, crossing his arms over his chest and glaring at his sister. "Why on which moon would Noliminan exile Michael?"

"Because he fell in love with Raguel." Camael shrugged as he reached for Uriel's hand to pull her into his arms so that he could bring her comfort. "And yes, dear." He kissed her forehead. "Haniel stopped by moons ago to tell me."

"Nonsense!" Metatron seethed. "I won't believe it."

"Believe it or don't." Camael grinned at him, not understanding the true depths of Metatron's rage. "He's being replaced by Lucias' bastard." He chuckled slightly at the fierce indignation that crossed the features of his brother's flaming face. "Michael, it would seem, is now in the service of our father."

"Say you *what*?" Metatron seethed. The flames that made up his body exploded all around him. "You lie!"

"Not a wit." Camael shook his head. He had the better sense to take a step away from Metatron as the small room flooded with the smoke of his brother's rage. "Lucias has offered King Noliminan a trade. The bastard monster for Michael."

"For Michael?" Metatron's flared.

"That's what our brother claims." Uriel nodded, her curly blonde hair dancing around her fairly made face. "Michael told Haniel so himself."

"For *Michael*!"

"Really, Metatron." Camael sighed as he casually placed himself between his wife and his brother. "You should be happy for—"

"Happy?" Metatron took a step toward Camael, his eyes wide and his anger all consuming. "*Happy*?!"

"Michael has served King Noliminan longer than any one of us but for Raphael." Uriel tried, her voice holding a note of pleading within it as she grasped her husband's shoulders far too tightly. "Camael is right. Michael deserves the reprieve."

"Michael doesn't deserve the reprieve!" Metatron cried. "Nor does he want it!" Camael felt Uriel cringe behind him. His hackles rose as his instinct to protect his wife outweighed his love for his brother. "*I* wanted the reprieve. And have asked Lucias for her succor time after time only to be told to bide!"

"Metatron—"

"No." Metatron seethed, his anger exploding around them all. Camael felt the hair on his brows singe; Metatron was that angry. "I will not stand for this."

"There's nothing you can do." Uriel whispered.

"Isn't there?" Metatron seethed, his body flaring again.

"Don't do anything stupid, brother!" Camael begged.

Metatron merely glared at him before storming out of the cottage that Camael and Uriel shared, slamming their front door behind him.

-17-

Gorgon faced his father, his strange and murderous eyes hidden behind dark glasses, shivering. He had the better sense to be terrified.

"I love you, child." Loki whispered. "And I'm sorry for the path I must set you upon."

The snakes on his head betrayed him. They flew in every direction, hissing. Yet he forced the words all the same. "I am proud to serve the King of Lords."

Loki snorted.

"Father." Gorgon swallowed the bile in his throat. "I will not fail you."

Loki smiled at him and raised his hand to run it along the contours of Gorgon's face. As he did so, one of the damned snakes that made up Gorgon's hair wrapped itself around Loki's wrist. The shame that Gorgon felt as the snake did this was overwhelming.

Yet, his father, who had never admonished him for his nature, merely rolled his eyes and turned his neck to kiss the head of the snake that wrapped around him.

"Gorgon." Loki whispered. "Mind me child."

"Yes, father."

"You are mortal." Loki raised his hand and brushed several of the snakes that were flying toward him behind Gorgon's ear. "You have powers beyond those of your peers." Gorgon felt his brow furrow. "Do you understand what I am telling you?"

"No." Gorgon choked back his fear. "Forgive me, father."

"There's nothing to forgive, child." Loki sighed. "Just know this."

"Yes?"

"You don't have to mind his every whim." Loki answered forcefully. "Do you understand?"

Gorgon shook his head.

"You're mortal, damn it!" Loki growled. "You aren't an archangel." Loki's lips pursed. "He can't make you do anything you don't want to do."

Gorgon frowned.

"Don't you understand?"

"No." Gorgon whispered.

"You are blessed with a will of your own." His lips thinned. "Your peers . . . aren't."

"I don't under—"

"You are a member of Noliminan's Quorum." Loki said, unwrapping the snake that had wrapped itself around his wrist and kissing it on the head before pushing it away. "It's true." His lips thinned again. "But you are my son. And I love you."

"I love you." Gorgon replied.

Loki smiled.

"Papa?"

"If he orders you to do something that offends you," Loki turned his purple eyes away from his son, "disobey him."

"Father!"

"He can't punish you!" Loki seethed, returning his gaze to Gorgon.

"But he is the King of *all* Lords!" Gorgon whispered.

"That may be." Loki smiled tightly. "Disobey him all the same." Loki looked swiftly away. "And protect your half brothers and sisters if you can."

"Half-brothers and—"

"There are eleven others whose pillows rest alongside his throne." Loki returned his gaze to meet that of his son's. "Never forget that you are the only one who can, for now, protect them."

Overwhelmed by the understanding of the responsibility that suddenly crashed upon him, Gorgon swallowed.

"Yes, Father."

-18-

The dathanorna watched the copper haired creature and his party pass through its forest with an empty belly and base desires. Though there were plenty of other creatures in its forest, none smelled as juicy and sweet.

It licked its lips and, in its wolf's form, which it was most comfortable wearing given it had been the form Lucias had given it as a babe, stepped lightly toward the edge of the tree line.

"Be wary, Iladrul." The silver haired angel said as he looked right and left. "We've entered the forest of the lost dead."

"Yes, my Lord." The sweet young thing said, looking over his shoulder with a strange expression upon his fair face. "Are we in danger?"

"We shouldn't be." The angel replied, his tones low. "But one never knows when walking amongst the children of Hades."

The dathanorna smiled, despite itself. The angel was right. Many a man or woman who had entered the boundaries of its forest had run mad.

"Just be wary."

"Yes, my Lord."

They walked on.

The dathanorna followed.

-19-

When the door opened and Loki stepped through, Aiken started. His violet eyes grew round and his thick lips split into such a grin as would never, again, be duplicated by any living creature. As for Ishitar, he merely looked at Loki with tired interest.

"You're home!" Aiken flew to his feet and ran to his friend, taking him in his arms in a warm embrace. Loki bore this with a tight, embarrassed smile.

"Why is it that every time I step through these doors after a bout of absence I'm molested by a fairy?"

Aiken laughed. He wasn't the child he had been when he had last pounced on Loki in this manner.

"Because I've woken from a dream." Aiken grinned and kissed his dearest friend on his cheek. "And this time, you've come home to save your Sam."

"My Sam." Loki swallowed and pulled away, planting his hands on Aiken's shoulders and looking him straight in the eye. "He survived Noliminan's terrors?"

"He did." Ishitar replied, standing and walking toward the pair, his hand extended. Loki released Aiken and shook it. "For a wonder."

"How are you, boy?" Loki asked, smiling slightly.

"Well." Ishitar cocked his head. "How is your mortal son?"

"Well." Loki grimaced at the question. "For now."

"Good." Ishitar's eyes narrowed slightly. "I hope you're hungry. Aiken's made a fine stew." Loki returned his gaze to Aiken, smiling. "And, anticipating your return today, I've made you one of my pies."

Loki's face split into a wide grin. "I've missed your pies."

"Have you?"

Aiken, turning his eyes in Ishitar's direction, clenched his teeth lest he frown.

-20-

"All of our ships!" Iykva screamed at Paul. "Burned asunder!"

"You can't have expected them to not bar our passage."

"Jackanapes!" The demon replied, spinning and storming toward the tent in which he meant to lay his head for the day.

Paul turned toward Jamiason, trying not to smile.

"Don't smirk." James muttered as his eyes turned to Thamores. "Any word from my twins?"

"None." Thamores shook his head. "Not a peep."

James' lips thinned.

"I'm certain they're safe." Paul tried to assure his Maker. "They are, both of them, cunning."

"Perhaps." Jamiason shook his head. "What do we do now?"

"Convince Iykva that the best course is to head for home." Thamores suggested. "We can't cross the sea. And we can't back trace our steps."

"The only means for going home from here without back tracing is the Forest of Spirits . . . " Paul whispered. "We can't possibly—"

"Don't tell me you're afraid of ghosts." Thamores scoffed.

"Unlike you," Paul snapped, "I'm mortal and will be damned when I die rather than raised up as a God."

Thamores grinned at that.

"The spirits can't harm you." Jamiason replied irritably. "And Thamores is right. If we back trace, the fairies will destroy us. As much as I want the elves to win this war, I don't want my people eliminated."

"Should we speak with Chiron?"

"He's moved his herd south." Jamiason shook his head. "They only promised me the one battle."

"Of course." Thamores sighed. "My wolves frightened them."

"They are a Heavens' bound race." Jamiason's smile was thin and tight. "And not at all on our side."

"I think it was the manner in which I licked my chops." Thamores chuckled. "Rather than the manner of God that they serve."

"Perhaps so." Jamiason, for the first time in a long time, gave a short, but honest laugh. "Regardless, this is now a battle of vampires and wolves." He flicked his gaze to Paul. "What have you heard from the humans?"

"Those against the Devonshires will continue to march with us." Paul shrugged. "So long as we promise not to bend their necks."

"Make your promises, then." James nodded at him. "And see that your people toe their plank."

"As you wish."

"So be it." Jamiason let out a long breath of air, unsettling Paul. "Come sun fall, we journey south."

-21-

Iladrul shivered as that odd sensation that he was being watched washed over him again.

"Lord Raystlyn?"

"Yes child?" The Silver Mage turned his strange eyes upon the elf.

"Do you . . ." He swallowed. "Am I mad? Or is something other than the spirits haunting our steps."

"You aren't mad at all." Raystlyn smiled softly at the boy. He had become fond of the elfin child, despite himself. "We've been followed for the last twenty nauckts."

The boy's green eyes, so alike to those of his mother, grew wide.

"It's a changeling, boy." Raystlyn whispered. "An abomination to the very Gods who protect or damn us."

"A . . ." The boy shivered again. "A dathanorna?"

Raystlyn nodded.

"But I thought—"

"None are known to exist." Raystlyn stopped the boy from speaking the words. "That doesn't mean that they do not."

"Are we in danger?"

"Most definitely." Raystlyn shrugged his shoulders. "It's been following us for days. Although, it hasn't eaten one of our party as of yet."

Iladrul pulled his horse to a stop. As he did so, the five doxies stopped their horses as well. "As of yet?"

Raystlyn smiled at him.

"Meaning that it may?"

"It may, indeed." Raystlyn nodded. "Best keep moving, boy."

-22-

After listening to Sam's newest reports on the goings on of Ishitar and Noliminan, Aiken's stomach ached as if he had just swallowed a boulder. Noliminan, it would seem, had become more than a little obsessed with the elves. And Ishitar, who always wore that strange, contemplative smile, seemed to care little and less about the outcome of the mortal war. His mind, Samyael advised Aiken, seemed trained upon Loki and some mysterious tree that he kept visiting to pick the fruit which made up Loki's pies.

"Curious." Aiken grumbled as his eyes trailed the contours of Samyael's face. "I've never heard of a tree such as you speak of."

"Have you ever seen the gourds such as he uses before?" Aiken shook his head. "Or tasted such sweetness?"

"Sam." He admonished. "Please do not tell me that you ate of Ishitar's fruit."

"Just one gourd." Sam shrugged.

Aiken shook his head. He had only had one slice of Ishitar's damn pie and he hadn't felt the same since.

"Keep that business to yourself." Aiken warned. "Whatever that fruit is, it's damning."

"Yes, my Lord." Samyael lowered his gaze, almost as if he were ashamed. As he did so, Aiken stood, startling him. "Where are you going?"

"To palaver with Loki." Aiken muttered under his breath. "To seek his advice."

"He won't give you any." Samyael warned him. "It is a mortal war."

"Mortal or not," Aiken frowned at him, "if I know Noliminan, he means to make his strike."

"Against the elves?"

"Doubtful." Aiken snorted and stormed out of the room.

He didn't understand Noliminan's obsession with the damned elf. It was true that he toyed with the mortals when it suited him. But never *male* mortals.

What is it about this damned elf? Aiken wondered. *That brings the blood of the very Gods to a boil. He isn't that damned pretty.*

He was beginning to loathe the creature. Though he promised Jami he would protect him—and, he would—the damned elf was causing him far too many concerns for his liking.

When he reached the library, he bent so that he could poke his head through the door. Loki, who was bound by obsessions of his own, sat at the desk, staring down at the strange tome, with his brows furrowed over his dark purple eyes.

"Can you spare a moment?"

Loki started at the sound of Aiken's voice and looked up at him with a nervous smile. Despite his annoyance that Aiken had interrupted him, he indicated the chair across the desk.

"Of course," he said. "You know I always have time for you."

Aiken smiled tightly at the dishonesty in that statement. He was coming to believe that he was being tolerated more than welcomed.

"I have a concern." Best to get it out without delay.

"Oh?" Loki reached for the book, slipped a ribbon over its parchment to mark its pages, and closed it. "About?"

"About Noliminan." Loki's brow rose high over his eye. "And about—"

He bit his tongue. He was about to admit that he didn't exactly trust Ishitar, but something in the back of his mind tickled, warning him not to say anything to Loki about that just yet.

"And?"

"I'm told that he's obsessing over the elves."

"The elves?" Loki frowned at him. "Queer."

"Indeed." Aiken's lips pursed. "Loki." He swallowed. "I've promised Jamiason that I would protect Iladrul."

"Foolish of you." Loki crossed his arms over his chest.

"Perhaps." Aiken admitted. "My people needed to choose a side."

Loki, who didn't govern a mortal race, so didn't understand the politics required to ensure their survival, merely shrugged.

"Regardless," Aiken continued, "If Noliminan interferes, he'll discover that Jamiason is no longer what he appears to be."

Loki frowned at him. "Are you telling me the rumors regarding Evanbourough are true?"

"I'm telling you that Noliminan will destroy Jamiason and his people without the first thought of them." Aiken replied, irritably.

What is wrong with me? Why am I so wary of Loki? Of all people under every moon?

"It's bad enough that he's been exiled." He continued. "I can't sit back and watch him—or his children—be destroyed."

"Stay out of it Aiken." Loki's tone held a warning quality to it that Aiken didn't much care for. "You don't want to be at odds with Noliminan."

"I already am at odds with Noliminan." Aiken snapped. "Or hadn't you noticed."

"Losing your daughter to serve Michael is not the worst he could have done to you for meddling with Moira." Loki shook his head. "Trust me on that."

"This isn't about Karma." Aiken glared at his friend. "And you know it."

Loki's eyes narrowed as he assessed Aiken for a long, almost torturous moment. Finally, he said, "You asked me for my advice and I have given it to you."

Frustrated, Aiken rose to his feet and stormed to the library door. When he reached it, he turned to face Loki, his anger brewing to a boil.

"Mark me." He said. "If we do not interfere—and soon—then there is going to be Hells' fire and damnation to pay." Loki blinked at him. Aiken had never, in all of the years that they had been friends, raised his voice to him. "And when it rains, I pray it falls on your head!"

-23-

Aminar stared into the depths of the forest, frowning. He didn't like the uneasy sensation that he had, lately, begun to feel. There was a threat in those woods. But it was invisible, even to his fairies eyes.

He heard the crunch of leaves behind him as the scent of a summer rain washed over him. He recognized the scent at once as belonging to one of the young Prince's doxies. As such, he didn't start with surprise despite the fact that he was on edge.

When the one called Osete stepped beside him, he turned to give the young elf a tired, wary smile. "You're up late."

"As are you." Osete replied. "Couldn't sleep?"

Aminar shook his head and returned his gaze to the forest. Osete, who was extremely perceptive in Aminar's opinion, did the same.

"What is it, do you think?" The elf whispered.

"Nothing that mine eyes are trained to." Aminar whispered. "It blends into the forest as if it were, itself, a tree."

Osete nodded and reached toward Aminar. This surprised the fairy until he saw that the elf held a peach in his hand. Aminar stared at it for a moment before reaching for it and granting Osete a tentative smile.

Where on which moon did this creature find a peach?

"Won't you be whipped for standing in the shadows with me?"

"Your people are chaste." Osete shrugged. His eyes flicked away as a blush crossed his fair cheeks. "And, you haven't the tools with which to shame me."

Aminar chuckled under his breath and returned his gaze to the forest as he took a bite of the peach. The sour and sweetness of it burst upon his tongue, causing him to sigh.

"Best not stay out too long." Osete warned as he turned, very gracefully, away. "Lest you find yourself in the belly of the beast."

His curiosity raised by that statement, Aminar studied the elf as he, rather quickly, darted away.

As Osete ducked into his Master's tent, Aminar knew one thing to be true: the elf knew exactly what the monster was that was haunting their trail.

-24-

Mihr watched the strange creature as he stepped tentatively into the room, turning his face this way and that, appearing as though he hoped to be overlooked. Seeing him, she felt a smile dance across her lips. He was, though oddly made, rugged of face and handsome of features.

Her brothers and sister seemed unaware of his arrival. They were caught up in their arguments over their displeasure that Michael had been stripped of his duties. None of them, including Mihr, understood what their brother could have done to displease King Noliminan to such a degree that he would trade him for the service of another.

She stood and walked, very attentively, toward the new member of her Quorum.

She didn't know if he would be friend or foe and she, gentle creature of the forest that she is, had heard rumors from Raphael that a single gaze into his eyes might drive her mad.

"Hello." She said as she approached him. He gave her a wary smile. "My name is Mihr. I am the youngest of the Quorum."

"You were the youngest." His voice was deep, causing her to smile. As she did so, his lips curled slightly as well and the snakes that made up his hair began flying madly around his face. "My name is Gorgon." His oddly made brow furrowed. "You're brown of skin."

Her smile grew at that. "Have you never seen a brown skinned woman?"

"No, my Lady." He replied, his eyes darting to her white, tightly curled hair. "I've lived a rather sheltered life."

"My father—" She stopped herself. Metatron had, by now, told them all that Lucias was no longer living as a male. "Your mother," her smile grew, "Lucias, used to say that Azrael and I were blessed because we were charred at birth by Metatron's hands as he caught us slipping from Raziel's womb."

He chuckled under his breath. "A likely conclusion."

"Indeed." Now her smile was wide and true. "Come." She reached for his arm. "Let me introduce you to the rest of the Quorum."

He gave her a shy nod and allowed her to lead him toward the fray in the center of the room. As they approached, Metatron waved his hand and the others each fell silent.

Metatron, in Michael's absence, was our leader.

He stepped forward, his flaming lips pursed. "You must be the gorgon."

"My name is Gorgon." Mihr watched as Gorgon bit his lip with his sharp, black teeth, correcting her brother and stepping toward Metatron with his hand outstretched. "Yes."

"You must know from the start that we aren't pleased that you are joining us." Barkiel, whose body was made of the blue light of electric lightening, grumbled. "You've displaced our brother and, as such, you aren't welcome here."

"Don't mind Barkiel." Raphael smiled at Gorgon. It was a smile so similar to that which our Master claims that they all coveted it. "He's just sore because he didn't have the opportunity to say goodbye. Michael's exile took us all by surprise."

"None more than Michael." Uriel stepped forward, her hand extended. "I'm Uriel. And this is Camael."

"A pleasure." Camael, who looked extremely surly in Mihr's opinion, frowned as Gorgon took Uriel's hand and raised it to his lips to kiss it. Still, he made the introductions around the room. "For the purposes of making your indoctrination neat, forgive me for repeating names. These are Metatron, Raphael, Gabriel, Haniel, Zadkiel—you've met Mihr and Uriel—Barkiel and

Cassiel." Next, he indicated what appeared to be an empty chair, making me smile. "And, we assume, Azrael has joined us as well."

"Azrael has." I chuckled under my breath.

"Never mind them, Gorgon." Mihr sneered at her brothers. "They're merely surly today."

"And every day." I grinned at her. She had always been my favorite sibling. "Trust me on that matter."

She smiled; although, I knew that smile wasn't for me. Camael, it would seemed, understood its secret meaning as well. His eyes narrowed on Gorgon and he gained an inch in height.

As for Gorgon, he seemed oblivious to her charms. I knew this to be because the only women he had ever met before her were his mother and sisters.

Perhaps it was his innocence around women which made me pleased by the prospect of this particular pairing.

"We're done here for today." Metatron announced. "I should show Gorgon where he will sta—"

"I can show him." Mihr turned to her brother to glare at him before returning to face Gorgon with a smile. "If he doesn't mind soft company."

"Soft company would be most welcome." Gorgon replied, brows raising high over his murderous eyes and snakes flying wildly around his head. "If it wouldn't be an inconvenience."

"It *would* be an inconvenience." Camael hissed, glaring at Mihr before turning his attention to Gorgon. "I will show you to Michael's cottage."

"Camael," Raphael sighed, "Really!"

"Stay out of it, Raphael." Uriel muttered the warning under her breath.

Her thoughts were teaming with discord. She understood that Raphael, out of all of us, had no business doling out advice when it came to the inappropriateness of relationships.

As Camael turned toward Raphael to chastise him, Haniel stepped in.

"I'll show Gorgon to Michael's cottage." He offered. "I've promised Michael that I'd pack his things for him and, thus far, haven't found the time." He gave Gorgon a tentative smile. "Seems a fair time to kill two birds with one stone."

Gorgon, who had turned many birds to stone, blushed. His grey scales turned dark as he lowered his face. The shame that he felt for the turn of his magic bounced off him in waves around the room. I was pleased to note that my brothers and sisters had the better sense to be embarrassed by their behavior toward him upon seeing him so.

Haniel, and rightly so given he'd meant to wound his half-brother, above all.

"I . . ." Gorgon swallowed the pain that welled within him at the immediate knowledge that he was not to be accepted amongst his peers. "Thank you."

Disgusted by them all, I allowed my admonishment against each and every one of them to explode within their hearts and minds.

All of them, of course, but for my dear, sweet sister, Mihr.

-25-

Sappharon watched with quiet fascination as Loki dismissed the children that he and Lucias had created while Countenance trapped them in their time. They were, all of them, so different from one another.

Not that this should have been a surprise.

The archangels that Lucias had sired were all very distinct from one another as well. Yet, that was, somehow, different in Sappharon's mind. They had been birthed for the purpose of serving Noliminan's throne. These children of Loki's were another matter. These children had been born to breed monsters of their own.

The second oldest, after Gorgon, is Siren. She is a beautiful creature with a voice more lulling than an entire choir of angels.

She can lure even the strongest of souls to her bosom has she the mind.

The third is Taurus. A creature born with the head and legs of a bull and the torso of a man, Taurus was bred to be a fierce warrior, much like Metatron and Michael. His heart is fiercely jealous, however, and he guards that which he believes to be his with warlike abandon.

Fourth is Djinn. A strange, mist-like creature, Djinn has the power to grant a being any wish that their heart desires. And he encourages mortals and immortals, alike, to lend as many wishes as he may grant. For he feeds off the greed of others and will consume the souls of those who ask for that which they covet but do not require.

Shade is the fifth. Like Djinn, his form is more mist-like than corporeal. Unlike Djinn, his powers only effect those who are mortal born. He does not consume a body, but he expels its soul and takes the body as his own so that he can walk about as if he were they. The soul, not having been touched by my hand, walks mad amongst the spirits who inhabit Hades' realms.

Loki's second daughter, at the time, was the youngest of his children. Her name is Banshee. Though beautiful of face and form, when she speaks to a mortal, that mortal's body and soul turns to dust. The soul, because it has not been touched by Zadkiel's hand, flies into the wind when it blows. Not even Hades' doors are open to these poor creatures.

My heart breaks for Loki's children. They have, all of them, been raised by his hand. Because of this, each of them lives daily in their own brand of Hell as they attempt to blend their nature with their understanding of right versus wrong.

"I must hold palaver with your mother." Loki tells them now, his purple eyes darting from one to the other. "The matter is private."

"Yes, Fete." It is Siren, oldest amongst them now that Gorgon is gone, who speaks on the behalf of all of them. I find myself smiling at this because of the dark parallel that these children have found to the structure of my own brothers and sisters in following Metatron without question. "Will you say goodbye before you leave us?"

"I wouldn't sleep a wink tonight unless I do." He grinned at her as he pulled young Banshee, who was barely old enough to toddle at the time, into his arms to plant a kiss on her well-made brow. "Go now. And put your younger siblings to bed."

"Goodnight, Fete." Those who could speak said in unison.

Loki grinned as he watched Siren herd them all away. I knew that, despite their odd magic, he loved each and every one of them in like kind.

"So early?"

Sappharon started at the sound of Lady Lucias' voice. She was pregnant with her seventh child. This one, it would seem, took a good deal of her energy to brew. She was always tired during this pregnancy. Something which troubled Sappharon to no end.

"You've slept the day away, met paken." Loki muttered under his breath, his eyes turning to Sappharon.

Though I could no longer read his mind, I had long ago come to understand his facial expressions. He was contemplating letting her stay or asking her to leave. Sappharon understood this as well and was waiting with curious intent to see which choice he would make. When he smiled at her and returned his attention to Lucias, she was pleased.

He was coming to trust her. It was a trust long, and hard, earned.

"Rumor has it that your husband is obsessed with the first bred elf."

Lucias' brow furrowed at that. As the baby in her belly turned, her thoughts reverberated through my mind.

With a male?

"Oh?"

"So Aiken says." Loki shrugged. "I understand he's been watching Noliminan rather closely."

Lucias chuckled under her breath and rubbed her belly. She wasn't, I suspected, surprised by this turn of events. "Aiken is a disobedient child."

"He is of your seed." Loki reminded her, unnecessarily. "He seems troubled by it."

"Why?"

"He keeps one foot in the mortal world." Loki shrugged. "He's sided with the elves in their war against the vampires and were-creatures."

"Against Jamiason?"

Sappharon was surprised by this question. It was no secret that the affair between Aiken and Jamiason ended upon Jamiason's exile.

"It would seem that was James' choice." Loki shrugged again. "He wants to raise against your husband." Sappharon noted that Loki's eyes narrowed slightly. He was waiting to see how she would respond, the demoness knew. "I told him to stay out of it."

"Yes." She muttered as she ran her hand over her swelling belly again. "Good advice."

"Is it?"

"Of course it is." She snapped, almost as though she were irritated with him. "You know that Aiken cannot stand against Noliminan."

"I do." Loki conceded.

"Well." Lucias seemed to be forcing herself to smile as she raised her hand to her brow as if to salute him. "Here's to hoping that Aiken, for once, has the better sense to mind."

-26-

The dathanorna was hungry. It had eaten bear and bovine, so it was sated. But, what it wanted was the sweet delicate taste of elf on its tongue.

It licked its lips and stepped toward the road.

Although it wasn't ready to be seen—it was a master tracker—it needed to ensconce itself in the scent of that sweet flesh lest it go mad. Especially that earthy, sugary taste of the young Prince that led them.

There was something salty in their taste tonight. Something different. It enticed the creature beyond telling.

Until it smelled something unassociated with the elves.

Something base and unclean.

Its nose curled as it turned toward the oncoming army.

There was death in the air. Death enveloped by the sweetness it coveted.

Smelling the death, a taste that should have been its, alone, it growled. And, though it did not know it at the time, flew toward its unsettling future.

-27-

Iykva felt the burn on his skin as he clashed swords with the young elfin Prince. The creature fought bravely for a boy. And with more skill than the demon could have ever suspected to have encountered.

The hunger burned within him as well. The smell of the elf's blood flowed within every bead of sweat that he expired.

It was distracting. As was the scent of smoke that beat off his own body as the sun rose in the east.

"Retreat!" He screamed as he clashed his sword one last time against the elf's. He turned and saw his men, smoke beating off their bodies. The frustration that had been burning in his mind since he had come to the realization that his prisoners had no intention of breeding overwhelmed him. "Now, the Gods damn you!"

One by one the vampires and demons fighting on Iyvka's side pulled away from the fray. And, one by one, the elves chased after them.

They were swift, these creatures. Being born of the forest, they were deft on terrain that tripped Iykva and his people up.

"Damn it." He muttered under his breath as he jumped upward and into the trees.

He didn't make it.

As his wings spread to take flight, the dathanorna changed its form from that of the wolf it was most comfortable wearing to that of a griffin. Its body collided with Iykva's as it let out a murderous cry and wrapped its claws around his neck, ready to rip his throat open to eat him.

Intent on its prey, it didn't see the branch that the pair of them were hurtling toward. Its head hit square on, knocking it unconscious and sending it into a spiraling huddle toward the ground.

Iykva, seeing no reason, followed. He meant to kill that son of a bitch griffin if it were the last thing he ever did.

It might well have been had the elf not interfered.

An arrow flew past Iykva's cheek, tearing into his flesh. The pain of this, coupled with the agony of his searing flesh, brought him to his senses. He hissed at the elf and spun around, his wings catching the air so that he could fly as swiftly as possible into the shadows of the forest

He entered the cave where the demons and vampires had determined to bide the day mere moments before he would have, otherwise, burst into flames.

-28-

"What do you mean to do with it?" Sezja whispered, shivering.

"We haven't time to worry about that now." Iladrul muttered under his breath as he watched the griffin return, unconscious, to its wolf form. "We have miles to make."

"You can't leave it." Raystlyn shook his head. "It will track us."

"Then let it track us." Iladrul snapped, glaring at Raystlyn. "Now is our chance to free the doxies! Another opportunity will not present itself!"

"They're still guarded by the wolves." Gregor reminded him.

"Aye." Pialoron replied, biting his lip. He turned his gaze to Xylon. "Isn't the leader of their pack friend to your people?"

"I wouldn't call Thamores a friend." Xylon shrugged. "But he and my father are amiable with one and another."

"Will you bring me to him?" Iladrul asked. "Can you get me near to the blonde king?"

"Lord Scrountentine?" Xylon blinked his strange, almost transparent eyes. "I suppose if I invoke my father's name." He shrugged. "But, then again, perhaps not. They aren't on speaking terms."

"Your father gave his people the benefit of his grove for the purpose of palaver." Trevor reminded him. "He owes Emissary Lord Darklief a favor."

"He owes him more than one." Raystlyn muttered under his breath.

"Pardon?" Iladrul frowned at him.

"Never mind." Raystlyn replied. He turned his attention to Xylon. "Trevor's right. Invoke your father's name and Jamiason will meet with the elves."

Xylon, having watched the dance between his father and the demon for the full of his life, was doubtful.

-29-

Thamores stood at the edge of the camp, scouring the forest with his wolfish eyes.

He had seen the changeling and he knew damn well and good what it was. He had the better sense to be troubled by his knowledge of its existence.

If the words whispered on the wind were to be believed, the Gods had taken enough of an interest in the war between the elves and the vampires to be troublesome. The last thing that they needed was for one of the damned ones to draw attention to them.

"We've lost this war." He muttered to Jamiason. "You do realize that."

"I realize it." Jamiason grinned at him. "I thought that was what we wanted."

"Ta." Thamores kicked his boot into the dirt. "But I'd as soon keep my soul intact if it's all the same to you."

Jamiason shrugged.

"You saw that changeling?" Thamores growled at him, incredulous that he was taking this matter so lightly. "You saw it transform with your own two glams?"

"I did." Jamiason's brow furrowed. "Everyone did."

"And, you saw the elf protect Iykva."

"He wasn't protecting Iykva." Jamiason assured him. "He was stopping the dathanorna from putting itself before the eyes of the Gods."

"Why would he care?"

Jamiason leveled his gaze on Thamores, making the benandanti shiver. There were few things that frightened Tham. Yet, lately, the intensity of Jamiason's gaze held the quality to do so.

"What are we to do now?"

"Give him what he wants." Jamiason muttered as his gaze flew to the mouth of the cave where his brothers lay sleeping. "Let him take the doxies."

"Iykva will never stand for—"

"There is little Iykva can do while the sun crests the sky." Jamiason reminded him. "And, given he retreated, he can't exactly blame you and your people if you retreat as well."

"I can lie to him." Thamores felt his nostrils flare. "Not to my own people."

"These aren't your people." Jamiason leveled his gaze upon Thamores. "These are werewolves. Not benandanti."

"There are no more benandanti!" Thamores cried.

"Yet, before me stands one." Jamiason replied, turning away from him. "And he is the God of his people." Thamores swallowed the bile that rose up into his throat as Jamiason walked toward the mouth of the cave. He stopped just at the lip and returned his gaze to the benandanti. "A God, as Aiken would counsel you if he could, with one foot in the mortal grave."

"As are you." Thamores whispered.

Jamiason merely gave him a tight lipped smile before slipping into the cave to join his brethren.

Their positions were nowhere near the same.

Jamiason, unlike Thamores, was an exile.

-30-

Xylon smelled the benandanti long before he saw him.

Above and beyond that, he smelled the flesh of elves.

"What . . . ?"

"Silence." The benandanti muttered as he turned his dark profile upward to look into the shadow of the sun. "Our time is limited here."

"I've come to—"

"Ask for the doxy elves." Thamores turned his yellow, wolfish eyes toward Xylon. As he did so, his nostrils flared and his tongue darted over his lips as if he were hungry. "Take them." He stepped out of the way, opening the camp to Xylon and his small band of fairies. "And be quick about it." The benandanti growled deep within his throat. "Before I change my mind and sup on them myself."

Xylon, although confused by this turn of events, directed his men in the manner in which a future King must.

-31-

At times the farce of the Council overwhelms me. Why do I bother to still attend? Yet, here I sat, on my pillow, watching my youngest brother as he lowered himself onto Michael's as though it belonged to him.

Not that I begrudged him the pillow. It was simply that he appeared as uncomfortable lowing himself upon it as he felt.

I sighed my pity for him and shook my head.

He looked down the line behind his dark glasses but found no comfort there. Until, of course, his eyes landed upon Mihr. She noticed that his attention had fallen upon her and her face split into a brilliant grin. A grin that was compounded, in my heart and mind, with her hope that he looked upon her out of desire and respect.

Smiling, I lowered my gaze.

As I did so, I felt Uriel's hand as it rushed through me.

"If you're there, hello."

"Hello." I replied, sending the word to her mind as well as verbalizing it.

She turned toward my pillow and smiled at me. "How is Ishitar?"

I wish I knew. Though, this, I did not say to her. "Fine and well."

"Good." She turned away and found her place in line. I watched her with interest as Camael entered the room, passed her without giving her the slightest glance, and found his own pillow.

I decided, watching him, that I was tired of the requirement that we play our games in regard to those whom we loved. I wanted nothing more in life than to share with my brothers and sisters that I had finally won the heart of my beloved Zamyael.

What a foolish proposition that idea was.

To tell them that I'd bedded a demon would put them in their own precarious positions should Noliminan ever press them for the information.

Especially when he learned that said demon was Zamyael.

I would be forced to witness as he destroyed my brothers and sisters for the sole purpose of punishing me.

I shivered at the thought as Metatron lowered himself into the pillow beside Gorgon. He gave our youngest brother a tight smile and then turned his stoic attention to the Great Hall as the Gods and their servants rifled in.

Perhaps twenty shifts later, Noliminan entered with Raphael close on his heel. Following languidly after him was Raziel, taking great pains to make a dramatic flurry as she lowered herself onto Lucias' throne. I rolled my eyes at her vanity and refocused my attention on my Lord and Master.

Lord Loki and Aiken were, very purposefully, the last to arrive. I assumed, based on the smug satisfaction on Loki's handsome face, this was because he knew that his gaggle of geese would draw attention to him as he lowered himself into the chair which was surrounded by them.

If so, his plan worked.

Noliminan stood with violent quickness and made his way with heavy steps to the podium. As his hands fell upon it, Gabriel stood and blew his trumpet to announce this Council meeting as open.

"There will be no votes today." Noliminan instructed the Gods. "There will be plenty of time for such foolishness later."

There was a disappointed murmur that ran through the Council. They had all anticipated making their desire to manipulate the sex of their servants known.

"Many of you may have heard that I've sent Michael into exile." He began. "My reasons are my own and not meant for discussion amongst the Council."

Glances were exchanged all about. No one had ever anticipated that Michael would do anything which would warrant the consequences of exile.

"His replacement," Noliminan continued, seemingly oblivious to the discomfort of the Council members, "is another of Lucias' sons."

There was a discontented murmur throughout the hall. Zuko, who was sitting behind Loki, shifted uncomfortable in his chair. His large, dark brown eyes fell upon Gorgon and his lips pursed as if he were angry. I knew that this wasn't the case, however. He was one of the rare few who knew that this child was Loki's son. Though he had never seen Lucias in her true form, he was uncomfortable with the knowledge that Lucias had never truly been the God that he had thought her to be.

"Rise Gorgon."

Gorgon, terrified and embarrassed, did as he was bid. As Noliminan called him forward he walked, rather gracefully, toward him.

"Michael's replacement." Noliminan growled, his lips thinning as his gaze fell square upon Loki. The proud expression on the younger God's face was undeniable. "It is my wish that he is treated with the respect equal to his station."

There was a murmur of agreement throughout the room, though glances were being exchanged all about. Noliminan, still seemingly oblivious, dismissed Gorgon to his pillow with a violent wave.

"The matter which brings us together today, however, is neither Michael nor Gorgon." Noliminan began. "As you may all well know, a new war has broken out amongst the mortals."

"The vampires are destroying the elves." Aiken crossed his arms over his chest. Noliminan glared at him. "Adults attacking children. It's a massacre. Not a war."

"Yet a mortal matter all the same." Noliminan replied, the anger clear in his tone. "One in which you have interfered, Aiken of the Oakland."

"No, your Grace." Aiken replied, standing. He was being addressed directly so custom demanded it. "My people were called to an alliance. I merely stepped out of their way and allowed them to keep the promises that they have made."

"It is a mortal matter!" Noliminan cried, pounding the podium. His eyes darted around the Council. "One that we, as Gods, will steer clear of."

"We, as Gods, have." Aiken replied, shrugging. "My actions were those of a mortal King."

"Six and half of twelve." Lady Moira groused. "You're always unstringing my tapestries."

"My people are mortals." Aiken replied, shrugging again. "I cannot control them when they chose to play with your knots."

"You can and you will!" Noliminan ordered Emissary Lord Darklief. "Stay out of it, Aiken. I'm warning you."

Aiken, who had learned long ago when the time for argument with Noliminan had come to an end, thinned his lips and took his seat. He made no vow, however, not to direct his people against the vampires. Nor would he. He had made a promise to Jamiason and he intended to keep it.

"That goes for each and every one of you." Noliminan seemed to make eye contact with each member of the Council in turn. "Be warned." His eyes fell on Lord Loki. "The consequences for disobeying me on this matter will be damning."

Loki, no longer necessarily afraid of Noliminan, merely smiled in return.

-32-

When the dathanorna awoke, some two sunrises later, it did so with a fuzzy head and an even fuzzier mind. The smells of the forest had returned to their rights. Gone was the sweetness of the elves and the bitter tang of the vampires.

It shivered, understanding clearly that the elves had done it a kindness. They had spared its life when to have taken it would have, by all accounts, been the wiser decision.

Understanding this, it comprehended something else as well: One day, the pretty copper haired prince would demand his repayment. It also understood that, no matter what the request may be, the dathanorna, damned from birth, would have no choice but to oblige.

-33-

Ishitar appeared to be unsurprised to see me wearing the face of another and sitting in the chair at Zamyael's side. Rather, he merely leaned over and kissed the demoness on the cheek, forcing her to put aside her needlework so that she might give him a motherly hug.

"You missed a farce of a counsel today, Ishy." Zadkiel muttered as he dragged himself toward the lad.

"Oh?"

"Ta." My brother indicated me with his chin. "Ask him if you don't believe it."

Ishitar smiled. "Why would I not believe it?"

"Your father demanded the Gods stay out of the war between the elves and the demons." I explained. "He was goading Aiken, of course."

"Of course." Ishitar's expression grew contemplative. "Why does he care?"

"Aiken has aligned himself with the elves." Zadkiel shrugged. Though he couldn't hear me when I spoke, and I hadn't signed my words, he had the wits enough to assume what I'd said. "And your father has taken a special interest in the first of their kind."

"Doesn't want Aiken and his people mucking with them?"

"Just so." I agreed.

"That elf had best watch himself." Zamyael prophesized. "Being the subject of Noliminan's fascination has never boded well for anyone."

I leaned toward her and kissed her temple. She, of all people, knew best what the Bwuet Va was capable of.

"Least of all, beautiful Goddesses." Ishitar winked at her. She blushed prettily and lowered her gaze. "I'm not overly concerned for the elf. He has Aiken on his side."

"And Loki." Zadkiel's eyes narrowed. "Which puts a target directly upon his back."

"Moira's business." I reminded him by signing with my hands. This was followed by a grin as Zadkiel snorted at me. "And she's a fickle Goddess."

"More fickle than you know." He threw my own words, said long ago and not to him, back at me.

I was helpless not to laugh.

"Perhaps I should pay a visit to this elf." Ishitar muttered under his breath.

"Careful." Zadkiel's eyes narrowed. "If your father has taken an interest in him, he won't want you meddling."

"What can he do?" Ishitar asked, grinning, "Spank me?"

316

"He can do whatever he wants to do." Zamyael, who wore a faraway expression, reminded them in distant tones. "If not to you, then to those that you love."

Ishitar's brow furrowed. His lips thinned slightly before he nodded. He understood what she said to be true. Zadkiel had been whipped, after all, for the mere fact that Ishitar had chosen Loki as his mentor.

"Stay out of it." Zadkiel warned. "That's my best advice."

Ishitar, who had never enjoyed being schooled in the manner in which he should behave, merely gave him a distracted nod.

-34-

When the great marble gate came into view, Iladrul's relief overwhelmed him. He had made it home safely. And, though, not all of the doxies had survived the long journey, enough had that, once the war was over, they could rebuild the doxy village.

"Let's get them to the castle proper for the time being." Xylon muttered under his breath, his strange, fairy's eyes darting suspiciously around the forest. "The Gods know we don't need them to fall at your very gates."

Iladrul nodded, dug his heels into the flank of his horse, and led his people to what he hoped was the safety of his home.

-35-

"What will you do?" I asked Ishitar, truly curious to know his answer.

"Nothing." He muttered as he paced the length of his room. "What can I do? My father will play his hand. Then I will play mine."

"Yours is a reactionary game, then?"

"It's the game my mother taught me to play."

Perhaps, I thought. *Or, perhaps, Aiken is right and you really are playing a game of your own.*

317

Not wanting to tip my hand to him, not wanting him to understand that I knew him better than he may have wanted, I opted not to respond.

-36-

The defeat that coursed through Iykva's veins was burning. As was the narrowed eyed judgment that passed upon him from his King. Yet, now was not the time to back down or turn tail from his passions.

"I can capture them again."

"And do what with them?" Jamiason asked, his cobalt blue eyes narrowing. "They didn't breed as you'd wished. They were far too young!"

"Then I force my patience this time." Iykva snapped. He was becoming irritated. He didn't care for the fact that his failure was being thrown at him as an excuse to keep the damned and blasted elf that Jamiason had become obsessed with alive. "I asked too much of children. So let them become men."

"Why can you not just let this matter go?" Paul asked, impatient. "I want to walk within the rays as well." His voice was flat and harsh. "But at what cost?"

"He does have Aiken fighting at his side." Jamiason nodded. "What God would forgive you?"

"I should hope the God that rules me." Iykva seethed. "And, if not him, then his pet wolf."

Jamiason and Paul exchanged an irritated glance and then returned their attention to Iykva. It was Jamiason who spoke. "We've told you from the beginning that your aims are foolish." His thick lips pursed. "Would you damn us all?"

"You damn yourself, Jamiason Scrountentine!" Iykva knew he would regret the outburst eventually, but, for the moment, he didn't care. "With your inaction and protection over a child that is not of your own blood."

"We fought as brothers." Jamiason's eyes narrowed even further. "And in an effort to be treated as one."

"We are not treated as one!" Iykva cried. "Even in exile! And you know that well!"

"The sun rises soon." Paul raised his hands, almost as if he meant to placate the demons. "And we're all war weary."

"I go, Jamiason." Iykva swallowed the bile that rose into his throat. "With our without your support."

Jamiason merely shook his head and waved his hand at Iykva, dismissing him.

-37-

Gorgon shifted uncomfortably from foot to foot as Raphael fastened the bell that was to be his summoning charm around his ankle. His eyes darted nervously to his Lord and Master and his heart thrummed in his chest. He had heard, for the full of his life, stories of the cruel acts that the King of Lords had committed against his servants.

"Hmm." King Noliminan's lips thinned as he stared into the large basin that Raphael had told Gorgon was called a Crect'antee. He had braved a look within when Raphael had told him its purpose and had found the liquid gold within its bowl to be fascinatingly beautiful. "These demons are tenacious."

"Your Grace?" Raphael turned toward him, smiling.

King Noliminan's eyes, identical to Raphael's, flipped upward. He gave his archangel a broad smile. Gorgon thought, looking upon that smile, he could understand why, despite his cruelty, the members of the Quorum had come to love their Lord and Master.

"They're marching toward Wisterian." As he spoke, his eyes flicked to Gorgon, who blushed slightly and lowered his gaze. "This time, I believe Iykva means to strike at the heart of the castle."

"It would be the wiser move, your Grace." Raphael, still smiling, replied. He stood and turned Gorgon. "Now you're properly ready to serve."

"And I have my first task for you."

319

"Your Grace?" Gorgon wished he could slap down the snakes that were flailing wildly about his face. He was growing to loathe the damned things.

King Noliminan, however, seemed amused.

"How do you kill a snake?" He asked Gorgon.

Gorgon didn't find that question very funny. Though, obviously King Noliminan, wearing a self-satisfied smirk, did.

"I don't know, your Grace."

"You cut off its head." He replied, stepping forward and reaching for one of the snakes that made up Gorgon's hair.

As he did so, his fingers bit into the throat of the little beast, smashing it. The agony that rushed through Gorgon's body made him cry out with horror and surprise. When the King of Lords dropped the snake, its head fell to the ground at Gorgon's feet.

"That hurt you?"

"Yes." Gorgon whispered as he tried to bite back the tears that were springing to his eyes. "Your Grace. It did."

"Interesting." He turned away as if bored.

King Noliminan bent over the Crect'antee again and narrowed his eyes. Gorgon realized, as he did so, that Raphael was looking at him with a sad, almost apologetic smile. Gorgon smiled weakly in return.

"What you are to do, my son," King Noliminan dipped his finger into the gold liquid within the bowl, "is travel to Anticata and look Iykva straight in the eyes. Turn the carvetek mouk into stone." He looked upward. Gorgon didn't care much for his smile. Nor did he care to be called 'son' by this man. "See how he likes being frozen in time for as long as it takes for someone to care enough about him to release him."

"Your Grace," Gorgon shivered. "I can't do that. My father always says—"

"You aren't in service to Loki!" He growled. His voice was booming. So much so that Gorgon felt like covering his ears. "You are in service to me and you will do as I bid."

"It does seem extreme, your Grace." Raphael's voice was shaking as he said these words. "Don't you think?"

"I didn't ask for your opinion on the matter." He spun on Raphael, his hand flying to strike him. Raphael, an old master of this game, dodged out of the way just in time.

"Forgive me, your Grace." He whispered.

This seemed to placate the King of Lords. He glared at Raphael for a moment and then returned his attention to Gorgon.

"Do as you are bid." He growled as he pointed to the snake head on the floor. "Lest you see more of your little friends join that one."

Before Gorgon could respond, he spun on his heel and stormed out the door.

Gorgon raised his gaze and met Raphael's. "I won't survive him."

"You will." Raphael sighed and walked toward the sofa. He threw himself upon it and raised his foot onto the table in front of it. "After all, you really don't have a choice."

Watching Raphael, Gorgon remembered his father's last words to him and wondered if his brother's words were true.

-38-

Sappharon's lips spread wide across her face as she opened the door and her eyes fell upon Lucias' son. She sprang toward him, wrapped her arms around his neck and planted a warm kiss on his cheek. He seemed pleased by this, as his snakes began attacking her fiercely, ticking her skin.

"Is my Mother home?" Gorgon asked her as he stepped away.

"She is." Sappharon signed. "In the garden; playing with Banshee."

Gorgon smiled at her, nodded and made his way into the cottage. Sappharon, who had never been one to respect the privacy of others, followed after him. When they passed through the kitchen and into the back yard, Gorgon looked over his shoulder at her and gave her a patient smile. "You don't have to follow. I can serve her needs."

"I don't mind." Sappharon signed at him.

Familiar with Sappharon's ways, Gorgon merely shook his head and proceeded out the back door.

When Lucias saw him, her face split into a wide grin. She sat the baby on her bottom and flew toward Gorgon, hugging him tightly. As she did so, she noticed the limp snake hanging from his head and recoiled.

"Piss on the Gods, Gorgon!" She cried as she reached for it; she had picked up Loki's sayings over the years. I always find this particular turn to be an amusing one, but more so when it escapes from her lips. "What happened to him?"

"The King of Lords happened to him." Gorgon replied frowning. "He snapped his head off to make metaphor."

Her lips thinned at that. "Always one to prove a point."

"He wants me to turn Iykva to stone." Gorgon told her, his voice heavy with his grief. "And, if I don't, he said he'll take the heads off of all of them."

"He'll do no such thing." Sappharon turned at the sound of Loki's voice. She smiled at Ishitar, who was following behind him. "If he touches a single one more, I'll have *his* head."

"There's nothing you can do about it, Fete." Gorgon sighed. "I must do as he has bid."

Loki's lips thinned.

"Perhaps the shadows have shifted their weight long enough." Lucias sighed. "Perhaps you should lay claim to Raziel's throne now rather than waiting."

"Without a full Quorum?" Loki asked, crossing his arms over his chest. "And with half of them not yet knee high to a pixie?"

"There is a way." Ishitar muttered under his breath. "If, that is, you're willing to trust Loki."

"What have you got on your mind?" Lucias asked, walking toward him.

"I can transfer a portion of your power to Loki." He replied. Sappharon's brow immediately furrowed. "It would be temporary. Just until you, yourself, are properly returned to your throne."

Lucias grinned at him. Sappharon shivered. She raised her hands in argument.

"That is a mistake!" She signed. "If you give your power away, there's no saying that Loki will want to give it back!"

"She has a fair point, Luci." Loki, who looked as uncomfortable with the idea as Sappharon felt, replied. "With power comes greed."

"The very fact that you worry about your potential actions tells me that you will not act upon them." Ishitar advised him. "But, if you are concerned, I shall keep control over the binding of it. If I believe you are taking advantage of the situation, I shall return Lucias' power to her. By then everyone will consider you as the Sovereign Lord."

"And what of Lucias?" Sappharon signed. "Who will protect her in her weakened state?"

"The one who always has." Lucias replied, stepping toward her and placing her hand on Sappharon's shoulder. "You've served me long and true, Sappharon. And I have been holding onto something to give you when the shadows shifted rightly."

"I don't want any gift from you!" She replied. "I want you to see common sense."

Lucias raised her hand and ran her finger lovingly over Sappharon's brow. As she did so, an electricity unlike any that the demon had ever known coursed through her veins. And, as Lucias came to the end of her brow, the heavy wings she had carried the full of her life fell from her shoulder blades to land with a heavy thud to the ground.

"I don't . . ." She spun around to look at them, horrified.

"I took Raguel's powers from her on the day I took her life." Lucias said, her voice gentle. "They belong to you now, met paken. And when Loki exchanges his powers with mine, we shall, at long last, be equals."

"It's not a gift that I can accept." Sappharon swallowed as she signed these words. "You are now, and always shall be, my Lady."

323

Lucias leaned forward and kissed her forehead. She then turned away to face Ishitar. Gorgon, who had watched all of this in silent confusion, stepped forward as if to stop her.

But he didn't. He allowed her to walk toward Loki and take his hand. When their fingers were entwined, Ishitar reached forward and grasped each of their wrists. The moment he did so, a bright light surrounded them both, blinding Sappharon with its glory.

The transformation in Loki was instantaneous. His back straightened and his dark purple eyes grew wide. By the time Ishitar dropped their wrists, Loki was looking down on Lucias with obvious love and quiet fascination.

"Go to him." Lucias placed her palm upon his cheek. "And claim the throne that is rightfully yours."

He leaned forward, kissed her gently and was, very suddenly, gone.

Sappharon stared at the spot where he had stood knowing one thing and one thing only: there was nothing about this blasphemy that could possibly work in Lucias' favor.

-39-

"I can't tell you what happened between Loki and Noliminan when Loki approached him to demand Raziel's old title and throne." I advise Charlie in reverent tones. "He approached Noliminan when no one else was about. And, since Loki had begun eating Ishitar's pies, I was able to train on him less and less without his allowance."

"When they both returned?" Charlie asked, his attention turned completely toward me. "Did Loki wear Raziel's crown?"

"Oh yes." I smile at him. "And Noliminan wore a wound upon his cheek which glows as a bright pink scar to this very day."

-40-

"I won't stand for it!" Raziel cried as she stormed through the library to pound her fists on Noliminan's desk. "Loki has no business being a member of the Small Council!"

"Lucias and Raguel must eventually be replaced." His lips thinned as he looked up at her. She saw, for the first time, the angry wound upon his face. She had the better sense to be frightened. The only one who could give him such a cut was Lucias. Clearly, the pair of them had argued hand to hand and Lucias, quite possibly, had won. "Lucias insists that Loki is the better choice to represent him as the Hells bound Lord of the Council. He has the right to pick your replacement. Just as I have the authority to determine who will replace Raguel."

"Whom?" She felt her teeth shake in her gums. She didn't like the idea of him sitting a Queen at his side. She thought of herself as his Queen now that she warmed both his bed and Lucias' throne.

"It's still under consideration." He replied. "The time for me to take a new wife is long overdue. Yet, my decision must be tempered with what is best for the Sixty Realms and not in the direction that my heart and mind would fly."

Her lips pursed. She bit her tongue to hold her anger at bay. It was no secret that, like Loki, Noliminan had a gaggle of his own. He merely showed more discretion than the younger God when slipping into their beds.

"Choose wisely, Nol." She warned him. "And make it clear to her from the start of it that she is to bow down to *me*."

His eyes flashed. She knew her words had been a mistake the moment he laced his fingers together and tented them under his chin. The calculation in those cold orbs made her shiver.

"And you, my dear, will ever bow down to Lucias." She lowered her gaze, terrified. "Or is a reminder of your true place required?"

"No." She replied. "Forgive me."

"You will tolerate Loki because it is what Lucias desires." He advised her, unwinding his fingers. She had never been more relieved in the full of her life. "And, when the time comes, you will tolerate whomever I choose to marry because it is what I desire. Do you understand?"

"Yes, Noliminan." She found a smile for him that seemed to please him. He hadn't said that she needed to respect or obey Loki or this new other. Just that she should tolerate them. Which meant that she still held the power to Lucias' throne. "I understand perfectly."

"Good." He sighed and sat back in his chair. "Now leave me. I have much to think about this morn."

"Of course." She leaned forward and kissed his cheek. "Will you be by tonight?"

His eyes trailed the length of her as he granted her a haughty smile. It was all the answer she required.

-41-

Metatron's brow furrowed as he stared at the door. The hour was late and he was unused to receiving visitors. As such, it wasn't until the second knock that he put his book aside so that he might greet his caller.

When he opened the door, his heart fell into his stomach. There stood Lord Loki, wearing a tight, uncomfortable smile.

"My Lord?"

"May I come in?" He asked, looking over Metatron's shoulder and into his humble cottage. "I won't take up but a shift of your shadows."

"Of course, my Lord." Metatron stepped back to allow him entry. He had never felt so uncomfortable in the full of his life. He and Loki hadn't truly passed any real words since what had become to be known as 'the incident'. "How may I serve you?"

"An announcement is going to be made at the next Council." He replied. Metatron frowned. He hoped beyond hope that it wasn't the announcement that they all feared was coming.

326

"Before it does, I want to give you the opportunity to make a choice about something."

"Oh?"

"You do know who Gorgon's father is, don't you?"

"Yes." His nostrils flared slightly. It was common knowledge that Gorgon was Lucias' child, but few knew that she had been the one to birth him. "I do."

Loki gave him a tight smile. "And how do you feel about that."

"How am I supposed to feel about that, my Lord?" He was curious as to this line of questioning. "Who Lucias beds is not mine to be concerned with."

"Do you understand why she is having children?"

"It is the natural order of things when one person loves another." He frowned at Loki. He had a child of his own that he had no business having seeded. Not that Sappharon had ever let him see it. "Planned or otherwise."

Loki smiled at him, raised his hand and grasped his bicep for the barest moment before releasing it. His touch burned Metatron and shame overwhelmed him.

"She's having children because she's building a Quorum." Loki advised him. "Michael became the first member, although I believe she means to wait to call him into service until such time as he's sired a son amongst the gargoyles."

Metatron nodded. He had visited Michael out of anger when he had learned it had been Michael, rather than himself, that Lucias had released from Noliminan.

"I've come to ask you if you want to be the second."

Metatron recoiled with surprise, "My Lord? She means to grant me her succor?"

"No." He sighed. "But, if you are willing to serve me, and serve me well, then I do." He gave Metatron a weary smile. "We'd be seeing quite a lot of one another."

"My Lord . . . I would be . . . grateful." He swallowed and shook his head. "But how are you to manage it? Noliminan will never—"

"Let me worry about Noliminan." Loki's lips thinned beneath his goatee. "He and I have come to somewhat of an . . . understanding."

Metatron wasn't certain, but he would have sworn that Lord Loki's eyes flashed as he said that last word. He didn't know if it pleased him or terrified him.

He thought, perhaps, it was the latter.

"You'll be hearing from me soon." Loki advised him before turning away and heading toward Metatron's door. He stopped when he reached it and looked over his shoulder to meet Metatron's gaze. "You and I? Are we past our . . . eh . . . issues with one another?"

"Of course, my Lord." Metatron, greedy for his freedom, replied. "It will never be thought of again."

Loki's brow furrowed slightly as he opened the door. As he left he gave Metatron a tired, almost wintery smile.

His parting words were, quite simply, "You know, I doubt that."

-42-

The twins had been attempting to return to the castle when they heard the stomping of many feet upon the road. They darted off, Louis pulling Melody behind him, and bounded upward and into the trees. From there, they watched as Iykva's army of vampires and fallen demons marched toward Wisterian.

When they had passed, Marchand pulled upon Louis' sleeve and asked, "Do we follow them?"

"It's what Jamiason would want." Louis agreed, turning his dark eyes to Melody. "What do you think?"

"I agree." Melody replied. "Judging by the expression on Iykva's face, he isn't up to any good."

"The pair of you should return to Jamiason to make a report that the elves returned safely home." Marchand lowered his gaze. It had become clear to them as they journeyed that the twin who Melody was interested in was Louis rather than him. Now, looking at Louis' eyes light up at the thought of being alone with her, he knew that the feelings were reciprocated. "I'll go back and warn the elf."

"Is it safe for you to travel alone?" Melody asked, blinking at him.

"Don't worry about my brother." Louis replied, grinning. "He can hold his own against anything."

Marchand, nodding, hoped that was true.

-43-

"You try my patience!" Noliminan growled as he slammed his fist onto his desk. "Trading Michael for Gorgon was one thing. He has use to me. But I will not trade Metatron for a near sighted bull!"

"I didn't offer Taurus to you." Loki snapped. "He's far too young."

"Surely you don't expect me to take Lucias' daughter!"

Mihr, who was serving King Noliminan in Raphael's stead while her brother saw to a task that he had been put upon, flinched. She understood all too well the displeasure that the King of Lords had felt upon first looking at her and her sister in their true female form.

"Of course not." Loki replied, eyes wild with fury. "She'd have you on your back and in her bed before you knew what hit you." He smiled then. "And we all know how you like your women submissive. She'd never suit you."

King Noliminan made to cross the desk to throttle Loki, but the younger of the two Gods didn't even flinch. He merely smiled and pointed his finger at the gash across the King of Lord's cheek.

Which, to Mihr's surprise, stayed her Lord and Master on his side of the desk.

"Why do you need Metatron anyway?" Loki asked, almost seething. "Simply to do your dirty business for you?"

"It would seem to me that it is you that is up to dirty business, Loki." King Noliminan groused; then he smirked. "Or perhaps you now have a taste for the flame."

"You know damn well and good that isn't the case." Loki flew to his feet. "But say it again. Let us see what I can do when I mean to strike you!"

"I know not where your powers come from, *nymph*." He leaned forward so that his face was about as close as it could come to Loki's without their noses touching. "But the barest moment I figure it out, I shall strip them from you. When I do, your soul will repay for the damnation of every sin ever made in your blasted name."

"Until that day comes," Loki shot back, "you will bide me."

"Not for a single shift more."

Loki backed away and lowered himself into his chair. Mihr, sitting quietly on the floor in her waiting stance, had become fascinated with this repast.

When had Lord Loki become so brave?

"I want Metatron."

"Take him then." King Noliminan, following Loki's lead, fell into his chair. "But in exchange, I keep Samyael."

Loki's face went purple with rage. "What good will Samyael do you?"

"He's proven useful." The King of Lord's smile was chilling. "You've trained him well."

"No good can come of a demon in your service." Loki snorted.

"Just as no good can come of an angel in yours." He grinned. "The next time you see Sam, he will be wearing wings of white. Upon sight of them, you *will* send him back to my service."

Loki, as angry as anyone Mihr had ever seen, flew to his feet. He glared at the King of Lords for a long painful moment before kicking his foot behind him and knocking over his chair.

As though he finally realized that common sense was the better part of valor, he stormed past Mihr and out of King Noliminan's library, slamming the door behind him. Mihr watched him until he was gone and then turned her surprised gaze in the King of Lords' direction.

As her eyes clashed with his, she realized that it would be she who would pay this night for Loki's disobedience. By morning, my sister understood, all too well and for the first time in her life, just how far Noliminan is willing to go to make his point.

Upon receiving her battered and broken body, Lord Loki, who had barely even noticed that she sat in the room, cried out in anger and fury.

As for me, I wept.

Scrawled upon my sister's forehead was a message that was meant to be a warning to all who looked upon her from that day forward. It was simply one word; it was my name.

Its purpose? To remind everyone what, ultimately, happened to those who eavesdropped on conversations that they weren't meant to hear.

Mihr, who had always been meek and mild, buried the message deep in her heart. Fearful of what might happen to her if she did, Mihr chose not to utter another word to anyone—about anything—for a very, very long time.

-44-

Metatron cradled Mihr in his arms, his fiery gaze dancing upward to look upon Lord Loki's profile. The young God had just explained to Samyael that he was meant to return to Noliminan's service in Metatron's place.

Samyael, having opened the door to Mihr when she had tripped her way to Loki's apartment, shivered.

"Must I?"

"You must." Loki sighed. "I'm sorry Sam. You no longer belong in the Hells. Not with wings of white."

Metatron swallowed and lowered his gaze. At his foot sat the dog that was always following Ishitar around. Its mismatched eyes were watching him with great curiosity. If he hadn't known better, he would have thought that its black lips were curled into a tight smile.

"I'll never obey him." Samyael whispered.

"You will." Lord Loki's tone was firm. "Sam. You must. You see with your own glams how he treats his own. One toe off the plank and he will punish you if only to destroy me." His eyes flicked to Mihr, who whimpered against Metatron's chest. His expression was immediately one of excruciating pain. "I've hurt enough innocents this day."

"Yes my Lord."

"Now go." He couldn't even look at Samyael. "Knowing you are always welcome here."

"He's been looking for an excuse to rid himself of her since Tristan made his mischief." Metatron corrected him after Samyael was gone. "And it won't be long before you have Uriel as well. Mark me on that."

"Can she be protected until that day comes?"

"Doubtful." Metatron muttered under his breath. "But she has Camael to defend her if needs be. He loves her fiercely."

"Ansibrius." Loki barked.

The dog turned away from Metatron and whined.

"I know that you love Ishitar." The dog whined again. "But you are needed elsewhere." Now she growled. "None of that. Go to Camael and Uriel's cottage and keep your eyes and ears peeled to them until you are certain that Uriel can weather this particular storm." He flicked his eyes back up to meet Metatron's gaze. "He'll destroy her if for their love of one another alone."

Metatron, his lips pursing, nodded.

"Before you go," he held his hand out to the dog, "I have a formal introduction to make."

Metatron watched with quiet curiosity as the dog padded toward Loki. When she reached him, she looked up at the God, her whines returning.

Loki smiled down at her and then looked back to Metatron.

"Enough of these games of deception." He said. "If you are to be in service to me, I demand complete and open honesty between us. On both sides."

"Of course, my Lord."

"And enough of that as well." Loki frowned at him. He returned his gaze to the dog. "Na'amah." Metatron froze. He had heard that name on Sappharon's lips once when she had slipped and spoken their child's name. "Meet your father."

The dog looked over her shoulder. As their eyes met, her form changed.

There was no denying whose child she was.

"Na'amah." Metatron whispered. "I'm . . . so pleased . . ."

She rose and walked toward him. When she reached him, she bent forward and kissed his brow.

Lord Loki cleared his throat. They both looked in his direction.

"I'm sorry, but there isn't time for a proper family reunion right now." He said. "Get to your task, Na'amah. And be quick about it."

She gave Metatron another glance, smiled sadly at him, then returned to her dog's form.

Metatron, overwhelmed with the pain of the years he had survived, turned his face into his sister's tight blond curls lest his weakness show and Loki judge him for it.

Loki didn't. Rather, he walked toward the pair of them, patted Metatron on the shoulder and made himself scarce.

-45-

Marchand clung to the side of the tower, hovering just outside of the window so he could listen to Iykva speak with the human. His fingers ached from the sheer effort it took to keep his body from being caught by the wind and hurtled to the ground below. The fall certainly wouldn't kill him, but it would break him to the point where it could take decades, if not a full century, for him to heal.

When the demons and vampires had turned off of the road that led to Wisterian, he had, at first, hoped this meant that they would abandon their course. Now, as he listened to Iykva speak of the Devonshires and their alliance with the elves, he knew better.

A chill ran through Marchand, causing him to shiver. He momentarily lost his grip and slipped slightly against the stone. He thought that Iykva might have heard him, but if he did he showed no sign of it. Perhaps, he thought Marchand to be nothing more than a bird pecking at the outside of the window.

Had the vampire a breath in him, he would have sighed with relief as Iykva and the human left the room.

He hadn't heard everything, but he'd heard enough to know what he must do.

As swiftly as his arms would allow, Marchand shimmied down the side of the building, jumping the last story to land with bent knees and one hand to the ground.

He had a falcon to send.

Not to any King or Prince, but to a doxy.

This falcon was meant to fly to the elfin girl named Sezja.

-46-

Aiken, who was paying more attention to both the vampires and the elves than was probably good for him, frowned as the pixie he had set upon Marchand returned to him with news of what the youngling had overheard. Shaking his head, Aiken thanked his tiny friend and allowed the creature to blend himself back into his skin.

"Damn it." He muttered. "And there's nothing I can do."

"My Lord?" Aiken turned toward Samyael, who was hovering in the doorway. "Ill news?"

What are you doing here, Sam?

"Nothing to worry yourself about." He gave Samyael a guarded smile. "And you?"

"Worry comes in spades." His eyes flicked around the room before landing upon Aiken. "The King of Lords . . ." Aiken's own eyes narrowed as he crossed his arms over his chest. "Loki told me I'm to serve him in trade for Metatron." Aiken's eyes darted upward and he noticed, for the first time, the change in the color of Samyael's wings. "And after what he did to Mihr . . ."

"What has he done to Mihr?" Aiken, who had been sitting, immediately flew to his feet. "What could *she* have done to displease him?"

"She was born a female, Emissary Lord Darklief." Samyael replied, his tone cold. "Could there be a worse crime where the King of Lords is concerned? Lest the female be his bedmate?"

Aiken heard a whistle fly through his teeth that immediately made him grant Samyael a sardonic grin. He sounded all too much like Lady Lucias for his own taste when he made that frustrated noise.

Samyael, whose wit could never be called into question, returned the smile.

"He has changed me."

"That isn't the worst thing that could happen to you." Aiken advised him. "Demons are looked down upon. You're being elevated socially."

"Would you feel the same where they to announce that you were to now be an elf?" Samyael asked him, his black eyes blazing. "Given the elves have stolen the favor that the fairies once claimed."

"No." Aiken agreed at once. He walked toward Samyael and stroked his cheek. He did love this demon, in his own way. "I'm sorry Sam. That was very insensitive of me . . ."

Samyael smiled up at him. "No matter, my Lord."

Grateful for the demon's understanding, Aiken turned away from him. "You'll be in a position to go on watching him." He looked over his shoulder, wary of Samyael despite the fact that reason screamed at him that he had no call to be. "If you wish to continue serving Loki, that is."

"I do." Samyael swallowed. "I love him." His eyes darted away. "I feel nothing for the King of Lords but disdain."

"You would do well to hold on to such." Aiken reminded him. "After your binding to him is complete."

"I am bound to Loki." Samyael whispered. "The color of my wings will not dispel such magic from my soul."

Pleased with Samyael on so many levels, Aiken stepped toward him, laced his hand through his hair to bend him forward, and kissed him, this time, on the lips.

-47-

Samyael approached Lord Loki very cautiously. He, above everyone else, had marked the changes in his Master since Lord Loki had lost his head. Yet, these changes seemed small in light of those that had come recently.

There was a power about Lord Loki, now, that was almost as intimidating as that which Lady Lucias and the King of Lords possessed. Having been warned by Emissary Lord Darklief to refrain from eating more of the forbidden fruit of the tree, Samyael had a small fear and idea where this power had come from.

"Excuse me," Samyael announced himself timidly. "My Lord?"

"Sam?" Lord Loki looked upward, surprise masking his features. He stood, almost at once, and darted around the desk. He ran forward, grasped Sam's shoulder's and looked, searching and imploring, into Samyael's eyes. "How are you? Is he treating you well?"

"Well enough." Samyael forced himself to smile. "And you, my Lord?"

"Well enough." Lord Loki grinned at him as he pulled him into a warm embrace before, all too quickly, pushing him away. "You put yourself in danger by coming here."

"I do." Samyael lowered his gaze. "But, my Lord, I must warn you."

"Warn me?"

"Emissary Lord Darklief . . ." Sam swallowed the betrayal that welled in his heart. He loved Aiken. He had even lain with him from time to time. Yet, his deepest loyalty belonged to Lord Loki. "He's . . . meddling."

Lord Loki chuckled deep from within his chest. "Totally out of character."

Sam had no choice but to smile at the truth of those words.

"Enough that it troubles you, however."

"Ta." Samyael felt a moment bit of relief wash through him. "He's . . . spying."

"On?"

"His betters." Samyael replied, eyes wide, as he shrugged. "The King of Lords and—"

He bit his tongue. Something deep within his soul told him not to mention that he had been set by Emissary Lord Darklief in regard to the Prince of Providence.

"And?"

"It troubles me."

Lord Loki, who hadn't a clue that Samyael had partaken of the fruit—or what the fruit had the power to do—grinned. He reached forward and clapped Samyael on the back of his shoulder with warm, masculine affection.

"I trust you will not let Aiken run amok where Noliminan is concerned." Loki winked at him. "Otherwise, you wouldn't be here."

"Emissary Lord Darklief is a storm that cannot be reigned in." Samyael reminded Lord Loki, though with a heart tinged of relief. "Which is why I come to you. He's meddling with the fate of the elves. Despite the King of Lords' orders that you Gods refrain."

"I'm aware of this." Lord Loki's brow furrowed. "For James."

"For James." Samyael agreed. "But also because it is the right thing to do." He swallowed. "You do know what the demons and vampires are doing to the elves?"

"I'm aware." Lord Loki's tone was flat. "I also know that I cannot interfere with this matter right now."

"I don't ask you to." Samyael met his gaze and held it. He wanted Lord Loki to know that he wasn't playing games with him or lying to him. "I only meant to warn you that Emissary Lord Darklief is not quite as cautious."

"Then keep an eye on him Sam." Lord Loki implored. "For me." He sighed and looked away. "Please."

"I shall." Samyael promised. "And will I continue to report my findings to you?"

Lord Loki blinked and returned his gaze to Sam. His lips were curling into a grin beneath the bush of his goatee.

"Yes, Sam." He replied, his tone gentle. "When you can."

"I am ever yours." Samyael reminded him. "No matter who, in name, I serve."

As Countenance's shadows pass him by Loki has learned, by Samyael's actions, that truer words could have never been said.

-48-

"You've gone to visit her Gods be damned grave again?" Karma stormed as she stepped toward Michael. "What is the damn fascination? She's dead, Michael! And you have responsibilities here!"

Michael ignored her. He wasn't in the mood to placate her, or anyone else. He had just learned that his sister had been attacked by Noliminan for the sheer audacity of being present in the room during a conversation she hadn't been meant to overhear.

And, no doubt, her presence had been required at his former Master's orders.

"Leave off." He grumbled, pushing her out of the way. "Unless you have news."

"News." She spat. "What news?"

"How fair my children?" Michael barked, irritated. "My gargoyles."

"Perhaps if you spent more time—"

"Karma." Max shook his head. "Don't agitate him."

"Agitate." She grumbled and spun away.

Michael watched her storm out of the room and turned his gaze to Max. His nostrils flared and his eyes narrow. Until he realized he wasn't angry with Maxium.

"Why is she so upset?"

"She doesn't understand your obsession with the Queen of Ladies." Max shrugged. "Given she died a Lord."

"She wasn't a Lord." Michael growled. "She may have been born that way. And she may have died that way." He shook his head. "She didn't live that way."

"Mortals don't have the luxury of waning and waxing their sex." Maxium shrugged. "You can't expect her to understand."

Despite himself, Michael had no choice but to agree.

"What must I know?" He asked. "About my children?"

"Haniel's stew has made the sickness pass." Max smiled at him. "Your children, what remains of them, should thrive."

Michael sighed his relief and nodded at his servant.

"I know it's a touchy subject."

"Then don't raise it." Michael warned.

Max only smiled at him. He had never been obedient.

"What?"

"Your new station." Max lowered his gaze. "Serving Lord Lucias."

"Hasn't been defined." Michael barked. "And now he has Metatron and Mihr."

"Mihr?"

Michael turned toward the sound of Karma's voice and glared at her. She had a damn nasty habit of getting under his skin.

"What on which moon could Mihr have done—?"

"What on which moon could I have done?" Michael seethed. "Or Metatron, for that matter!" He shook his head. "He's a fool."

"Michael!" Max cried. "Don't say those words. It's blasphemy!"

"Then blasphemy it is." Michael grumbled before turning away from them both and storming toward his room. He stopped at the hall and returned to face them. "Damn me for it. But I see him for what he is now." Karma and Maxium exchanged a guarded glance that Michael didn't much care for at those words. "And I am grateful that I shall never be forced to supplicate to him again."

-49-

Sezja read the letter, crumpled it up and threw it into the fire.

Be on the lookout, its author had warned her. *Trust no one new. Especially if they wear the face of a human.*

She raised her gaze to the orphan that Prince Trevor had found wandering the Great Road. He was a young thing of eight or nine and he had the innocent face of an angel.

Still, she thought, *he bears heavy watching.*

She raised her hand and set it upon the swell of her belly. The babe would be coming soon.

Closing her eyes she raised her face to the Heavens, sought out the Lady Theasis and prayed.

-50-

Aiken was beginning to get extremely irritated with Ishitar's constant presence in Loki's apartment. It seemed, to Aiken, as though he was no longer to be afforded a private conversation with his friend. It was almost as if Ishitar was aware of Aiken's growing mistrust of him and so made it a point to be ever present to prevent the fairy God from sharing his concerns with his friend.

Not that he would.

He was aware of the special bond that had formed between Ishitar and Loki. There was nothing that he could say to Loki to break that bond. Because of this, he decided to bide his time and simply watch.

Quiet defiance, he had learned over time, could sometimes take a person further than direct confrontation.

"You just missed Sam." Loki grinned at him. "He would have loved to have seen you."

Aiken forced a smile. He had seen and talked to Samyael before Sam had sought out Loki. "That's bad luck."

"Indeed." Loki smiled in response. "He looks well."

"I'm pleased to hear that." Aiken meant that sentiment. He worried every day that he would hear that Samyael had somehow been molested by the King of Lords. If Noliminan knew that Sam were spying on him, all manner of every Hell would reign down upon the child. "How does he feel about the new color of his wings?"

Loki chuckled and shook his head. "That one's a survivor." He grinned. "Always has been. He'll be fine."

Aiken gave him a curt nod and turned his gaze to Ishitar. He sat quietly on his favorite chair, watching Aiken with that strange, contemplative smile he always wore.

The dog, Aiken noticed, was queerly absent.

"Have you been watching the goings on between Jamiason and his elf?" Aiken asked, turning his attention back to Loki. "It would seem that Iykva's aligned himself with the House of Fyrsoth."

"Has he, now?" Loki replied, distractedly, as he turned his attention to the tome on his desk. "That promises to be entertaining. Aren't they sworn enemies of the Devonshires?"

"Ta." Aiken bit his tongue. He had just about enough of Loki's obsession with that fucking tome. Especially when he was trying to make a point and was being ignored for it. "They are."

"What does James intend to do about it?" Loki seemed almost bored by the conversation as he turned the page that he had been reading.

Aiken was ready to explode upon him with anger.

"I'm certain he'll call in the elves' allies." He snapped. "What do you intend to do about it?"

"It isn't my war, Aiken." Loki raised his gaze at the tone of Aiken's admonishment. "There's nothing I can do about it. Unlike you, I do not govern a mortal race that I can direct to Iladrul's aide."

"You're the Sovereign Lord now." Aiken reminded him, unnecessarily. "Raise the issue to the Lady Regent and demand that she asks Noliminan to interfere."

Loki assessed him with his dark, purple eyes. His expression was unreadable. Finally, he let out a long sigh and shook his head.

"He told us not to interfere." He muttered. "Now is not the time to test him."

"If not now, then when?" Aiken's frustration with his friend was overwhelming. "You obviously have his ear! Otherwise you wouldn't be wearing Raziel's crown!"

"A crown that's been newly set." Loki leaned back and crossed his arms over his chest. "I know you want to help James. And, although I understand why, now is not the time. I can't risk losing my position. Lucias needs me where I am. I can't give Noliminan a reason to change his mind."

Aiken shot an angry glance in Ishitar's direction. The strange smile he wore made the fairy shiver. He was enjoying this little diatribe.

What are you so damn smug about?

He shook his head and returned his attention to Loki.

"Fine." He groused. "Don't help me; don't help James. Just sit there and do what you've always done: let Lady Lucias manipulate your moves and then blame everyone else around you when it all goes horribly wrong."

Frustrated and angry with his friend, Aiken spun on his heel and stormed out of the room. As he slammed the door behind him, he very nearly tripped over Ansibrius. He glared at her, not liking the fire burning in her strange, intelligent eyes.

Knowing kicking her would be an unwise move, he stormed out of Loki's apartment to seek counsel from one of Jamiason's old friends.

-51-

Ishitar excused himself from the room almost immediately after Aiken left them. Na'amah slipped in when the door opened, watching him with a slight frown before turning her gaze to Loki. Loki, who had been staring at the door with quiet interest since the moment that Aiken had left him, lowered his gaze to meet hers.

"I thought I put you to task."

"I came to report that they've both, wisely, returned to their own quarters." She advised him. "I believe if they are both careful they shall be overlooked."

"Good." He muttered. His eyes flicked to the door and then back to meet her gaze. "Do me a favor, Na'amah." She whined. "Follow one or the other of them—I don't care which—and report back to me anything that they do which you find curious."

"I refuse to betray Ishitar."

"Then perhaps it's best you follow Aiken." Loki suggested with a raised brow. "As I said, I don't care which." His eyes narrowed slightly, causing her to shiver. "Given Aiken's temperament just now, perhaps he bears the most watching, anyway."

Na'amah, who had seen the fire in Aiken's eyes as he looked upon her, couldn't have agreed more.

-52-

I must admit that I would have preferred that Na'amah followed Ishitar rather than Aiken. My eyes were already glued to the fairy God, whereas my boy passed out of my sight until such time as he wanted to be seen.

The buzzing nest of Aiken's thoughts had been clear to me for some time. As I've said before, Aiken no longer trusted the Prince of Providence. And I, who oft times looked upon Ishitar and saw the face of both his mother and father, was beginning to wonder if he were up to his old games.

If the King of Lords could fool me into believing he was Lord Loki, who was as different from Noliminan as night was to day, then he could fool me into believing he was anyone.

Sighing, I pushed the thought from my mind.

There was nothing I could do to calm my ever growing doubts now. Ishitar was out of my line of sight and I couldn't read his thoughts or emotions even if he were not. In this particular matter, I was left to form my own opinions based on personal observations and my maddening ability to read others.

Aiken's course would have been predictable even if I hadn't already known where he was going. He meant to see Evanbourough to convince him that he must speak with Jamiason and warn him to force his people to stand down. With Ishitar, Lucias and Noliminan standing on polar opposite corners of a triangle of disagreement, nothing good could come of the demons and the vampires in their attempt to oppress the elves.

"He'll listen to you." Aiken grumbled as he fell into one of Evanbourough high backed chair. "You're his God! His ruler! He can't tell you no."

"You were his Master and he managed to slough you off." Evanbourough snapped at Aiken. He found it pointless to remind Aiken that Jamiason was now, also, a God. "Don't underestimate that child's will."

Aiken gave him an impatient glare but made no response. What response could he give? Evanbourough was right. There was no controlling Jami when he had a burr stuffed up his backside.

"Why is this so urgent for you, anyway?" Evanbourough asked, his curiosity thrumming through his mind. "What interest have you in the elf? Other than Jamiason's happiness, that is?"

Aiken thought about his response for a long moment. He had never really trusted Evanbourough after Evan had jilted Theasis. Even if he were Aiken's main link to Jamiason's salvation, he didn't much trust him now.

Evan was one of those men, in Aiken's estimation, that used what he wanted when he needed to and then threw it into the wind like a piece of muddled trash.

"My people are involved in this war too."

"At James' request." Evanbourough smiled thinly at him.

"Perhaps." Aiken agreed. "But now that they are—and one of them is my future son-in-law—what choice do I have but to see it has a quick end?"

Evanbourough considered him for a moment, wondering if he were being lied to. Emissary Lord Darklief could be a very tricksey God. Never mind that he had an angelic face that was often times difficult to read. In fact, Theasis had often warned Evanbourough that, if it were Aiken's will, the fairy God could convince a thirsting mortal into giving away the last cup of water from his long drying well.

He finally settled on, "I see."

"I'm not asking much from you."

"You're asking me to interfere in a mortal war that we were all, very specifically, ordered to avoid." Evanbourough shook his head. "No. I'm sorry, Aiken. But I'm already on the short list of candidates to soon face the King of Lord's rage."

Aiken snorted at that. The list that Evan spoke of could roll out for miles. I found myself smiling at the God as this thought crossed his mind. After all, on that score, Aiken was right.

"Fine." Aiken scoffed as he found his feet. "Be as you ever have been, Evan: a hypocrite and a coward. And let's see how we all fare when this fracas is over."

-53-

When trouble came, it came not in the form of soup or wine. Nor was it at the hand of the boy that Sezja had been watching so carefully. Rather, it came in the form of a silk shirt. Delivered to Iladrul from the hand of someone that Sezja had not suspected.

Though she had been told at her selling that she must wear the clothing that was given to her Prince before it ever touched his flesh, she seldom took this warning seriously.

And, honestly, the only reason that she threw the shirt over her shoulders, now, was because she needed to make her necessary and didn't want to walk through Prince Iladrul's apartment completely naked.

Smiling, she leaned toward her man—she did think of him as *her* man now—and gently kissed him on his brow. He stirred slightly in his sleep but did not waken. When the time came for searching for something to be grateful for, it would be this that she would settle upon as her greatest relief.

After reflecting upon his handsome features for as long as the press of her child's foot against her bladder would allow, she spun on the bed and walked, with a smile on her face and a hand on the swell of her belly, toward the golden box with the pretty silver bow which bore the name of someone that Iladrul counted as a friend.

She ran her fingers lovingly over the fabric for a moment before raising it out of the box and wrapping it around her shoulders. She relished in its smooth softness, lack of weight and cool, caressing properties as she buttoned it over her aching breasts and bulging belly.

Smiling—feeling, in his shirt, that she truly *was* his woman— she made her way out of his bedchamber and toward the bathing pools where he kept his chamber pot. In the depths of their grief, her brothers would later conspire amongst one another with theories of what her fate might have been had she chosen the dressing room or the smaller room that was meant for whichever brother was in care of Iladrul that night.

Questioning Moira, however, was a useless proposition.

Sezja had chosen the chamber pot in the bathing room and all of her brothers were grateful. Even Haidar, who still fought and bucked against his station in life, kept silent toward Iladrul about how bad things might have been had it been otherwise.

The burning didn't start right away. In fact, she made it through her necessary, humming and rubbing her belly, before she realized something was not quite right. Even then, it was little more than an itch.

Feeling that itch, she pulled the shirt off of her shoulders languidly believing that the thing had been laundered incorrectly. It wasn't until she saw the pulsing, puss filled wound on her arm that she understood with sudden clarity that her beloved Prince had been betrayed.

She bolted to the bathing pools, choosing the hottest so it would scald the poison from her body. Though it did remove the effects from her outer skin, the intended results could not be mitigated.

The chemicals on the shirt was meant to kill a body from the inside out and that is exactly what they were doing.

"Thirty Hells and Sixty Realms." Sezja muttered as she realized the truth of what happening to her. "Iladrul . . . I'm . . . sorry." Then in a whisper. "I failed you with my contentment."

"Sezja!" It was Jeavlin who was on duty that night and so it was Jeavlin left to comfort his sister and inform his brothers there was a problem. "Tell me! What—?"

"Bring the guard." She whispered as she scraped sloughs of skin off of her body as they burned from the acid on her flesh. "But, first . . ." She pulled herself out of the water and looked upon Jeavlin with imploring eyes. "First . . . Make me presentable to our Lord and Master." She looked up with him with haunted eyes. "Hide my condition as best you can."

Jeavlin, ever as obedient as he had been trained to be, complied.

-54-

Ishitar turned up where I least expected him—his father's library.

When he stepped through the door, Samyael turned his gaze to Gorgon and the two shared a silent, concerned exchange. Sam

347

didn't miss that the strange creature's black lips twitched slightly as the snakes that made up his hair began to dance.

"Father."

"Ishitar." The King of Lords' tone was laced with surprise over Ishitar's appearance. "Your visit is unexpected."

"What is your interest in the elves?" Ishitar asked as he lowered himself into the seat across from his father. "What is the story with the demons?"

"It is a mortal concern, Ishitar." Noliminan's eyes narrowed. "Stay out of it."

"It's not a mortal concern from my point of view." Ishitar crossed his arms over his chest. "And certainly not a moral one."

"This happens every time a number of angels and demons are exiled all at once." Noliminan advised him. "You saw this yourself when the benandanti went after the mages."

"You've managed to dissipate that race rather nicely, haven't you?"

"I've nothing to do with the bronzies and their carnivals."

Ishitar's eyes were the ones to narrow now. Zadkiel had told him, once, how the bronzies had been brought into creation. The fact that the man that he thought of as his Da had been humiliated had infuriated Ishitar at the time. I'm certain he still dwells upon his ill will toward his father over Zadkiel's pain.

When he spoke, he surprised me.

"Then you aren't the one responsible for orchestrating Corline's disappearance?"

"Corline?" Noliminan's lips twitched. "Who would that be?"

Gorgon and Samyael exchanged another one of those looks. As for me, I snorted. Ishitar, turned his gaze to me and asked, "Did the bronzies take her, Az? And add her to their collection?"

I glared at him. He knew I couldn't respond to that question.

As if I had, however, he nodded and returned his gaze to my Lord and Master. "And you're to tell me that you're not responsible for this."

"What, precisely, did he say?"

I started. I turned my gaze in Noliminan's direction.

THE SCRIBING OF ISHITAR: ASHES TO ASHES

He can't see me? He can't hear me? Even though Ishitar can?

Samyael and Gorgon had the same thoughts as I and exchanged another one of those looks. As for Ishitar, he merely watched his father with great curiosity. I couldn't tell if he was surprised or if he were not.

I decided that it didn't matter.

"She bore Loki's child." Ishitar lowered his gaze slightly. I believe it was out of respect for Loki, rather than his father, but I cannot be certain. "By any road that is important, I'm certain she has by now."

"Too bad for her." Noliminan's mouth curled into a bitter smile. "And too bad for him." Then as an afterthought, "The babe. I could piss in the wind over Loki."

"Never mind Corline. Or the babe." Ishitar leaned back in his chair and uncrossed his arms. "What is your position on the elves?"

"It will play itself out." Noliminan shrugged. "These things always do." Then, cocking his head, "What is your position?"

"Oddly enough," Ishitar replied. "I agree. Gods should not meddle with the fates of the mortals. Not now that you have given them free will."

"What is your mother's position?"

Ishitar appeared to consider him for a moment. Finally, he said, "She has decided to make it Loki's concern rather than her own." He gave his father a tight smile. "But, then, I gather you've already come to that conclusion."

"I suppose that I have." Noliminan's lips grew thin. "And his position?"

"At the moment, he doesn't wish to raise your ire any more than he already has." Ishitar shrugged. "I'm certain he would assist the elves otherwise."

"He's growing overly bold." Noliminan replied cautiously. Ishitar only smiled. "Is your mother in danger by his will?"

"No." Ishitar shook his head. "I do not think he would play against her."

349

"Very well." Noliminan said. As he did so, he pulled open one of his desk drawers and removed an envelope. He raised it to his son and shook it at him. "Give her this when you next see her. She needs to replace Mihr."

I felt my lips purse. Gorgon and Sam exchanged another guarded frown.

"Do you have a preference?"

"No." Noliminan replied, standing. "How could I? They are her sons. I must love them all in equal measures."

"And daughters." Ishitar reminded him with a cocked head, ignoring my scoffing snort at Noliminan's last sentiment.

"Then I lied." Noliminan glared at him as he leaned over the desk to stare down at the youngling. "I prefer to be surrounded by sons."

Ishitar gave Noliminan a very guarded smile as his eyes flicked to Gorgon and then back to our Lord and Master. Sensing our discomfort, he gave Noliminan a curt nod.

"Very well." He replied, a strange, amused lilt to his tone that I rarely ever heard coming from him. Though, it must be said, I did recognize it. It was a perfect mimicry of how Lord Loki would have responded to him. "I shall ask the Lady to offer up only my brothers."

-55-

Gorgon entered his mother's cottage with a feeling of great trepidation. He had been ordered not to visit Lucias by the King of Lords, yet it wasn't an order that he could comply with. He loved his brothers and sisters far too much to stay away from them for overly long.

Never mind that he needed his father's guidance more often than he would care to admit.

As he closed the door behind himself, he heard a young boy squeal with childish glee as he ran toward him. He turned around in time to lower himself to his hunkers and throw his arms wide apart. Shade collided with him, hard, and Gorgon wrapped his arms around his little brother to pick him up as he stood.

"Gorgon!" Shade squealed. "Have you come home to stay?"

"That is an impossibility, little brother." Gorgon turned his face to kiss the lad's plump cheek. "Just to visit." He smiled as his brother made a sour face over the kiss. "Is Fete here?"

"No." Shade replied.

Gorgon sighed his disappointment. He wasn't surprised, however. Loki had been spending less and less time in Lucias' company since Gorgon had left his home to serve Noliminan.

Not that he had wasted any time trading Samyael for Metatron; something that troubled Gorgon greatly. He had become fond of Samyael. The demon—nay, angel, now—was clever and dry with his wit. He was a rare soul who found humor in the same things in which Gorgon, himself, could be amused.

"Any plans for a visit?"

Shade shrugged and pushed himself away from Gorgon. Taking the hint, Gorgon lowered the lad to his feet.

"You know Fete." Shade looked up at him with eyes that swirled in rings of black and grey. "He comes when it suits him."

"That he does." Gorgon patted him on the head. "Mome?"

"Sleeping." A troubled expression crossed his brow. "I think we are to have a little brother or sister very soon now."

Gorgon nodded. The snakes that made up his hair hissed with irritation.

More children for her to trade into slavery.

"Brother."

Gorgon turned toward the sound of Taurus' voice. As his gaze fell upon the minotaur's bullish face, he found a true grin. As strange looking as Gorgon was, his brother had the worst of it out of all of them.

At least so far.

There was no saying what monstrosity grew in their mother's belly at the moment.

"How are you, brother?"

"I bide." Taurus' bullish mouth split into what looked like a grin. It was an ugly and gruesome thing to behold, but Gorgon would never say so.

How could he? His grin was just as gruesome.

"How goes it on the side of the Heavens' bound?"

Gorgon chuckled and rolled his eyes under his dark glasses. "You wouldn't want to know."

"I am to begin training with Sir Metatron." Now the grin turned into an all-out smile. "On the morrow."

"I'm pleased!" What he actually felt was jealousy, but he wasn't about to ruin his brother's good mood. It was a rare enough thing for the brooding creature. "There is no finer swordsman."

"But for Michael." Taurus agreed. "But Mome prefers he sees to his babies." His brow furrowed. "Strange little beasties, that lot."

"Strange indeed." Gorgon tried to suppress his grin. Either of them calling another creature strange was hypocritical at best. "Will you tell Fete, when he shows, that I seek his counsel?"

"I will." Taurus promised. "Shall I tell him what it is about?"

Gorgon considered for a moment before deciding that he had nothing to hide.

"The Price of Providence." His lips pursed. "And . . . the King of Lords."

"What about them?" Siren, who Gorgon hadn't heard enter the room, demanded. "What about Ishitar?"

Gorgon frowned at her. He was aware that she had a girl's fascination over their half-brother. It was innocent enough, yet still ill-advised given his great station and power. He would never count any one of them as his true siblings.

"Never you mind."

-56-

Macentyx watched with anxious anticipation as Prince Iladrul paced across the room. Sezja had gone into labor after having been poisoned by the shirt.

Though, at Sezja's request, Prince Iladrul did not know this to be the reason why the babe had chosen to come early.

No matter the circumstance, a little Prince or Princess, bastard, bastardess or doxy that they may be, was about to be birthed into the world. A child who was to be the rightful heir to Iladrul's throne until he sired a babe in his, not yet negotiated, marriage bed.

The nurse wives were darting in and out of the birthing room, doing nothing to calm Macentyx's nerves and serving to further agitate the young Prince. Every time the door opened, Iladrul would spin around and beg for news.

It was slow coming. This child meant to take its time before pushing its way, squalling and red faced, into the world.

"My Prince?"

Macentyx turned toward the sound of Gregor's voice. He had come to respect the stable boy and his skills at war. Yet, he didn't care for the expression the lad wore now.

"What is it Gregor?" Prince Iladrul asked, irritably.

"You have a guest." His lips pursed slightly.

"I am in no mood for receiving." Iladrul snapped at him. "You should have known better than to approach me in a moment like this."

"Still." Gregor's eyes flicked to Macentyx. They were burning with discontentment. Macentyx passed him a silent question by turning his chin slightly. This only caused Gregor to break their gaze to return his attention to the Prince. "He says he's here on Lord Scrountantine's behest." He shivered. "And I believe him."

"Is he . . ." Macentyx shuddered as he posed the question, "one of them."

"Ta." Gregor nodded. "But young. Our age."

"Our age?" Haidar who had been silent, for a wonder, asked. He turned toward Iladrul. "One of the fabled twins, do you think?"

"I do." Iladrul frowned at him and returned his attention to Gregor. "Show him to the throne room. And be hospitable. I must ready myself to meet him."

"Yes, my Prince."

Gregor bowed to him and turned to swiftly escape the room. When he was gone, Prince Iladrul turned his attention to Macentyx.

"I know Osete or Jeavlin generally see to my grooming." His eyes flicked to Macentyx's brother. "But I need that trap that is your mind."

Macentyx smiled at the compliment. They were few and far between and he had found, over time, that he cherished every one.

"If news comes," Prince Iladrul advised Haidar, "bring it to me on swift feet."

"Of course." Haidar shrugged.

Macentyx rolled his eyes. Prince Iladrul had been patient with his brother's tongue, but the day would come when he'd catch their young Master in a foul mood.

He hoped, when the business of the birthing of the babe was over and the truth regarding Sezja's condition was discovered, today would not be that day.

-57-

Iladrul flicked his eyes upward to look upon Macentyx's face in the looking glass.

None of the doxies were acting as they normally would. Haidar was uncommonly silent. Jeavlin, though generally shy, was behaving morose. Osete's absence was far too poignant. And Macentyx seemed distracted from his tasks.

Never mind that he had yet been allowed to look upon Sezja in her birthing bed.

Though, he supposed, the birthing of a baby brought about strange emotions and guarded expressions. He knew Sezja was strong in both sprit and constitution, but the business of birthing was a challenge she had not yet conquered.

"My crown." He muttered.

"Hmm?" Macentyx's brow furrowed. That faraway look in his eyes blinked out momentarily as he met Iladrul's gaze in the mirror. "My Prince?"

"My crown." He replied, an octave higher.

"Oh." Macentyx gave him a nervous laugh and then reached for the bauble. He raised it upward and gingerly set it upon Iladrul's brow. "Yes. Of course."

"What's the matter, Mac?" Iladrul sighed. "You seem distracted."

"I'm to be an uncle." He replied. His eyes darted away and his skin paled. "It's an exciting day."

"It is." Iladrul replied, his brow furrowed. He turned on his seat to face his doxy. "So why are you—and your brothers—so damned melancholy?"

Macentyx gave him a weak smile. "We lose our little sister today."

A chill ran down Iladrul's back.

"She'll be a woman now." He looked away again; his skin paled even further. "Once the babe is birthed." He swallowed and returned his gaze to meet Iladrul's. "And you'll have an heir." Again, the swift flight of his eyes. "Until you wed and sire a proper son."

"Nostimun will be a proper son." Iladrul replied, frowning at him. "I love your sister. Why would I wed another?"

That weak smile returned. "Love and politics have never lasted."

"What do you know about either?" Iladrul asked, irritable. Macentyx swallowed and returned his gaze to meet Iladrul's own. "You're not a Prince. And you've never been in love."

355

"No, my Prince." He lowered his gaze this time. "Of course not. Please forgive me."

"There's nothing to be forgiven." Iladrul snapped as he stood, still irritable. He had the distinct impression that Macentyx was lying to him. Or hiding something. Whatever was taking place, he didn't much care for it. "But now is not the time for this conversation. We've an important guest waiting." Then, as an afterthought, "Most likely with ill news."

"Of course, my Prince." Macentyx's smile was apologetic now. "Forgive me. There are more important matters at hand."

"Not more important." Iladrul sighed, shaking his head. "Just more . . . pressing. And far reaching."

"Yes, my Prince."

Iladrul gave him a last, mistrustful glare and made his way out of his dressing room. Not a word passed between them as they navigated the halls of the castle to the Throne Room.

Once at the door he warned, "Be ready for anything."

Macentyx nodded at him before opening the door and leading his Prince within. When Iladrul's eyes fell upon the young vampire, pacing the length of the room, the chill that he had felt when Macentyx had spoken about the loss of Sezja returned to him.

"Prince Iladrul." The creature stopped its trek and turned toward Iladrul to give him a respectful bow. "Forgive my intrusion."

"I hope that the message that you bring from Lord Jamiason is one of peace." Iladrul replied to this, walking toward him. "We tire of your people and your war."

"My message is not from my Maker." The vampire's dark, brown eyes darted nervously over Iladrul's face. "And it is a word of warning rather than peace."

"What warning?" Macentyx's hand immediately flew to the hilt of his sword. Iladrul knew that, if he didn't like the vampire's message, all that would be left of the child monster would be soot and ashes. "Speak swift and true."

"Iykva and his people have allied themselves with the House of Fyrsoth." He lowered his gaze slightly. "I overheard a conversation between Iykva and Lord Fyrsoth. Their intent is to strike where you'll least see it coming."

Iladrul felt his brow furrow. His doxy, he noted, paled. He turned toward him.

"Mac?" He reached for the other boy's wrist. "What is it?"

"Sezja, my Prince." Macentyx's eyes darted to the vampire and then returned to meet Iladrul's gaze. "She's . . ."

"What?" Iladrul demanded.

"She didn't want us to say anything until after the birthing—"

"Tell me *now!*" Iladrul rounded on him.

"She's been poisoned."

The rage within Iladrul upon hearing these words was stronger than any emotion Iladrul had ever, before, experienced. For the first time since he had taken on the responsibility of being the master of doxies, his hand flew free and he struck the other boy.

It would not be the last time.

He would never forgive Macentyx, or any of the others for that matter, for the moments with Sezja that they had stolen from him.

Her last moments; her last breath.

Nor would he ever forgive the baby that, at that moment, was ripping her womb apart.

He stormed out of the throne room, forgetting his manners where Marchand was concerned.

He didn't care.

To the Hells with the vampire. If he knew that Sezja was in trouble, he should have made haste. If he were really on the side of the elves—if Lord Scrountentine were—Sezja's life would never have been put at risk at the hands of his people.

He ran past the angel who guarded the royal apartments without giving him a second thought or look. This, he would later regret. The guard had always been kind to him; had always been kind to Sezja. Had he realized that he would never see the angel again, he would have taken the few extra seconds to acknowledge his proud, secret smile.

But Iladrul's thoughts were on one person and one person only: his beloved Sezja. The true depths of his grief over others he would lose that day would not be understood for years and years to come.

For now, his only hope was that he had not arrived at the birthing bed too late.

-58-

Unlike those around me, I had time to grieve for them both. Iladrul burst through the door to the birthing room to find Sezja alone and breathing her last breath.

She reached for him with what she feared what was her last bit of strength, taking his hand in her own. It was with her final reserve that she whispered his friend's name.

His eyes widened.

Hers closed.

Chaos, though he did not know it then, reigned around them.

-59-

Osete did not wait. The moment the child had squalled its first cry, he yanked it from the angel who had assisted with the birthing, swaddling it as he went rather than waiting for the babe to be properly bundled. These precious few seconds, the doxy would later reflect, saved the girl's life.

These precious few seconds and his penchant for wandering around the castle when he was bored.

He had found the secret passageway that led from Wisterian's room, beneath the expanse of the castle grounds and into the cave beyond. He was certain that few, if anyone else, were aware of it, but he took no chances and made haste.

The cool air rushed through the mouth of the cave to overwhelm him. It invigorated him, giving him the extra push he needed to put the required speed upon the balls of his feet so he could sprint that extra mile through the cavern, out of the mouth of the cave and into the darkness of the recently fallen night.

-60-

From the window of the cottage that was set upon the land just outside of the mouth of the cave, the face of a young boy, not quite yet in his tween years, watched as Osete darted across the yard beneath him with the bundle of Iladrul's baby clutched within his arms.

The scene was familiar to the child, though he could not place it. Some distant memory lost in the land of nod.

Perhaps, he smiled as the strange creature with the bundle in its arms darted into the forest beyond the young boy's lands, another one of his dreams.

Turning his gaze in the direction of the flames that brightened the night sky to the far west of the cottage, he shrugged his shoulders, pulled the curtains closed and did what he ever did when he was confused by his surroundings.

He crawled into his bed and fell, blissfully, into a dreamless sleep.

-61-

Iykva stood in the middle of the courtyard, his thick lips curled into a satisfied grin. He was surrounded with a litter of bodies ranging from whores to royalty. Though some of them were the soot and ash of his people, he felt not the first lick of regret on the back of his neck.

The Fyrsoths had promised him that they knew the weaknesses of the elfin kingdom and they had made good on that promise.

He hadn't believed that it would be as easy as the humans insisted. Given it had been, he intended to pay them not only the gold that he had promised, but an extra chest or so more.

Three extra chests if they handed over that damn brat of a Prince's newly born baby.

The news that the doxy bitch was pregnant had surprised Iykva. He wasn't certain why. Perhaps it was the fact that he had tried to force hundreds of them together and not a one of them had conceived. He supposed that he believed, after such a defeat, that the elves couldn't breed. That they were mutant in some way, like the vampires, who passed their lineage in a manner other than by the natural method.

Now that he knew better, the anger that he had felt from the moment his ability to find his pleasure by way of the hungers of the flesh had been stripped from him returned, compounded exponentially.

He felt cheated all over again. Lied to all over again. Shamed all over again.

Enough so that, even now, with the taste of victory on his lips and warm blood still flowing through his mouth, his only thought was that of revenge.

Revenge and, finally, laying the damn angels, who had always held themselves above Iykva and his kind, low.

-62-

"Lucias, you aren't listening to me." Sappharon frowned to herself as she pressed her ear against their bedroom door. She had long since grown past the point of spying on Loki and Lady Lucias. Yet, when he raised his voice to the Lady, she found that she couldn't resist. The only other time he'd done so was when he had learned she'd traded Gorgon for Michael. "Your husband is watching the demons toy with the elves like a dog watches a cat play with a rat in a trap. This attack on Wisterian's lands—"

"Hasn't played itself out." The Lady replied with a weary sigh. This last baby that she had birthed had depleted her now limited source of energy. Sappharon, who still disputed Lucias' decision to give Loki a portion of the source of her power, rolled her fiery eyes and shook her head. "Let one side or the other win. Then let us discuss what next steps will be."

"My words to Aiken." Sappharon heard Loki sigh. "And I was wrong."

"No." She sounded irritated. "We can't tempt Noliminan now, Loki. You must wait!"

Loki's silence stretched between them for far too long. Finally, he let out a frustrated sigh.

"I am still to be your golem then?" He asked, his tone sharp. "And your husband's marionette?"

"Loki, I—"

"Sometimes I wonder, my Lady," he growled, the sound of his voice moving away from their bed toward the door leading to the chamber next to it, "which of you it is that pulls my Gods be damned strings."

At the sound of a door slamming crashed on the other side of the door behind which she hovered, Sappharon's brow furrowed.

It was a question she had asked, within her own mind, on several occasions. She wished desperately that Loki had given Lucias the courtesy of time to deliver her answer rather than storming out of the room.

Not, Sappharon supposed, that she would have.

She turned away from the door and walked toward her own room, biting the inside of her lip as she did so. She had the barest of a glimmer of what she must do. It would go against everything that Lucias would have wanted of her.

When has that ever stopped you?

If Loki believed that he couldn't interfere—and if Lucias wouldn't—there was only one person left to stand up to Noliminan who might see reason.

And reason must be seen.

The great will of the Gods had more important things to resolve its focus on than a pointless, mindless, mortal war.

- 63 -

Iladrul stormed through the castle, the three doxies who remained in his service beating off demons to his left and right. Losing Sezja had been a devastating blow. Finding his father, drained of all blood, cut from stem to sternum, had driven him into a madness that stole all of his reason.

And now I know who is responsible! Who has always been responsible!

His blood was pounding through his skull, darkening his vision in a shadows of red. His fury, as he made his way through the castle grounds, whirled around him. His sword flew through the flesh of his enemies, though he didn't waste time watching them turn to ash beneath his feet. There was only one man whose death he would relish this day.

Relish and savor.

Forced to follow him, I reflected upon the fact that the last remnants of the boy that had resided within him, the boy who had hid under his bed in utter terror, was completely gone from him now.

The boy would have shown his friend mercy; the boy would have asked why.

The man—the King—wanted only revenge.

Iladrul flew the door to the chamber open, his sword split and swinging in front of him in circling arcs. When he stood before the cowering elf, his rage overcame him.

"It was you then!" He cried. "You all along! You who told them where we would be! You who let them in the castle to slaughter your own people!"

"I would rather die," Faunus replied, standing tall now, his eyes blazing, "then bow down to a King who cares more about protecting the cities whores than its people and who trusts the world of a stable boy over his rightful General at Arms!"

"A wish I shall gladly grant you!"

THE SCRIBING OF ISHITAR: ASHES TO ASHES

The silver of the blades of the split sword in Iladrul's hands swiped through the air, cutting neatly into Faunus on either side of his neck. They continued their circling arch through his body, barely passing one another, before escaping just above the bone of his hips.

As if gravity no longer existed, his torso and arms, where he had been cut, slid slowly downward until they fell with a disturbing thud at the boy's feet.

The boy, himself, did not fall right away. Rather, he stared at Iladrul as if surprised that any threat would be made good, before a gush of blood escaped as vomit from his mouth and began pouring down his chin.

It was then that his knees buckled beneath him and he fell in a crumpled heap to the ground.

The sound of it was not nearly satisfying enough. The bloodlust had taken hold of Iladrul now. He swung around, glaring at Haidar, whose brown, gold ringed eyes were wide with fright. Had Jeavlin not stepped before him, Haidar would have joined Faunus in whatever traitors Hell waited for him on the other side.

"Your Majesty!" Jeavlin's voice trembled. It was that tremble, rather than anything else, that brought Iladrul to his senses. "There are still vampires—demons—raiding your lands. Would you turn on one loyal to you? When there is real justice which must be wrought?"

Iladrul, slapped back into reality by Jeavlin's words, shook his head.

"Take me to Iykva."

How he managed to hold such a calm tone to his voice, I shall never know.

Forgetting that his threat was an impossibility given vampires turn to ash when they die, "His will be the first head to stand on guarded spikes at my castle walls!"

-64-

Zamyael looked up from her needlework as she heard Ishitar sigh. She hadn't been paying attention to Sappharon, who had burst into their little cottage with her chin cocked in defiance and determination burning in her flaming eyes. She knew her sister well enough to understand that, although Sappharon always acted with good intentions, the consequences of her ill wrought interference in the games of her betters always ended poorly for all involved.

Zamyael, who had lived through enough of her own trials, thank you very much, had no intention of getting caught up in Sappharon's latest motives and schemes.

"Lady Sappharon," Ishitar's tone was patient, causing Zamyael to smile. "If my mother and father will not interfere, and if Loki believes that he cannot interfere, why, precisely, do you intend to meddle?"

Unable to resist, Zamyael raised her black eyes to watch.

An old and persistent hunger—mixed with a new passion that I had never in life believed I would ever know—exploded within me. I had come to love Zamyael as no man has ever, in the history of all worlds and times, loved a woman. The turn of her curiosity, mixed with her amused apprehension, brought me great joy.

"Must there be a reason aside that it is the right thing to do?" Sappharon signed. "The war your parents and Loki should be fighting is amongst each other and for the right of the Divine Crown. Instead, they play games with the mortals, turning demon upon angel or angel upon demon. Time after time it is the same thing. These are mortal matters, your Royal Highness. They became so the moment that Noliminan exiled Jamiason and Wisterian."

"And," Ishitar reminded her, "it is Jamiason and Wisterian who are at war."

"No, Ishy." Zamyael shook her head.

She was loathe to agree with Sappharon in this matter, but the brat of a demon—*Goddess, now*, she reminded herself—had the right of things. Just as Noliminan had culled the mortal worlds of the benandanti by way of the bronzies, he was now culling the elves by way of the vampires.

"It isn't right," her tone was low and motherly, "Your father demands the right of free will for the mortals. And, yet, he yanks it away for the turn of his amusement."

She lowered her gaze so that he would not see the loathing that she felt for his father burning within her eyes. I sensed she needn't have bothered. Her story was not a secret one.

"He toys with them; teases them. Each time a new batch of exiles is born, he picks one side or the other and manipulates them to destroy the other race."

He looked doubtfully upon the demoness before turning his gaze toward me. He had barely acknowledged my presence since Sappharon's arrival. I sensed that this was because he did not want to give away my mortal disguise rather than that he resented my presence.

I smiled at him. He gave me a weary smile in response.

"Do you feel the same?" He asked. "Do you agree with Lady Zamyael?"

I met his gaze, my smile tightening. This was, as Zamyael and Sappharon had both pointed out, a mortal war. Though I was prone to side with the elves in this instance, it was not my place to judge or interfere until the time of aether came. No more than it was my place to interfere with the bronzies' abduction of the benandanti.

"I believe that there is no stopping or interfering with the designs of either one of your parents." I replied, knowing that he was the only one who could actually hear me speak. "And I believe that your only recourse, if you wish Loki to do so, is to grant the trickster the favor of another one of your Gods be damned pies."

He chuckled at that and lowered his gaze.

"Ishitar," Sappharon was watching me with guarded interest. She knew that Zamyael was courting a mortal man but she didn't know that mortal man was actually me. So it was, she didn't understand why Ishitar would bother with asking my opinion on the matter or why I would, seemingly, merely grin at him without granting him the courtesy of a response. "I understand your reluctance to stand against your mother and father."

I rolled my eyes at that, though she didn't see. Zamyael, however, gave me a guarded, narrowed eyed glare. Her admonishment only served to please me.

"But do you wish to have the race of elf completely removed from all worlds and times?" Sappharon implored. "There is but one benandanti left which we are aware of! Breeding with a wolf whose blood is so diluted that the race will never reach the glory it had once known."

Ishitar sighed and turned his gaze to Zamyael. She was watching him wearing an expression which should have told him, if it did not, that she not only agreed with Sappharon, she would have him stand up for the pretty elfin creatures if she were to have it her way.

"You wouldn't be alone." Sappharon continued when he failed to agree to her demands immediately. "The elves do have allies."

"Fairies and humans." Ishitar reminded her.

"The Devonshires and Emissary Lord Darklief." Zamyael corrected him. "One of the most noble line of Adam and the other a living, mortal God."

"And Jamiason." Sappharon nodded. "Don't forget that the very King of the race that attacks them would see to the elves' protection."

"Yet he cannot convince his own people to behave." Ishitar scoffed. "Why should I assist?"

"He called on Aiken knowing it was his only course." Zamyael reminded Ishitar. "He is outnumbered! He can't stand directly against his people when his own guard would slay him the barest moment that he tried."

Ishitar gave her a doubtful smile before turning his attention to me. I shrugged, telling him, in my own way, that I wasn't going to get involved in this discussion any more than I already had. Nor was I about to spill Lord Jamiason's secrets in regard to the rumors that circled around him.

"The elfin city burns now." Sappharon reminded them all, her hands flying. "There isn't time for debate or discussion."

Ishitar assessed her for a long moment before his eyes landed first on me and, then, on Zamyael. I sensed that it was Zamyael's soft, encouraging smile that finally seemed to convince him.

"Very well," he told us as he stood. "I'll speak with my father about the matter again." His eyes narrowed as they returned to Sappharon. "But no guarantees, my Lady. I may, after hearing his side of things, change my mind."

Zamyael and Sappharon, who knew both Noliminan and Ishitar better than the two Gods knew one another, exchanged a weary smile.

-65-

The moment that Louis had explained to Jamiason and Paul what they had come across in the forest, James had disappeared in a flash of light, the smell of electricity burning the air. Paul's mode of transportation to Wisterian's lands had not been quite as swift. Still, he was only half a night's march behind Iykva and his murderous band of demons as Faunus let the Hells' fires reign within its walls.

Though he was not where he wanted—or intended—to be in time, Moira, for once, had given him her blessing. Had he been with Iykva, rather than on his trail, his path wouldn't have crossed that of the frightened doxy with the baby swaddled tightly in the grasp of his arms.

He recognized the lad at once as being one of Prince Iladrul's servants. For the barest of moments he thought to let him run by. After all, he was running at breakneck speed through the forest clutching at his trickla as if his life depended upon it.

Then Paul heard the baby cry and he understood, all too well, what the doxy's presence in the forest, without the escort of his master, must mean.

He swerved into the doxy's path. The lad almost collided into him. He would have, had Paul not jumped swiftly out of the way. As it was, Paul had to grab him by his long brown hair and yank him backward lest he fall, crushing the baby beneath himself.

The doxy screamed as Paul flung him around by the hair so that he was facing him. The baby, sensitive to the lad's fear and confusion, lent its howls to the boy elf's, ringing a horrifying chorus into the night.

"Stop." Paul seethed, shaking the lad by his hair. "I don't intend to harm you."

The elf, not believing this, suddenly had the presence of mind to reach for the blade at his hip. Though he was fast, and surely a force to be reckoned with on the battle field, he had the disadvantage of the baby in his arms. Contrarily, Paul had years of feeding from Jamiason's neck, which had made his curse strong.

"I'm on your side!" Paul tried again. As he spoke he heard the pounding of horses' hooves in the distance. The centaurs of this forest were growing short on patience. And they—Paul and this blathering boy—were growing short on time. "Quiet boy! And hush that baby as well! We'll have an entire herd of wildered centaurs upon us if you don't pull yourself together."

Whatever fear the child had of Paul was clearly minimal to his fear as to what would happen to him if he were to be dragged away by wildered centaurs. He let out one more hitching sob, pulled the baby close to him and glared definitely up at the vampire Prince.

"Better." Paul muttered, letting the boy's hair free. His eyes flicked to the baby, whose face the doxy was covering with the blanket to muffle its cries. "Whose babe is that?"

The doxy pulled her even closer as his gold rimmed eyes gleaned in what light shone through the leaves of the forest from the moon above them.

"Is that Prince Iladrul's babe?" Paul demanded. "We'd heard rumors that your sister was fat with child."

"Hers is a neck you shall never sink your rotted teeth into!" The doxy seethed.

An amused, somewhat surprised, chortle escaped Paul's lips. He knew it was an ill timed laugh, but he was helpless not to let it loose.

The boy had found his brevity, for all the good it would do him.

"I have no intention to sink my teeth into her neck." He tried to keep the amusement from his tone and utterly failed. "No more than I do yours." He shook his head. The sound of hooves on moss and leaping over underbrush was drawing nearer. "Do you mean to protect her?"

"With my life."

"That may not be necessary." Paul replied, turning his back to the elf. "Come. And be quick about it. I know a place where we can hide until the herd passes."

Having no other choice if he wished to avoid the raging madness of the wildred herd of centaurs, the boy did as he was bid.

-66-

Jamiason bent over Wisterian's body and begin to weep. He knew there was no time for such nonsense, but he also understood that once an angel or demon expired it was a permanent thing. Wisterian, unlike the mortals who had fallen this night, would never grace Martiam's halls or Loki's cages. Certainly, his feet would never touch the sacred marble tiles which, it was rumored, made up the Guf. He had had his chance to rise to glory. And he had, according to the laws of the King of Lords, abused it.

Zadkiel, James knew by the cold, rigid flesh of his friend's body, had already claimed him and willed his soul to the portal that would take him to the world beyond the Sixty Realms.

That there must be another world beyond the one that he knew, he was certain. It was incomprehensible to him to believe that, when the immortal death breathed upon you, it all just came to an end.

"Goodbye, old friend." Jamiason whispered before leaning forward to press his lips to Wisterian's brow. "Wherever one goes after failing the tests of the Heavens, I hope that you finally, and at long last, find peace."

Screams swelled all around him, forcing him out of his reverie. Standing, he keened his ears in the direction of those that were nearest to him.

One thing, he knew, was certain: his friend's death would not be in vain.

-67-

Raystlyn ran on swift feet, his wings catching the wind so that he might take flight, the barest moment that he heard her scream.

Men were not allowed in the Temple of the Charbala; it was a place where women prayed.

He didn't care.

He knew this tradition belonged to the exiled angels of Wisterian's rebellion. But, then, Wisterian had never had the relationship with Theasis that Raystlyn had shared with the Goddess. As a result, Wisterian misunderstood her general silence toward them as lack of care. In the minds of the angels of this exiled generation, the only time the Lady visited was when she overheard an elf or an angel's prayers. And she only answered, they believed, if the prayers came from another woman.

Because the Temple doors were locked to him, he was forced to revert to the magic that had been granted him to burst his way through. He allowed a ball of silver energy to form within the palm of his hand, which he pulled backward and flung with all of his strength toward the door.

It exploded in spray of marble and glass, littering the steps so that those Priestesses who came running from within would cut their bare feet as they escaped the monsters who had made their way into the Temple to see to their slaughter.

He heard her scream again, this time louder; more desperate.

"Helena!" He cried her name, desperate to find her. Despite the pain she had caused him when she had chosen to stay with her husband after their affair, he did still love her. "Where are you, my angel?!"

"Raystlyn . . ." Even though she was screaming, her cries were muffled. She had locked her door to sit Charbala. And now, because of her foolish traditions and beliefs, she was trapped. "Please, Rayst! Help me!"

Knowing that the doors to the Priestesses chambers were as locked to him as the front door had been, Raystlyn began flinging balls of silver light to the right and the left of him. His arms crossed gracefully over one another as chaos reigned in his wake. The women, all of them terrified, flew from their prayer chambers to run like lemmings to the front of the Temple.

Every one of them smelled the burning wood and flames as the castle and the city burned around them. Every one of them understood that, trapped in their chambers as they had been, if the Temple, itself, had caught fire, they were little more than the kindling wood that was the structure of the building around them.

She was in the last chamber on the right. As the door exploded in front of her, the fire that they had all feared caught and shattered the window behind her, blasting into the room. She escaped with just enough time for him to slam the door shut to contain the fire long enough for him to wrap his arms around her waist, lift her into his arms and take flight.

Had anyone still resided in the Temple to see him, he would have appeared to them to be little more than a blur.

As it would turn out, his speed, which had been born from his love for her, saved them both.

-68-

The barest moment that the pixies landed on Aiken's palm to advise him that his charge was in trouble, the fairy God willed himself into the center of the chaos. He stood in the courtyard, his eyes wide, looking right and left and wondering how, in the name of all of the Gods that he had ever loved, hated or been indifferent to, things had gone so horribly wrong so terribly fast.

He saw demons rushing to angels; angels rushing to demons. He saw elves—*still babies, Gods, they are all still babies*—standing around with wide, terrified eyes and vampires pouncing on them, grabbing them by the sides of their necks to twist them before sinking their teeth into the children to drain them of their blood.

"Piss on the Gods . . ." He muttered, swallowing the bile in his throat.

He had known that if it ever came to this it would be bad. He simply hadn't understood that it would ever be *this* bad.

He knew then, without a doubt, that if Loki could see this . . .

If Loki saw this . . . If he understood . . . He couldn't, then, deny me.

Hoping the gamble was worth the delay, he willed himself to Loki's library.

Much to his dismay, he came face to face with—not Loki, as he had hoped—Ishitar.

-69-

Na'amah gave a foolish girl's cry of surprise that sounded more human than canine as Emissary Lord Darklief appeared before Ishitar with an expression of pain and desperation on his brow. He flicked his eyes to her, started momentarily, then, to her great relief, dismissed her.

"Your Royal Highness—"

"Aren't we past that, Aiken?" Ishitar sighed. Na'amah, watching them both, fidgeted. "I don't wish your adulation. Not in your own home."

"It isn't my home." Aiken reminded him, his violet eyes narrowing. They flicked to Na'amah once more, then returned to Ishitar. "It's your mother's."

"Semantics."

Another swift look in Na'amah's direction before Emissary Lord Darklief, clearly, decided that he didn't have the luxury of time to be curious about the sound of her squeal.

"Come with me." He said. "I need your aide."

"My aide?" Ishitar gave him a tight smile.

"I came for Loki." Emissary Lord Darklief seemed to seethe whilst still holding his tone. "But you'll have to do."

Laughing, Ishitar reached for his hand and allowed him to take him where he would. Na'amah, not a Goddess, was unable to follow.

-70-

Ishitar wasn't laughing for long.

From the eyes of a child who was reaching up to him, her body battered and broken and her blood draining from her— blasphemy in such a war as this when it would have been lapped up by her enemy had they the luxury of time—I saw the pure expression of horror first dance, and then crawl, over the lines of Ishitar's handsome face.

Knowing there was a war, with all of its destruction and devastation, was one thing. Standing in the center, smelling the stench of burning flesh and listening to the screams of children, put an entirely different light upon his perspective.

"Please," the child reached for the hem of his shendyt with her small, delicate fingers, "help . . . me."

Ishitar, swift to react, bent over to will the health back into her.

She had lost too much blood; he was too late.

Standing behind him, I had no choice but to step forward and take her soul from her expiring body. As I did so, I raised my gaze to meet his. He looked at me as if I were the greatest of all his enemies.

"This," I schooled him, "is a small cost of a mortal war." I swallowed as he blinked at me. "Perhaps now you can decide, for yourself if you wish to interfere."

-71-

It would seem that he did.

He was gone in a flash, raging through his father's apartment, throwing the door to the library open without so much as a knock.

"Father!" He roared. "Do you see what is happening?"

"The demons are winning." Noliminan shrugged. "One side or the other always does."

"And you do not care about the means by which they do?"

"The demons run this war, Ishitar," Noliminan raised his gaze to look deep into his son's eyes. "What would you have me do about it?"

"Bid that every last one of the blasted demons, from the first to the last of them, be ever, hereafter, turned to ash!"

-72-

With Ishitar's command tossed carelessly into the wind, a new brand of chaos ensued.

-73-

The masked, corporeal part of me lay with Zamyael, content and trying to ignore the things I saw, felt and heard with the rest of my being. I snuggled my face into the warmth of her neck, loving her more in that moment, for distracting me from the war with the elves and the demons than I had ever, in all of my long years, loved her before.

I was about to tell her so. I was about to give myself over to her completely. I was about to bind my soul with hers for the remainder of eternity.

Before I had the opportunity to do so, my beloved lady, the one bright star in my overly long, miserable life, exploded in flames and turned to ash in my arms.

-74-

Through the blood red of his rage, Iladrul saw the demon responsible for this madness. He sprang forward, his split sword flying, with every intention of cutting Iykva down.

Iykva, seeing him, gave him a malicious grin.

This only served to drive Iladrul's rage all the more.

He sprang forward, his blades flying—

Deprived of the satisfaction of taking the demon's life, he screamed with rage as the creature burst into flames and fell into a pile of ashes at his feet.

Reason lost on him, Iladrul ran forward and kicked at the pile of ashes that had, a moment ago, been his greatest enemy, scattering them into the wind.

-75-

Never before, in all of my days, had rage overcome me as it did when Ishitar called her name.

What right did he, the one who had caused her immortal death, have to now seek comfort from her?

I ran toward him, able to do so in my corporeal form, and let my fist fly. The satisfying sound—feel—of my fist meeting his jaw gave me a minute bit of peace as he first cried out and then glared at me with a mixture of anger and surprise etched in the lines of his handsome face.

"Think twice, Azrael!" He growled at me.

"To the Hells with you Ishitar." I replied, spinning away from him. "And may Countenance's shadows dance *twice* upon your grave."

I dissipated the mortal body I had been cloaking myself within and willed myself out of his sight.

I didn't know, until that moment, that I had the ability to do so.

In my grief, I did not recognize the significance of this gift at the time.

-76-

Not that I had left him completely.

Through Zadkiel's eyes, I watched him continue to scour the cottage in search of the comfort of the woman he thought of as his true mother. When he couldn't find her, he made his way to the kitchen, where Zadkiel—patient father that he was—waited for him.

"Where is she?" He asked, more irritated than desperate.

"Gone." Zadkiel swallowed the pain of the word and raised his gaze to meet that of the God that he thought of as his son. "Ishitar. She's gone."

"Gone where?" Ishitar snapped at him.

Zadkiel blinked at him, confused.

Then, understanding dawned upon him.

Ishitar didn't realize the extent of the damage that he had wrought.

"Ishitar . . ." He shook his head and reached for Ishitar's hand. Ishitar stared at him, at the hand that grasped his, frowning. "You . . . bid that they all . . ."

"That they all what?" He snapped, his anger and impatience clearly overwhelming him.

Zadkiel, who had, until that moment, feigned strength and wisdom, swallowed the hitch of his sob.

"She's gone." Ishitar's brow furrowed. "You bid that they all turn to ash." He looked swiftly away. "From the first . . ."

Ishitar's eyes widened. He glared at Zadkiel with an expression of pure horror. He realized, in that moment, that his beloved mother was the first.

A fact he should have held in his mind all along.

"She's in Azrael's bed." Zadkiel was finally able to say the horrible words. Then, unable to hold his anger at bay. "Go, boy. And see for yourself the reality you are capable of creating when you have the mind."

-77-

I was laying on the bed, my body curled around what was left of her, when he opened the door.

"Azy?" His voice trembled.

I ignored him.

In that moment I loathed him. As such, I was in no mood to placate him.

He walked around the bed, slowly. When he stood at the other side, he fell, gracelessly, to his knees.

As his eyes fell upon her, I knew he needed my comfort.

I couldn't offer it to him.

And, to my horror, I found great satisfaction in the sound of his guilty, self-condemning screams.

-78-

Iladrul took stock of the damages before making his way to the throne room. He would be expected, he knew, to give comfort and counsel to those whose loved ones had been lost.

That his own family was now gone to him would mean little and less to his people. He was their King now. And he must, from this point forward, put his own happiness and pain to the side of himself.

Though he hadn't seen his mother's body, he assumed she had fallen. The Temple, after all, was now little more than soot and ash.

Ash . . . He thought distractedly as he looked around himself. *Ash is everywhere . . . Blotting out the sun. Blackening the day.*

As were the rotting bodies of angels and elves.

The first order of business, he knew, was to instruct the healers to bring the bodies of the dead to the Priestesses.

And to build a pyre . . .

More ash, he thought.

Then he shivered.

-79-

Osete stood on the border of the lands of Wisterian, his niece clutched tightly in his grasp. He turned his gaze to Prince Paul, swallowing.

"The soot of this place is smothering." The vampire Prince muttered. "My face will not be welcome."

"Will mine?" Osete asked, swallowing. "Will Nostimun's?"

"Nosti*man*'s." Prince Paul turned to meet his gaze and gave him a tired smile. "She's a girl. She requires a girl's name."

He raised his hand and ruffled Osete's hair.

The doxy bit his lip and lowered his gaze.

"No, Osete." Prince Paul replied. "I don't think so."

Osete shivered and buried his face into the girl's hair. She smelled like fresh tobacco leaves, oddly enough. The scent of her did not comfort him.

He raised his gaze and met that of the vampire Prince. When he spoke, his voice was little more than a whisper. "Where are we to go?"

Prince Paul continued to smile at him. As he did so, he extended his hand. Osete looked upon his palm, confused.

Prince Paul's smile grew as he raised the hand and wrapped it around Osete's neck.

"Come with me, Osete." He entreated. "And bring the girl with you."

"With a vampire?" The horror that coursed through Osete's veins was undeniable. "For your food?"

Prince Paul shook his head and returned his gaze to the castle. He raised his hand and pointed in the direction of Wisterian's lands.

"My people perish tonight." He muttered under his breath. "As may yours, for all I know." He shrugged and returned his gaze to Osete. "We can return to the castle and the lands that I rule in truce." He grinned. "Vampire and elf. Allies." He flicked his eyes to the burning city before them. "And Iladrul's daughter will return to him, when she is ready, a Queen."

Osete flicked his gaze to the babe in his arms and shivered. She slept, peaceful in dreams, despite the Hell raining down upon them. He licked his lips, looked toward the city that had ever been his home, and then returned his gaze to Prince Paul.

He saw no ill intention on the vampire's face.

Hoping his decision would not damn the girl, or her race, he gave Prince Paul a tentative smile.

"A second city of elves." Osete muttered. "Raised at the hand of a vampire."

Prince Paul chuckled and laced his hand around Osete's neck again. Osete, despite the cold shiver that passed over him, smiled at Prince Paul in return.

"A second city of elves." Prince Paul agreed. "And vampires, who I believe have no right to nest, will be forbidden from its walls."

"All vampires?" Osete asked, curious.

Prince Paul's smile grew.

"Mayhap all but one."

-80-

Gabriel stood next to Ishitar, his eyes imploring.

"Are you certain?" He asked. "It's a heavy choice."

Ishitar leaned forward and kissed Gabriel's cheek. When he pulled away, he wore a tight, desperate smile.

"You do understand that you shall be stuck in your mortal body until Moira's will be done by you." Gabriel reminded him. "You're mother's barter with her before you were born—"

"I understand, well, the cost I must pay for my choices." His expression was painful to look upon. "Yet, it is the only course I can take."

Gabriel nodded at him, raised his hand and ran his finger over Ishitar's brow in an attempt to draw Ishitar's memories from him.

"As you command me," Gabriel smiled at him, "thy will shall be done."

He raised his hands, setting them upon Ishitar's shoulders and, with all of his strength, pushed.

$\mathcal{A}$ZRAEL

"I didn't know where he went." I raise my gaze to look upon Charlie's profile. He had long ago become lost in the story and was attempting, now, to reconcile its meaning within his mind. "Nor, I must admit, did I care."

Charlie nods.

"I have nothing more to say to you."

He raises his face upward to imply that he is giving me his full attention.

"Where do we go?" He asks. "When Zadkiel takes us?"

This question surprises me. And I, not one who is easily surprised, let out a confused chortle.

"I don't know." I admit.

He nods.

"But he went to Gabriel." Charlie mutters. "Not Zadkiel. So he was still . . . alive?"

"He is still alive."

"Still mortal?"

I grant him a tight smile.

"And . . . Sappharon?" He swallows. "Samyael?"

"Sappharon has been made a Goddess." I remind him. "And Samyael's wings are now white."

He nods.

"I'm . . . sorry."

He reaches for my hand. He cannot grasp it. This seems to frustrate him but he says nothing about that. He realizes, for the first time, that I am either who I say I am or he has lost his mind and I am a figment of his imagination.

"For your loss. I grieve for you."

"Thank you." I whisper.

The pain is still acute. Whenever I think of her, I am felled.

"It's getting late." I tell him. "And I am unable to continue with this story."

He tries to reach for my hand again. This time he grunts his frustration and shakes his head. But his words, despite his confusion, are kind. "I understand, Azrael."

I smile.

"Will I see you again?"

"Oh, yes." I grant him a regretful smile.

Hearing my voice raise above him, he takes my cue and finds his feet. His legs have gone numb, so he shakes them, one at a time. As he reaches for Rocky's harness, he gives me a weary smile.

"Until then," he says, a shudder passing through him.

Unable to bear the heavy weight of the air around us, I grant him a final, regretful smile.

*C*HARLIE

Charlie sat at his kitchen table, spinning his cup of tea, his mind racing.

He had more questions for Azrael, damn it. And he should have asked them while the strange man had been standing at his side.

"*If* he was standing at my side." Charlie scoffed. Then he laughed at himself. "I must be losing my mind."

The knock at the door roused him from this thought. He stood and walked toward it, opening it to stare with blind eyes at the man on the other side.

He knew who it was, well enough. He could smell him. The faint order of mixed spices permeated the room. Not precisely a cologne that Charlie was familiar with.

But, then, given Joshua's accent, he supposed the cologne has come from whatever lands the man, himself, had risen.

"Am I intruding?" Joshua asked him.

"No." Charlie took a step back, his smile coming easy. "Please, Mr. Silverstone. Come in."

"I've come to replace the bottle of scotch I drank the last time I visited." Joshua's voice was tinged with a note of amusement. "Perhaps you can entice me to a glass before I go."

"If I must twist your arm." Charlie chuckled, taking the bottle and turning away to walk toward the cupboard. "I was wondering if I'd ever see you again."

"I'm like a bad cough." Joshua teased. "Just try to get rid of me."

Charlie laughed out loud at that.

"Have you received any more packages from your friend?"

"Better than that." Charlie replied as he led Joshua into the kitchen. "He approached me at Liberty Park."

Joshua started. Charlie turned toward him, surprised by his sudden movement. "You actually saw him?"

"Yes." He said, not correcting the man over his semantics. "He spoke of a mortal war this time."

"Which?" Joshua sounded eager.

"Elves." Charlie muttered, curious with regard to Joshua's tone. "And the demons who would destroy them."

Joshua flinched, causing Charlie's brow to furrow.

"Yes." Joshua replied, his tone flat. "I am overly familiar with that particular fable."

"Then I'll spare you the gruesome details of the ending."

"I'd . . . prefer that." Joshua swallowed. Charlie heard the click in his throat as he did so. "How did he seem? Your friend?"

"Fine." Charlie's brow furrowed even further. "Are you alright, Josh?"

"Yes." His tone wrapped around a smile now. "Forgive me. Since you found the lost Tome, I've found myself getting wrapped up in history."

Charlie did not know how to respond to that particular statement.

"Well." Joshua laughed under his breath. "Legend." He leaned forward, toward Charlie. The warmth of him—the smell of him—brought Charlie an odd comfort. At the same time, the unguarded intimacy of the gesture intimidated him. "Will he be back? Your friend?"

"I don't know." Charlie admitted. Then, remembering the heavy quality of the air that surrounded Azrael before he bid Charlie goodbye, he shivered. "He said he intends to."

"When he does," Joshua's tone had a pleading quality to it, "tell him I'd very much like to speak with him."

Charlie, tipping the bottle of scotch toward an empty glass that had been sitting in the rack to dry, was unable to utter any such promise.

*L*ESSON *O*NE:

*Malicious Intent is the
Best Friend of Your Enemy*

*L*ESSON *T*WO:

*The Cut of the Tongue is Mightier
Than the Sting of the Sword*

$\mathcal{A}$UTHOR'S $\mathcal{N}$OTE

Although the core of this story was written as it had been originally drafted, the ending, when it came to me about half way through the novel, took me by complete surprise. As did the moves on the kings' board being made by the players. Characters, just like friends and lovers, sometimes have the strangest habit of heading off in the direction that best suits them, sometimes leaving those that love them behind.

There are still many loose ends to tie up, but I hope that I have managed to share this round of the game with a successful conclusion.

Regardless, I want to thank you for taking the time to read Ashes to Ashes. As a self-published author, I depend upon word of mouth and recommendation to promote my books. That being said, whether or not you enjoyed the story, I would appreciate an honest review on social media, such as Facebook, Amazon.com and Barnes&noble.com.

If you have a particular question in regard to any one of the installments, do not hesitate to contact me on the series' Facebook page at:
https://www.facebook.com/#!/TheScribingOfIshitar
or you can contact me at TheScribingofIshitar@comcast.net.

$\mathscr{A}$BOUT THE $\mathscr{A}$UTHOR

Carrie F. Shepherd (1971) was born in Salt Lake City, Utah but currently resides in Highlands Ranch, Colorado. The single mother of one, she enjoys taking advantage of the hiking trails when it's cool out or curling up with a book next to the pool on warmer days. Twenty years of scribing have brought the personalities of the people who most inspire her to life within the characters in these pages.

The Scribing of Ishitar:

Fall From Grace (Volume I)
Ashes to Ashes (Volume II)

Made in the USA
Charleston, SC
22 July 2014